AN UNFOLDING SOUL

A tale of Bath

by

Douglas Westcott

Valley Spring Press
P O Box 2765, Bath, BA2 7XS
gordon@douglaswestcott.com

ISBN 978-0-9926397-47

Printed and bound by CPI Group (UK) Ltd, Croydon, CR0 4YY

By the same author:

GO SWIFT AND FAR – A NOVEL OF BATH

Hardback: ISBN 978-0-9926397-09
Paperback: 978-0-9926397-30
e-book: Kindle Edition - Amazon

ACKNOWLEDGEMENTS

The author gratefully acknowledges the contribution, often very substantial, of Vikki Annett, the Bath Chronicle, Bath Newseum, Alice Beazer, Stephen Bird, Janet Bradley, Dr Bruno Bubna-Kasteliz, Simon Burrows, Judith Cameron, Martin Coulson, The Combe Down Heritage Society, Stephanie Dodd, Dr Amy Frost, Alastair Giles, James Hillman, Greg Ingham, Anna Jacka-Thomas, Colin Johnston and his staff at the Bath Record Office, Caroline Kay, Penny Knowles, Donna Lodge, Patrick McCloy, Cynthia O'Hara, Yvonne Palmer, St John's Foundation, Sebastian Stafford-Bloor, Dr Margaret Tonge, Cecil Weir, Steve Wells, and Richard Wyatt.

The support and encouragement of the 100 or so other real Bath citizens, who are in the story so far, has been much appreciated over the years of writing.

My gratitude and congratulations to the Arvon Foundation on becoming 50 years old in 2018.

For Liz

£1 received from the sale of this actual book will be donated to Julian House, which for over a quarter of a century, has helped hundreds of homeless men and women to get off the streets of Bath and into a new life.

And a man said, Speak to us of Self-Knowledge.
And he answered, saying:
Your hearts know in silence the secrets of the
days and the nights.
But your ears thirst for the sound of your heart's
knowledge.
You would know in words that which you
have always known in thought.
You would touch with your fingers the naked
body of your dreams.

And it is well you should.
The hidden well-spring of your soul must needs
rise and run murmuring to the sea;
And the treasure of your infinite depths would
be revealed to your eyes.
But let there be no scales to weigh your un-
known treasure;
And seek not the depths of your knowledge
with staff or sounding line.
For self is a sea boundless and measureless.

Say not "I have found the truth," but rather,
"I have found a truth."
Say not, "I have found the path of the soul."
Say rather, "I have met the soul walking upon
my path."
For the soul walks upon all paths.
The soul walks not upon a line, neither does it
grow like a reed.
The soul unfolds itself, like a lotus of countless
petals.

"The Prophet" by Gibran Kahlil Gibrain

PROLOGUE

The City of Bath, England, 2 March 1966

The city of Bath is unique. Much of it was built during the reigns of four kings all called George over a period of only one hundred years. Its three thousand or so Georgian buildings form the heart of one of the most complete and beautiful cities in the world.

But for how much longer?

As dawn broke at 6.43 am on Wednesday, 2 March 1966, Jason Jenkins gunned the engine on his crane and raised the forged-steel wrecking ball. He released the rope drum clutch and sent the ball, weighing over a thousand pounds, plunging down through the six ancient properties opposite the Guildhall.

At twenty-eight years of age, Jason was an experienced demolition man, for he and his gang of workers had learnt their trade well in similar operations in the city, undertaken countless times in the last five years: they had become efficient, fast and ruthless in the destruction of old Georgian buildings. With the roofs destroyed, Jenkins released the lateral clutch and sent the ball, now swinging like a pendulum, crashing into the walls. From time to time, he paused, allowing a bulldozer to clear the accumulation of shattered stone and debris onto a waiting truck. The splintered wood was separated and piled high awaiting the torch.

The crew of unshaven, long-haired youths worked happily; they were the masters of their own universe, relishing the instant gratification of their devastation. After the sun went down, the Guildhall was illuminated by the flames from a huge bonfire on the bare ground, which was pitted with uncovered basements. The men packed up, content with the promise of double pay for finishing the job in a day and without disruption from the preservation protesters. Tomorrow, they would go across town to Twerton and flatten the house where Henry Fielding had written much of *Tom Jones*.

CHAPTER ONE

The beating had been savage; the knuckleduster and steel-capped boots had done the job only too well. A broken nose and torn lips adorned the heavily-bruised and swollen cheeks crowned by a shaven head. Its angry six-inch skull wound secured with heavy black stitching was hidden beneath a white bandage dressing. The young man had been unconscious since his arrival at Bath's Royal United Hospital late at night two days earlier when staff feared for his life. It was touch-and-go in the during those early hours, and he had stopped breathing on more than one occasion.

Charge Nurse Piggott came on night duty at five o'clock and looked at his patient. The face was still so engorged and twisted that it was difficult to discern whether he had been good-looking before the attack, although the bruising was starting to yellow.

What a mess, he thought but appreciated that the casualty department team had done a brilliant job in saving a life. He checked the red rubber tracheal tube and the curved steel cricoid inserted into the airway through the hole pierced below the Adam's apple and began deflating the attached balloon. The rhythmic sound of the leather bellows in the ventilator providing the patient with vital oxygen filled the small room. Piggott did not hear the door open behind him.

"Good evening, Charge Nurse." Piggott turned to greet the Senior Consultant surgeon.

"Good evening, Mr Medlock."

"They're a bit worried upstairs and asked me to pop in. I go back a long way with this young man – to the day he was born when his mother went into labour under the rubble of her home in New King Street. It was after the German air raids in April 1942 and a close run thing for mother and child."

Piggott looked back at the inert body. One of nature's survivors, he thought.

"I had a look at the x-rays," Medlock continued as he picked up the metal clipboard of notes hanging on the iron bedstead at the foot of the bed. "It's a miracle they're clear. The jaw isn't broken, and there's no depressed fracture of the skull."

Piggott watched and, where necessary, assisted as the consultant performed a thorough examination of the comatose youth.

"A vicious attack," the Consultant remarked afterwards as he vigorously washed his hands in the basin. "And there seems to be no change at all since he was admitted?"

"No, sir, I was on night duty when he was brought up." Piggott was of slight build and always immaculate in his starched white tunic and trousers. Pale skinned with neatly-trimmed, strawberry-blond hair, he had recently grown a beard that he habitually stroked as if to make sure it was still there. He did so now, and his fingers reached for his chin.

"As you've seen from the notes, Casualty restarted his breathing at four fifteen on Wednesday morning, two days ago. I know he was heavily sedated at the beginning, but I'd have hoped for something as the dose of curare was lowered. But there's been nothing, not even an eyelid flutter."

"I agree – most worrying." Medlock sat down by the bedside and penned his note for the clipboard.

For a young man of twenty-four years of age and in good health before his admission, it is of concern that Ian Morris remains deeply comatose, seventy-two hours after the attack. He displays no signs of regaining consciousness, which may indicate widespread cerebral damage. The next seven days are critical. If things remain unchanged, there is an increased risk of permanent brain damage and associated paralysis.

David Medlock

CHAPTER TWO

Since Roman times, Bath and its curative spa had simply been a place of rest and recreation. This was particularly the case during the eighteenth century, but its popularity fell dramatically because of the Napoleonic Wars after the French Revolution of 1789: banks and the entire building trade were pushed into bankruptcy, causing a complete halt in all development. Fashionable society deserted the mineral water of the spa to follow royalty to the saltwater of the new English seaside resort of Brighton.

The rich and famous no longer came, and for a hundred and fifty years Bath declined into insignificance, becoming a mere shadow of its former glory.

Then, in 1939, the city became strategically important when, for the first time in its history, the Admiralty left London and moved to Bath. It commandeered major hotels and schools to accommodate its burgeoning administration.

As many Bathonians know, the roof of the former Empire Hotel in the centre of the city was designed in three parts: a miniature castle, a house and a cottage. They represented the upper, middle, and lower born citizens in a class system so beloved by the Victorians. Completed in 1905, on the site of the Athenaeum for the hotelier Alfred Holland, the building was described at the time as 'a monstrosity and unbelievably pompous', but soon became an important landmark.

Rear Admiral David Jellicoe Fisher DSC used the original bridal suite as his office at the Admiralty HQ and shared the hotel's birthdate. Some maliciously even suggested that Fisher merited the building's description, for he certainly considered himself important and liked to be addressed at all times as rear admiral.

He looked at the clock – two minutes before six – and sighed with relief. Screwing the top back onto his fountain pen, he returned it to his inside jacket pocket. He closed the manila file marked "Ships Postal

Services", pushed his chair back, and stood up to return it to the metal filing cabinet until his return on Monday morning. Sitting on its top was the photograph taken in 1942 on the submarine HMS Dolphin: in twenty-four years, he had progressed from surviving German dive bombers in the Mediterranean, climbing through the ranks of Her Majesty's Royal Navy, only to be reduced to sorting out its postal service.

He returned to his desk and collected his cigarettes and gold Ronson lighter, which he dropped into his trouser pocket before reaching for his overcoat and hat. It was wintry outside and he struggled to do up his coat buttons over his suit as he lumbered down the staircase towards the former hotel's grand entrance doors. Throughout the day, he had watched the endless line of removal lorries outside the building next door. The Bath police constabulary was decamping from Orange Grove to its newly-built headquarters in Manvers Street, and he was keen to hear what Detective Inspector Romer had to say about the move.

It was Friday night, and Fisher was going for a drink with Jack Romer – they were fellow freemasons in the city's oldest and largest temple.

Unknown except to the initiated, Bath was regarded as the Premier Masonic Provincial City of England. Founded early in the eighteenth century, the first anywhere outside the London, the Queen's Head Lodge met at the pub on the corner of Cock Lane, now Union Passage, and Cheap Street. It had been started by a very prestigious membership – six Dukes and Earls, five Fellows of the Royal Society plus numerous Baronets. All were existing London Freemasons and came regularly to the city to take the waters: the remaining forty-two founding members were made up of local luminaries, including the City's Master of Ceremonies, Beau Nash, and six gentlemen who either had been, or would go on to be, Mayors of the City.

Now renamed the Royal Cumberland, Rear Admiral Fisher was Master when Romer was inducted into the Lodge by his Chief Superintendent. Over several years of drinking together, he and Romer had discovered many shared values despite the differences in their age and backgrounds.

Fisher, whose wife had died of cancer three years earlier, was pleased to have established this weekly ritual. Rosemary, his eldest and favourite daughter was now married and had gone to Australia, while his youngest, Anne, was often away. Nevertheless, he enjoyed other recreational activities and particularly those offered through a local escort agency that he planned to telephone later in the evening.

Romer was waiting on the pavement, similarly attired to the rear admiral, but his suit was ill fitting and baggy and the overcoat had seen better days.

"How goes it, Jack?" Fisher shook the younger man's hand before they both headed down to their usual watering hole at the corner of York Street.

Romer was clearly unhappy about having to move from the classical beautiful building, where the police station had been for over a hundred years, to the dreadful "biscuit tin" in Manvers Street.

"Well, David, as you know, the new station is a brute of a building which is hardly a surprise given that it was designed by the city's planning department. I reckon the only happy people tonight will be the prisoners. They've swapped their 1865 damp old basement cells for spanking new ones"

There was a group of youngsters milling about the triangle on Terrace Walk. Nicknamed Bog Island after its two splendid, underground, Victorian public conveniences, it was a favourite among the undergraduates as a Friday night gathering place before embarking on pub crawls.

The two men looked out of place threading their way through the loud mouthed, 'fucking this and fucking that,' scruffy bunch of eighteen and nineteen year olds. But they were settled in the Huntsman, ready to put the world to rights, accompanied by their pints and cigarettes.

"What's happening to the world, Jack?" Fisher was barely seated behind their usual corner table before he began. "Did you see that unwashed rabble outside? And what does our bloody prime minister do, but grant four of their kind honours? I know men who gave their lives for less. Do you know what John Lennon said after receiving his MBE? He said he deserved it more, because he got it for entertaining rather than killing people – to think that I fought a war for him and those louts out there."

"The world's changing," Romer replied. "We've got to accept that. I mean, those louts, as you call them, aren't doing any harm – you should see some of the estates that we get called to, that's something else. In the old days, a good thump from a rolled-up bobby's cape in a dark alley was enough, but that's not allowed now – law and order don't seem to matter anymore."

"So, what's gone so wrong?" Fisher already knew some of the answers – the rising birth rate when the armed services had returned from the war. Then there was the introduction of the welfare state, free education, and endless state money.

In his opinion, the country had fundamentally changed for the first time in over two hundred years. It was no longer the case, as in past centuries, that only the sons of the elite got the chance of good schools and a decent living. Nowadays, the working class young were financially independent and what was once vulgarity had become vigour. Previously, being parents gave you authority over the young and earned their respect, but not today. Change, and more importantly the speed of such change since the war had left adults bemused and floundering. His own children had been protected, but only because the girls attended the Royal High School, mixing with their own class – or *plus*, as he liked to call them. Fisher looked around and saw the youths from outside were beginning to fill the pub.

"There's something else," Romer added. "Young men have always felt it was their duty and an honour to fight and die for their country. But where's that gone to? Now that conscription's been abolished, I can't see any of this rabble volunteering to fight. In fact, quite the opposite, they're mostly a bunch of pacifist hippies."

"We'll have to find another place to drink in future." Fisher glumly took a gulp of his bitter.

"I agree," the policeman said. "Look at them, it's like they're a different species from us – with the long hair, it's difficult to tell boys from girls. And what about the music? Well, if you can call it music …"

"I sometimes think I'm part of a dying breed," Fisher said. "Did you know that *Time Magazine* actually gave over a whole edition to 'Swinging London'? I saw it when I was last in my London club. It was full of tripe about the pop groups drinking and doing goodness knows what else at some place called Ad Lib, together with photographs of men and women wearing each other's clothes in Carnaby Street. Such nonsense, they say, has made London the cultural and fashion centre of the world. 'A Tourist Honeypot' with … It's so depressing." The older man finished his drink and stood up.

"Are you off to get another round?" Romer drained his pint and grinned. "I'll join you, squire," he proffered his glass.

"OK, but I'll need to relieve myself first." Fisher made his way to the gentlemen's lavatory at the back of the pub, squeezing his bulk between the group of youths. He disliked being surrounded, but enjoyed pushing through the scantily-clad young women, and rubbed up against one ample-breasted girl, no older than his daughter, who obviously was not wearing a brassiere.

"Fuck off, you old letch," she hurled at him. Finally, he pushed open the toilet door only to encounter a young man heaving up. The sour-smelling vomit disgorged down the rear admiral's trousers, splattering onto his highly polished shoes.

Lost for words, he staggered back into the pub and saw the voluptuous girl smirking at his predicament. He decided that the second pint would have to wait, and fled to find a taxi home to change his stinking trousers.

Unmarried and no one to go home to, the policeman waited patiently, knowing that his drinking companion was no longer as quick on

9

his feet – unlike in his younger days, when the rear admiral had distinguished himself during the war. Romer's call up some years later was uneventful: he became a military policeman in the army, so after demob, it seemed natural that he join the police force.

Like Fisher, he did question what would happen in the coming years as a result of the growing freedom and prosperity now enjoyed by the young and their wealth. Especially because the prosperity was not shared equally. The police force's continual interaction with the poor made them only too aware of the growing gulf between the haves and have nots of Bath. But the issue was ignored in divisional reviews and at the Masonic Chapter meetings attended by many of his fellow officers.

Starting in his army days, Romer had always been a strong believer in self-preservation. For him, being a detective was perfect and the only job he had ever wanted: learning the habits of those who thought themselves his betters gave him power that could be wielded if and when necessary. Unmarried, Freemasonry would allow him to become one of them, for eventually, he would be both Master of the Lodge and Chief Superintendent of the Bath Police – but until then, he kept quiet and observed.

Seeing the prospects of his second pint disappear out of the pub in disarray, he stood and looked at the girl who Fisher had bumped into.

CHAPTER THREE

The members of the Wessex Property Club entered the Abbey Hotel – not through its palatial foyer on North Parade, but by way of the little known poorly lit courtyard to the rear where it was not unusual for the odd vagrant to bed down for the night.

Last to arrive, as Romer noted from his unobserved nearby car, was Malcolm Austwick, one of Bath's leading solicitors. This noticeably-tall man had aged well, maintaining his good looks, an enviable golf handicap, and was fit for his age. He was no longer as slim as in his younger years, but his handmade suits were beautifully cut and he continued to favour gold cuff links over buttons.

He inserted his member's key into the building's shabby, unmarked door. Out of sight, out of mind, he mused. Until around the time of his birth at the turn of the century, the destitute had been hidden from view in this building. Nothing had changed, he thought, recalling the recent vociferous public opposition to creating a homeless shelter in a nearby middle-class city street.

Austwick never ceased to marvel at what Ian Morris had achieved in the guise of upgrading the back of the hotel: with the owners Ian and Christa Taylor more than happy to find a use for the derelict space. No expense had been spared to transform the old Victorian poor-relief blockhouse into a very plush members' club. Completely separate and inaccessible from the hotel, the décor was pastiche Georgian with matching reproduction furniture. Ostensibly a private gentlemen's dining club, the paraphernalia of gambling remained out of sight until needed after ten o'clock each night. The only clue to its true identity being, as in most casinos – no natural light nor any clocks.

Owned and converted by the Wessex Property Club, the so-called Georgian Rooms had proved a superb investment. Away from prying eyes, it also made a perfect venue for their three monthly meetings on the Friday before each quarter day – agreeably for the Property Club members, the four days in every year when their tenants had to pay rent.

Austwick entered the private dining room and took his seat at the table next to Patrick McCloy, a highly-successful property solicitor from Bradford on Avon. The other members were already seated. At the head was Tom Scotland, Managing Director of Ardent Scotland Limited, the oldest building company in Bath, and believed to be handling every major project in and around the city. On his right was Roger Palmer, the city's most successful property developer. Next to him Christopher Johnson, the Manager of the Old Bank of Bath: opposite the Guildhall since 1760, its financial backing assured the members' continued dominance in all matters involving land and property in the city. The last place was taken by Peter Groves, who chaired the meeting and whose accountancy practice shielded so many secrets.

McCloy greeted him.

"Good evening, Malcolm. We were just discussing the dreadful business about young Morris. He's still in a bad way."

"Really, I only got back from the West Indies last night. What's happened to him? Has he been in an accident or something?" Austwick asked.

"He was attacked outside his home nine or ten days ago and is still unconscious in hospital. The police think it may be a property deal that went sour. I'm not sure I agree with them, despite Ian having upset a few people on his way up. After all, this is Bath, not Chicago!"

"Gentlemen, may we proceed?" Peter Groves addressed the meeting.

"Item one on the agenda is 'Apologies'. Apart from Morris, who obviously can't make this evening, our friendly civil servant wishes to remain in the background and so isn't with us either. I'm sure you'll agree that he's proving most helpful, especially in relation to the Board of Trade."

Everyone nodded, remembering the Building Certificates needed and so easily obtained for the last group of factories.

"Let's move on to item two and the redevelopment of the Harvey Block in the High Street. You will recall that this involves the demolition of those decrepit properties facing the Guildhall, where we have planning consent for a block of six shops with three floors of offices and flats over. How's this going, Roger?" He looked to the developer.

"Fine, our guys moved in at the crack of dawn on Monday and took the protesters by surprise. I passed the site on my way here – it's all been flattened, and we plan to start laying the foundations on Monday next."

"Excellent, are there any problems you've come across?" Groves asked.

"Just the usual grouses from the preservation lot, but we managed to keep the town planners sweet with a few design alterations. We just turned the top floor into a sham mansard roof and put a break in the front façade. They bought the idea, and it's actually reduced costs. It should all be up and ready in about eighteen months."

"Well done!" Groves tapped on the table, and the other members duly joined him in a muted round of applause. "So, onto item three and yet again Buchanan's tunnel. What should we do about it? Tom, what have you been hearing from your people on the Council?"

As always the builder spoke his mind. "Professor Buchanan might be England's greatest planning and traffic boffin, but his idea of building a tunnel under the centre of Bath is barmy. It'll cost millions, destroy hundreds of houses, and cause years of disruption. So, it's the usual battle lines – rabid preservationist versus greedy developers wallowing in a soup of self-interested house owners. There's been petitions galore, Bathwick Ward, Walcot Street, and Kingsmead – no one wants it. Apparently, Buchanan has threatened to throw his toys out of the pram and go back to London. He might have the Planning Officers behind him, but the Council's deadlocked: the vote was twenty-three to twenty-three last week – after a four-hour debate. Bath in bloody blunderland. I can't see it ever happening. And, more to the point, I can't see that there is or ever will be any money in it, just mayhem for years. Steer well clear and move on."

"Next ... BAD," – Groves referred to the Bath Against Developers protest group run by Lord Lundy and loathed by all present – "is working itself up to its usual frenzy, but with the Harvey Block underway, he is no longer a problem for the moment, thank God."

"Item four looks like being much more interesting. It's not public knowledge yet, but the chairman of the Planning Committee will shortly announce that fifty more acres of land inside the city boundaries are to be re-zoned for much needed factories. BAD and others did their best to scupper the project, but Stothert & Pitt and Darlington's report has prevailed."

Stothert & Pitt, the substantial engineering firm founded in 1785 on the Lower Bristol Road was one of the city's largest employers: it manufactured cranes that were located in docks all over the world, and during the Second World War had produced Challenger tanks and miniature submarines. Its outspoken managing director, Dr Darlington, was known to all of them.

"I believe you have something to say on this, Patrick?"

"Thank you, Peter," McCloy responded. "I've had a word with one of my clients, who owns eighteen acres of the relevant land off Locksbrook Road. He's willing to sell, and I've established off the record that the Committee will give consent for twenty factories. My client will do a deal on a fifty-fifty profit sharing basis – with nothing up front."

Christopher Johnson spoke for the first time. "The bank is prepared to put up all the money."

"That's a good site," Scotland said, "and factories are easy to build, cheap and fast. I'm sure you'd agree with me, Roger." He turned to the professional developer in the group.

"We'd be in and out in nine months, and with twenty factories costing, say, a million to build, there's got to be a profit of three hundred thousand split between the land owner and ourselves. Not bad, a profit of a hundred and fifty thousand pounds in a year."

"Much more interesting than a tunnel," Groves said to jocular approval before continuing. "Item five. I had a word with Edward about the General Election in three weeks' time." Edward Brown was the Conservative Member of Parliament for Bath, elected two years earlier following Sir James Pitman's retirement. "He reckons that the socialists and Harold Wilson are heading for a landslide."

Scotland could not contain himself.

"Thank God my children have finished their education. The hypocrisy of Anthony Crossland," – he was referring to the Education Secretary – "privately educated himself, but hell-bent on destroying every grammar school in the country; some of them have been going for five hundred years or more. What's wrong in separating out the best? Oh, no, that's unfair, must reduce everything to the lowest common denominator – fucking comprehensive schools, a tragedy, an unmitigated disaster.

"But while the country might choose his lot's crackpot ideas, we have to be grateful to know that Bath will remain rock-solid Tory ..."

Groves interrupted. "On that note, gentlemen, I suggest we end the meeting and head for the bar."

CHAPTER FOUR

The first thing Charge Nurse Piggott did when he came on duty was to check on Ian Morris. The coma had lightened three days ago and now that he could breathe unaided they had unhooked the ventilator, although the tracheostomy in his neck remained. His face was no longer swollen but there was still a bruised tinge to his skin. The injuries to his nose, mouth, jaw and soft tissue all seemed to be healing, as well as the scalp wound.

As usual, the young woman was sitting close by the bedside. She was attractive rather than beautiful, petite with short dark hair, regular features, a ready smile, and clear hazel eyes. Always cheerful on arrival, she would first look for a response from his inert body, before slowly removing her fawn mackintosh and placing it over the back of a chair, all the time continuing to search for any sign that he acknowledged her presence. Then she would move the chair to the bed, sit down and clasp Ian's hand in both of hers. His only visitor, she had been given permission to stay beyond visiting hours, in the hope that her presence might somehow hasten his return to consciousness.

That morning's edition of the *Bath & Wilts Evening Chronicle* and a burgundy binder lay on the bed. She had introduced herself on the first night as Trish Traynor and explained that her boss, for that was their relationship, loved history, British and American, especially anything and everything to do with Bath. The idea had been hers and so, every night, she read to the young man, loudly over the noise of the wheezing ventilator, now thankfully no longer needed. But all to no avail.

As the days passed, she and Piggott got into the habit of chatting for a few minutes during his hourly check-ups. She rarely left before midnight, and the conversation revolved around Ian. She had worked for him since leaving secretarial college and clearly worshipped the man. Piggott thought the relationship was purely professional given that everything talked about was work-related. However, despite never mentioning social involvement, he wondered if she might harbour more personal feelings.

"How are you this evening, Trish?" he asked. "Have you noticed any difference?"

Ian had heard the faint answer, "Nothing."

It was pitch-black, and Ian could not breathe. His head was heavy and stuffy as if filled with cotton wool. His tongue felt glued to the roof of his mouth and there was something in his throat that felt cold and raw. He tried to open his eyes but could not. He sank back into the darkness.

Having read aloud the *Chronicle* from cover to cover Trish picked up and opened the burgundy binder. She had discovered it on Ian's bedside table when checking his house on the morning after the attack. It had been with two other books, one called *The Prophet*, the other a biography of Winston Churchill, and contained about twenty hand-written pages, the first of which was entitled,

PROPERTIES OF NOTORIETY IN BATH
by
Ian Morris

She started to read aloud.

"Two Bath Street, William Smith's Millinery Shop hides the shameful secret, which Jane Austen's family had endeavoured to keep for over a hundred and fifty years."

Consciousness returned, although still in utter darkness and with an excruciating sore throat. Ian thought of his mother but couldn't picture her face. Was he blind? Was she abandoning him again? Then, there was a voice. A familiar voice speaking familiar words …

"Jane, her brother Edward and his wife had been warmly welcomed by her uncle and aunt, James and Jane Leigh-Perrot, at their home at number one Paragon, when they visited Bath in June 1799. On this glorious day in August, Mrs Leigh-Perrot made her way to her favourite milliner's shop on the corner of Bath and Stall Street: the previous day, she had been much irritated by its owner, Miss Gregory, and her refusal to lower the price of some white lace, costing twenty shillings."

Trish paused and looked up. She thought she'd heard something in the stillness of the hospital settling for the night. Had there been a slight cough? She waited. Nothing – she must have imagined it, so she went on.

"Unable to move her on the price, Mrs Leigh-Perrot bought some black lace and left the shop. She had barely gone a few yards when she was accosted by the enraged shop owner accusing her of theft, for there, poking awkwardly out of the package of black lace made up by the clerk, was the card of white lace so coveted.

A few days later, Jane Leigh-Perrot was arrested for shoplifting. If found guilty, the penalty for stealing anything over five shillings was hanging or deportation to Australia. Being a gentlewoman, she was not put into the public jail but had to endure the very squalid conditions of living with the jailer and his wife for eight months until she came to trial on March 24ᵗʰ 1800."

He had to move his tongue: he wanted to swallow, but there was something stuck in his throat.

"In 1801, Jane's father retired from his church living and moved the whole family to Bath. The rent of a hundred and fifty pounds per annum for four Sydney Street consumed a quarter of the family's meagre income. When this lease ended, they were forced to Green Park Buildings, cheaper because of flooding from the nearby river. Malaria was the reason for the fever that resulted in her father's death in 1805. Poverty drove the family ever downward, first from Gay Street to Trim Street, and eventually out of Bath completely to Southhampton in 1806."

Suddenly, the hand resting in hers twitched, and Ian groaned, then very quietly enunciated, "F …, F …, Fo …, Fo …"

He was trying to tell her something. What was it? She put her ear to his mouth and listened to the barely-audible sound. Triumphant at last, she rose, opened the bedside locker door, and took out the framed, faded photograph of his mother, which again she had brought from the house, and placed it under his lifeless hand.

CHAPTER FIVE

Exhausted, hungry, and unwashed, apart from what had been possible in the public convenience wash basins of airports, bus and railway stations, the Honourable Fiona Symons, the thirty-four-year-old daughter and eldest child of the late 3rd Earl of Lundy, had caught the milk train from Paddington to Bath Spa. She'd checked in her purse and found just five pounds and some loose change. This time, she would choose more carefully.

She hauled a rucksack onto her back and walked down through the station subway and into the booking hall. It was two in the morning, and despite the stark area being brightly lit, there were several people bundled and asleep on benches. She went out into the dark forecourt and crossed the road to the Railway Inn, rang the doorbell, and went on ringing it until she roused the night manager. Like others in unloved railway hotels, the room had seen much better days, when steam had been king and the motor car was nothing but a pipe dream. She did not care and simply wanted a bath and a bed. The low budget flight back from Southern California had taken four days with the polar route and had involved long transit delays in places like Banff and Reykjavik.

As she stripped off her clothes and loosened her long blond hair, she realised it had been four years almost to the day since she'd last set foot in her home town. In March 1962, her privileged world had come crashing down; the grand country manor and estate in Limpley Stoke, her home in Great Pulteney Street and even the virtual sinecure of running her father's estate office. She'd paid dearly for her Christmas fling with the housekeeper's son and fled Bath in shame. Four years, where had all that time gone?

It had started with the disaster in Geneva, but Linda had come to her rescue and scooped her up from the clinic. They'd known from when they had first met at finishing school that their friendship would be forever, and sure enough, they'd picked up exactly where they'd left off in Switzerland ten years earlier. In some ways, they were like one another; both were tall, slender and had thick, long, straight hair parted in the middle. But where Fiona was blond and fair skinned with blue eyes, Linda was dark, almost olive skinned, and had deep brown eyes.

"I'm so pleased to see you and can't thank you enough," Fiona told her friend as they drove along the lakeside, away from the clinic and towards Linda's home.

"I always knew something would bring us back together, but not this," Linda replied. "I feel terrible about recommending that butcher."

Linda's home was an impressive penthouse on the top floor of a low-rise block in central Geneva that looked directly across the lake. It made Fiona wonder what her friend exactly did – perhaps it was owned by her father.

"I am in banking," Linda told her once they'd kicked their shoes off and were spread across the black leather sofas. "Particularly for American clients or more specifically in this case a Mr Frank Duffer Junior from the Windy City."

"The Windy City?"

"As in Chicago, Illinois. He's made a fortune in supplying the US Army in Vietnam. His speciality is attack helicopters, or more precisely things you put in and on them. His problem was that, according to a Senate hearing, they were costing Uncle Sam a fortune and often didn't work that well. So, my Mr Duffer solved the problem by moving the whole company here and has somehow managed to sell it back to the American Government for a vast profit."

"How did you get involved?" Fiona asked, vaguely remembering that Linda had always excelled at figures and money.

"It was really down to Daddy: he knew a director of one of the small banks here, and got me a job. Six months later, one of the big American East Coast outfits bought them out, and being bilingual with a home here, I got the job of explaining the Swiss to Mr Duffer and vice-versa. Long may it last."

"Will it?"

"I doubt it. I think the work's coming to an end, but I'm not worried. Something else will turn up." She stood up and went to the kitchen, returning moments later with a bottle of champagne in an ice bucket and two glasses.

"Now it's time for us to have a bit of fun like we used to – with those young Italian gardeners at finishing school, remember, the scoresheets?" They both laughed. "It's good to see a friendly face, a chum from the old days. I've missed you, and the least I can do is make amends, so, we're off to dinner with my very handsome Bostonian banker and his friend."

"I don't think …" Fiona was still tired from the operation and sore too.

"Don't you even think of ducking out. You've been through a tough few days and now it's time to put the past behind and enjoy yourself."

"What's his name?" Fiona asked.

"Mine's Ford Fraker, but here's to yours," she raised her glass, "a commodity dealer with more money than sense."

CHAPTER SIX

After the Friday evening debacle, David Fisher woke early on Saturday morning and was determined not to let the unpleasant incident ruin his weekend. He had not been up to arranging for a whore the night before but would do so now. As long as it was a young filly, he'd make sure his frustration was effectively dealt with.

The phone started ringing at one minute past eight and startled the cat that was still dozing in front of the fire on the first floor of the elegant Brock Street house. She was not expecting a busy day, Debbie Smith thought – amongst other things, Bath Rugby was playing away this weekend. She drained her coffee, put the newspaper down, and picked up the receiver.

"The Roman Experience Escort Agency."

"Good morning, Miss Smith." She immediately recognised the voice, David Fisher was a regular of several years' standing. Well heeled, discrete, knew the ropes and in many ways an ideal client. But there was something about him that was distasteful, condescending, falsely charming – but then the girls said he was meticulously mannered and often attentive in surprising ways.

"Good morning, Rear Admiral. How may I help you?"

"A weekender would be most welcome. I meant to call last night but would be grateful if you could help me out today instead."

"Anyone in mind?" she asked.

"You know me, Miss Smith, I love a change every now and then. How about someone new?"

Debbie Smith knew that he liked younger girls. "Sarah joined us last week. She's a twenty-four-year-old beautiful blond."

"Usual rate?" he asked. He always accepted who she suggested.

"Well, she won't be able to get there until lunchtime but it will still be the two- day special rate. Shall we say seventy pounds per day plus the cost of the room?"

"That would be perfect, Miss Smith. And will it be the same venue as my previous appointments?"

"Of course, Rear Admiral. I'll get her to call the Cathedral Hotel for the room number before she sets out, and please remember the receptionist's commission."

"I certainly will do. As always a pleasure Miss Smith – many thanks and goodbye."

After letting Sarah know about her appointment, Debbie made another cup of coffee.

According to those who knew about such things, Debbie Smith's women were the best in the city. Each was chosen with great care and 'no previous'. Avoiding criminal prosecution depended on discretion and the ability of her girls passing as totally-respectable escorts, as some often were, at Bath, Bristol, and, occasionally, London's grand functions. There could be no hint of sexual favours on offer to the various men. Some clients just yearned for work colleagues' envy, others were in sexless marriages or used her agency to hide their homosexuality.

Debbie had never envisaged herself running an escort agency but was quite happy with her comfortable home, her cat, and the financial independence it brought. Accustomed to a solitary existence – her parents had always lived abroad – after leaving La Sainte Union Convent School in Pulteney Road, she had started work in a Milsom Street bookshop and found a bed-sitter on Lyncombe Hill. A year later, she lost her first job after fighting off the middle aged married owner's advances.

Naively, she placed a small personal advertisement in the *Chronicle* as 'a Girl Friday willing to turn her hand to anything'. To her horror, every reply was from men wanting sex, until there came a telephone call from a Colonel Marcus Rose seeking a 'personal secretary'. As soon as she went through the gates of Widcombe House and was greeted by the striking retired army officer, she knew it was exactly what she'd been looking for.

From the start of the interview, the chemistry had worked, and she began the job two days later.

Intelligent and quick to learn, little by little, day-to-day menial tasks and errands were replaced with ever more responsibility. She willingly gave up her weekends and frequently took unfinished work back to her tiny home. Sometimes, she accompanied him to meetings in London, often arriving back in Bath late at night. There was no time for a social life, but she didn't care, and on the rare occasions when a date was sought by a passing young man, it was rejected out of hand. She was happy to give her all to this distinguished-looking man with his extensive business empire and numerous charitable endeavours.

Marcus grew to depend on Debbie more and more, and his wife, Susan, at first suspicious of her youth and good looks, accepted her as she realised the workload she was taking over from her husband. Acceptance turned into friendship as the girl became a part of the childless couple's household.

After four years, she was indispensable, and Rose appointed her his personal assistant, with which came a generous salary increase, her own shorthand typist, and a beautiful, rent-free cottage on the estate.

Debbie went back to her Daily Telegraph crossword and pondered eight across, 'the square of nothing cubed (3)'.

CHAPTER SEVEN

David Medlock went straight from the Sunday morning service at Bath Abbey to the Royal United Hospital. He was keen to see if there had been further progress since his visit twelve hours earlier.

No longer unconscious, Ian was breathing normally and the tracheostomy had been removed, but he had yet to open his eyes. As usual Piggott was on duty, and the doctor asked if there was any improvement, while he made an examination of his patient.

"No, sir, but he does seem slightly more restless and occasionally groans or coughs."

"I do hope we see something positive soon. I'm growing ever more concerned about permanent brain damage."

"Do you know him well?" the male charge nurse asked.

"Not personally, but some of my wealthy private patients, especially those involved in the Bath property scene say he is a force to be reckoned with. There was a big article about him in the *Chronicle* last month when he qualified as a Chartered Surveyor – so ambitious and successful, but look at him now."

Medlock turned to leave the room but paused at the open door and glanced back at the young man prone on the bed. "Let me know immediately if there is any change either way." He was clearly worried about the patient's prognosis.

Piggott was fussing around the already immaculate bed when Trish Traynor came in five minutes later and, after her usual cheerful greeting, sat down on the bedside chair.

Little by little, she and Norman Piggott had got to know and like one another. There would never be any sexual chemistry, but a friendship was developing between the two who spent several hours together on an almost daily basis. Their concern for this particular patient was mutual, hopefully recovering, albeit slowly, in this side room of the men's surgical ward.

"Hello, Trish," Piggott smiled tentatively, bringing both hands up to touch his beard. "I … I was wondering if you could possibly help me in a couple of ways for a good cause."

"Try me, Norman," she smiled in return, wondering why he always seemed so nervous.

"Well, first of all, I want you to know that this isn't really for me. I am lucky enough to live in a cosy little flat at the bottom of Bathwick Hill, but for the women who work here: they do such a caring job, work incredibly long hours for very little, and have to live in the Nurses' Home – a great big, old, dilapidated building in Sydney Road. The rooms are stark and tiny – stand in the middle and you can touch the walls – just a bed, chair, and small chest of drawers; if you are lucky, really grotty communal washrooms, but worse of all, endless narrow corridors with bare stone floors.

"Working shifts, staff come and go at all hours, and no one gets much sleep: just carpeting these floors would make such a difference, but the NHS has no money to spare for such 'non essentials'."

He continued in great detail about how the place had opened as the Bath Spa Hotel in 1915 before being requisitioned by the Admiralty in the Second World War and then bought by the Ministry of Health in 1948 – low priority – only minimal improvements had been made since the nurses had moved in nearly twenty years ago. Trish immediately explained that if it was money he was after, she couldn't help, but that was not what he wanted.

"No, nothing like that, just some typing if you can spare the time. We need to raise five hundred pounds through a Christmas Ball, and we're producing a little pamphlet. I volunteered to provide the history of the hospital," he picked up a couple of sheets of paper lying on the windowsill, "and after days in the library, I've come up with this." He handed her the two sheets of blue Basildon Bond writing paper, each side covered in his beautiful, black-ink script, using an Osmiroid pen. Trish started to read.

Following in a great tradition – The Nurses' Ball at The Royal United Hospital

After sixty years, the Bachelors' Ball is to be resurrected. Re-christened the Nurses' Grand Christmas Ball, it will take place at seven o'clock on Saturday, 22 December 1966.

Until the eighteenth century, Bath was simply a provincial city with a population of around a thousand five hundred that offered few facilities. But then came the Georgian invasion that transformed the centre into the most famous health resort in England. The Bath General Infirmary, or as we know of it now, the Mineral Water Hospital, opened in 1742 for these rich visitors from out of town.

As for the lower classes, there was the Bath Pauper Trust founded in 1747, with its dispensary in Wood Street, which moved to Lower Borough Walls. Later, following countless accidents caused by Bath's dangerous building boom, a new casualty hospital opened in 1788 on Kingsmead Street, and the two merged into the Bath United Hospital in 1826, in what is now Beau Street.

When its new wing was named the Albert Wing after the Prince Consort's death, the grieving Queen Victoria bestowed the title Royal, and so, the Royal United Hospital came into being in 1864, moving to its present site in 1932.

The hospital has always depended on the generosity of the citizens of Bath, often through novel ways of funding. There were the penny-admission charges from Penny Readings given in church halls. Local magistrates often directed the fines paid for poaching, petty theft, and slander to the hospital.

Until 1905, wealthy citizens paid an annual subscriptions, which entitled them to vote for the doctors in the hospital, in exchange for 'tickets of relief' which they could hand out to their favoured sick. The Bath Cycling Club raised funds, and it was only with the advent of the National Health Service that ...

"This is really interesting, Norman. I'm more than happy to type it out for you." she said. "What was the other thing you wanted?"

The charge nurse paused and brought both hands up to his chin again. "Would you come as my guest?"

Surprised, Trish thought for a moment – why not? "I'd be delighted," she replied.

CHAPTER EIGHT

Fiona had hung the *Do not disturb* sign on her door and slept for thirty hours. Eventually resurfacing, she had another bath, unpacked the last of her clean underwear from her rucksack, and then went in search of something to eat. It was just midday and she was the first guest to be seated for lunch in the shabby restaurant.

Like a cloud, the smell from the previous evening's smokers and fried food filled the room, but she didn't care – she was starving and was not disappointed: the prawn cocktail was followed by a large rump steak, chips with all the extras, and then the slab of Black Forest gateau smothered with whipped cream. Finally, the Irish coffee accompanied by a couple of After Eight mints, and she knew she was truly back with English cuisine. She left the dining room and took her purse of coins to the public telephone in the hall.

Fiona knew that she'd been remiss in not keeping in touch with her old crowd, and was not surprised to find that the first two friends she called had both moved. She was lucky with the third because, whilst Rosemary Fisher had apparently married and emigrated since they'd last spoken, the phone had been answered by her younger sister, Anne. Fiona remembered that the young girl had been rather in awe of her.

"Fiona! How lovely to hear from you."

"You too. I've just got back, but …" She took a breath and cut straight to the point. "I'm a bit desperate and need somewhere to stay until I get myself sorted out." Anne could not have been more friendly – it was as if it had been four days, not years, since they'd last spoken.

"That would be no problem. Father's away for the weekend on Admiralty business, but I know he won't mind. The house is so empty these days – why don't you come over straight away?"

An hour later, Fiona arrived in Lansdown Crescent. After walking up from town via the Circus, she cut up through St James' Square, and slightly out of breath, she dropped her rucksack to the ground and gazed back down onto the Georgian heart of the city. "What an amazing place to call home," she thought and smiled when she noticed the new lambs among the handful of sheep grazing in front of the Crescent. For the first time, she felt glad to be back in her beloved city and pulled the old iron bell handle by the Fishers' front door.

"My, you've grown up," she said when Anne appeared and welcomed her in. Fiona had always been the good-looking one who attracted the men in the old Bath crowd. Anne had been too young, but now the two women were much the same size, and Fiona sensed a potential rivalry. At twenty-four, Anne was tall and slim with long, blond hair – altogether another classic English beauty.

Unaware, joyously Anne hugged Fiona and then went about settling her into one of the guest bedrooms. Now they were seated, cups of tea in hand, in the drawing room, Anne chatting furiously, telling her all that had happened since she had been gone. Fiona felt she owed her young friend an explanation for her unexpected arrival and need to start at the beginning.

"As you know, I ran off to Switzerland after everything collapsed. A friend from finishing school put me up, saved my life, even got me a job as a receptionist in the bank she worked for." But she left it at that – she was not yet ready to say any more.

CHAPTER NINE

The creamy stone obelisk reflected the early morning sunlight. Trish remembered Ian had told her that it had been a thank-you present to Beau Nash from the Prince of Wales, in exchange for a gold-enamel snuff box.

It was Monday, 14 March 1966, and she could not believe that it had only been a month since she and Ian had first opened the office. She unlocked the front door of fifteen Queen Square, where the brass nameplate shone.

FORSYTE MORRIS & COMPANY CHARTERED SURVEYORS

She'd ordered the new one on her own initiative. It replaced the original with the word 'Chartered' added after Ian passed the final examination.

She walked past the magnificent wooden staircase and went through the daily ritual of opening the wooden Georgian shutters to the windows of Ian's empty ground-floor office overlooking the square. Then she returned to her back office and worried about her future.

There was mail to open with a new instruction to sell a property but also a worrying final demand for the unpaid rent of the offices. With a sense of foreboding, she stood up from her desk and returned to the silent magnificence of the enormous front office. The good luck cards and telegrams following the opening announcement were still spread along the mantelpiece either side of the brass mantle clock, which she had forgotten to wind and consequently had stopped. Most were from local businesses eager for a fresh source of work, or rival agents mindful of Ian's contacts in the city and hypocritically wishing him well. Then she saw the one from Susan Rose. She was the wife, now widow, of Ian's lifelong mentor and hero, Marcus Rose. Childless, they had treated Ian as a son, and Trish had accompanied her boss to occasional meetings at their beautiful home in Widcombe House.

Calamitously, Marcus had died of a heart attack the very day they had opened the new office in Queen Square. Nevertheless, Susan had rushed to the hospital in the morning immediately after Ian's attack, his only other visitor.

Trish decided to ask her advice and rang Widcombe House.

"That won't be possible, I'm afraid Miss Traynor. Madam left for London ten days ago," Jennings, the butler, replied.

That would explain why she hasn't returned to visit Ian, Trish thought. "Do you have any idea when she'll be back?" she asked.

"No, Miss Traynor – unlike the late Mr Rose, Mrs Rose does not confide in me." The resentment was audible. "You could try the Grosvenor Square flat, do you have the number?"

She tried the London number, but the telephone had been disconnected. At a loss to know what else to do, she closed up the office and made her way back to the Royal United Hospital.

The weekend had been a roller coaster: on Friday night, they finally removed the tube from his neck, saying Ian was regaining consciousness. But then, nothing more happened except for him making strange jerking movements. She stayed late, but he still had not opened his eyes when it came time for her to leave.

The small hospital room was crowded on her arrival with Mr Medlock, Norman, and the Ward Sister at the bedside. Ian was restless with his eyes still closed, his face and limbs twitching and making occasional rasping noises.

"What's wrong? What's happening to him?" She was unnerved. Piggott looked round and grinned.

"It's good news, Trish." Norman's face was flushed. "It looks like your boss is finally coming round."

Mr Medlock started talking and writing on the clipboard at the same time. "Nil by mouth, continue to feed intravenously into the thoracic vein, so as to ensure a more rapid flow. This will allow for fast dissemination of the elemental food, dissolved fatty acids, proteins, and vitamins as well as trace elements like magnesium and zinc without clogging up a smaller vein."

He replaced the clipboard at the foot of the bed and smiled at Trish.

"Thank goodness. At last, we're making progress, but there's still a long way to go yet …" The Staff Nurse gasped, Medlock then looked back at his patient.

Ian Morris had opened his eyes.

Trish's immediate joy and relief was then replaced by a sense of bewilderment. Ian did not recognise her and just stared blankly at all about him. It was as if he'd woken up to an unknown world.

"Amnestic syndrome," the Consultant said, gently took Trish's arm, and walked her into the hallway before continuing. "He probably doesn't know who he is, but hopefully it will be short-lived."

He then explained that amnesia was common after severe head injuries. But what alarmed Trish most was that the eminent physician could not say when or even if any of Ian's memory might return: it all depended on the type and severity of the brain lesion.

CHAPTER TEN

Fiona continually had to avoid the rear admiral rubbing his thigh against her knee under the breakfast table and tried not to flinch every time he groped her. Anne seemed oblivious to her father's inappropriate behaviour, but Fiona remembered, even when his wife had been alive, how she'd always had to fend off the old man's wandering hands. He really was an old letch.

Otherwise, staying with the Fishers was proving to be good news, and knowing her destination that morning, Anne had kindly lent her a smart trouser suit. The brown velvet fitted jacket was double-breasted with wide lapels, and the trousers were fashionably bell-bottomed. Under it was Fiona's favourite flowered blouse, chosen on a boutique shopping spree in Carmel quite early into her Californian adventure with Linda.

A little later, as she walked down into town, Fiona felt quietly confident that she would make the appropriate impression on the man she was going to meet. The central garden of Queen Square was as beautiful as ever in the early spring weather, and she noticed two magpies dancing around its obelisk and one another, in what she assumed was a mating ritual. It made her smile until shocked she noticed, tucked along the railings between some bushes in the garden's corner, a pile of cardboard beneath which someone was apparently asleep: she could never recall ever seeing anyone sleeping on the streets of Bath before. Totally ignored by passers-by, it was as though the unfortunate person did not exist. She shuddered, grateful in the knowledge of her good fortune to have friends that she could turn to in need.

Austwick & Company was on the northern side of Queen Square and had been solicitors to the Lundy family for over fifty years. The senior partner, Malcolm Austwick was Fiona's guardian, godfather, and trustee, having advised her throughout her life. She still counted him as a favourite among her late father's friends, and he was obviously delighted to see her:

untypically, he gave her a hug and then the more expected paternal kiss on the cheek.

"It's good to see you back home and about time too, young lady." He looked her up and down, smiling. "You look as beautiful as always. Tell me your news, where have you been and what have you been up to?"

He sat behind the large partner's desk in the window of his first floor office and listened, as she related a sanitised version of her travels over the past four years. Wondering how honest she should be with this lovely old family friend, she sometimes paused to look beyond him and through the bare trees to the Francis Hotel. But she finally reached the end of her epic trip back to Bath.

"Such adventures!" Austwick said enthusiastically. "And what are your plans now, my dear?"

"I'm staying with the Fishers. The rear admiral says I can stay as long as I like, and I've always got along well with Anne but … I need some money, and I was wondering … if my trust had survived the bankruptcy."

"Yes," Austwick sighed before continuing, "but sadly the only things left in it aren't worth very much, if anything at all. There are some long abandoned and derelict houses in Corn Street here in the city, then there's the old Lundy nursery farm. That's largely made up of exhausted and unlettable fields in Combe Down. But don't fret, my dear, I always promised your dear papa and my dear friend, the 3rd Earl, that I'd keep you safe. How much do you need?"

"Twenty-five pounds a week." She hesitated. "But only until I get a job."

"Let's make it thirty – I'll put it into your trustee bank account and organise for you to pick up a cheque book. That might take a week, though, so …" He paused, took out his wallet, extracted fifty pounds, and handed the notes to her.

"Thank you so much, Uncle Malcolm." Fiona tried not to show the relief she felt in her smile. Now she could afford some clothes and to have her hair done, much needed if she was to make a fresh start in the city.

"I'm delighted to be of assistance my dear and only wish your brother's financial problems could be so easily solved."

"I haven't yet spoken to Alistair. Is he all right?" She wasn't looking forward to catching up with her brother – nor her mother.

"Ah." The elderly man lent back in his chair and told her how the whole sorry story had played out after she had left.

"Do you remember Ian Morris?"

Fiona nodded.

"Well, Alistair blames him for the whole catastrophe, but he's quite wrong. I explained to him that while your father was a delightful chap and wonderful company, he really wasn't a businessman, and I'm afraid he made some very poor decisions. But young Alistair won't see reason. He seems obsessed with young Morris … Anyway, it looks as though his wish has been granted."

"What do you mean?" Fiona was intrigued.

"Oh, you wouldn't know, of course. It must be … oh, about two weeks ago now that Morris was battered and left for dead outside his own front door. That was your old house, of course, in Great Pulteney Street. The last I heard, he's still unconscious, and the police have no idea who attacked him. When I first heard, I thought it could've been Alistair's doing and asked him straight out. 'Good riddance and got what he deserved,' he told me but swore he had nothing to do with it – not sure I totally believe him. Personally, I think it's a great pity, because I like Morris. He's fought against great odds and done extremely well for himself – and others."

Fiona sat quietly while her guardian extolled the virtues of Ian Morris until she had the chance to change the subject.

"Well, thank you once again for the cash, Uncle, but I need to get on and face mother and Alistair. Anne Fisher has offered to drive me over there."

"A word of warning: be prepared. Your mother is not the woman she once was, sadly – much changed. The bankruptcy hit her very hard, and she is not at all well. Anyway, it's been a pleasure to see you again, my dear, and please stay in touch."

"I promise," she said and kissed him goodbye.

CHAPTER ELEVEN

Fiona and Anne returned to Lansdown Crescent in the early evening.

"I hope you had an enjoyable day." David Fisher perfunctorily kissed his daughter and greeted Fiona, with his hands all over her in his embrace. "It's so good for Anne to have company again. I can't remember the last time she looked so happy."

"I'm pleased." Fiona disengaged.

Fiona had been shocked by the pokey little flat in Monkton Combe where her brother and mother now lived, and it had been a difficult meeting. Her mother had become forgetful and clearly was not coping without the retinue of staff she had been so used to – Alistair did not seem to notice the mess and accumulated grime. Fiona and Anne found some cleaning equipment and spent hours trying to bring a state of order to the chaos.

In contrast, Fiona saw that the rear admiral appeared to have recovered from his wife's death, and was coping well with life as a widower.

"Why don't the two of you help yourselves to gin and tonics, and we can then decide where I take you to dinner?" Fisher suggested.

"Thank you, Daddy. That would be lovely – let me fix you a drink too." Anne said. "Then we'll go and get cleaned up."

Anne brought the drinks up to Fiona's bedroom where she was sitting at the dressing table applying makeup.

"Thank you so much for coming with me to mother's flat and everything, Anne. I feel so ashamed." Fiona looked at her friend through the mirror's reflection.

"You don't need to be. Many of our old set have just disappeared."

"Where to?" Fiona reached for a pale-pink lipstick from her toiletry bag.

"Like me, lots went to London, and after Daddy sent me to Lucy Clayton, I would've stayed there too if he hadn't been on his own. But I couldn't after Mummy died and Rosemary went to Australia," Anne said. "It's awful. There's absolutely nothing to do here, now that so many of the old Bath families like yours are either broke or have little money, and their children have left. It all happened so quickly. Everyone's gone – if it's not London, it's Birmingham, Manchester, or even Newcastle, would you believe, to become solicitors, accountants and bankers – anywhere and anything to just get away from this sad old city."

She took a drink from her glass, swilled its ice cubes, and looked again at Fiona in the dressing table mirror.

"I'm not kidding. It's all so depressing with just money grabbers left, leeches who just want to bleed the place dry. I am so bored, I would leave if it wasn't for father."

Fiona thought for a moment as she pressed her lips together and re-applied another layer of Pink Mist.

"What do you know about my brother's campaign to stop the property spivs, the leeches as you call them, destroying Bath?" she asked.

"Oh you mean Bath Against Developers?' Anne gave a little grin, seemingly on safer ground. "I have to admit that I think your brother is amazing, and I joined it right at the beginning – I was even a steward at its first meeting. But it seems to have gone quiet recently."

Something her brother had complained about earlier occurred to Fiona.

"I have an idea." She stood up and turned to Anne. "Do you think your father would mind if I used the phone? It'll be a really short call."

"Of course not, there's an extension in my bedroom."

Fiona went out, closed the door behind her, and returned a few minutes later.

"How would you like a job as secretary to my brother Alistair, and his anti-developers movement?"

"Really? Your brother? That would be great!"

"The pay would be a pittance," Fiona grimaced.

"That doesn't matter. It would be so good to have a reason to get up in the morning and I can't think of anyone I'd rather work with. I've always thought your brother clever and interesting."

Hardly the words that Fiona would have readily used to describe her useless brother, but she did agree with the BAD ethos and was really pleased if she could help repay Anne's kindnesses.

"I'll ring him back and say you accept and can start Monday. Then we can go and have dinner with your father."

"And will you tell us more about California?"

"All right, but not tonight, not with your father there."

Anne was growing on her, but there was so much to tell, and it was important she understood. Linda was right when she'd advised her in Switzerland to always "be careful, be straight, and tell it how it is."

CHAPTER TWELVE

Overlooking the village of Monkton Combe, two-and-a-half miles south of the city of Bath, is Combe Grove Manor, so named because of the groves of fir trees first planted across the valley in 1520.

This large, imposing house, bought and altered in 1706 had fallen on hard times and since the early 1800s had been let to numerous tenants. The latest, the eccentric Audrey Easter, had turned it into private apartments for "ladies and gentlemen who declined housekeeping". Like a modern-day Miss Havisham, she occupied the former orangery and lived her life in an ever diminishing reality, recalling famous past tenants, such as the film stars Rex Harrison and Kaye Kendall.

Alistair, the 4th Earl of Lundy looked out of the window of his tiny office in the flat he was forced to share with his widowed mother, the Dowager. There was not even room for a proper desk or any filing cabinets – he had just two chairs and a small coffee table surrounded by files stacked high against the walls.

Across the Limpley Stoke valley stood Rowas Grange, his magnificent ancestral home surrounded by its four hundred acres of land, farm cottages, and woods. Every day, he looked and felt the shame of the family's bankruptcy in 1963 with the humiliation of the very public sale of its entire contents, all the wonderful antique furniture, pictures, and even his personal possessions. He craved revenge, especially against the housekeeper's son, Ian Morris, who had been the cause of the family's downfall. Although if what he heard was true, someone had got there before him.

That awful Roger Palmer had outsmarted him – again. He'd not expected the demolition opposite the Guildhall in the High Street to start until next week at the earliest. All his plans that were geared to kick off in three days' time were now useless. He had lined up dozens of eager pickets and sit down protesters, with the *Chronicle* photographer straining at the leash. It had been designed to attract headlines and maximum publicity, and draw in new members and much needed cash – but all to no avail.

He'd set up Bath Against Developers two years earlier following a chance remark by the elderly Colonel Bradshaw over a drink at the County Club – and the thousand pounds the old chap offered in funding. At twenty-two years old, Alistair was effectively a redundant aristocrat – broke, unemployed, and virtually unemployable. So, he had jumped at the opportunity to do something, anything, to help redeem his family name and establish his standing in Bath.

Everyone had underestimated the level of the hidden anger felt by Bathonians at what was happening by stealth to their city. The inaugural packed meeting at the Pump Room was explosive with noise, stamping feet, and so many willing volunteers. He was amazed: he'd touched a community nerve that mobilised a dozen committees of volunteers.

Its news-sheet, *The Battlefield,* launched by a sympathetic newspaperman, had gone from strength to strength, attracting hundreds of new recruits. To begin with, the subscriptions and donations poured in, but then, it was no longer newsworthy and stagnated.

With his ever supportive sister back, hopefully to help with their embittered and difficult mother, perhaps BAD could prosper again. Fiona's first step in finding him a secretary, or personal assistant as he would call her, was an excellent move. Girls had never been high on his agenda, but Anne was perfect in the role – perfect background, perfect image, and even more perfectly, and for reasons he had not yet worked out, prepared to work for next to nothing.

As if on cue, Anne Fisher came in to place a cup of coffee on the table and hand him the post.

"I think this one will make your day, Alistair." She indicated the top of the small pile.

Christopher Kane & Partners
20 Quiet Street
Bath

15 March 1966

Dear Lord Lundy,

We have not met, as I have only recently moved my practice down from London. I understand no solicitor acts for Bath Against Developers, and so, I am taking the liberty of writing to you directly.

A client of this firm much admires what you have achieved and continue to achieve in preventing the wholesale demolition of Bath's historic buildings. He wishes to assist you, but requires to remain anonymous.

He also suggests that 'Bath Against Developers' is a rather negative name for such a worthy cause. He wonders if you would consider renaming the organisation to emphasise the more positive aim of preservation and restoration: the choice of name to be entirely yours.

With this aim in mind he has put my firm in funds to the extent of five thousand pounds, and I am authorised to pay this to you so that your admirable venture can be put on a more secure footing. How you employ these funds is left to your discretion.

Assuming the above is acceptable, I should be obliged for your banking details, so I can arrange for the transfer of these monies.

It occurs to me that from time to time you might like to let me have copies of the Minutes of your Board Meetings.

Naturally, I will treat these as confidential, but so I can pass them onto my client. I suggest this so that his continuing interest and possible further support of your venture can be fostered.

Yours sincerely,

Christopher Kane

For the first time ever, Alistair felt the thrill of self-achievement – he was numb and simply stared at the letter in front of him.

"Who do you think the donor is?" Anne asked.

"I don't know but wouldn't be surprised if it turned out to be someone like Champagne Charlie or Charlie Ware. I noticed him sitting quietly at the back at our last meeting and wondered what he was doing there – he's made a fortune out of restoring old buildings and loves Bath. He lives in the Royal Crescent and is involved with the Theatre Royal, so it makes sense." He leant back on the chair, looked at his personal assistant, and smiled.

"Ring Christine Penny at Bath Office Agents in Margarets Buildings and tell her to expect me in a couple of hours. At last, we can get out of this rat hole and into a proper office in Bath, with a real wage for you and a managing director's salary for me." Coffee forgotten, he stood up. "I'm off to see Mr Kane," he said, walking past Anne towards the door before turning back to her. "And thank you for believing in me." Then, he was gone.

Anne picked up the untouched coffee and sat in the chair Alistair had just vacated. She brought the cup to her lips and looked back across the Limpley Stoke valley as he had done minutes before. *I'm getting there,* she thought, *and it's easier than I'd imagined.* Despite her father's misgivings, she knew she was in touching distance of the Lundy title.

Thank you, thank you, Fiona, she thought again, sipping the coffee. You've brought me Alistair and all I have to do now is slowly reel him in.

CHAPTER THIRTEEN

Trish's relief when Ian had opened his eyes after fourteen long days turned to fear and bewilderment, as more time passed during which he blankly stared out at them all but didn't appear to see anything.

Everybody at the hospital was very understanding as she continued to sit by his bedside looking for just a flicker of recognition. Norman tried to keep her spirits up by pointing out the physical progress, as mouth and throat swellings went down and the reliability of the gag and cough reflexes returned. He was a wonderful nurse and always positive. But for her, the lifeless unrecognising eyes were desperately sad.

At first she saw little point in attending the office, but after another week passed she returned to Queen Square and a mound of unopened post on the doormat. She picked it up and was hanging up her coat when the bell rang. Returning to the front door, she was confronted by a tall man sombrely dressed in a dark overcoat. He lifted his bowler hat and smiled pleasantly.

"I wonder if you can assist me, I am looking for Mr Ian Morris. I have been to his house on Great Pulteney Street several times over the last week, but I can't seem to raise him there."

"I work for Mr Morris," she replied. "Maybe I can I help you."

"Oh, yes, excellent." He reached into his briefcase, took out a manila envelope, and handed it to her. Then, without another word, he lifted his hat again, turned, and was gone.

She took the envelope back to her room and opened it.

THE COURT OF REPOSSESSIONS

LONDON

CLAIMANT: *Woods & Partners*
              Chartered Surveyors
              Wood Street
              Bath

DEFENDANT: *Ian Morris*
              12 Great Pulteney Street
              Bath

The Claimant Messrs. Woods and Parker requires vacant possession of 12 Great Pulteney Street Bath and making a claim for an unpaid mortgage debt of £5,000 plus costs of this action.

THIS CLAIM WILL BE HEARD ON THE MORNING OF WEDNESDAY, 30 MARCH 1966 AT PRECISELY 10 O'CLOCK AT THE STRAND, LONDON WC2. IF SUCCESSFUL THE DEFENDANT WILL BE ORDERED TO LEAVE THE PROPERTY IMMEDIATELY AND ANY GOODS THEREIN WILL BE DETAINED.

Her immediate reaction was pure fear. She had never seen a writ before and its sheer brevity and formality scared her: to give her time to think she put it to one side, sat down and started to open the remaining mail. The first two letters were agents' particulars of properties for sale, but the third was from a firm of solicitors.

Christopher Kane & Partners

20 Quiet Street
Bath

Forsyte Morris & Company
15 Queen Square   <u>BY HAND</u>
Bath

14 March 1966

Dear Sirs,
                        <u>15 Queen Square, Bath</u>

 *We act on behalf of your landlords, who inform us that the rent arrears
amounting to £300 remain unpaid despite numerous reminders and a
Final Notice, all of which have been ignored. Accordingly, unless the
sum plus our costs of £20, namely a total of £320 is received at this
office within the next seven days, namely by close of business on
Monday, 21 March, we are instructed to take the appropriate action for
full recovery without further notice.*

Yours faithfully,

Christopher Kane & Partners

The next was addressed to Ian personally, and she carefully slit open
the long vellum cream envelope.

The Royal Institution of Chartered Surveyors
12 Great George Street, London SW1

 I. Morris A.R.I.C.S.
12 Great Pulteney Street
Bath   *14 March, 1966*

Dear Mr Morris
                    <u>The Pilkington Medal</u>

*As advised in my letter of 1ˢᵗ March, you are the winner of the Pilkington
Medal, which is awarded to the candidate who obtains the highest marks
over 75% in the Advances Property Valuation Papers of the Final
Examination. The medal is accompanied by a cheque for £75.*

*I write now to confirm the arrangements for the presentation. I would
request that you present yourself here on April 24ᵗʰ to receive your
Certificate of Admission, the Pilkington Medal and cheque from the
hand of the President, Mr Frank Knowles PRICS.*

Yours sincerely,

ROBERT IRONS FRICS (Secretary)

Terror, bravely contained since the assault on Ian, now overwhelmed her. Everything was spinning out of control, and there was nothing she could do. Slumping onto the desk, she finally gave in and sobbed. There was no one to turn to, no one to advise her, and she could cope no longer.

CHAPTER FOURTEEN

For five thousand pounds, Alistair had no problem with his donor's suggestion of renaming. The new brass nameplate on the front of fifteen Queen Square, *Traditional Bath,* looked very impressive, and while unwise to shorten the name to TB, it was certainly more positive than BAD.

"What shall I do with this?" Anne asked, holding out the nameplate taken down and left on the hallway table by the sign makers when she and Alistair had moved in four hours earlier.

"Put it on the mantelpiece in my office."

Two days later, the presence of the redundant nameplate puzzled Fiona, who was sharing a pot of coffee with Alistair in the magnificent building's ground floor front office: the top of the building was being made into a separate flat for Fiona and himself.

The office was the same reception room that Ian Morris had used just a few months earlier. She was surprised that her brother wanted to keep everything as it was, the desk, vast conference table, chairs, sofas by the fireplace and even the double locked cabinet in the back room: all paid for by 'the housekeeper's son and to remain exactly as he'd found them – a constant reminder of his victory.

"A trophy from my first battle with the working class," he replied, getting up from the desk and walking across to one of the sofas. "And a reminder of how dangerous they can be, when they forget their place and get above their station."

"Ah, your nemesis, Ian Morris," she said. "Don't you think he's got enough to deal with at the moment?"

"Right in one, Sis. Flat on his back and unconscious in the Royal United Hospital." He sounded jubilant. "As far as I'm concerned, it couldn't have happened to a nicer guy."

Fiona decided no useful purpose would be served in pursuing the subject and sat down on the other sofa.

"So what have you asked me here for? I can see that you have an impressive office now but what do you want from me?"

"I've got an idea," he said. "The City Council has contacted me, asking if I knew of anyone who could assist their planning department in deciding which buildings to preserve and which to demolish. They've got a backlog and need an outside consultancy urgently."

"I don't know a thing about property." She lifted her coffee cup to her lips and waited to hear what Alistair had in mind.

"That doesn't matter, you can always hire others. What's needed is someone to front the whole thing up." He lent forward eagerly. "Your credentials are perfect. You're from an aristocratic family that's been in Bath forever, and your brother heads up a popular preservation movement in the city. The Council will love it. Especially at the right price – remember grandfather's maxim of 'bid low to secure the deal, then add the extras later to make a pile'?

"Grandfather's expressions were fine sixty years ago, when he owned, terrified, and controlled everything and everyone, including the Council." She wasn't sure she wanted to work so closely with her brother but had no other plans. "Anyway, where would I work from? I can hardly set up in the Fishers' guest bedroom. And what about staff?"

"The first floor here is empty, and as for staff, until the money starts to roll in, I'm sure we can share Anne." Obviously he had worked it all out.

"I wouldn't be sure of that at all," she said.

"Why not?" he replied. "She seems really happy."

"Oh, come off it, Alistair. Remember I'm your sister, and that I've seen it all before. She's all over you, but you've not told her that she's wasting her time. Or am I mistaken? How is your love life these days?"

"OK, OK!" His confidence suddenly crumpled, and Alistair looked decidedly uncomfortable. "You're right, there is someone, but it's all very discreet. He's got his own little flat over the shops at the bottom of Bathwick Hill, so you don't need to concern yourself."

"But I do worry – even if I've not been around to show it, it only takes an ambitious young policemen armed with information from a disappointed young woman who's interested in marrying for a title ..."

"Well, don't." He reached into his pocket for a cigarette and then picked the silver lighter from the coffee table. "I've learned to take care of myself in your absence, so let's get back to what's important." He lit the cigarette. "So – the consultancy role?"

"Oh, all right then." Fiona was warming to the idea of earning some money and liked the idea of doing something to help the floundering city.

"Great – I'll get back to the Council and let them know."

To celebrate her new job, Fiona took Anne out to dinner at the Firehouse Rotisserie. Only recently opened by Richard Fenton, with its American ranch décor and dishes which Bath had never seen the like of before, the restaurant was proving an enormous success.

They were shown to a table opposite the massive open ovens. Seconds later, two Californian nectar cocktails on the house appeared in front of them.

"Welcome, ladies. Don't worry, non-alcoholic – hopefully that will come later – just apricots, pears, and unsweetened pineapple juice," the ebullient young owner advised and handed them the menus.

"No more stalling, Fiona – California."

Fiona laughed. "Oh, all right – now, where did I get to?"

"Nowhere. You were staying with your friend Linda in Geneva. She worked for a big American bank on a deal with an American in the weapons business, with the unlikely sounding Frank Duffer Junior."

"Oh, yes, the DNM," Fiona said, slowly enunciating the letters. "The Duffer Nature Movement."

"The what? It sounds like a nudist colony." Now it was Anne laughing. "Being in the buff … or being up the duff …"

Fiona continued and explained that, as Linda had predicted, the American Bank ended her contract a few months after Fiona's arrival. In the meantime, Frank Duffer had grown dependent on Linda and offered her a job as his personal secretary. With a little persuasion, he also agreed that Fiona could be taken on as a junior assistant. But rather than return to chilly Chicago with his ill-gotten gains, he had decided to relocate to the laid back beaches of California.

"To begin with, Duffer's California dream was basically a holiday, but after a while he got drawn into one of the numerous small cults that were springing up on the west coast of the United States. It was called the Free Nature Movement and was all about the use of self-realisation to stop the world going to hell in a handcart before the appointed date."

"The appointed date?" Anne interrupted.

"Yes, the end of the world, midnight on 31 December 1999 – and on that note, I suggest we order. The menu looks fabulous."

"So, what is it to be?" Richard had returned.

Fiona answered first.

"The Texas-spiced, rubbed rotisserie Norfolk chicken with Jalenjo coleslaw with hickory barbecue sauce, if I may."

He looked at Anne.

"Very American, but I am afraid I am going to be less adventurous. The seared fillet of Scottish salmon with crab risotto and extra-virgin oil, please."

Fiona continued. "Duffer was a shrewd businessman. Within three months, he'd paid off the movement's so-called Shaman, taken it over, and renamed it after himself." Although some said he was obsessed and been sucked into the cult, Fiona knew otherwise. "He spent a lot of money and turned DNM into a Charitable Religious Foundation, which meant he avoided paying a cent of tax on the enormous profit from the sale of his armaments business."

With a flourish, their meals arrived and were set down with an "Enjoy" – they lived up to their exotic descriptions.

As they waited for the coffee, Anne tried to persuade her to continue, but Fiona had other ideas.

"I'll tell you more another time, but tonight, we're celebrating that we have both become financially independent, and I want to suggest something." She stirred her coffee. "I can't carry on indefinitely staying in your guest bedroom but wondered how you'd feel about us renting a place together."

"That's a great idea," Anne said, "I'd love to move out, and I think Daddy would be OK on his own if I am nearby. Do you have anywhere in mind?"

"My old place in Great Pulteney Street. Alistair told me that it's available at a knock-down rental if we can move quickly due to a repossession order."

"How exciting! I'm definitely up for that."

Anne and Fiona took the house. Later, she was to find the auction particulars when she had been evicted and it had been bought by Morris: twelve Great Pulteney Street was lot three hundred and forty-one on the second day of the sale, which had seen every single thing owned by the Lundy family sold off to the public.

The hammer had come down at ten thousand six hundred pounds, weirdly exactly four years earlier on 28 April 1962.

CHAPTER FIFTEEN

Barely conscious in a hospital bed, he lay unaware that his creditors had seized his beloved home in Great Pulteney Street: he was still struggling to return to the land of the living two weeks later when his business ceased to exist. The Court Sheriff's people unceremoniously evicted Trish from the Queen Square offices, allowing her to take only personal possessions, armfuls of files and unbeknown to them, her key, one of the two to the map cabinet in her office.

Six weeks after the violent assault, Ian was finally able to take fluids by mouth, and the ever-attentive charge nurse, Norman Piggott, began to feed him with a porcelain-spouted cup.

Ian was aware of the man leaning over him with an overpowering smell of soap and the small watch pinned to a white tunic. He could feel something pressed between his lips, a warm sweet liquid trickled over his tongue and down his throat, forcing him to swallow. He was drowning. He fell back into darkness. Who was the young women sitting by his bedside? Darkness … He tried to talk to her, then his head would throb and his eyelids become heavy. Tiredness overwhelmed him, and darkness would return …

Ian's bouts of semi-consciousness continued for four weeks, his twenty-fourth birthday passed unnoticed. Having exhausted her meagre savings, Trish was forced to sign up with a temping agency. A nomad going from company to company, she worked as a copy typist during the day but returned each evening to his bedside.

One morning, Norman Piggott found Ian wide awake when he came on duty. Now, the eyes followed his every move and, as usual, the charge nurse started his one sided commentary.

"How are you this morning? Let's get you sat up ready for breakfast. That's better, pillows comfortable?" Piggott turned away to pick up the hated feeding cup from the top of the bedside locker.

"No," came the hoarse interjection.

"So you *do* have a voice!" Piggot's delight was evident and his hands sprung up to his chin.

Ian nodded his head slowly.

"Welcome back, Mr Morris."

The ringing telephone broke her concentration on the document she was copy-typing.

"Trish, it's Norman from the hospital."

"Hello, Norman, what's wrong?" It was the first time he had ever called her from the hospital.

"Nothing, quite the reverse. Your boss has started to talk, and Mr Medlock said it's time to make plans to get him out of bed for some proper physiotherapy."

She didn't hear any more: she dropped the receiver into its cradle, picked up her handbag, and ran out of the door. If she'd continued to listen, the charge nurse would have told her that she was the first person Ian had asked for.

Trish took one look at him, propped up on the pillows, grinning at her, before throwing her arms around him. It was such a joy, and she couldn't help but smile as she later watched him struggle valiantly to tackle a bowl of soup and eat a slice of bread.

After he'd been tidied up by Norman, he faced her. Ian looked a wreck, not the confident smart businessman he'd once been – for a start, he was missing two front teeth – but Trish could see the bright eyes, the look she knew so well when he was working on something important.

"Got your note book?" he croaked.

"No," she said, surprised. "Never be without one" had been the first golden rule he'd given her when she first went to work for him. "Take it to bed with you, more useful than sex," he had joked, or at least she'd thought he was joking at the time.

"Well, find something to write on," he said, his voice improving slightly as he gestured to the clip board hanging at the foot of the bed. Instinctively, she did his bidding and found a blank temperature graph.

"So, first things first. Hopefully, you've managed to keep the business ticking over?"

She was so taken aback by the question that she couldn't find her voice to answer.

"The business," he asked again. "It's okay, isn't it?"

Trish shook her head, swallowed, and finally managed to speak. "You've been here for over three months, Ian. It's been a nightmare. There's been no work, and so there's been no money. It's just been problems, debt, angry creditors, landlords …"

"Surely, some people were able to help – Sue Rose, the Wessex Property Club?"

"No, there's only been me," she faltered, it had never occurred to her to look elsewhere. Tears began to gather both at her own helplessness and his ingratitude; he had no idea what she had been through. He had strove to make something of himself, to make sure that he would never be poor again, but so had she. She'd done her very best, and yet she'd had been unable to stop the bailiffs, the debt collectors, the evictors – it had all come crumbling down.

"What the hell do you mean?" It came out as a hoarse, accusatory whisper.

She listed the category of disasters and explained that there was nothing left – even his beloved sports car was gone.

Already pale, he turned grey as the blood drained from his face, and he sunk back onto the pillow. He grunted rather than spoke again, and Trish realised that she was being blamed for the catastrophe. On this sour note, she left, her proffered goodbye kiss on the cheek rebuffed.

Returning the next morning after a sleepless night, she found him in a more positive mood. As requested the evening before, she'd brought the writ, eviction notice, and the enforcement papers. He spread them over the bed, paying particular attention to those relating to the repossession of his home and office. Trish knew he was searching for a way to bargain himself out of the fiasco. After all, that was what he'd always been able to do – to get what he wanted.

When he realised that the three month delay had been fatal, he sank back into the bed, scattering the various documents and papers onto the floor, and rolled over to face the wall. Totally ignored, Trish gathered everything up and left.

When she returned after work the next evening, Norman was waiting for her in the corridor, out of Ian's earshot.

"I thought you should know that I found him in tears this morning, and he's obviously extremely depressed. Strangely, the loss of his home has affected him less than the news about his business: for him, it's a severe bereavement. He has to learn to accept it, but that may take some time.'

"So, what can I do to help?" she asked.

"Well, let's get him back on his feet – the physio starts tomorrow, and we can start by helping him get his independence back. With luck, he'll be up and walking, and then he will be able to get out of here in a few weeks."

She wondered if Ian would ever accept the situation. Was he finished, going nowhere, washed up at only twenty-four?

Reality came a step closer when the question of his discharge from hospital arose in late June.

"Trish, they want to discharge me at the weekend, but where to? I've got nowhere to live." The cracked ribs had healed, and Ian was walking unaided – albeit slowly – beside Trish on one of their walks in the hospital garden.

"Given that I took all that was left of your few personal belongings to my place, it probably makes sense for you to come and stay with me for the time being.

"In Gay Street?"

She shook her heard. "I wish. I'm afraid not – I ran out of money after your accident, and so I had to move back with my mum."

"I am so sorry, where are you living?"

"In Snowhill, Mafeking Street, number thirty."

"Mafeking Street? I'd never realised that was where your mother lived."

"Do you know it?" Unlike Ian, she had never denied her humble background and that she'd grown up in one of Bath's rougher areas. Her main ambition had always been to eventually buy a house of her own – in the centre of town, but obviously, this now wasn't going to happen any time soon.

"Do I know it?" He laughed, but without mirth. "My mother and I lived at number thirty-six when I was about twelve – I wonder if you were there then." Somehow, knowing this made her feel even closer to this man.

"They're very small houses, are you sure there is room?"

"Mum and I have already discussed it," Trish replied. "We'll be fine. You're more than welcome until you get back on your feet."

Three days later, Ian went back to live in the shabby little street of terraced houses that he'd taken twelve years to try and forget.

CHAPTER SIXTEEN

"Bloody disaster," Tom Scotland said after Peter Groves opened the June evening meeting of the Wessex Property Club at the back of the Abbey Hotel.

"The Tories are a complete shambles. It's the Suez fiasco and Anthony Eden all over again. At least McMillan found a good dentist and understood the press. Then came Christine Keeler, Profumo, and that blasted programme, what was it called?"

"*That Was The Week That Was*," Roger Palmer chipped in.

"That's the bugger. McMillan had no choice but to resign, and so they get Douglas-Hume. Lovely chap, a laird from some remote Scottish island, whose family goes back hundreds of years and has no idea how the real world works. He was nothing but a two-minute wonder, and now we've got a grammar-school boy – Ted Heath, unmarried – bang goes our women's vote!

"Kiss goodbye to the Tory aristocrats and statesmen who have run this country brilliantly for centuries: six Baronets lost their seats – swept away. The grammar schoolboy is more interested in sailing his beloved boat, Morning Glory. No wonder the country is going down the pan."

Just seventeen months earlier, Harold Wilson's Labour Party had been elected with an unworkable majority of only four seats, reduced to two at subsequent by-elections. But when Wilson called a snap election at the end of March 1966, it was a landslide – he gained a majority of ninety-six.

"These are desperate times," Scotland lamented. "Wilson's clever like MacMillan was and knows how to work television. They've re-invented him into 'the man of the people – your workmate in the pub with pipe and a pint', although the swine never goes in pubs and doesn't like either: his tipple is brandy, and he loves his cigars.

"Did you see yesterday's Financial Times? The economy's in crisis with continuing Treasury cutbacks, and all we get is desperate short-term fixes. Another four years to soak the rich, of disastrous rampant socialism, kowtowing to the Trade Unions, more regulation and red tape administered by vast numbers of new bureaucrats, financed by increased, sky-high taxes from you and me. How we are going to make, or more importantly, keep, any money we make? You tell me!"

Groves had let the rant run long enough and interrupted him. "Nearer to home and more worrying is what happened in Bristol – Alan Hopkins and McLaren lost their seats – it's a sea of red."

The faces round the table were glum until the banker, Christopher Johnson, broke the silence.

"One good piece of news: Ian Morris came out of hospital yesterday. I bumped into his old secretary, Trish Traynor: she told me that he's made a remarkable recovery but is understandably feeling very low, having lost everything in the months he was unconscious, bed ridden and out of action. I'm arranging for him to come and see me next week, and will offer him something to keep him occupied in the Bank."

It wasn't an unusual story where a one-man business overstretched with debts falls down easily, and Johnson knew that several around the table would have sympathy for Morris.

"Good idea and give him our regards," Scotland said. "And let us know if there's anything we can do to help him get back on his feet, better late than never."

"Now, let's move on." Groves cleared his throat. "Malcolm, I think you have something to discuss." He looked at the solicitor.

"Thank you, Peter. Something I learned at a recent legal dinner," – many knew about the monthly get-together of Bath solicitors – "Lord Lundy's Bath Against Development has been renamed Traditional Bath and has received an anonymous donation of five thousand pounds. Regrettably, I would anticipate therefore that his protest operation will become more active: ironically, the new set-up has moved into Ian Morris's old offices at fifteen Queen Square …"

"And something that may be relevant – or should I say coincidental," Tom Scotland interrupted, "is that while the Council is in favour of demolishing vast tracts of the city, it can't be seen to encourage this policy. It's done the usual thing, appointed a firm of consultants to hide behind and do their dirty work for them. A firm called the Bath Regenerating Practise has won the contract – if 'won' is appropriate: it bid so much lower than anyone else – others are complaining it was a fix."

"I've never heard of them," Palmer said. "What's the coincidence?"

"The Bath Regenerating Practise is a part of Lundy Enterprises Ltd."

Everyone present knew the name of the company set up sixty years earlier by Michael Symons, the iron fist of the 1st Earl of Lundy. A monopoly to deal solely with his vast business empire of shops, factories, hotels, pubs, and thousands of feudal ground rents and rent charges, not to mention the swathes of workers' terraced houses let on weekly tenancies – a tenth of the whole city. In addition, it owned twenty thousand or so acres of agricultural land and woodlands around the city, much of the Somerset and Bristol coal fields, the Fuller Earth works, and the stone quarries.

Tom Scotland went on. "You'll remember that everything went under the hammer at the three-day auction in the Assembly Rooms about four years ago, but not the Bath Regeneration Practice given that it owned nothing and had been dormant since the outbreak of the Second World War. Anyway, Lundy's sister bought it for a pound and is operating from the first floor of fifteen Queen Square."

"I didn't know she was back in Bath," Palmer said. "Didn't she leave in a bit of a hurry after Morris evicted her and then bought her big house on Great Pulteney Street at the auction? Remind me, what was her name?"

"The Honourable Fiona Symons – and my god-daughter," Austwick answered him, "and you are correct, although the tables have turned again, and she is back living in her old home."

Palmer nodded and went on. "Clever, what better credentials for the Council to hide behind – the titled sister and her brother who heads up the only populist preservation movement in Bath."

"On that depressing note, I suggest we, gentlemen, bring the meeting to a close and retire to the bar. I'm sure we can all use a drink," Groves said.

"Your usual, Peter?" Austwick asked the accountant.

"Thank you," Groves answered. "And tell me, Malcolm, how serious a threat do you think this Labour Party is?"

"Oh, Tom's right in my opinion – if anything, he underestimates the danger. Wilson has done a very clever rebranding exercise – do you remember the Labour Party Conference in Scarborough three years ago? Labour had been lost in the wilderness for years until his "technology forged in white hot heat" speech: that catapulted the party forward fifty years. A young Grammar-school technocrat versus all the old Tory buffers in their tweeds on grouse moors. To me, Wilson is putting himself in the mode of President Kennedy – and that photograph of him with the Beatles must have been worth a million young votes."

The elderly solicitor brought the glass of the twelve-year-old brandy to his lips and relished its warmth for a few moments before continuing. "Actually, Peter, I think the whole political, social, and cultural landscape is about to be utterly transformed."

CHAPTER SEVENTEEN

It was a glorious June evening, and the elegant, large, high-ceilinged first-floor drawing room was bathed with light from the windows overlooking Great Pulteney Street. Fiona was joyful to be back in her old home with so many good memories. She looked up from reading Country Life as Anne came into the room; it was gone seven.

"Sorry I'm so late – Alistair asked me to put in some extra hours. Traditional Bath's membership is booming."

"I've got fish." Monday was Fiona's night to cook.

"Marvellous – I'm famished."

They went down to the kitchen with its dark-brown flag stones and cream AGA. Anne sat on one of the bar stools by the central, polished-wooden work unit. Fiona opened the bottle of chilled Chablis and poured each of them a glass.

"So, how do you find working for my brother?" she asked, taking the tray of seasoned trout from the fridge and placing it in the AGA's top oven.

"Well, the actual work is really interesting, and Alistair knows everyone and so much about Bath: it's been a real education in many ways." Anne took a sip of her wine and pursed her lips before continuing. "But he's quite distant – somehow different from most men, but then I've mixed mostly with sailors from Daddy's office."

"How do you mean?"

"Usually, I don't have any problem in attracting the opposite sex, but I think Alistair's just shy around women – sometimes I wonder if he actually likes me." She sighed. "He's a bit secretive – he plays his cards very close to his chest."

Fiona busied herself in preparing a salad and, deciding best not to discuss Alistair, she changed the subject.

"You're right. I was always more touchy-feely than Alistair and loved living in America – at least to begin with." She went on. "Life in California was extraordinary. Everything was so casual and laid back. I was surrounded by beautiful young people from all over America willing to try anything new. Duffer's Nature Movement became a huge success, attracting hundreds of followers every month: the training was weaning all these insecure young Americans off expensive and ineffective counselling.

"It wasn't Linda's scene, and before long, she followed her handsome banker back to Boston and got married. I, on the other hand, became more and more drawn into the Movement and did the training."

"The training?"

"This meant sitting for hours in a large hall with about two hundred complete strangers from different backgrounds confronting our conceptions of the world. If and when you achieved this, you could turn your whole life around for the better. I really 'got it', as Duffer would say. I was so happy; mentally as high as a kite and without a single pill or regret – to such an extent that I decided to become a trainer and teach others.

"This involved three months of a hotchpotch of deep meditation, spirituality, philosophy, Buddhism, and Zen. Oh, I had an amazing time, but now we must eat," and she took the fish from the oven. "I'm starving. After dinner, I'll show rather than tell you what I learned from the Nature Movement"

"I thought it was Duffer's Nature Movement?"

"It was, but Frank then got mixed up with Republican politics and sold it all to a Hollywood studio. He went to Washington DC, and I thought it was probably time to come home." She didn't mention that once Duffer disappeared, so did her job and income.

Anne and Fiona sat opposite each other, about six feet apart in the drawing room. Night had fallen, and the window shutters were closed to keep out any extraneous street light or noise; a single side lamp provided a dim glow. Fiona had become very serious and looked at Anne.

"Before I start, we have to exchange promises," she said.

"In a moment, I'm going to ask you to shut your eyes, and no matter what happens, you must promise not to open them, nor to use your hands, or move any part of your body until we finish. I, in turn, make two promises. Firstly, I will not move from my chair, touch you, or allow anything to harm you. Secondly, I will never tell anyone what, if anything, transpires in this room. Do you agree?"

Anne nodded.

"OK. So, relax into the armchair and please close your eyes. I want you to think about the thing that has upset you most in the last few weeks. Take your time."

But Anne didn't need time, because she instantly answered. "I know."

"When and where was this?"

"Last Friday in Alistair's office at fifteen Queen Square."

"Now I want you to go back and be there when this happened." Fiona said. "Describe the office to me."

"You know the office – you've been there a million times."

"Forget me. I need to see it through your eyes."

"It's a very spacious room with high ceilings, a magnificent marble fireplace with a clock on the mantelpiece, deep blue carpets, and matching curtains that hang down the two full length-windows overlooking the square. There is a long, wooden conference table with twelve matching chairs, and Alistair's big mahogany partner's desk in the corner," Anne replied

"OK. What are you doing?"

"I'm closing the shutters to the windows, so no one can see in from Queen Square."

"Are you on your own?"

"No. Alistair is sitting on one of two huge blue sofas that are either side of the fireplace."

"What's happening?"

"He's saying what a great week it's been with new members flocking to join and donations pouring in. He says that much of this is down to my hard work and support."

For a moment, Fiona hesitated. Should she continue given this was about her brother? A situation involving one's own family had never come up during her time as a trainer, but she knew the therapy often helped to bring things into the open, and having started, she was loathed to stop.

"So, you are in Alistair's office. It's last Friday evening, and you're looking at him. What's he wearing and saying?"

"As always, he is beautifully dressed," Anne smiled.

"Tell me exactly."

"He's got a dark grey suit, a white shirt with stiff collar, an Old-Etonian tie, polished black shoes. He's saying, 'I don't know how to thank you' …" Anne's voice petered off.

"So, why are you so upset?"

"It's what happens next …" Anne stopped again.

"Which is?"

"I go and sit next to him, and put my hand on his and say, "I know what you can do, Alistair. Why not take me out for dinner?" Now she was silent, her smile gone.

Knowing that they had reached 'Moment One', Fiona let the ensuing silence hang for a moment before responding.

"You have all the time in the world, Anne, just keep your eyes shut and go at your own pace."

"I'm all right," Anne whispered.

"Stay in Queen Square and tell me exactly what happens next. What can you see?" Fiona prompted softly.

"Alistair goes red in the face, flustered, angry. He violently shakes my hand off his:

'Are you mad? You are my secretary, not a friend, and nor will you ever be anything more.' He hates me and storms out: I just sit there, crying; I'm so upset."

66

Fiona then remembered how, unusually, Anne had come in and gone straight to bed without a word on the night in question. She hadn't seen her until she came down late Saturday morning.

"Tell me how upset feels," she said

There was silence before Anne asked, "What do you mean?"

"Let's start with where you feel it."

Anne started to raise her hands.

"Remember, Anne, no movement – just tell me."

Finally, she said, "In my stomach."

"Good. I want you to imagine looking into your stomach as it was last Friday, after Alistair left. What can you see?"

"A great big ball."

Fiona recognised that 'Moment Two' had been reached.

"How big?"

"About two feet across." The fact that Anne's abdomen was nowhere near that wide was irrelevant.

"What colour is the ball?" Fiona asked.

"Deep, blood-red crimson"

"What's it made of? Reach for it in your imagination, but don't move your hands."

"Thick, red, sisal string."

"So, your upsetedness is a big, red ball of thick string about two feet across." Fiona let the silence hang for a full minute, then said,

"Now look at your stomach again and tell me what's happening to the colour."

"The red colour's fading."

"How big is it now?"

"Smaller, about eighteen inches."

"What about the sisal?" Fiona knew the exercise was working.

"Much thinner strands."

So they went on.

"And the colour now?"

"It's pink and it's still getting smaller."

"And the strands?"

"They've become thin cotton."

Soon, the ball had reduced to the size of a pea and was white and misty before it disappeared completely, and 'Moment Three, Completion' had arrived.

"Open your eyes, Anne." Fiona looked at her watch, thirty-four minutes had passed.

"Are you still upset about it?"

"No. It's completely gone – that's amazing."

CHAPTER EIGHTEEN

The physiotherapy and occupational rehabilitation were working. He could stand without a stick and no longer had to suffer the indignity of asking Trish's mother help him wash and dress. Life was definitely looking up, Ian thought, as he picked up his copy of the day's *Chronicle* in the Royal United Hospital's shop, following his final morning speech therapy session. At last, he could talk properly again without a lisp and looked half normal.

His mouth was still a mess, but the weeks of specialist treatment and the temporary dentures made by Edward Boursin and his team in Brock Street had restored his face. He was grateful to Jenny Lippett in her Bridge Street salon who had patiently battled with, trimmed, and coaxed the wild-sprouting hair until it covered the scarred scalp.

He opened the local daily newspaper on his way back in the bus to Snow Hill, and as it stopped in the High Street, a small article on page six caught his eye.

BATH – FROZEN IN TIME

Research into the damage to the city by the German Bombers in April 1942 at the Bath Record Office in the Basement of the Guildhall has resulted in a most extraordinary discovery. Aerial photographs covering the whole of Bath in the nineteen thirties have been uncovered. Taken before the Second World War, they are keyed into a series of large scale Ordinance Survey maps and show every building in and around the city about thirty years ago. The curator has very kindly agreed to make the photographs available for inspection by any interested party. Normal opening hours: Monday to Friday, 9am to 1pm & 2pm to 5pm. Telephone number: 01225 477421

Maps had always fascinated Ian ever since he had learned to map-read in the Air Training Corp at fourteen. Facing yet another boring afternoon alone at Mafeking Street, he was intrigued and, on an impulse, got off the bus, crossed the road, and made his way down to the basement of the Guildhall.

The ever-eager and enthusiastic Colin Johnston settled him at one of the large oak tables and brought out the map with the faded brown label stuck on its front – *Property of the Royal Air Force – Luftwaffe Intelligence Berlin 1945*. Beautifully backed on linen, which when unfolded extended some six foot square and overhung the table's edges, it covered the whole city and was divided into thirty-six numbered squares. The curator handed him the battered box file containing thirty-six photographs, each of which was about twelve inches square and numbered to correspond with the numbers shown on the map. He laid the numbered photographs out on the appropriate squares on the map. Bath was there with every feature crystal clear, snapped from about five hundred feet above the city.

Utterly absorbed, he picked out familiar landmarks, dwelling on his personal triumphs over the past few years – those properties bought and sold that had made him and his clients so much money now all lost in his case. He discovered old buildings that had stood for centuries before being reduced to rubble in the 1942 German bombing raids and, more recently, by developers.

Wistfully, he thought back to those good times after he'd returned to Bath in 1961, when everything he got involved with turned to gold. Now penniless, there seemed no way back.

His finger idly traced across the images, following the route he would walk back to Mafeking Street, turning right half way up Lansdown Road, and then onto Gay's Hill and Snow Hill.

Suddenly, he stopped. Why didn't he recognise some of the buildings shown in this photograph? They weren't houses but big sheds, he guessed, surrounded by a large area of land on which there seemed to be huge piles of little boxes. The enormous site was completely enclosed by terraces of artisan houses with its only opening between the end of two of them, down a narrow pathway from Pera Place. He guessed the entrance would be hidden at ground level; hence he'd never noticed it. He glanced from the photograph to the map and located the correct square; it was marked *BREWERY*. He looked back at the photograph and realised that what he had thought were piles of boxes were barrels – hundreds upon hundreds of beer barrels. A tap on his shoulder from Colin interrupted his thoughts – the office was closing, four hours had passed.

Half an hour later, Ian turned off Gay's Hill and walked into Pera Place; he found the narrow lane that had served as the entrance to the brewery. The light was fading as he peered through the head high weeds and piles of rubbish. Clearly, the brewery was no more. Intrigued he would come back in the morning and discover what had happened to the land and buildings surrounded by these houses.

It was a warm night, and the house in Mafeking Street had settled. Wearing her lightest cotton nightdress, and sitting at her mother's dressing table bought with wartime-ration coupons, Trish had removed her makeup and was brushing her hair – she was thinking about the change in Ian over the previous twenty-four hours.

Since he had been discharged from the Royal United Hospital, he was never up by the time she left for work. According to her mother, it was unusual for him to be washed and dressed by noon, and he rarely went out unless he had a physio, dental, or hair appointment: some afternoons, he would take himself off to the local library.

His afternoons were generally spent with his nose in a book, and he had little or nothing to say to Trish when she got back in the evening. But this morning, he was up and gone before she'd even got down for breakfast. When she'd returned in the evening, he'd greeted her with a big smile and produced a bottle of wine, which they had drunk with their supper of shepherd's pie.

Had something changed, she had enquired. No, the police still had no idea what was behind the vicious assault he'd suffered, although it was clearly not robbery. Nothing had been stolen – except his memory. The last thing he could remember from that fateful evening was listening to the news on the radio. Mr Medlock had explained that this memory block was common in the case of severe head injuries, and sometimes took years to come back or never returned.

Then he stood up from the table, saying that he had an early start in the morning and did something he had not done for a long time: he'd kissed her goodnight on the cheek and went upstairs.

Ian returned to the brewery site early the next morning. After battling his way through the nettles and around the piles of rubbish, he found the half-opened, rusty gates over which stretched the wrought iron nameplate of the Alpine Brewery Company. Below was a weathered and just-legible plate with the name and address of a firm of solicitors in Frome. Unusually, he had never come across the firm in his previous property dealings in this small market town about thirteen miles from Bath, and located at the eastern end of the Mendip Hills.

Behind the gates everything, was derelict; a vast yard with weeds and even small, self-seeded trees growing between the dozen metal vats, around which were stacked hundreds of wooden barrels. Alongside were abandoned buildings with broken corrugated asbestos roofs, smashed windows, and full of rusty old machinery. Apart from small rodents, the only evidence of habitation was the remnants of bonfires, along with some piles of dirty blankets, suggesting where tramps may have slept years ago.

On the following day, Ian went to Frome and located the solicitor's office in Cheap Street. It was housed in two first-floor rooms that were reached by walking through a funeral directors on the ground floor. The black-clad undertaker, who had enthusiastically welcomed him on entering the premises, rapidly lost interest and pointed to the glass door marked,

STEVEN TURNER

Solicitor

Commissioner of Oaths

Ian climbed the narrow staircase and entered a small, deserted room with a second door opening into a further room.

"Can I help you?" An elderly man looked up from the desk in the adjoining office.

"Mr Turner?" he asked.

"Indeed it is," he said, standing up and slightly bowing before coming round to greet him.

"Good morning," Ian said. "May I introduce myself?" He handed the solicitor the single, shiny business card that he had made the night before using Letraset and a varnish spray. It read,

IAN MORRIS

Member of Brewers Society

Bradford Ales and Stouts
4 The Shambles
Bradford upon Avon
Wiltshire

It was a trick he'd used many times before to disguise his real motive and, as usual, bore his solicitor's address.

Turner peered down at the card in his hand.

"And what can I do for you, Mr Morris?"

"I believe you act for the Alpine Brewery Company?"

The solicitor's manner immediately changed. He became cautious, mention of the name filled him with foreboding.

"I'm afraid you're mistaken, Mr Morris. The company went bankrupt before the Second World War."

"That's a pity," Ian replied, "because I'm interested in buying its derelict site in Bath. I don't suppose you could put me in touch with the present owners?"

"Ah." The man paused. "That's a different matter. After the bankruptcy, the land passed back to the Alpine Family Trust, for whom I have acted as sole trustee for many years." The solicitor became attentive: Ian rightly guessed it was the prospect that the years of worry about his personal liability for rates, trespass, injury, and the host of other dangers of a derelict site, might finally be about to disappear.

"Tell me, what do you have in mind, Mr Morris?"

"Well, I want to brew a new pale ale called *Wood's Best*. You know, after Bath's famous father-and-son architects." Ian smiled, and within the hour a deal had been struck – at a ludicrously low price.

Again at supper that night, Ian had been animated. It had to be the prospect of the meeting with Christopher Johnson, Trish thought. Initially, Ian had shown little interest in a meeting at the bank, but yesterday, out of the blue, he had changed his mind, and she had fixed the appointment for the next morning.

CHAPTER NINETEEN

The building in the High Street still bore the inscription *The Old Bank 1760* carved into the stone above the entrance door. Not for the first time, Ian wondered about the other banks, which had occupied the building at some point in its two hundred years. He knew that historically-obsolete signs over business premises were often left in place when a building's occupiers changed.

Some dated back a century or more, you had only to look up as you walked down any city street, and you could be transported back to the trades of yesteryear. Yet another idiosyncrasy of Bath were its first, rather than ground-floor street signs, more-easily read by high-mounted coachmen.

Christopher Johnson came down to the bank's ground floor to greet Ian and personally accompanied the young man back to his office.

"It's good to see you looking so well. Please have a seat," he said, gesturing towards a small conference table.

"You've been missed at the Wessex Property Club's gatherings, and everyone sent their best wishes at our meeting last week. So, how are you?"

"Much restored, thank you." Gone was the relaxed voice Johnstone remembered. A slightly hoarse and more strained register replaced it. The bank manager looked at the scar above Ian's left eye, the changed mouth, and the slightly unruly black hair.

"Have the police still no idea of who attacked you that night?" he asked.

"None, except they believe two men were involved, and I've been of no help as I can't remember anything." Ian swallowed before continuing. "Anyway, thank you for your invitation here, but what can I do for you?"

Johnson was glad to see that the young man had lost none of his confidence and self-assurance.

"It's the other way round, actually," he replied softly. "I wondered if the bank can be of assistance to you. I hear it's all gone, the house, the business ..." He saw no reaction on the young man's face: he also knew that Ian's few savings at the County Bank were exhausted, and that Ian had reached his overdraft limit of five hundred pounds. Despite supposedly offering client confidentiality, banking was a small, close-knit affair in Bath, and there was always gossip.

"I would like to offer you a job at the Bank," he said. "Nothing grand, just something to help get you back on your feet."

Ian's eyes narrowed before responding. "That's very kind, Christopher, but what sort of job?"

"The Bank has decided to set up a Property Loan Book and needs someone to run it, a valuer. It has initially earmarked a fund of a millions pounds, using a 'Bath Abbey lending policy'."

"What's a 'Bath Abbey lending policy' when it's at home?"

"We will lend on any property that can be seen by someone standing on the top of Bath Abbey. In other words, nothing outside the city."

"And are you suggesting that I manage the fund?" Ian asked.

"We want to limit the bank's risk, and so, under no circumstances can any loan exceed three quarters of a property's value. I believe that you are one of very few people who know how much Bath buildings are worth, so I'm happy to offer you a starting salary of a thousand pounds a year, and the usual inducements and pension."

"A pension?" Ian laughed. "I'm only twenty-four!" He paused. "Would a mortgage be on offer?"

"Well ..." Johnson hesitated because usually, a mortgage was only on offer after an employee had been with the Bank for five years. "I dare say we can stretch a point. What do you say?"

"It won't surprise you when I say that I do not see my long term future as a Bank employee." Ian smiled. "I'm happy to forgo the pension, and all the other perks, if the Bank will simply take me on as self-employed with a retainer of, say five hundred a year, and an office here at the Bank. I would charge a fee of one percent for every valuation wanted. This would be cheaper for the Bank, because you could get the lender to pay my one percent."

"That sounds an attractive option." Johnson was pleased to note that it wasn't just Ian's confidence that remained as before. The attack hadn't affected the young man's ability to negotiate a deal to everyone's advantage.

"Anything else?" the manager asked.

Ian clicked back the two catches on the black leather briefcase which he had laid on the conference table before sitting down. He lifted the lid and extracted an old, yellowing plan, one of many provided by the Frome solicitor. It was dated 1938 and had been drawn up by the Bath Regeneration Practice at five Gay Street.

"What's this?" Johnson asked.

"Hopefully the Bank's first property loan," Ian replied. "Six acres of prime housing land, which I've agreed to buy for about a quarter of its worth. I've set up a company, Bath Surplus Land Ltd, and I need a loan of twenty thousand pounds to buy and cover all my costs, including getting the planning consent for sixty houses. It will be for two years at most – I don't propose to build these houses – just sell the development on. I'll offer it first to Tom Scotland because, while he's not over-generous, he is fair and reliable."

Within two weeks, Ian had moved into an office in the Bank, obtained the loan for twenty thousand pounds and bought the old brewery. With the ink barely dry on the loan agreement, he struck a deal with Tom Scotland to immediately buy the whole site for five thousand pounds more than it had cost and, more importantly, Ian would receive a further payment of twenty-five thousand pounds, if and when planning consent was granted.

He had even managed to move the hundreds of barrels on for five hundred pounds to a London gardening company specialising in rain water butts.

CHAPTER TWENTY

Just around the corner from the bank at the Empire Hotel, Rear Admiral Fisher had a difficult morning concentrating. A group of retired naval officers had asked for his comments on the Nelson Tour which they were putting together. Yet again, he read the first paragraph.

Naturally, this will start from Nelson House at two Pierrepont Street, the home of apothecary, Nicholas Spry, and where the great man came in 1781, invalided back from Nicaragua with fever. The tour should then cross the street to number nine, where his father, the Reverend Edmond Nelson, lived ...

Despite his utmost effort, his mind kept returning to the woman. He had been with many whores during his naval career, and normally, the memory of such encounters soon faded. He regarded them in much the same way as a meal – some were good while others were not, and you would only return to a restaurant if you had eaten well. But Sarah had been different, and he couldn't focus on anything without remembering her smell, her taste, her very essence.

It wasn't just what she had done during those twelve hours after they first met at the Cathedral Hotel, it was the way she'd done it: so eager to please, and she evidently enjoyed the sex. He was flattered that she appreciated his maturity and strength of character – after all, she was the same age as his daughter Anne, but instead of seeing him as a father figure, she had appreciated his experience and virility.

There was a knock on his door, and the Wren from the signals department came in.

"A message from the Admiral, sir," she said, handing a document to him.

"Thank you." He was still reminiscing as he unfolded the paper and noticed the *Confidential* heading.

CONFIDENTIAL

FROM: THE ADMIRALTY . WHITEHALL . LONDON

DATE: 2 June 1966 (1100 hrs)

TO: REAR-ADMIRAL.D.J.FISHER (RESERVE LIST)

         THE ADMIRALTY, EMPIRE BUILDINGS, BATH.

FROM: ADMIRAL M.J.T. BYWATERS

REF: HG/AUX . V . NOS: 1/5

(A) BACKGROUND BRIEFING

1. In early September 1940, when the threat of a German invasion appeared imminent, the Home Guard set up the Bathampton Platoon, which was based at the church hall in Bathhampton with a sandbagged machine-gun post and slit trench on the Warminster Road, just south of Bath by the Old Dry Arch, east of Claverton Wood.

2. Within a matter of months, this became an Auxiliary Unit (AU), with its Operation Base (OB) about 2 miles east of the Claverton Manor, (now the American Museum), anti-aircraft gun battery. Its headquarters was in Bath at Bathwick Street. As you probably know, all AU's were top secret, with everyone in or connected to them sworn and signed up under the Official Secrets Acts.

3. At Winston Churchill's direct instructions in 1940, AUs had been set up all over England by Colonel Colin Gubbins and formed the British Resistance Movement to await the arrival of Hitler's invasion forces.

4. Despite the depleted state of the army after the Dunkirk evacuation, these AUs were given priority and were very well equipped, with Smith & Wesson 38 pistols, P17rifles, sticky bombs, hand grenades, gelignite and plastic explosives. Much of this was kept in a bomb store at the top of Bathwick Hill, with the rest in an old explosive hut in the disused quarry at Claverton Hill.

5. The Bath Resistance Movement was run by a Sergeant Jack Wilde, under an Intelligence Officer called Captain John Shackle and its OB, which was to be used as a hideout when the Nazis arrived, was cleverly disguised in the old mines on Hampton Rocks in the woods, just off the tenth fairway of the Bath Golf Club.

6. The Admiralty had 5 AUs of its own, headquartered at the Empire Hotel, where you are now based. Most were disbanded by the end of 1942, when the threat of invasion had disappeared.

(B) COMMEMORATION CEREMONY

1. With the declassification of the whole operation under the Official Secrets Acts, it is agreed that the Royal Navy will be part of the Combined Services 25th Anniversary Ceremony commemorating those that served in the British Resistance Movement.

2. The evacuation of the Admiralty to Bath before WWII and the establishment of the RN's AUs, in 1940 in the city, make your location a natural choice for such a celebration.

3. An inter-services liaison committee has been
   established at the Ministry here at
   Whitehall, London. My recommendation that you
   represent the RN has been accepted by Their
   Lordships, and your regular attendance in
   London will be required.

(C) REQUIREMENT

Attached are the names, addresses, and service
details of the six surviving members of the Bath
AUs: hopefully, they may know of others. I
suggest you meet with them in the next 14 days and
report back with your proposals.

SIGNED: MICHAEL JAMES THOMAS BYWATERS (ADMIRAL)

He thought for a moment and checked that his diary was clear for the afternoon before pressing the button on his intercom.

"I'm going out for the rest of the day." He had just been given the perfect excuse to get away.

"Yes, Rear Admiral," the Wren replied. "What shall I put in the log?"

"Commemoration Ceremony: The Bath Resistance Movement – initial recce. And open a new file for it," he looked back at the paper. "HG/AUX. You'll find the first order on my desk – and remember to put it under lock and key when you've finished with it."

He left the office and cut rapidly through Upper Borough Walls and Quiet Street onto Queen Square, and then round towards Queen's Parade and up to Brock Street.

The grey Ford Anglia parked twenty yards down the street went unnoticed as the senior navy officer breathlessly removed his hat and pushed the doorbell. Nor did he see its occupant, Detective Jack Romer, photograph him, as the front door opened and he was shown in.

"This is a pleasant surprise, Rear Admiral," Debbie Smith lied, taken aback by his sudden appearance at her front door. She discouraged all visits, insisting transactions be done by telephone, thus avoiding any issue with neighbours. Although reasonably confident that her exclusive business was acknowledged and would be ignored by the city authorities, she ensured discretion.

She had met Fisher just the once in person when introduced by Marcus Rose at the Widcombe House Christmas party a few years back. He was a big man in every sense; tall, heavily overweight, and overbearingly arrogant.

"Yes, I thought I'd come in person." He didn't wait to be invited but walked past Debbie and into the house. "Because this is important and not something I would wish to discuss on the telephone."

Apprehensive of where the conversation was going, Debbie said nothing and led him into the drawing room.

"It's about the girl last weekend," he said. "I've decided to buy her from you."

"Buy her?" What on earth could the man mean?

"I don't want her going with anyone else." Fisher sank heavily onto the leather chesterfield, reached for a handkerchief from his coat pocket, and wiped perspiration from his brow and cheeks. He was evidently flustered, out of his depth but determined. "I want her completely for myself. I'm prepared to set her up in a little flat. I imagine she has a contract with you, and I want to buy it and her – please name your price."

Debbie couldn't initially think of a suitable response to the man's supercilious and conceited self-importance. He seemed to think that nothing had changed in a hundred years, that women were the property of others, and that prostitutes were worse, sub-human and merely items of trade. She found her voice.

"Did you speak to her?"

"I thought I should talk to you first, sound out the position – I mean, I assume that it's your decision."

"No, Rear Admiral, it's not my decision." Debbie spoke slowly, trying to control her anger, as she reminded herself that this awful person sitting on her beautiful sofa was a good customer. "I'll mention your proposition to her, although I don't think it will be of interest."

"Why ever not?" The rear admiral was obviously taken aback. "I'm offering her a comfortable life with a generous stipend. It's a very good offer!"

Debbie debated whether or not to answer his question but decided she would, if only to end the conversation and get the odious fool out of her house as quickly as possible.

"Because she's married."

DI Romer photographed Fisher leaving and wrote the time down in his police notebook.

CHAPTER TWENTY-ONE

In his new office overlooking the Guildhall, Ian was pondering the best way of getting the town planning consent to build the houses on the Pera land, when the telephone rang – it was Tom Scotland. Sometimes blunt to the point of rudeness, the businessman had little time for small talk.

"Good morning, Ian. I'm pleased to see you're around again as I need your help about a place I have just bought. It's called Widcombe House. Do you know it?"

"I certainly do." Ian was surprised. "It is one of the grandest private houses in Bath. Its owner, Marcus Rose, was the father I never had. I assume you're buying it from his widow, Susan."

"She's scarpered," Scotland said. "According to Luke Brady, who's dealing with the sale, gone abroad with some American at least half her age."

Ian was shocked: she hadn't even been in touch before leaving the city. But she'd chosen the right agent in George Street – probably the city's most prestigious; established for over a hundred years, part of a global network, and the very fabric of Bath. Discreetly dealing with all the best houses, acting for royals and the famous, with or without their mistresses and wayward heirs, the properties concerned often never came onto the market. He went back a long way with Luke Brady, its senior partner.

"The Old Bank has agreed a mortgage," Scotland went on. "And Christopher tells me you're their valuer, so I just want to run the figures past you."

"That's fine." Ian reached for pen and paper. "How much did you pay for it and how much are you looking to borrow?"

"I've agreed two hundred thousand pounds and want to borrow a hundred and seventy-five thousand."

"Sorry, Tom, but the Bank's maximum is three quarters of the value, namely the two hundred thousand pounds you've paid, so a maximum loan of a hundred and fifty thousand. The Bank has made it very clear that under no circumstances can I exceed a loan of more than three quarters of the price paid."

"That's not enough, Ian, I need a hundred and seventy-five thousand. So, how can we manage it?"

"I don't think you can." Ian deliberately replaced the "we" for "you".

"To get a loan of a hundred and seventy-five thousand pounds, the value would have to be at least two hundred and thirty-five thousand. As it stands, no self-respecting surveyor can value a property at thirty-five thousand more than the price paid on the open market." There was an awkward silence, then Scotland said,

"I got the property cheaply because Susan Rose couldn't wait to run off with her toy boy. I assume the same applies if say the sale price had been two hundred and fifty thousand: you'd have to value Widcombe at a quarter of a million and lend me a hundred and seventy-five thousand."

"Absolutely," Ian smiled.

"It will be," Scotland said. "In the meantime, where do you want the trunk delivered?"

"What trunk?" Ian had no idea what he was talking about.

"The sort my parents took on cruises around the world thirty years ago. Apparently, Mrs Rose left it behind on the understanding that I deliver it to you. Her late husband wanted you to have it – Luke's got the keys."

Completely bewildered, Ian said, "Maybe it's best brought here to the Bank."

"Also," Scotland said, "What are you doing on Saturday 30th?"

"Nothing I can think of."

"Good. We're holding a combined house warming with the World Cup final. Come and join us."

"Well, I would," Ian replied, "but I've promised my old secretary that I'd watch the game with her.'

"That's no problem; Trish is a good looking girl, bring her with you."

Without a goodbye, the phone line went dead, and barely ten minutes later, it rang again. This time, it was Andrew Phillips, an old friend who wasn't only nuts about cars but also a brilliant mechanic. Ian had helped him buy a garage in Bradford upon Avon, where he'd set up the now very successful T&A Motors.

"Andrew, how are you?" They hadn't seen each other for at least six months, well before the attack.

"More to the point, how are you? Have the police caught the bastards yet?"

"Much better, thank you – and no, not yet."

"Well, I've got something that belongs to you," Andrew said. "*IM 21.*"

For a moment, Ian was lost for words as he thought of his sleek blue convertible MGB, a gift from his dead friend and business partner, Henry Lieberman. Like everything else of value he had owned, it had been seized by the creditors.

"I was at a car auction this morning …"

"And?" Ian could feel his heart starting to pound with excitement.

"It was so cheap – about half what Henry originally paid me for it. But don't worry about the money – I am happy to wait – it's the least I can do after all you have done for me. The Wheatsheaf, say, eight tonight?" This was Andrew's favourite pub at Combe Hay, a few miles south of Bath. "I'll bring the car along, and we'll take it from there."

No loan had been needed thanks to the money from the sale of the barrels from the brewery site, and that night with the hood down, Ian knew his life was on the mend. Mildly drunk, he drove along the Midford Road listening to Kenny Everett's Audio Showcase on the local pirate radio station, with the disc jockey playing non-stop Beatles songs.

It took him back to the only time the group had played in Bath four years earlier and his one night stand with the German girl.

"Day Tripper", "I Want to Hold Your Hand", "Help!", "She Loves You" and "A Hard Day's Night" … Together and in that order, they perfectly described that wild, amazing night – a lifetime ago.

CHAPTER TWENTY-TWO

Ian slowed the MGB and, as he had done countless times before, turned right between the two stone pillars and up the long gravel drive: it was bordered on each side by immaculate, sweeping lawns with hedges of purple rhododendron and orange azalea bushes. A variety of other cars, all expensive, were parked on the perfect circle of apricot-coloured stone chippings surrounding the large marble fountain.

The symmetry of the Georgian house was perfect: Widcombe House was as magnificent as the day he, when a boy of sixteen, had first met Marcus Rose. Ian remembered how his mentor would bid him farewell from the front door, set into the magnificent Doric front-elevation of the honeyed Bath stone rising up some thirty feet.

Trish had scrubbed up beautifully in the plain-white linen tunic dress; she certainly had the legs for the mini skirt and handled her exit from the low-slung car perfectly. But nothing stirred in him as it would have once – his libido had disappeared along with his front teeth on the night of the attack. He pulled the large wrought-iron bell, and a moment later, the front door opened.

"Welcome, Mr Ian, it's been a long time." Clearly, the butler had been hovering.

"Jennings, good to see a familiar face." It had never occurred to Ian that Tom Scotland would re-employ this trusted retainer, but it made perfect sense given the years that he'd been at the place. He was amused to see the butler so formerly attired – something Marcus had never required, but then Scotland was very old school. "You know Miss Traynor."

"Indeed I do; welcome, madam." His gaze returned to Ian. "I'm so glad to see you back on your feet after that dreadful episode. Now, if you would like to follow me, drinks are being served in the main drawing room before the match commences."

They went down the familiar corridor and into the room where Ian had spent so many enjoyable evenings with Marcus and Susan. Now, everything was different. At the far end of the room was a large screen, and it took Ian a moment to realise it was live television, courtesy of those wizards of technology, Paul and Angie Lewis, who were hovering behind the massive projector. Rows of chairs were facing the screen, and elsewhere, people were drinking and talking. Many were known to him – some very well, being his fellow members of the Wessex Property Club and their wives.

"Ah, Ian and the lovely Miss Traynor."

Although hard as nails with men, Tom Scotland was a charmer with women, especially the young, pretty ones: on cue, a waiter appeared carrying a tray with flutes of champagne.

Scotland handed each of them a glass before turning to Trish. "I do hope you don't mind, but I need to steal him away for a moment," and then expertly guided Ian, hand on arm towards a group across the room.

"I'm so glad we were able to resolve that little valuation problem for this house; the loan from the bank came through on Tuesday." To meet the bank's minimum loan requirement, Scotland had simply transferred the house to one of his other companies for sixty thousand pounds more than he'd paid for it.

"I know the match is about to kick off, but there's someone I want you to meet. She could be very useful in getting the Pera Road consent for building the houses."

They came up behind a woman with short, blond hair. She turned round: she had had long hair when they'd previously met.

"Ian, may I introduce you to the Honourable Miss Fiona Symons, the owner of the Bath Regeneration Practice."

How long had it been since he'd last seen her or received the postcard from the Swiss clinic? Was it three years? No, it had to be more. He gazed at her perfection, speechless.

"Ian Morris." She put her hand forward to shake his. "How good to see you again." She was as beautifully poised as ever, and before he knew it, Scotland had seated them together, just as Kenneth Wolstenholme's BBC commentary began. Everyone's eyes were drawn to the enormous screen.

"Her Majesty arrives in the Royal Box ..."

Ian stared at the television, but his thoughts were very much elsewhere: his arousal flooded back, his libido no longer in any doubt. He found it impossible to concentrate on the football with Fiona sitting next to him. He thought back to the night she'd picked him up at the Lundy Estate office Christmas party and taken him back to her house in Great Pulteney Street.

"A goal! West Germany have scored! After twelve minutes, Helmut Haller has put West Germany in the lead."

How old had he been? Not even twenty and she nearer thirty.

Seven minutes later:

"In it goes – Hurst with the equaliser!"

She'd fucked him out of his mind.

78th minute:

"A chance ... A goal! Peters!"

They hadn't got dressed for three days.

"And that undoubtedly was a well-scored goal from Peters. England 2-1 in the lead now, deservedly so because they've been piling on the pressure. He stabbed at it ... Kept his knee over the ball ..."

Walking to the bedroom or kitchen as hunger or lust demanded ...

"They must do ... They have done ... Weber has scored in the last seconds! Thirty seconds from the end, Weber has equalised ..."

Boxing Day and that last bottle of wine when she cautioned silence and dismissed his protestation of love ...

101st minute:

"A here's Ball, running himself daft ... And here's Hurst ... Can he do it? He has done! Yes! Yes! No, the linesman says no. The linesman says no ... It's a goal. It's a goal. The Germans are going mad at the referee ..."

He recalled his anger and humiliation at being sneaked out through the tradesman's entrance, her bit of rough, never to be seen together in Bath's class-ridden goldfish bowl. Then, his sweet revenge when he engineered her eviction from the Great Pulteney Street house and bought it at auction himself; seized it when the Lundy family lost everything.

120th minute:

"And here comes Hurst. He's got ... Some people are on the pitch! They think it's all over ... It is now, it's four!"

A great cheer went up, and everyone was clapping. Fiona turned her eyes from the screen and faced him. She wore a slight smile. He initially thought that she, too, had been recalling their fabulous few days together but realised how wrong he was immediately when she spoke.

"Tom Scotland has told me about Pera Road and what you want. You've always been smart, and the old brewery, hidden away like that, was a great purchase – especially so cheaply."

How the hell did she know what he'd paid for it? Ian thought, but he had forgotten how dazzlingly green her eyes were.

"I've no doubt that the Bath Regeneration Practice and I can help you achieve the planning consent for sixty houses," she carried on, "but I'd need something in return."

He tried to concentrate on what she was saying rather than what she looked like: it was as if she knew.

"You need to forget the past, Ian. This is about the Bath Regeneration Practice and is purely business. Think about it and give me a ring on Monday." Then, she leant towards him and quietly spoke into his ear.

"Now, I suggest you give your sweet little girlfriend some attention. She's looking rather unhappy."

Trish and he drove back to Mafeking Street in silence.

His first boss had warned him all those years ago when he'd been sent to work in South Wales away from London. "Never get your feet too far under the table, or the next thing you know, it'll be pregnancy and marriage."

Ian had to find somewhere else to live.

CHAPTER TWENTY-THREE

The brown steamer trunk sent over by Tom Scotland was still waiting unopened in his office when Ian got in on the following Monday morning. He hadn't got round to getting hold of the keys, but now that he had a second reason for calling, he finally rang Luke Brady.

"I urgently need somewhere to rent," he explained to the agent. "A minimum of three months, preferably somewhere furnished and cheap."

"Your timing is perfect, Ian. How does St James' Square suit you? It's a bit run down but basically a beautiful town house."

"It sounds perfect, but I couldn't afford that sort of rent. The attack and everything has left me struggling, so anything I take has got to be cheap, I mean dirt cheap."

"Is free cheap enough?" Luke offered. "You've just got to cover the running costs – at most a few pounds a week."

"Are you kidding?" Ian couldn't believe what he was hearing. "It sounds too good to be true. Tell me more."

"Number thirty-five, built by John Palmer in 1793, one of the great residential squares in Bath, fully furnished …"

Ian interrupted the agent's polished patter.

"Thirty-five St James' Square – why does it sound familiar?"

"Because you'd be the latest in a string of worthies to live there. We did some research for its recent sale and they include Charles Dickens, Alfred Lord Tennyson, Longfellow, and Prince Louis Napoleon. Dickens fled there from London, after Nicholas Nickleby was serialised in 1839 and became successful. Apparently, he based *The Old Curiosity Shop* on the house."

Brady explained that it was a probate sale after the death of the very old woman who had grown up and lived in the house all her life. It had been bought lock, stock, and barrel by a couple of American bankers called Ford and Linda Fraker. Luke was obviously impressed by the buyers, describing

Mr Fraker as 'definitely top drawer', a Princetown alumna from an old Boston family.

"His wife is English, super bright, and sounded delightful from my long distance telephone calls with her. An absolutely lovely couple, who happen to be Charles Dickens enthusiasts. They can't get here for at least six months and need someone to keep an eye on the place. They specifically asked that I find someone I can personally recommend. So, when do you want to look at it?"

"I don't need to see it, Luke. When can I move in? Today?"

"Really? Well, ..." The agent paused for what seemed like an age, and Ian hoped Brady hadn't changed his mind – the place sounded perfect. But then, he said "Looking at my diary, I could meet you there in about an hour."

Ian was over the moon and about to hang up, when he remembered the key to the mysterious trunk – Brady agreed to bring it with him.

Leaving the bank immediately, Ian bought a large bunch of flowers on his way to Mafeking Street. He knew that Trish would be at work, and to his relief, her mother was out too. He packed his few things and left the bunch of flowers, door keys, and brief note on the kitchen table.

The one-hundred-and-fifty-year-old, five-storey Georgian house was in quite a sorry state but exquisite. Ian felt very fortunate as he stood in the first-floor drawing room and looked out over the square with its residents' garden of mature trees and flowers in full bloom. The dining room and pre-war kitchen were on the floor below and four bedrooms above – all with their original cast-iron fireplaces and Edwardian radiators. He was more than happy to live with the shabby furniture, patched linen, chipped crockery, and varnished wallpaper.

He picked up the telephone and dialled Fiona to discuss the Pera Road project.

"It will have to be late in the afternoon, shall we say four o'clock here at the Bath Regeneration Practice?" she'd asked.

"No – why don't you come to my new office at thirty-five St James' Square?" Ian replied, and she agreed.

The letter with the steamer trunk key left by Luke Brady was lying on the dining room table. He opened it.

Dear Ian,

By the time you read this, Widcombe Manor will be gone and I will be in America without Marcus. Bath holds nothing for me, and I shall start a new life.

In clearing the study, I found these books and a note from Marcus requesting that they should be given to you upon his death.

God bless you,

Susan Rose

Intrigued, he called the bank, but the switchboard put him through to Christopher Johnson before he could arrange for the trunk to be sent over.

"Hello, Ian. A new customer from London has set up an advertising agency in Bath and wants a loan. I know this isn't a property valuation, but I am floundering and seem to remember that you've used such firms in the past. He's coming here tomorrow at two thirty, and I'd welcome your help – as a favour."

"I can be there." Ian was happy to oblige. "But can I ask a favour in return? Could you arrange for the old travelling trunk in my office to be sent across to my new home?'

"I'll get someone to sort it out now – what's the address?"

"Thirty-five St James' Square, and before you wonder how I can afford it, I can't. I'm just house-sitting for clients of Luke Brady's."

Before the trunk arrived, Ian walked around the corner from his new home to the nearby grocery shop for some basic needs. It was exhilarating to be independent again in his own place: to celebrate, he made a pot of tea and a cheese-and-pickle sandwich.

Ian opened the trunk which had been delivered and lay on the dining room floor. He recognised the red leather bindings with the large, golden, printed Roman numerals on their spines and unpacked each of the ten heavy volumes. He had wondered what had happened to these treasured books after Marcus Rose died. Rose's Bath Bibles had always been kept under lock and key on the top shelf of the oak bookcases lining the study at Widcombe House. He opened the first and thought back to when he'd first been shown the tomes five years earlier.

THE LUNDY ESTATE
VOL. I: FIFTY-ONE CITY CENTRE FREEHOLD
AND LONG-LEASEHOLD PARCELS OF LAND

The Lundy trustees had approached Rose to buy the whole estate when the 2nd Earl had died in the 1940s. But despite spending several months and a great deal of money exploring different angles, it was impossible to take the suggestion forward: the 1st Earl's bar on any disposal for fifty years was unbreakable.

Once again, Ian was staggered by the detail included about each lease, the beautifully-coloured plans, dimensions, the allowable use, and the then value for each and every one of the hundreds of properties.

He moved to Volume II, ever more excited. Unable to absorb any more, he stopped reading after Volume III but quickly scanned the indices of the remaining seven books. It was two in the morning. He went to bed realising the enormous potential of Marcus Rose's gift – a unique and detailed modern Domesday Book for vast swathes of Bath.

While Ian had been engrossed in St James' Square, at fifteen Queen's Square, Alistair had some important news for his sister. He walked into her first-floor office and closed the door.

"Got a minute, Sis?" He didn't wait for an answer. "I think you're going to be pleased with me and agree that congratulations are in order." He stopped to take a breath before announcing, "I'm going to marry Anne Fisher."

"What?" Fiona tried to fathom how things had changed so much between her brother and her friend. After all, it was only a month earlier that Fiona had dealt with Anne's conviction that Alistair didn't even like her. And now they were going to get married? "When did all this happen? Have you told Mother?"

"I'll let her know later today, and I know it's been quick, but I'm keen to get the deed done." He sat opposite his sister with his legs crossed and, rather than looking at her, was concentrating on his hands placed on his knees. She thought he was going to say more, but he didn't.

"I know Anne's very fond of you and the title is an obvious attraction, but do you really think this is a good idea?" she asked. "She isn't pregnant, surely?"

Alistair gave a short, mirthless laugh and shook his head but continued to look down at his hands as he spoke. "Not that I know about – and if she is, it's not my doing. But there's a detective – a chap called Romer – who's been asking questions about me and my friends." He looked up to her face and sighed. "I thought it might be sensible if I got married – I'd have to sooner or later, and the flat upstairs is a good size for us both to have some space. This way, hopefully, Romer will move on to some other poor bugger."

"You're probably right." Fiona had sympathy for her brother. "And you could do a lot worse than Anne Fisher."

"I thought we could get down to Lundy for the ceremony without much fuss – maybe next month, before autumn sets in and the weather turns." Although the wedding was his idea, Alistair didn't seem particularly overjoyed about it, and Fiona wondered if Anne had any inkling of what she was letting herself in for.

"That's a good idea – it won't cost much and shouldn't raise too much interest in the press." She remembered the awkward questions asked when Alistair had been asked to leave Eton.

He stood up and sighed again. "Well, that was my news, and I'm off to have a chat with my future father-in-law, Rear Admiral David Fisher."

Fiona came round the desk and put her arms around the slight young man.

"Congratulations, Alistair. Life isn't always straight forward."

She sat for a while after her brother left and wondered what hope there was for an heir to the Lundy title and the dynasty founded by her great grandfather.

CHAPTER TWENTY-FOUR

Michael Symons's peerage had cost him one million pounds in the early 1920s, the going rate required by Maundy Gregory, Lloyd George's whoremaster in such matters. He had chosen the title Lord Lundy following his first visit to the quite extraordinary tiny island of Lundy in the Bristol Channel in 1919.

Three miles long and half a mile wide, this lump of granite rising four hundred feet above the Atlantic Ocean lay just eleven miles from the Devon coast, with nothing between it and North America.

Symons was profoundly affected by the discovery of somewhere so beautiful, timeless, and unspoilt by modern civilisation. Its owner was an eccentric colleague from the city, Augustus Langham Christie, who had bought it on a whim because an ancestor had owned it a hundred and thirty years earlier.

Since every single thing needed to survive had to be shipped to the island, Christie purchased the seventy-one-ton Lowestoft drifter *Lerina* as the island's lifeline. In need of further investment to reopen the eighteenth-century hotel, he invited Symons over to stay with him in the owner's residence, Millcombe House – 'a modest little pastoral mansion built in 1836 in the Georgian style' was how the sale particulars described it.

The sole passenger, Symons felt a strange thrill as the little white two-master slipped her moorings and sailed out of Instow harbour. The feeling of adventure was only heightened when, some hours later, the *Lerina* sailed into Old Man's Cove. The crew then started the slow, laborious job of unloading into the small lifeboat, which had to be rowed back and forth to Lundy's only sandy beach.

Over the next few days, he experienced the total tranquillity of the eleven hundred acres with its majestic cliffs, ruined castle, three lighthouses, coastguard station, and a dozen or so very basic cottages.

St Helena, the incongruously-large stone church had just two worshippers, and the only farm had been long abandoned. The island's pub, the Marisco Tavern, simply ignored closing times for serving alcohol given that there had never been a policeman on the island to enforce the law since it was introduced in 1914.

After the unremitting horror and grief of four years of the Great War, and without any communication with the mainland, Symons found the tranquillity and magic of Lundy irresistible.

It was the beginning of a lifelong love affair, with the first Lord Lundy returning to the island whenever he wished to escape the demands of his vast mining, shipping, banking, and property empire.

During the next two generations of the Lundy dynasty, the close links to the island survived, and every August, the entire family sailed across to spend a month's holiday at Millcombe House. Occupying their own pew in the church, camping and playing cricket matches, they effectively were the island's royal family.

Thus, when Rear Admiral Fisher raised the question of where his daughter Anne was to be married to the 4th Earl, Alistair simply replied,

"Why, at St Helena on Lundy, of course, where my grandparents and parents were married. It will be a quiet family affair." He had no intention of making more of the ceremony than was necessary and was relieved that Fisher did not demur.

"I've already spoken to the vicar of Bideford in whose parish the island lies, and we've fixed eleven o'clock on Saturday, 13 September. I assume that suits." It was a statement rather than a question, and Fisher just nodded. "Millcombe House is the only hotel, and I suggest we all sail over two days earlier and pray for calm weather."

They had a glass of champagne to celebrate the forthcoming nuptials. The rear admiral then excused himself, pleading the need to go to London for another meeting of the Bath Resistance Movement Commemoration Ceremony Committee. He explained that it was an onerous task, presently requiring frequent nights away from home.

CHAPTER TWENTY-FIVE

Ian went into the Bank's small conference room where Christopher Johnson introduced him to Al Giles. He was a tall, well-built man, who Ian judged to be of similar in age to himself but dressed far more casually. He wasn't surprised when the advertising man went straight to first names.

"Ian, nice to meet you."

"And you, Mr Giles." Until he got to know someone, Ian preferred the security and seriousness of purpose that formal business etiquette required.

They all sat down and Johnson started.

"Mr Giles has moved recently from London and set up his new business."

"The Bath Marketing Company," Giles interrupted.

"Quite so," Johnson agreed. 'Now, Mr Giles wants to borrow a thousand pounds to fund a specific project but has no assets, so the Bank would be relying on a charge on the company and his personal guarantee. I would welcome your comments, Ian."

"Do tell me about the project, Mr Giles," Ian said.

"We've been asked to arrange the Nurses' Grand Christmas Ball later this year – a fundraising event by the nursing staff at the Royal United Hospital."

Ian was puzzled as he thought he knew the city's social calendar well but couldn't recall such an event in past years.

"And what is your proposed fee?"

"What's normal for this type of event – nothing payable up front and then ten percent of the total sum raised after deduction of all costs. We're on a short lead time-wise – it's just over three months away, so I calculate I could repay the loan by the end of January next year." Giles had a file of papers in front of him that he opened. "If you'd like to have a look at …"

Ian held up his hand and declined the proffered papers.

"We can look at the figures later, but as this would be an unsecured loan, can you tell us more about yourself? For instance, what's brought you to Bath?"

"I'm originally a journalist and worked for *Tatler* until it closed last year. You know, the monthly glossy magazine."

Both men nodded – it was probably Britain's most prestigious publication, beloved by the English upper classes and covering high-society balls, charity events, race meetings, shooting parties, fashion, and gossip.

"I went there straight from Winchester and worked my way up under four different editors. But our customer base had largely disappeared and was replaced with *London Life*, so I decided to call it a day and move on."

"So, why Bath?" Ian asked again.

Giles paused for a moment to reply.

"Well, the Nurses' Ball isn't the long-term reason that brought me to Bath, but I do think that event organising can help finance my idea for coming to the city. I'm willing to share this with you in confidence." He looked at both men.

"Of course," Johnson answered, and Ian nodded.

He pushed the file of papers in front of him to one side and reached into his briefcase to put a glossy mock-up cover on the table.

"Gentlemen, my brainchild, *The Bath Way* magazine.

Ian liked its look and picked it up, thinking the idea clever: its print style, font, and design were very similar to *Tatler*.

"People have always loved to be seen in society magazines," Giles said. "But until now, they've been national publications. There is little or no chance for provincial worthies to appear in them unless they take themselves up to town for the season with Wimbledon, Henley, Ascot, Lords, etc. So, I'm imagining a local, top-quality magazine – just for Bath. Everyone who is anyone in this city would buy it, and more to the point, want to be seen in it."

The marketing man had done his homework and was bright as well as personable. In Ian's experience, Wykehamists, the old boys of a school dating back over five hundred years, could generally be divided into two types: academically brilliant in a world of their own or absolutely charming. He quickly decided that Giles fell within the latter category and undoubtedly had a great network of acquaintances, many high up in the organs of government – a valuable future contact.

"My plan is to start monthly with a run of five thousand at a cover price of half a crown. There will initially be sixty-eight pages, twenty of which will be advertising, but I aim to build up to, say, eight thousand copies fortnightly with one hundred and eight pages, and at least half advertising, launch costs, and–"

Ian stopped him in mid-flow. "When would you expect to break even?"

Giles reached back into his briefcase for a sheet of figures that he passed across the table.

"I'm confident that we would get any investment back within a maximum of three years, possibly twenty-four months. Whilst we would charge a cover price, initially, there would also have to be lots of free copies for the advertisers who could then be lured in by the usual content."

"Which is?" Ian was curious now and keen to learn more.

"Cradle to grave ..." But before Giles could continue, Johnson had interrupted him.

"Thank you very much for coming in, Mr Giles. If you would like to leave it with us, I should be able to let you have the Bank's decision on the initial thousand-pound loan in a day or so." He signalled the end of the meeting by standing up. "Now, do let me show you out."

Ian waited in the manager's office until Johnson returned.

"So, what are your thoughts, Ian?' Johnson sat down again. "He's certainly an interesting man, don't you think?"

"I think the thousand-pound loan is safe and the local magazine is a superb idea but more risky, not for the Bank. I wouldn't mind getting involved personally. Would you object?"

"Not in the slightest."

Later that day, Ian was still thinking about *The Bath Way* while browsing in Mr B's Emporium of Reading Delights in John Street, when he noticed the very old book *The Story of the Malakand Field Force* by Winston Churchill. A hero of Ian's since childhood, it was not only a first edition dated 1896 but also the first book that Churchill had published. It described his part with the British Army dealing with the unrest on the North West Frontier – now western Pakistan and eastern Afghanistan.

"How much, Nick?" he asked Mr B, the former lawyer who'd given up his career for his love of books.

"Churchill's out of favour at the moment – you can have it for ten pounds," he said. "When did you start collecting Churchill?

"I hadn't until now."

"Do you want me to keep an eye open for anything else?"

"Please do," Ian replied.

CHAPTER TWENTY-SIX

"This is pleasant, Ian, a very different image to Queen Square."

Fiona was opposite him in the drawing room of thirty-five St James' Square, with her long legs tucked demurely to one side and crossed at the ankles. She wore a pale-green ribbed roll-neck over a rust-coloured short tweed skirt, looking elegantly poised as she inhaled on her cigarette. "And you say it isn't costing you anything at all."

This was the first time they had been alone, and he simply sat marvelling at her beauty: it took him a moment to register what she'd said.

"Yes – well, only the running costs. It's because I'm house-sitting for an American couple – well he's American, she's English – they're bankers from New England called Fraker."

"Not Ford and Linda Fraker?"

"Yes – do you know them?" he asked.

"Well, that's amazing – I was at finishing school with Linda, and we met up again later in Switzerland before moving to California together. She's absolutely lovely, and Ford's a darling too. I've lost touch since she moved back to Boston to get married, although I knew they planned to spend some time in England eventually. What a small world. When do you expect them to arrive?"

"They are due to move in about six months." He smiled and would have loved to keep the chat personal but felt it wise to move onto business.

"Now, let me tell you about Pera Road."

Fiona listened as Ian outlined the planning consent he needed.

"As I told you on Saturday," she said, "if I recommend Bath City Council to approve a scheme to build sixty houses and they grant permission, you and Tom Scotland will make a great deal of money. So, I would want something in exchange."

Ian was surprised by her bluntness: his only previous experience of such a blatant request for a back-hander had arisen when he'd worked abroad in Jamaica.

"So, you want a bribe?"

Now it was her turn to be shocked.

"Goodness me, no. Something that will benefit the whole city, not me personally. I'm simply asking that a part of your profit be used to subsidise the preservation of our Georgian buildings. They need to be treasured, and we need to maintain our heritage for future generations.'

"I thought you were an independent consultancy firm, not part of your brother's set up." Ian took a puff on his own cigarette.

"I certainly am independent," she retorted. "A totally-professional consultancy that needs to justify its existence with realistic demands on developers. Alistair is against any development, which is not what I advocate. On the contrary, I want to work on regenerating our city, and what better way than by persuading developers to donate a small part of their huge profits to fund restoration?"

"And what is your idea of a small part? What percentage do you want for Pera Road?"

"Fifteen percent."

"But that could be ten thousand pounds!" Ian spluttered, coughing on his cigarette. "Scotland will say it's blackmail, and I would agree."

"It's not blackmail – it will be fully accounted for as part of the Restoration Fund. Take it or leave it." She sat up as if getting ready to leave. "You can let your cronies at the Wessex Property Club know that without a donation, there won't be many planning consents forthcoming."

Ian had never experienced Fiona's business side before and wondered if she was calling his bluff or whether she meant it. No raised voice, just quietly tough, unlike her brother, no bluster or theatrics. Far more dangerous, he thought, absolutely stunning.

"I'll talk to Tom Scotland, but I really don't think we could go above five percent," he countered.

"No chance." She stood and started to collect up her papers. "Forget it, we have nothing more to talk about."

"Six percent?"

She stopped and looked at him. "I'll accept seven and a half."

Ian held up his hands in surrender. "Let's make it a firm figure. How about six thousand five hundred pounds and we call it a deal?" Fiona hesitated long enough to worry him.

"Agreed."

Ian was relieved. The figures would still add up, and he would have to persuade Scotland that there was no alternative.

"How many other developers have agreed to pay into the Restoration Fund?" he asked.

"None. You are the first; a virgin donator, you might say," Fiona said, smiling. "And where you lead, I believe others will follow."

He had to admire her self-confidence. Fiona was a shrewd negotiator and had played her hand superbly, an excellent poker player. Mind you, there were more worthy causes than maintaining old buildings.

The growing homeless problem in Bath came to mind: he'd been reading about in the *Chronicle*. A local housing-officer-cum-social-worker, Cecil Weir, wrote an occasional column about his work and the problems he was encountering. Ian had met up with Weir about a year ago, having been touched by one such article about a retired ex-soldier who slept rough in Bath. He bedded down in shop fronts, derelict properties, and, in winter, by the heating vent behind the new Forum Cinema.

Weir recounted the story. Regimental Sergeant Major Daniel Morgan had joined the Somerset Light Infantry as a lad of sixteen at the outbreak of the Great War, or, more precisely, fifteen years and eleven months. A large, well-built boy, he was over the minimum height of five feet three inches and chest size of thirty-four inches. As for the minimum sign up age of nineteen, the recruitment officer was more than happy to turn a blind eye in exchange for the half-crown he received for each new recruit. After all, he told himself, he was only doing his patriotic duty given the size of the German army of nearly four million – over five times that of the British at the time.

A foundling, Daniel had simply walked out of the Dr Barnardo's home in Gloucester, hopped on a train, and found his way to the recruitment office in Bath. He joined the First Battalion on the Western Front where, over the next two years, he was lucky. Wounded with shrapnel, he survived and proved to be an outstanding soldier. As a corporal, he was posted to Northern Ireland after the Armistice, and then to Egypt and Hong Kong. At the outbreak of the Second World War, now a Sergeant, Morgan found himself in India, where he was to remain until Independence.

The First Battalion was the last British infantry battalion to leave the sub-continent on 28 February 1948. Eight years later, he had to accept compulsory retirement after over forty years with the Regiment.

Like many before, his world collapsed. The army had been his life and his family, providing an understandable routine, discipline, and anchor. But now, no longer of any use, it abandoned him.

For years, he drifted, and only the rigours of his previous army life kept him alive. He became well known in the homeless community of Bath, his size and obvious military bearing giving him the nickname Desperate Dan out of the Beano comic.

CHAPTER TWENTY-SEVEN

It was a glorious morning, more like July than September. Life was good, Ian thought as he walked from his home to the Old Bank. He took the longer route, turning right instead of left into Julian Road and then down Marlborough Buildings, past the Royal Crescent, and then left again into Royal Avenue. He was not in a hurry but enjoyed his solitude and the surrounding beauty of Royal Victoria Park. He sat on a bench to reflect on the day ahead.

Almost immediately, a grey squirrel caught his eye at the broad base of a nearby copper beech tree. It was eating a nut held between its paws for several seconds before dropping the husk and scuttling up the tree's trunk and into the branches above. For a moment, Ian envied its simple life where the only thing that mattered was the next beechnut. But then he thought again and changed his mind – far too boring an exercise.

Ian loved the challenge of crafting clever deals unseen by others and benefitting all involved. But he was beginning to realise that there was much more. Obviously, he was capable of earning a living, but he was seeking more, perhaps as a result of his desire to please Fiona Symons. To thrive, Bath needed to preserve the beauty of its architecture and find a way to pay for such preservation.

But for today, his priority was sorting out Al Giles and the new loan needed for his *Bath Way*. He had promised Christopher Johnson an answer when he got in, but the numbers didn't add up given the bank could only lend three quarters of the money needed. Yet it was such a great idea with enormous potential …

He got up and carried on towards the Bank, passing the war memorial down Queen Parade, and crossed Queen Square.

The scheme needed another thousand five hundred pounds injected into it, but Giles had no money.

He walked down Barton Street into Saw Close and, on a whim, stopped outside the Theatre Royal. *Gaslight*, the famous Victorian thriller, was showing, and he fantasised about taking Fiona to see it. She'd recently called to say the planning consent for Pera Road would be granted in the next few days. He strolled back to Borough Walls and along the High Street, and pushed open the door to the Bank.

Twenty-five thousand pounds from Tom Scotland would be in his bank account within a week, and then there was the six thousand five hundred to be donated to Fiona's Restoration Fund. That still left over eighteen thousand pounds – perhaps he'd call Al Giles.

"Oh, Mr Morris," the receptionist stopped him as he crossed the bank's lobby. "There's a policeman who's been asking for you, and I've taken the liberty of putting him in your office."

The plain-clothes officer introduced himself as Detective Inspector Romer and proffered a plastic wallet containing his identity card.

"Bit excessive, sending a DI."

Romer looked puzzled.

"I beg your pardon?"

"All I did was cross on amber."

"Oh, no, sir; I'm nothing to do with traffic. My enquires relate to a couple of London rogues bringing their bad habits onto my patch a couple of weeks ago, now locked up in our cells. Enforcers trying to collect an unpaid gambling debt from a bookie at the Bath Race Course – August race meeting, rather a large amount, on Chance Your Arm in the third race."

Romer reached into his inside pocket and handed Ian two grainy black and white pictures.

"Do you recognise either man?" he asked.

Ian looked at the photographs. The older seemed familiar, but he wasn't quite sure why: it was something to do with his slicked-back hair.

"That one," – he pointed at the picture – "I remember the hair; it was plastered with Brylcreem."

"Anything else?" the policeman asked.

Ian shook his head.

"Does the name John Forrester mean anything to you?"

"Yes," he replied. "That's a name from the past. A client, I haven't seen him for about two years."

Ian remembered Forrester, but it was his second wife, Clara, an Italian beauty less than half her husband's age, that immediately came to mind. On one occasion, Forrester couldn't make a meeting and Clara took her husband's place, and then had tried to seduce Ian. She was furious at his rejection, the torrent of Italian abuse following him as he fled the house down Winsley Hill.

The detective stood up. "We have reason to believe that those two worked for Mr Forrester and may have been in the country earlier this year. We think he's in Italy and have alerted other forces, and would very much like to interview him. Do give me a ring if you see him again or you remember anything else."

The detective handed Ian his card and left just as Christopher Johnson arrived.

"Good morning, Ian." The manager closed the office door. "So, what do you think about Mr Giles and *The Bath Way*?"

"I think it'll work, and I'm happy to sign it off on the usual basis, with the bank lending up to three quarters of what he needs."

"Fine, I'll give him a call," the manager said. "But personally, I'd be surprised if it actually happens. I think he'll struggle to find the remaining money needed to get the magazine off the ground."

"Would you be unhappy if I put up the rest of the money?" Ian asked.

Surprised, Johnson shook his head.

Giles came into the bank at the end of the afternoon to sign for the loan and suggested they adjourn for a drink to celebrate the birth of *The Bath Way*. Johnson excused himself on the grounds of a choir practice at the Abbey, but soon, Ian and Giles were sitting in the cosy, oak-panelled rooms of the Old Green Tree pub in Green Street. Built in 1716 as part of a bowling green, it was originally even smaller, with its own brewery on site. Nowadays a free house run by Tim Bethune, it served a very decent pint and was a perfect venue for confidential chats.

Giles raised his tankard. "Thanks for your help, Ian. Here's to 'The Bath Way.'

"Cheers," Ian replied. "So, have you worked out where you can get the rest of the money from?"

"Not yet, but I do have the perfect scoop for the first edition," he said. "Anne Fisher, Rear Admiral Fisher's daughter, is getting married and has promised me an exclusive."

Ian had met the rear admiral on a few occasions at official functions and was aware of his daughters but didn't personally know either.

Giles went on. "And it's not just any old wedding. She's marrying her boss, the young Lord Lundy and it's all very sudden, so I wouldn't be surprised if he's got her in the pudding club – especially given the venue."

Having known Alistair since childhood and being aware of his rumoured predilection, Ian was bemused and asked, "What's so special about the venue?"

"The island of Lundy in the Bristol Channel – it's in the middle of nowhere, and there are hardly any guests. It should be a fabulous photo opportunity, so I'm going over beforehand to check everything out."

Ian hadn't ever been to the island but was aware of its significance to the Symons family: it would make a great story for the first edition.

"Would you be interested in me putting up the extra one thousand five hundred pounds personally for a half share in the *The Bath Way* company?"

"Would I? More to the point, would you be prepared to do that?"

Some rounds later, the deal was clinched and, Ian recorded it in a single sentence of ten words on the back of two of the pub's beer mats. The two men each signed and exchanged mats, shook hands, and Ian wrote out a cheque for one thousand five hundred pounds.

"By the way, Al," Ian was now happy to use first names. "I should be grateful if you could keep my shareholding confidential. I'll tell the Bank of course – but I'd like to remain a sleeping partner."

CHAPTER TWENTY-EIGHT

Ian picked up the telephone. It was Fiona Symons, thanking him for the cheque. All his attempts to take her out had hit a brick wall, but he thought six thousand five hundred pounds was worth another shot.

"How about dinner tonight to celebrate our first deal?" he asked, trying to sound matter-of-fact.

"I'm afraid not," she replied evenly. "I'm tied up this evening."

Well, she wasn't unpleasant about it, he thought – perhaps another time.

"I do have something for you. Is there any way you could collect it sometime later today? It's here at my office in Queen Square."

It still rankled that his old office where all his dreams had turned sour was now in the hands of the despised Alistair Lundy.

"Will your brother be there, or is he still away on his honeymoon?"

"Oh, sorry, I forgot about you two still being at daggers drawn," she replied. "But you don't have to worry. He didn't really have a honeymoon but is away for a few days. So, do please come and collect it – I think you'll find it interesting."

"All right, but what about getting together?"

"Persistent as always." She laughed. "I tell you what, call me later in the week and tell me what you think of my present. By the way, the office shuts at six o'clock."

"OK," he replied. "I've got a meeting with my accountant round the corner, but that should be well over before six."

In the evening, Ian didn't leave Peter Grove's office until gone six. His accountant had been very sniffy about the two beer mats recording the *The Bath Way* transaction and insisted both men visit the office to sign a conventional contract. Giles was still very excited about getting his first edition to press.

"How did the Lundy trip go?" Ian asked as Groves sealed the papers.

"It didn't. I couldn't get out to the place early due to the only boat already being booked for the wedding party and a force-seven gale. When I finally caught up with the bride, now Lady Anne Lundy, she was less than enthusiastic. She seemed disappointed: it didn't look like her first days of married life were proving to be a bundle of fun. So, all I've ended up with is a portrait photo of her and a brief announcement."

Ian was surprised that Giles seemed unperturbed about his failed exclusive but acknowledged that it probably would not matter.

Once they were finished, and being only two minutes away from Fiona's office, Ian decided to try to collect the package, even though it was later than planned. He crossed Queen Square, as regal as ever with its fine trees having turned an autumnal, burnished gold.

It was twilight as he pressed the bell and heard it echo around the building. There was no immediate response but seeing an interior light on an upper floor after a minute or so, he tried the bell again. Finally, he gave up and started to turn away when he heard footsteps and the door was opened by a young woman. What first struck him most about Lady Anne Lundy was the luxuriant, long, blond hair – similar to Fiona's when he had first known her.

"Ah, the notorious Ian Morris." She had a broad and perfect smile. "Fiona said you'd be popping in, but I expected you earlier. Come in."

She held out her hand that was surprisingly cool to the touch when Ian shook it.

"I don't think I like the 'notorious'." He smiled in return and stepped into the hallway.

"Oh, don't worry, that's just my husband's description – everyone else I know, including Fiona, think you're probably all right. Anyway, come on, the parcel's upstairs," and without waiting for a reply, she strode up the magnificent staircase. He followed, the memories flooding back, until he reached the second floor which had been separated from the rest of the building and now had its own front door.

The flat had been furnished in a modern, Scandinavian style – all glass, chrome, cow hide, and maple-wood furniture. Anne shut the door behind him and sank onto the long sofa, motioning to him to sit down next to her. On the glass coffee table in front of them was a large, flat, brown parcel neatly tied up with string. Next to it was a cut-glass crystal tumbler with a half-finished drink with ice and a slice of lemon. Obviously not her first, he thought as she giggled before picking up the package and placing it on his lap.

"Go on, open it. Fiona's been so secretive, I'm dying to know what's inside," she said. "But where are my manners? What can I get you to drink? I'm afraid it's either gin or whisky." She gestured to the two decanters on a sleek black sideboard. "I gather the single malt is very good." The idea of consuming Lundy's expensive liquor appealed to him.

"Thanks, just neat would be good," Ian nodded, but his attention was elsewhere as he undid the string and removed the brown paper to reveal a large, black, leather album.

He opened the front cover.

It contained about thirty transparent plastic envelopes, each holding large photographs or closely-typed text with blown up headlines. The first in bright-red capitals read,

THE DESTRUCTION OF BATH

It had been superimposed on a foolscap-sized black-and-white picture of utter devastation. Gutted, roofless, and windowless, once-beautiful Georgian Buildings were surrounded by piles of rubble from half-finished demolition. The debris rose high above what had once been gardens. Perhaps as a result of the recent graphic television news coverage of the Americans battling in Vietnam, it reminded Ian of a war scene after a bombing raid.

He sipped from the rather full glass of neat whisky Anne had placed in front of him, turned the page and started to read. Headings caught his attention.

Bath is being ruthlessly destroyed

*2000 historic buildings – many of importance –
demolished since 1950*

*Driven by the determination of the Corporation
to see city expansion*

*Imposition of a new road system and tunnel which
will result in destroying much of the inner city*

*The implementation of totally-inappropriate
comprehensive development of motorways and
industrial estates*

Before-and-after pictures of building after building before demolition and development followed. Two particularly caught his eye; St James' Church built 1769, now Marks and Spencer and Woolworths, and the beautiful eighteenth-century houses replaced by the raw concrete of Northwick House in 1961, isolating southern Bath from its Georgian centre – and much, much more.

He was totally absorbed, and once again, it struck him how well-founded Fiona's arguments were for the regeneration of the city. Then, he became aware of Anne, replenished glass in hand, moving closer to him so that she could look over his shoulder at the album.

"Oh, dear," she said as Ian continued to turn the pages exposing the destruction. "It looks like she's been taken in by another cult."

Surprised, Ian looked at her. "What do you mean?"

Deftly, she lifted the album off his lap and started to flick through it.

"Well, it's bad enough that Alistair is obsessed with bottling the whole city in aspic around Jane Austen, but Fiona has become much more involved." Her speech was slightly slurred, and then, to Ian's alarm, she let the album fall to the floor and burst into tears.

"I can't believe what I've done – I'm such a fool." She covered her face with her hands, her body shaking as tears turned to sobs.

At a complete loss, Ian instinctively tried to comfort her and drew her towards him. Weeping women always unnerved him – he always felt so inadequate.

After a moment, the sobbing stopped, and she laid her head on his shoulder, holding herself tightly to him.

"I've made a terrible mistake," she said before turning his head to hers and kissing him lightly. But then she went on kissing him, harder and harder. Instinctively, his arms went around her, he opened his mouth, and found her tongue. She twisted round to sit across his lap, clasping him urgently and pressing down on his groin. For the first time since his accident, he felt the pleasure of an erection – and so did Anne. She placed her mouth to his ear.

"Fuck me," she said, now raising and lowering her body slowly and rhythmically. "Please fuck me."

She stood up and led him up the short flight of stairs to what was obviously a bedroom, and sat him on the single bed – Ian didn't protest as she bent down to unlace his shoes and undress him. He was equally eager until she, too, was naked squatting over him and gently started to guide him into her. Unable to wait, his hands went around her waist, and he pulled her hard down. It was unlike anything he'd known before, because instead of the joy of fulfilment, she resisted penetration. When, in frustration, he pulled her violently down again and he was fully inside her, she screamed. Instantly, he climaxed.

Afterwards, he gently stroked this beautiful woman who lay whimpering beside him. He'd never before felt regret. Since Fiona had seduced him that Christmas in 1961 before dumping him, he'd taken sex as and when he wanted it from willing women. This was a totally new experience.

Over the following hours, Anne recounted the horror of her marriage from the very first night of her honeymoon.

Alistair had drunk a great deal, and it was very late by the time the bride and groom had struggled through the storm to the tiny, isolated Lundy cottage of their honeymoon suite. There was no electricity, and although basic, Anne thought it so romantic by candle-light, and a fire had been lit in the grates of both the bedroom, and the sitting room so it was cosy and warm. There was an unopened bottle of brandy and a single glass on the table, and Alistair wanted a drink before retiring.

So, the new Lady of Lundy went to ready herself in a wonderfully-new, luxurious, silk negligee and lay patiently on the bed, waiting for her husband. She looked forward to discarding it and showing her husband of a few hours how happy she was to be his wife and how much she loved him. But he didn't arrive, and finally, she drifted off to sleep, only to be woken later by the howling wind.

She got up, checked in the mirror that she still looked desirable, opened the bedroom door, and walked back into the sitting room. She found Alistair sitting in the glow of the fire and staring out of the window at the raging storm. The half-empty bottle of cognac was beside him. During their engagement, she had encountered no complaint with her wish that their relationship remained chaste and her virginity intact. Now they were married, it would be different, she thought as she approached him, put her arms around his neck, kissed him tenderly, and went to sit on his lap. But he roughly brushed her aside and, tripping on the rug covering the flagstones, she fell back onto her bottom in front of the fireplace.

"Don't do that!" he barked. "Ever!"

She was too shocked to respond, but now, he was shouting.

"Don't you understand that I can't bear to be touched by women? You stupid bitch. You've worked for me for months, and you should've worked out by now that the man you've chosen to marry is a homosexual, a homo, a queer, a raging poofter! You wanted to be Lady Anne, and you've got it, but leave me alone! You're nothing but a whore, willing to trade your body for a title."

Hours later, Ian awoke to find her softly weeping, and he felt deeply moved by this beautiful woman he'd known for just a few hours. He took her into his arms and began comforting her. Fearful of hurting her again, he stopped short of making love, but she took hold of him and slowly pulled him into her. This time, there was no scream, and afterwards, she slept, her blond hair splayed across the pillows.

Very early, he gently disengaged and, careful not to wake her, got up from the bed, picked up his clothes, and went downstairs. A few minutes later, with the photograph album under his arm, Ian let himself quietly out of the house and listened to the dawn chorus as he walked across Queen Square and headed up Gay Street towards the Circus. He was a fool to have become entangled with the bride of a man who hated him and would stop at nothing to destroy him.

Would she tell him? Or worse still, would Fiona find out?

The sky was brightening as Ian walked back to St James' Square and the sanctuary of his house, but he was deeply troubled. He'd broken one of his golden rules to never become involved with a married woman. This thought stirred the memory of Cara Forrester and then the Brylcreem Man at the front door saying 'a present from John Forrester'." For the first time, he could remember lying helplessly on the pavement in Great Pulteney Street trying to protect himself while being kicked time and again. But he couldn't see his attacker. Then, in his mind's eye, there was the dazzling white light as he arrived at the hospital and felt the pain, the awful pain.

CHAPTER TWENTY-NINE

Ian came to the conclusion that Anne had said nothing to Fiona Symons, for her telephone call a few days later was concerned only with his reaction to her gift. Nor had he heard anything from Anne herself, for which he was grateful and sincerely hoped her silence would continue.

The photograph album, depressing as it was, drew him back time after time, and he became increasingly affected by its contents. He promised to let Fiona have his views at the reception they were both attending by chance at the University on the following Tuesday evening and decided to spend the weekend working out his position on the issue. Later, he questioned the awful coincidence of him spending time considering the destruction of Bath when, less than a hundred miles away, a human catastrophe was unfolding.

It was the shocking disaster in the Welsh village of Aberfan, near Merthyr Tydfil, on 21 October 1966. More than five million cubic feet of water-saturated debris broke away from a colliery spoil tip and slid into the village. It covered houses and, most tragically, the Pantglas Junior School, under forty feet of slurry. The children were attending morning assembly, and the death toll was a hundred and twenty children and twenty-eight adults. An hour earlier, and the children wouldn't have been at school: later that day, the school was due to break up for its half-term holiday. Like many others, Ian would never forget exactly where he was and what he had been doing when he first heard of the tragedy. It remained seared in his memory, joining that of his mother's death and the assassination of President Kennedy.

Tuesday evening arrived, and everyone was there to celebrate the grant of the Charter for Bath's own university. The original idea in the mid-nineteenth century had been for the University of Oxford to build a college in the city, but this had never happened. Instead, the University had taken more than a hundred years to emerge out of the Merchant Venturers Technical College in Bristol.

Ian looked at the display in the reception's lobby and envied what he saw. His own higher education had been a full-time job at seventeen, with the following six years of relentless evening and weekend study by correspondence courses and night school as he strove to obtain an external qualification.

Noting that the speeches were due in a few minutes, he turned towards the bar for a drink, where a tall slim man introduced himself. In his twenties and immaculately dressed in a beautifully-cut Italian suit, he didn't look like an academic.

"Toby Stafford," he said, handing over a business card. Instinctively, Ian ran his thumb over the engraved, quality card. The italic script read, *Tobias Stafford, Cassofiori Bank, Leadenhall Street, London EC3*. Ian had come across the prestigious private bank when he'd worked in London. It served only the very wealthy and was renowned for its absolute discretion. Ian introduced himself, and each recognised the other as a born networker in a sea of dowdily-dressed academia.

"You don't look like a teacher, so what brings you here?" Stafford asked

"Property – I was involved in the land sale on which the University is built, and you?"

"I'm the guest lecturer, seconded by my employer in London. The Chancellor wants to set up a Faculty for Business Studies which the bank has agreed to sponsor with an eye to future graduates joining Cassofiori. I'm here to start the process with a series of evening lectures starting in the New Year. My brief is to present a global overview, as seen from the City of London. I'll send you an invitation if you're interested; do come and have a listen."

"Will do," Ian said. "Reality would make a pleasant change." The two men chatted on for a few minutes before Stafford was invited to take a seat on the rostrum.

"You didn't go to university, did you, Ian?" Fiona Symons had slid round from behind him. His longing for her caused him to take a slow intake of breath. She was so elegant in a black shift dress and a simple silver rope necklace with matching earrings. Everything he so desperately wanted, needed, and loved was before him.

She turned to the stage as the reception room hushed and a balding distinguished-looking man with a moustache mounted the platform. It was the university's first Chancellor, Lord Hinton of Bankside. Ian half listened, with his eyes still on the back of Fiona's head where her hair had been cut close to the nape of her neck. She'd had it fashionably styled like Twiggy, the face of 1966, but Fiona was so much more beautiful and feminine than the famously-thin teenage model.

"Ladies and gentlemen, who would have thought it? All this from a technical school founded over a hundred years ago in Bristol. Set high up on Claverton Down, overlooking the city, we are opening our doors to over a thousand undergraduates, over a hundred postgraduates, and nearly five hundred staff ..."

The speech came to an end. As the applause died, Fiona turned to face Ian, those familiar green eyes boring into him, where he felt his inner most thoughts and motives were exposed. No other woman had ever made him feel so vulnerable.

"When are you going to let me know what you think of my gift?"

For a moment, his thoughts went back to receiving the album from Anne and what had happened afterwards between them. His heart pounded with fear that she could have confided in Fiona, but her friendliness and the light-hearted tone of the question made him believe otherwise.

"I'd never previously considered Bath from this perspective and agree with much of your argument," he said. "I went through it again over the weekend – it really is shocking."

"But it doesn't have to be, Ian." She spoke earnestly. "You could help to stop the destruction – that's why I put the album together. With your influence, we would be a formidable team and could make sure that what's important in this city is kept safe: it wouldn't just disappear under the guise of modernisation when, really, it's desecration and purely destruction for profit."

"But I don't think I'm your man – I might have been before the attack. What money and influence I once had here has gone," he smiled ruefully. "After all, you and your brother are comfortably settled in my old centre of operations in my wonderful office on Queen Square."

"Come on, Ian," she smiled back. "Don't be so melodramatic – I'm not trying to diminish the horrific attack you suffered, but I hear that you're definitely a man on the rise again ..."

He let the silence hang. He wanted her more than anything else, and her reference to a team was encouraging, but could he risk getting involved with her crusade? There was no way he could ever work with her brother.

"I'll tell you what," she linked her arm in his. "How about you take me out to that dinner you are always promising, and let's see if I can change your mind?"

"Of course, when can you make it?" He couldn't believe his luck.

"There's no time like the present, they say," she laughed again. "So what are you up to tonight – somewhere private?"

On reaching Bradford on Avon, eight miles south east of Bath, Ian parked the MGB, and they crossed St Margaret's Street to the Duke of Monmouth, originally a pub named after the eldest illegitimate son of Charles II: local folklore would have you believe that his rebellion reached this early-seventeenth-century building.

Its ebullient manager, Antonio, was there to welcome them and confirmed that the little-known private dining room had been reserved, away from prying eyes and wagging tongues. He escorted them across the busy, oak-panelled dining room and through an almost hidden door into another, much smaller room that again had oak panelling and a single table set for two diners. He settled them and lit the candles.

"What would the signorina like to drink?" He bowed slightly towards Fiona.

"A glass of good red wine would be most welcome," she answered. Antonio turned to Ian.

"Your usual, Mr Morris? The Margaux from Pierre Ginestet 1947?"

Fiona enjoyed the surroundings, and was impressed by the manager's professional flattery and his knack of making her feel special. Soon returning with the claret for tasting before filling both glasses, he almost danced around the table with the bottle, his evident sommelier skill elevated to an art form. Leaving menus with them, he then disappeared, sensing they were best left alone for a while.

The Honourable Fiona Symons sipped the deep red wine: it was soft, full-bodied, floated in the mouth, superb. She looked across at the man sitting opposite her. He was so different to the naive and rough nineteen-year old she'd enjoyed for a bit of fun that Christmas – almost a dare because of his nickname given by the girls in the typing pool, where he was known as the Monk. But that was 1961, before the fateful trip to Switzerland – she wondered if he had ever guessed what it was all about from the postcard she had sent. She, too, was different now – the family bankruptcy and that awful abortion: she had not only survived but become so much wiser.

Ian was also thinking about their wild sexual experience nearly five years earlier, and the hurt when she dumped him afterwards and disappeared abroad without any explanation. Why was he still so attracted to her? He realised that he knew very little about her or what she'd been doing since they'd first known one another. In many ways, she was an elegant stranger, and this made him feel unusually awkward and tongue-tied. But he needn't have worried, because Fiona, with the social skill she had doubtlessly learnt at her mother's knee, came to his rescue.

"So, where did you learn about wine? We always left such matters to the butler." But then, she quickly added, "I do realise that we were very privileged in that way."

Unoffended and grateful for the proffered ice-breaker, he answered.

"I go to wine-tastings at Great Western Wine in Bath – on the Wells Road – Alan Nordberg is absolutely brilliant." Ian planned to lay down a cellar should he ever have a son, in the old aristocratic manner. Every year from the day of his birth, it would involve one hundred bottles of the best young vintages being laid down until the boy's twenty first-birthday, not a single bottle to be drunk. Then, by judicial selling and buying, it should enable the young man to drink the very best wines free for the rest of his life.

Antonio returned just as Ian had finished talking, unfolded Fiona's linen napkin, and placed it on her lap.

"Your recommendations, Antonio?" Ian asked.

"Is there anything the signorina doesn't like?"

Fiona shook her head. "Then I would suggest foie gras with apple compote dusted with hazel nuts to start, followed by the speciality of the house, Salisbury Plain loin of venison roasted with red lentils, figs, and jus."

"That sounds delicious," Ian said.

"Perhaps with roasted potatoes and herbs and some buttered green beans?"

"Perfect," Fiona said.

Ian filled the silence left by the restauranteur's departure for the kitchen. "I met a real nutcase this morning. He's starting a campaign to preserve holes caused by the Luftwaffe from the bombing in 1942. Not the building itself, just the shrapnel and bullet holes. Would you believe it?"

Fiona laughed. "Where's that?"

"James Street West – the old Labour Exchange – and even you must agree that it is a really ugly building."

"Trust you to dwell on an extreme and ignore the triumphs." She picked up her wine glass: he loved the way she looked straight into his eyes.

"Think about the Royal Crescent, the Assembly Rooms, the Roman Baths; or then again, how about the Paragon, Lansdown Crescent, or Great Pulteney Street? Have you ever stopped for a moment and asked yourself why people are so passionate about Bath?"

He didn't want to admit that he had been asking himself a lot of such questions recently and ventured, "Status quo?"

"What do you mean?" she asked.

"People don't want anything to alter." This was familiar territory, but part of the doubts caused by Fiona's album. "They want to keep everything as it is. Most of those I come across aren't even Bathonians but retired Admiralty, retired couples growing older by the day, terrified of change."

"That's a bit harsh, Ian." She sipped her wine again before continuing. "I may be older than you, but I hope you don't think I love Bath because I'm in my dotage."

"No, of course not, but ..."

She interrupted. "People cherish Bath because the buildings are magnificent, beautifully proportioned, irreplaceable, and in the wonderful setting of seven green hills. Everything is on a human scale, not some vast, towering, and sprawling metropolis – and most importantly, the city is a living reminder of our history, heritage, and ancestors."

"But that doesn't explain the fanatics such as my holes man," he countered. "How can you justify them?"

"I can't. Nutters aren't unique to Bath or preservation, but at the same time, there's nothing wrong with conviction. I've spent a fair amount of time in the United States – many things to loathe there but a few so very good. For instance, I discovered that believing strongly in something binds people together and creates a spirit of community. I also saw that sometimes conviction becomes an obsession, and people become intolerant and intolerable.

"Where Bath is concerned, this has happened on both sides. You and I both know developers who think Bath is totally unsuited to the twentieth century. They want the Georgian streets completely flattened to make way for houses, blocks of flats, hotels, and massive concrete shopping-malls with their attendant cars, delivery lorries, and car parks."

She finally took a breath, and Ian was about to respond when she continued.

"Believe me, Ian, I'm new to this and hadn't really considered any of it until I got back here six months ago. But views have become so polarised that we're at an impasse: I am sure there is room for both old and new. This is why you and I need to work together on it."

Ian had never heard it explained so logically and was pleased to discover that she was a fellow fan of some aspects of the American way of life.

As the dinner progressed and ranged over many subjects, it began to dawn on Fiona that she was not only making progress in explaining the issues with Bath's heritage but enjoying herself. This man was very good company. She knew not if it was because time had passed and so he had grown up in her absence, or the assault had caused him to reconsider his priorities: Ian had changed.

His ambition to simply make money was no longer so naked: he even admitted to enjoying a good game of Scrabble. His interests were wide, and he displayed a considerable grasp of modern politics and history. She was particularly impressed by his perception of the relationship between England and the United States. He held strong opinions of how Churchill's vision and his mixed, British-American parentage had been instrumental in much that the United Kingdom had achieved and continued to achieve as its influence declined.

It had been a great evening, and Antonio kissed Fiona's hand in a dramatic farewell at the door of the restaurant.

"That's so typically Italian and way over the top," she said as they laughed their way back to the car. "And I love it."

"I suppose I should tell you about our Antonio Brioni, we go back some years. He was just plain Brian Anthony when he opened his sandwich bar round the corner from my office in London. With the name change and

Italian accent, he knew that he could attract a different class of clientele, and it's worked. He deserves the success."

Fiona's life of luxury and privilege as a child had been swept away with the loss of the family's wealth, but this hadn't seemed to matter in the anonymity of California where youth and money, not background, counted. Now back in Bath, she was expected to resign herself to being entertained by boring men, part of the faded gentry that struggled to adapt to a rapidly-changing world. She hadn't previously considered any alternative and, at thirty-four, was already considered on the shelf by some. As Ian drove her back to Bath in the open-top car, she couldn't help but be aware of his close proximity. She thought of the raw sex she'd enjoyed with the boy and considered what it would be like with the man.

Ian thought the evening a success and congratulated himself on not even having attempted to kiss Fiona goodnight. Once he returned home, he poured himself a very large malt whisky and started to listen to another great woman in his life.

He had come across her one night in New York, on his way back from Jamaica in 1963. First, he'd watched Nina Simone from afar at the Carnegie Hall and then up close at the NAACP gathering at the Village Gate in Greenwich Village.

"I Put a Spell on You" boomed out from the record player, and it brought back the violent images he'd seen on television of the Birmingham, Alabama bombings.

The next song was "Mississippi Goddam", and he thought of the black suffering at Selma.

Starting to feel fuddled from much alcohol, Ian remembered – sitting alone with the haunting voice of Simone in the background, he became maudlin: how could mankind be capable of such hatred, destruction, and violence?

CHAPTER THIRTY

Although not widely known, Robert Adam's original design for Bath's Assembly Rooms had been rejected by the citizenry as too costly, but John Wood the Younger had used the notorious tontine scheme to raise the money to get the celebrated venue built in 1771.

In June 1963, Princess Marina of Greece and Denmark, Duchess of Kent re-opened the grand Georgian party location and its new Museum of Costume – described as "the largest display of costume in the world".

It was the second time she had done so, the first being in 1938. After the City Council had taken out a seventy-five-year lease with the National Trust, it had completed a thorough and successful restoration of the great building – all gutted in less than an hour during a German air raid four years later.

Now, once again back to its full splendour, it was a magnificent setting for the Nurses' Grand Christmas Ball. The young staff of the Royal United Hospital had done a wonderful job of decorating the hundred-foot-long ballroom and the twenty-five dining tables. It had been Norman Piggott, Ian's charge nurse, who had come up with the clever idea for each table to be named by the guests, and a prize awarded for the most original.

Al Giles looked at the seating plan by the door and was amused to see that the Twelve Tribes of Bath, as he called them, were each named and now gathered in all their glory.

The *Healers and Feelers* had taken three tables. Perhaps reflecting the falling congregations, the *God Squad* had managed just one. Appropriately, next to them was the Do Gooders table for Bath charities. Sport was represented by four tables of *Heavy Breathers*, with two of them exclusively for *Rugger Buggers*. Stars and the elite from the Theatre Royal, festivals and other literati were to be seated on the *Arty Farty* tables. Next to them were two tables of *Cops and Robbers*. Giles smiled: the latter included the legal profession. Five tables for the *Wheelers & Dealers*, factory owners, traders, and businesses; *Those who can't* had academia covered, while *Hackers* represented the press and broadcasting. The *Guineas Club* was there for the professions, with the military on a table titled *Pips & Stripes*. Lastly, there were the *Three-line Whips*, which left one wondering about the peccadillos of local councillors and national politicians.

Superb sub-divisions for *The Bath Way*, he thought as the doors opened and the good and not so good of the city swept noisily in.

The quality and quantity of party-goers had much changed over the hundred and fifty years since the Assembly Rooms had first opened their doors. The type of ball described in *Northanger Abbey* and *Persuasion* involved around eight hundred guests of which ten percent could be deemed from the aristocracy. But looking down the guest list, Giles doubted there was even a handful of the present-day nobility, only the Fourth Lord Lundy's party apparent. Alternatively, handshakes betrayed just how many Freemasons would be attending.

Ian had asked Debbie Smith to partner him for the occasion. They'd known one another ever since she had become the personal assistant to his late mentor, Marcus Rose. They'd often been thrown together while jointly progressing Rose's schemes and had become friends.

After Rose's death, Ian had helped Debbie buy her Brock Street home. She had been frank with him about the type of business she proposed to set up, and he never raised the question of why she had chosen that line of work. On occasion, they would have lunch together. They called these their Dough lunches, because they took place in the pizza restaurant of the same name; highly-entertaining affairs as they each quietly exchanged gossip – he about the business activities and she concerning the bedroom habits of many of Bath's upstanding citizens. He was staggered at how prostitution had penetrated every aspect of Bath and sometimes became distracted at meetings, knowing what Debbie had told him about the upright citizens sitting opposite him.

They enjoyed an easy and relaxed relationship, avoiding the temptation of sex, and thus it was that they sat together at the high table of the ball. Trusted by Al Giles with many secrets concerning *The Bath Way*, Ian was one of very few who knew that Debbie had been hired to write the 'Tittle-Tattle' column of the magazine. It was based on the pillow talk reported back by her girls and was both light-hearted and enlightening.

After the meal, Debbie fell into conversation with Toby Stafford, and Ian excused himself. The dancing was in full swing, and he made his way through to the Card Room. With pride, he picked up the inaugural copy of *The Bath Way*, one of which had been placed at every guest place.

The first page had been the striking photograph of Anne Fisher with the description of her wedding and her becoming the 4th Earl's wife. Much of the remainder was a triumph for the provincial class-system, with photograph after photograph of unimportant Bath gatherings. They showed many wives in their best frocks with husbands who'd been seduced into buying the interspaced advertising. It was all cleverly broken up by occasional articles about the city, one of which caught his eye.

BATHWICK

On a summer morning in 1725, William Pulteney stood by Bath's east gate and looked across the river Avon.

On a whim, he took the ferry across to the far bank and spent the day strolling around the village of Bathwick, along with its surrounding parish.

Bath was bursting at the seams, and it was obvious to him that sooner or later, the six hundred acres of meadowland would be needed for housing. He decided to have a word with his agent and explore the possibility of a long-term investment, and within two years, he had purchased the whole area. "Long term" was to prove an understatement.

He had foreseen the need for a bridge to replace the ferry and the necessity of clearing the land of tenants before building but failed to solve either problem before his death some thirty-eight years later. His only achievement was the creation of the Spring Gardens Pleasure Resort, not so far removed from its present use as the Recreational Ground two hundred years later.

Frances, the daughter of his cousin Daniel, inherited the land, and her husband William Johnstone did two things: he took his wife's name, becoming William Pulteney, and ordered the bridge.

Robert Adams's design took Bath by surprise: bridges with shops were medieval and a thing of the past rather than suitable for a modern Georgian city. Finally, work on Pulteney Bridge began in 1769 but when completed five years later, the only places it served were the original, and still undeveloped, meadows and village.

(to be continued)

Clever man, William Johnstone, Ian thought, buying respectability by adopting the family name. He felt a tap on his shoulder, and from behind him, a woman's voice said,

"Hello, stranger." He turned to see a radiant Anne Fisher. He hadn't seen or spoken to her since that night at Queen Square three months earlier. Sometimes, he'd thought about calling her but decided against it, partly because he didn't know what to say and partly because he wanted to forget. In any case, she appeared to be on sparkling form, so presumably, her marital problems had been overcome.

"I was hoping you might be here," she said and, looking towards the bar, added, "Mine's a gin and tonic. Please."

A few minutes later, they took their drinks to the Octagon where tables and chairs had been set out for those wanting to avoid the noise and melee of the dance floor. Ian wasn't sure what to say and was glad when Anne started the conversation.

"Now, please don't be worried, but for obvious reasons, you're the first and only person I've decided to tell," she began. "I'm pregnant."

CHAPTER THIRTY-ONE

After Christmas lunch and the Queen's Speech, Alistair Lundy was enjoying the rare luxury of a good cigar – a present from his father-in-law. Contented, he watched its smoke weave its way up to the ceiling of the rear admiral's drawing room in Lansdown Crescent.

He had grown to like Fisher and counted him as one of the few tangible benefits of his marriage – the only other being the lack of interest in him by the police since the wedding. Like Alistair, the old boy was old school, utterly committed to Bath's heritage and preserving its tradition. Fisher's late wife had also been a snob, and he relished the rank Anne's marriage had brought to the family and was therefore only too keen to please Alistair.

"Are we still OK for our Thursday game?" the older man asked.

"You realise that it's New Year's Day?"

"Definitely," Alistair replied. "I'm looking forward to it."

Both members of the Bath Golf Club, they had got into the routine of playing a weekly round high up on Bathampton Down.

Founded in the 1880s, the club was affectionately known by locals as Sham Castle, including as it did, Ralph Allen's folly – the advert for his beloved Bath stone, which had dominated the city skyline for two hundred years. Many frustrated would-be members complained that, it being the sole preserve of the Admiralty, one would remain on the waiting list forever if you weren't a navy man. However, given his lineage, the 4th Earl had encountered no such problem.

"I want to discuss Mary Shelley and my idea about Frankenstein with you," Fisher said.

Alistair didn't respond but took a puff on his Montecristo.

"It's not that I'm into horror stories," Fisher continued, "but it's quite clever – especially when you stop and realise that the book was written by so young a woman. We're trying to get a plaque put up for her in the Abbey Courtyard but have hit a brick wall."

"What's her connection to Bath?" Alistair asked. "I didn't know she'd ever been here." He assumed the "we" that Fisher was referring to was the local branch of the Lord Byron Society of which his father-in-law was chair.

"Mary lived here in September 1816 after she returned from the Continent where she'd been with Shelley and Byron. She said the idea came to her in a nightmare after they'd been telling ghost stories in a thunderstorm."

"Fair enough," Alistair replied. "Let's chat about it on Thursday."

As with a number of other things, presumably due to the concussion caused by the attack, Ian had completely forgotten his old school-friend's generosity until the letter arrived.

Ramsden & Company
Mount Street, London W1

I Morris Esq   *BY HAND*
12 Great Pulteney Street
Bath   *31 December 1967*

Dear Mr Morris,

Beaconsfield Properties Ltd

It has been my sad duty to deal with the estate of the late Mr Henry Liberman, who as you know was lost at sea, when the TSMS Salamis foundered in the spring of 1966.

Under the terms of an Option Agreement dated 21 February 1962 and signed by Mr Liberman and yourself, you have the right to acquire 5% of his company for £5 on 1 January 1967.

We should be obliged to hear from you if you wish to exercise your option, as we shall shortly be putting the whole company up for sale.

Yours sincerely,

DAVID RAMSDEN
Executor

Beaconsfield Properties had bought all the surplus land and buildings from British Railways when Lord Beeching had closed the Old Somerset and Dorset Railways. Starting with Green Park Station in Bath, the company had purchased every station, goods yard, railway house, and piece of land adjoining the seventy miles of track to Salisbury and terminating at Bournemouth.

Ian and Trish had spent days going up and down the line surveying the doomed stations of Frome, Wells, Castle Cary, Blandford Town, and Christchurch. What was the value they reached – one million pounds or more? He wasn't sure but knew the answer would be in his old files. Hopefully they hadn't disappeared in the eviction – he'd have to ask Trish.

He remembered Henry's dream for Green Park Station, one of the new-fangled supermarkets, surrounded by its own vast car park in the enormous abandoned railway goods yard, enclosed by the river and James Street. He looked at the letter again and knew that he'd be a fool not to exercise his option. He wondered what price Mr Ramsden wanted for the whole company.

The first day of 1967 was a crisp January morning and the golf ball's trail in the heavy frost on the greens had demonstrated the waywardness of Alistair's attempts to putt.

They were making their way around the latest archaeological dig by the ninth hole, the third in the previous sixty years. This one was necessary because of the additional university buildings proposed to be constructed just south of the course.

"So, do you think it's all been worth it?" Alistair knew that the rear admiral, chair of the History Society, kept in regular communication with the excavation committee.

"Most definitely," Fisher said. "I went to have a look just yesterday. You've got remains from the Bronze Age Round Barrows dating back to 2000 BC, an Iron-Age fort, a Roman villa, and even the Georgian racecourse. But let me tell you about the interesting Mary Shelley.

"Percy Shelley was up to his eyes in debt and still married to his first wife when he took up with Mary, a teenager of seventeen. The couple fled abroad because of the scandal; it wasn't long before she became pregnant.

"Upon returning to England, the lovers parted in Southampton, and Mary came by mail coach to Bath where she took up lodgings at five Abbey Courtyard. It was a boarding house at the time, but is long gone, replaced first by a concert hall and now by the entrance to the Pump Room.

"Anyway, she and Shelley married three months after his first wife committed suicide by throwing herself off a London bridge. By the time Mary left the city in February 1817, much of Frankenstein had been written – she was still only nineteen. It really is quite brilliant – especially when the monster takes on the role of Adam and his creator is God, who of course was her ... Anyway, the City Council say a plaque commemorating Frankenstein isn't compatible with Bath's image."

"Leave it with me," Alistair said. "I'm sure a compromise can be found."

They played on. Fisher won the tenth hole, they halved the eleventh, and finished the twelfth all square. The rear admiral had gone on to explain about a Doctor Williams who, just fifty yards from Mary Shelley's lodgings, gave shows about the magical new forces of electricity and galvanism which were claimed to bring the dead back to life.

Alistair tried to hit the ball far too hard off the thirteenth tee with the result that he sliced it into the undergrowth, a good hundred yards off the fairway. It had landed into scrubland not owned by the golf club, and after Fisher hit a perfect shot onto the green, both men went to look for the lost ball.

For all the years he'd been playing the course, the rear admiral couldn't recall anyone going so far adrift but was more than happy to assist his titled son-in-law with the search in the long, dense grass. After about five minutes of frantic club hacking, Alistair discovered the ball's resting place. It had been stopped and held slightly proud on a piece of rusty metal. Even though out of bounds, the lie was good, and Alistair couldn't resist trying to hit it.

The club head, moving at a speed of over a hundred miles per hour, hit the tail fin of the enormous unexploded German bomb which had lain unnoticed and undisturbed since it had been dropped in the air raids of 1942. The detonation wave from the blast hit the two men at over twenty thousand feet per second, causing both to evaporate. The story occupied the complete front page of the *Bath Chronicle*.

TRAGIC DEATH
OF TWO LEADING BATH CITIZENS

REAR ADMIRAL DAVID FISHER & THE 4TH EARL OF LUNDY KILLED.
DEVASTATED WIDOW EXPECTING FIRST CHILD

* * *

WORLD WAR II BOMB EXPLODES

* * *

HUNDREDS EVACUATED AROUND GOLF COURSE

BOMB DISPOSAL TEAM IN ATTENDANCE

Just after 1 pm yesterday afternoon ...

Both the mother and sister of the late Earl were surprised that Anne had achieved pregnancy but had no intention of airing their concerns.

"For once, the boy put duty before pleasure," was the old Dowager's explanation to her daughter. "Let's hope it's a boy."

CHAPTER THIRTY-TWO

The memorial service was packed and sombre with mourners overflowing into the Abbey Courtyard where a Royal Navy band was playing the 'Dead March' from *Saul*. There had been nothing found of either man to bury.

Ian knew many people but was surprised to see Trish Traynor sitting next to Norman Piggott as he was shown to a pew near the memorial recording Beau Nash's burial over two hundred years earlier.

Looking up at the magnificent fan vaulted ceiling as the organ played Elgar's *Nimrod*, Ian felt a profound sense of insignificance. A nearby wall plaque only emphasised the fleeting nature of life: it recorded the death of a Joseph Maycocks in 1860 from wounds suffered after the Indian Mutiny together with four of his children, who had all passed away before reaching the age of six.

As Mozart's *Lacrimosa* played, the young widow entered in the Bishop's procession, her long, blond hair emphasising the black clothing she wore. Fiona was by her side, elegant and poised in mourning.

Hymns, tributes, Psalm 121, prayers of intercession, the Lord's Prayer, and finally a blessing – the inevitable ending of all lives, Ian thought. His stomach tightened in memory of his mother's death seven years earlier when he hadn't even been able to pay for a proper funeral.

As the service concluded and they sang the Naval Hymn, the principle mourners rose and slowly filed back down the centre aisle past the congregation. Fiona noticed him with a slight nod of her head, and so, despite his misgivings of confronting both women together, Ian decided that he ought to attend the reception in the adjacent Pump Room.

The line of mourners moved slowly past the relatives, and when Ian's turn came, he mouthed the usual platitude of condolence.

He had first addressed Anne but had been met with an unknown blank stare, but Fiona held on to the outstretched hand and quietly spoke.

"There's something that I need to talk to you about urgently. Are you free later?"

"I'm going to a lecture at the university but could come onto you afterwards," he said. "Would that be OK?"

"Yes. Great Pulteney Street." She spoke gravely.

"I look forward to it," he lied. He assumed that she'd found out about Anne's pregnancy.

Four South was an angular building that had been designed like many of the so-called plate-glass post-war English universities: it was functional, modernist, and constructed of raw-concrete blocks.

Ian took a seat in the lecture hall now rapidly filling as the Vice Chancellor introduced Toby Stafford. He waited for everyone to settle.

"Good evening, Vice Chancellor, faculty members, and guests." He was speaking from a small rostrum with all but his lectern light dimmed. The projector clicked, and the first slide of his presentation slid from its carousel to become illuminated on the large screen.

MAKING SENSE OF THE SIXTIES
POLITICS
URBANISATION
DEMOGRAPHICS
TECHNICAL REVOLUTION
GENDER
ECONOMICS
THE STATISTIC - 4d : £100,000

"This establishment is charged with teaching undergraduates in a world that has changed fundamentally from when you grew up and that has existed following the Second World War, just twenty-two years ago. My aim this evening is to summarise the extent and ever-increasing speed of this transformation as recorded worldwide and often daily in numerous sources."

Ian was impressed by his articulate confidence – he was a born public speaker.

"Politically, the world of empires had already disappeared, be they European such as the Austro-Hungarian, Ottoman, and Russian, or worldwide such as those colonised by the English, French, and Dutch.

"Everything changed after the First World War when so many colonies were swept away and new nations came into existence in less than twenty-five years. After the Great War and the Russian Revolution, the elite and privileged classes who had governed Europe and therefore most of the world, largely disappeared, thereby exposing the falsehood that democracy had ever existed.

"Since then, slowly and with difficultly, the world is becoming democratic – where universal suffrage is the aim and expected norm." He paused to sip from a glass of water.

"I talk about the world. But we must remember that a hundred years ago, more people lived in Europe than in any other region, but that is no longer the case. Britain's imperial status, like that of our western European allies, has evaporated. Like it or not, the modern world is controlled by Russia and the United States of America, not Western Europe. And we shouldn't ignore Chairman Mao Zedong's China that is rapidly developing into a powerful global force: India is close on its heels.

"So much of the political reality of sixty years ago has gone forever. Then, the only country on earth with more people living in cities than in rural areas was Great Britain. Now, in every developed country and a growing proportion of developing countries, the majority of populations live in cities. As I speak, seven out of the top-thirteen world cities of ten million or more inhabitants are in the Third World; with Mexico City, for example, having over twenty million citizens.

"The demographic change this century is unprecedented and due to numerous factors. Firstly, there is the huge growth in global populations despite the two World Wars. This had previously been controlled by such things as conflict, famine, and natural disasters – but most of all, disease, which has massively declined due to sanitation, immunisation and antibiotics.

"Closer to home, here in the United Kingdom, a child born today has a life expectancy of twenty years more than a child born at the turn of the century – a staggering third longer." Ian remembered Joseph Maycock's plaque in the Abbey. Toby continued. "At the same time, birth rates have plummeted, incomes have risen, and therefore, the average family has much more disposable income.

"I don't propose to dwell on technical change. I think we are all aware of the considerable advances over the last twenty-five years with transport, communication, media, leisure, and, of course, the workplace.

"More important, I would suggest, is that this rate of change is quickening, and some reckon more will be achieved in the next ten years than in the last fifty."

He stopped and looked around the audience of about a hundred or so mostly middle-aged men.

"I count at most eight women here. But beware the male of the species: there are already moves afoot that are changing the established order that you have grown up with. The good wife and mother, never to stray out of her kitchen and away from home, will soon be a distant memory.

"It is nearly fifty years since some women gained the vote, and ten years later, they were allowed the same voting rights as men. We need to remember that until then, a woman wasn't only denied the vote but also the right to own property, buy or sell anything significant, or even get a job without her husband or father's consent. This has changed, and we can forget the 'angel in the house' who needed our protection but has been effectively exploited since time began because it suited us men.

"Why? Because women demonstrated throughout both World Wars that they are more than capable of being a man's equal in the workplace. Their daughters, who are my generation, are now demanding equal employment opportunities and for them to be protected by law.

"Now, what does this all mean? Well, I believe that true liberty is beginning to replace forced repression. The individual is becoming more respected, with governments realising and recognising that they are not here to rule but to serve people, no matter race, religion, class, or gender. This should result in economic growth and private wealth on an unprecedented scale over the coming years. But there will be risks, great and many ..."

Stafford went on to describe the potential dangers he could foresee before winding up with a few questions.

The first came from a man who explained that he was head of the university's Social Sciences department.

"Would you be kind enough to say a few words on what you feel the role of the welfare state should be over the coming years?"
Stafford thought for a moment before responding.

"The British people came out of the Second World War craving social change, which was only reasonable given the enormous sacrifices made over the previous six years. Above all else, they wanted fairness for everyone, with decent employment, housing, and health services as a priority. The working classes in particular felt they'd been betrayed by the politicians and cheated of these basic needs following the Great War and didn't want a repetition of the Great Depression.

"This explains the Labour landslide victory in 1945 and the birth of the welfare state. The National Health Service, social services, and a public rebuilding and education programme all were put in place, together with the nationalisation of virtually every major industry. No matter which party has been in power since, this has been at the top of every politician's agenda.

"Sadly, history has shown us that radical policies often fail to deliver. And, with the notable exception of the National Health Service, this is the case with the welfare state. With little accountability, spiralling costs, and few evident benefits, I foresee a reversion to the norm in the near future. In particular, I see the denationalisation of most of the grossly-overmanned and inefficient utility companies in order to encourage competition, and a scaling back of the inhumane, towering council blocks which have been springing up across our cities in recent years."

The next question was from the single black man in the audience.

"What are your views of immigration, especially from the Commonwealth?"

"Starting all those years ago with the first wave of immigration on the Windrush from the Caribbean, I believe it should continue without limit. There has been no shortage of employment since the last war, and we sorely need a fresh young labour force with aspirations, particularly for our hospitals and our public transport systems. Also much needed are those with entrepreneurial drive who will join our middle class and help break down traditional barriers.

"So, to conclude, I believe and hope that we are heading towards a multicultural society here in Britain, because it is to the benefit of everyone, and this should be a global aim for every country.

"Lastly, the statistic of the month: the Bank offers a prize of a bottle of champagne for the first correct written answer – why are four pennies and a hundred thousand pounds a matter of life and death?"

Ian was still pondering the content of the lecture and the statistic of the month as he walked towards twelve Great Pulteney Street with the photograph album about the destruction of Bath under his arm. Then the memories came flooding back – particularly that Christmas weekend five years earlier when he had fallen in love with Fiona Symons. His stomach churned as he recalled the pain of her rejection, and how empty and painful the revenge of evicting her had actually proved.

He reached his former home and looked down at the pavement lit by the street lamp in front of the house where he had lain unconscious after the vicious attack. Why couldn't he remember anything? He tried yet again, concentrating his mind, but as always, there was nothing except that strange smell every time he thought about it. What was it? Tincture? Hair oil? Then it came to him: it was the odour of Brylcreem, as in the Brylcreem man –

the older man in the pictures that the Detective Inspector had shown him those months ago. It had all finally fallen into place. He would ring DI Romer in the morning.

He pushed the bell which brought back the anger of his creditors stealing the house from him, even as he lay unconscious. What goes around comes around, he thought. Now, Fiona was back where she had been before they had even met, where she – not he – belonged.

All was forgotten as the large panelled door opened and his heart leapt. She was no longer wearing the sad clothes from that morning but had on a pair of jeans and a bright-red pullover. As beautiful as ever and lit by the warm glow from the entrance hall, she looked like an angel.

CHAPTER THIRTY-THREE

It began in the familiarity of the first-floor drawing room, sitting opposite each other in front of the fireplace with drinks in hand. The Beatles LP "Revolver" was on the turntable, the curtains were closed, and Fiona was working out what to say to him. His heart pounded, and he was still trying to work out how he could explain away the night he'd spent with Anne when she picked up the album and opened it at the page with the photograph headed *THE DESTRUCTION OF BATH.*

Thank goodness, he thought, and his heart started to slow, perhaps Anne has not told her, and she just wants my support in preserving Bath. But when she put it down again as if she'd remembered something else, he swallowed hard and tried to quell his anxiety.

"Before we talk about important things, I wanted to tell you that I've heard from Linda Fraker and gather they're moving here soon." She smiled. Already aware that his house-sitting days were numbered, he felt calmer as he replied,

"Yes, Luke Brady told me. I'm looking forward to meeting them."

"So, what do you think, Ian?" She turned back to the album. "One thing I have learnt about you recently is that you are a thinking and reasonable man."

"It's very well put together and does paint a dreadful picture. It's extremely pessimistic and over the top in places." He loved this woman and didn't know how he was going to appease her and at the same time not antagonise many of his business associates. "I mean, there does have to be change, but there is a price to pay for dragging Bath out of the eighteenth and into the twentieth century. A compromise is unavoidable."

"I disagree, I think it is avoidable." She put her glass down and looked at him. "May I ask you a very serious question?"

Ian nodded and she paused. "Think very hard before you answer. Our whole future relationship depends on it."

He said nothing, just looked at her.

"Don't take this the wrong way, Ian." She looked him straight in the eyes. "Have you ever regarded this city as anything other than an exercise for making money out of property? Simply a game of Monopoly on a huge scale? Have you ever considered Bath as a community worth preserving rather than just a number of sites that can be torn down and rebuilt to make as much profit as possible? I don't believe you are like other property men.

"Yes, I know you're from an underprivileged background and have known real hardship, but surely by now you must have worked out what is really important in life. To others, Bath is just one endless honeypot to be exploited and out of which vast sums of money can be made without regard to the consequences. I wouldn't have wasted my time making that album for you if I thought you were like them."

Suddenly, the atmosphere had completely changed, and Ian was reminded of the Fiona he had glimpsed when they had dealt with the Pera Road project – utterly serious, not to be toyed with or evaded with platitudes.

Surprisingly, she changed the subject.

"A few problems have arisen since my brother's death that have become my responsibility." She was so matter-of-fact that Ian could not work it out – she was either incredibly pragmatic or still in shock after the deaths.

"My sister-in-law's inability to cope with the grief from the loss of her father rather than her husband has been made worse by her pregnancy. I'd hoped her sister would have come back from Australia to lend support, but she hasn't been able to." Ian felt a frisson of fear at the mention of Anne's condition but said nothing.

"She has very high blood pressure and therefore unable to continue to work. So 'Traditional Bath' is rudderless and at the same time, my own consultancy business is being overwhelmed. I urgently need someone who understands property, and importantly knows the Bath scene. But it has to be somebody with empathy."

Untypically, her voice started to quaver, and she stopped to bite her lip. Now she was close to tears. Instinctively, he put his whisky down, moved across to draw her to him, and stroked her hair and neck.

"Of course I'll help. I can't immediately change my view of this extraordinary city, but I'll do anything for your happiness." He held her close. "Don't you understand that I love you?"

She seemed content for a moment but then asked, "How can you be in love with me? Apart from a weekend of sex years ago, you know nothing about me."

"I just know I am."

Fiona pulled away and came back from a different direction. "All right, why do you think you love me?"

"I don't think, I know." He paused to pick his glass up again before adding, "Maybe partly because you're so beautiful."

"And so what will happen as my looks fade as they've already begun to? Remember, I'm nearly ten years older than you."

"That's rubbish," he said. "You're more beautiful now than when we made love together."

"Oh, Ian." She laughed, but it was mirthless. "We didn't make love together – that's the last thing we did. We fucked each other in every possible way, everywhere, and at every opportunity for a short period of time. I was very horny, and you were very young and, I'd say, inexperienced – at least you were when we started. You don't know what love is."

"Yes, I do." Why wouldn't she believe him? "I know I love you because I've loved before, and I've been loved."

"Who by?"

"There was a girl called Rachel for a start," he said. "We loved each other very much and were going to get married."

"And what happened?" She wasn't laughing now.

He paused. "She changed her mind and left me for show business and another man."

"That must have been hard." Fiona said. "But have you heard the saying 'Hurt people hurt people'?" Ian didn't know what she was talking about, but it didn't matter, because she didn't wait for him to answer the question.

"Something that you don't know about me is that I trained in a form of therapy when I was in California. I was very good at it, and that's how I know that you cannot possibly love me. In fact, until you learn to love yourself, you are not capable of loving anyone else."

"What do you mean?" He didn't know where this was going and, with the whisky mellowing his resolve, didn't really mind as long as they were still talking and he was with her.

"Love is a reflection of another person's feelings, and this increases the self-esteem of the person loved. Excluding your mother, there have been at least two occasions in your life when you have been abandoned by people you loved and, and more importantly, who you believe loved you."

Ian remained silent.

"Tranquillity following great sex matters, but only when you truly love … Ian, do you trust me?" This time, she waited for a reply.

"Of course I trust you. I've just told you that I love you."

"I want to try something. Please shut your eyes."

Ian did as he was bid, hoping for a kiss or something along those lines, but instead, she carried on talking.

"Now, I'd like you to think of the saddest moment in your life."

"What?" He opened his eyes.

"No, it's important that you don't open your eyes."

He complied.

"So, back to the saddest moment in your life, and I want you to tell me where you are."

"I'm in Holcombe Cemetery."

Fiona softened her tone. "Who is with you?"

"No one, I'm on my own."

"What are you doing?"

"Watching the grave diggers lower my mother's coffin into the grave. It's so small … The cancer had reduced her to the size of a child."

"What's the person conducting the service saying?" Now she was whispering.

"There isn't one; I couldn't afford a rabbi." He paused. "It was a pauper's funeral. It cost thirty-eight pounds, but I didn't have that much money, so I paid twenty pounds up front, and the undertaker agreed I could pay the rest at seven shillings a week."

CHAPTER THIRTY-FOUR

Dawn was breaking, and wearing nothing, as was her wont in bed, Fiona gently kissed Ian awake.

It had been three months since she had been taken him into her bed on the night of her brother's funeral, after he'd broken down in anguish when recalling his mother's death. She had been gentle in drawing out his sorrow, and he no longer felt the weight of guilt that he'd previously carried. Now, he only marvelled at his good fortune in having the affection of such a wonderful woman.

"Happy birthday, my darling."

They made love languorously before getting ready for work. Afterwards, he struggled to concentrate on getting himself dressed as he watched her wander around naked, looking for the day's outfit. Finally, he was all set, and Fiona was still applying makeup as he bent to kiss her goodbye.

"So, what does your twenty-fifth birthday hold for you apart from our dinner tonight?" She asked as she lifted a peach-coloured lipstick to her face.

She had arranged for them to return to the Duke of Monmouth, not alone this time but with the Frakers with whom Ian got on so well with. He particularly liked Linda's laid-back, yet sophisticated American husband, Ford.

"A mystery meeting with Malcolm Austwick. He described it as 'a personal matter best not discussed on the telephone'," Ian replied as he picked up his wallet and keys from the bedside table.

"Uncle Malcolm, do give him my love – did I tell you he's my godfather?" After putting the lipstick on, she pressed her lips together. "I didn't know he acted for you."

"He doesn't; I use Patrick McCloy, so that makes it even more mysterious. I only see him from time to time at our little property meetings."

"The Wessex Property Club?"

"Now that would be telling." He smiled and turned to go, half tempted to ask how she knew about something that was supposed to be a secret. While he had no interest in Freemasonry, which he knew to be rife in Bath and practiced by many of his acquaintance, the discreet nature of the property club had always seemed worthwhile.

Ian was shown into the empty conference room that overlooked Queen Square. He sat down at the long mahogany table on which lay six large cardboard boxes that were labelled *BATH ESTATES LIMITED*.

The door opened and Malcolm Austwick entered, and to Ian's surprise, he was accompanied by Christopher Johnson. Austwick took the seat at the head of the table and Johnson the one next to him, directly facing Ian.

Austwick placed the manila folder, tied with the red ribbon so beloved by his profession, on the table in front of him. Out of habit learnt from numerous negotiations, Ian read the upside-down printing in black capital letters on its cover – *DR ISAAC ABRAHAMS, DEC'D*

He was surprised. His uncle's name had not come up for years; he had been killed with his wife, Aunt Naomi, when Ian was nine. He had a moment only to wonder what this was all about before the solicitor started to speak.

"Many happy returns from both of us on your twenty-fifth birthday, Ian." He was intrigued that the two men knew his birthdate, but before he could raise a query, Austwick continued.

"It is of consequence to Christopher and myself because of a company called Bath Estates Ltd, which was set up in 1944 by a group of ten Bath gentlemen, including Isaac Abrahams. To say the least, it was an exclusive gathering chaired by the Second Lord Lundy, and it was not an insignificant venture. Each of the ten paid just over ten thousand pounds for their preference shares – a considerable sum of money then.

"Whilst winning the war was still well over a year away, the aim of these ten shareholders was to be in – if you will excuse the pun – on the ground floor of Bath's redevelopment when the Allied victory arrived. They already owned nearly half of the nineteen thousand buildings damaged or destroyed in the German air raids of April 1942. To their enormous advantage, they had obtained an advance copy of the as-yet-unpublished and secret plan showing all the development areas in the city. The venture was backed by numerous trusts represented by this firm. The trusts invested three million pounds, and Christopher's bank gave the company a facility of another seven million.

"Only three of the ten original members are still alive – Peter Groves, Christopher, and myself. Sadly, the company failed in 1948, owing the bank about two and a half million pounds. This is where Christopher comes in."

Ian was mystified by what he was hearing. Clearly, the two older men had scripted the meeting and discussed their roles, because Johnson seamlessly continued.

"At the time, I was the general manager of the bank which ended up owning Bath Estates Limited – that is, except for the original ten percent of the shares held by your uncle. When everything had been sold that could be, the bank was only too happy to sell your uncle what was known as the rump – in other words, the remaining ninety percent of the "worthless" ordinary shares. Isaac bought these for a nominal sum not long before he and Naomi emigrated to Israel in 1950."

On cue, Austwick picked up the story. "Your uncle and aunt were good and kind people, and I was very sad when I heard they had been killed in a bus, blown up by a land mine a year later in 1951. You would only have been a young child at the time."

Ian nodded, remembering the letter from his mother. Perhaps affected more than he realised by the long-forgotten memories, he spoke for the first time. "But what has all this got to do with me? I don't understand why am I here."

Austwick's tone softened. "Because twenty-three years ago in this very room, I made a promise to Isaac and Naomi Abrahams that I would ensure that the shares in Bath Estates would pass to you on your twenty-fifth birthday." He paused, untied the ribbon, and opened the file. "So, true to my word, I give you this," Austwick handed him a piece of paper, "and all of these." His hand swept over the boxes with a flourish.

Ian looked at the faded share certificate dated 1 January 1950. At its top was an oval blue logo depicting a line of three stone-castellated towers, a large one in the centre with two identical smaller ones each side. They were encircled by a broad garter ribbon on which was printed,

THE SECURITY OF LAND - BATH ESTATES LIMITED

"I don't know if the company has any value – probably none after all these years – but these," – Austwick again pointed to the six boxes – "contain all that is left of Bath Estates and now totally belong to you. Would you like our porter to deliver them to your home at St James' Square?"

Somewhat stunned, Ian nodded and, without thinking, said, "That would be much appreciated, but to twelve Great Pulteney Street." At Fiona's suggestion, he'd moved in with her when the Frakers had arrived to reclaim their house.

Austwick looked surprised. "Isn't that where Fiona Symons lives?"

"Yes, we're working together on a few things now," Ian replied quickly – too quickly – adding, "I am helping out with her business and on the preservation side following her brother's death."

Both men glanced at each other. As her banker and solicitor, both knew full well of Fiona's obsession about personal privacy and her insistence that work only be conducted at her offices at fifteen Queen Square – never taken home.

CHAPTER THIRTY-FIVE

"With Uncle Malcolm in the picture, everyone in Bath will know by closing time tonight," Fiona said, having squeezed past the six boxes in the entrance.

"Sorry." He had explained his gaffe as soon as she'd arrived home.

"I'm not. I was going to talk to you about our situation anyway. It's fantastic what you've achieved behind the scenes in just a month. My business is back on course, and Alistair's crowd are now taking me seriously. I'm so grateful for all your help but would much prefer it was all in the open. Why don't you come back to fifteen Queen Square? We can then get rid of all this stuff," she waved vaguely in the direction of the boxes in the hall.

"You can have your old ground-floor office back. I know you love it – and as things stand, it is just sitting there, shuttered, empty, and sad. It would also mean we would keep your ever-increasing stream of business people and paperwork out of our personal lives and home. What do you think?"

"It would mean going public about changing sides, and I'm not sure that my business associates are ready for that." As always, Ian was cautious, afraid of making a wrong move which could affect his business.

"What are you saying?" she asked.

"Well, how would it look to others on the property scene? 'Opportunistic trader always on the make becomes conservationist', 'poacher turned gamekeeper': it wouldn't make any difference how it was presented – preservationist, anti-developer, or whatever, it all means the same thing."

"Now, let's not get carried away," Fiona kissed him lightly on the lips, "one step at a time. Just give some thought about whom you spend your time with." She paused. "But I would suggest that you have outgrown the Wessex Property Club: maybe not immediately – it needs you more than you need it."

He knew he had no choice and would do what she asked. Whilst his self-preservation instinctively surfaced, he was haunted by the fear that he would lose her if he didn't agree.

"All right, I'll come back to Queen Square. When?"

She pulled him to her, and kissed him deeply and long. At last, she pulled back and looked at him.

"There's no time like the present, but we have your birthday dinner this evening. So, first thing in the morning, it shouldn't take more than a couple of hours for Mike Goodwin and his lot to move you."

Ian nodded in agreement. For once, his heart was most definitely ruling his brain.

Fiona and Ian stood in his old office. It had been over a year since the landlord's agents had seized it from him, and he'd forgotten how large it was. Fifty feet long and some thirty feet wide, it had been the reception room of the grand house. It was huge. As with many of the great buildings of Bath, number fifteen was a Grade I listed building, and any sub-division of the space was totally forbidden. Nothing could be tampered with, especially the magnificent original fireplace.

Fiona's late brother had changed nothing during his brief tenure. Pleasantly surprised, everything was as he had last used it. The deep-blue carpets, perfectly matching the curtains to the two full-length windows overlooking Queen Square, were as sumptuous as when Trish had arranged for them to be hung. His old desk was in the same position across the front corner, and the two large, blue sofas, nicknamed his Hollywood casting couches by Trish, were on either side of the fireplace. Even the locked, custom-made map cabinet hung, untouched, on the wall.

The ever-helpful driver from Me and My Van had unloaded all the boxes and other paperwork onto the huge reproduction dining table and chairs, a bargain when he and Trish had bought them at auction from Aldridges in Cheltenham Street, because small modern homes had no use for such large pieces. He sank into one of the sofas. It was so good to be back, but then he remembered that something – or rather someone – important was missing. He turned to Fiona.

"Would you mind if I asked my old secretary, Trish Traynor, to come back and work with me? I was on the point of asking her before I moved out of St James' Square."

"I can't pretend I'm that keen – not given the way that she never took her eyes off you at the World Cup party."

Ian laughed. "Will you believe me when I tell you that Trish was always too valuable to sleep with?"

Fiona wasn't laughing. "That can change. Are you sure that nothing could ever happen between you? Can you promise me?"

Now deadly serious, he took both her hands in his, and they looked into each other's eyes.

"I promise," he said solemnly, knowing that he could never be unfaithful.

"Let me think about it." She sounded a little more convinced, but before any more was said, the door from the hallway opened slowly.

"Oh, thank goodness it's you, Fiona – I was wondering who could be down here."

Ian looked round over the high back of the sofa to see Lady Anne, heavily pregnant, in the doorway. Although the fine features were still visible, her face was puffy and pale. Her hair, once lustrous, hung limply over her shoulders, and her whole body seemed to have swollen, including her legs and ankles. She looked down at him.

"Ian, what a nice surprise," she said, and Ian thought back to how hollow his promise to Fiona might sound if she knew the truth about Anne's pregnancy.

After the appointment with the bank, Ian returned to fifteen Queen Square later that afternoon and found DI Romer parked outside. The policeman got out of the small, grey car.

"I had a problem finding you, Mr Morris, but we've had some good news," he said, shaking Ian's hand. "You were right about Mr Brylcreem being the culprit in your assault."

The two men went into Ian's office.

"Will there be a trial?" Ian asked when they were sitting down. "Will you need me to testify?"

"No need for you even to attend," Romer replied. "Unless you want to, because the younger one admitted to the whole thing in exchange for a leniency plea – brought the older man down with him. Both are pleading guilty and, in my opinion, will doubtlessly remain in prison for quite a while."

"That's a relief. Presumably Forrester ordered the beating?"

Romer nodded. "But we don't know what's happened to him. He's probably back in Italy, but that brings me to the second reason I'm here." He paused and looked to the closed office door before asking. "What's your connection with the Georgian Rooms? I'm talking about the gentleman's dining club behind the Abbey Hotel."

"I'm a small shareholder and use it for meetings from time to time." Ian wondered if, somehow, Romer knew about the existence of the Wessex Property Club. "Why do you ask?"

"I am grateful for your help in nailing Mr Brylcreem and his friend. One favour deserves another, and I'm not telling you this officially – I suggest that you disconnect yourself as quickly as you can. You really don't want to be associated with the place any longer."

Ian was taken aback. "Why?"

"I really can't give any details – just something about Forrester that has come to light. Trust me, get out as soon as you can."

"When you say soon, Detective Inspector, just how soon would you suggest?" Rumour had it that the policeman kept notes on everyone of influence in Bath.

"Yesterday." Romer said no more, collected his hat, and left.

Ian knew that simply selling his shares would be too obvious if trouble was brewing so quickly: it had to be done subtly. Picking up the telephone, he dialled Tom Scotland's number. Despite his approaching retirement, the builder could never resist a bargain.

As always, Scotland came straight to the point. "What do you want?"

"I need to quit the Wessex Property Club," Ian replied.

"Why? It's always served us all so well."

"I've joined Fiona Symons," Ian said.

"Yes, I heard you'd shacked up with her," – Ian could almost hear the smirk – "but that shouldn't affect your business."

"No, I mean in business. I've become a director of the Bath Regeneration Practice in Queen Square – you know, the Planning Consultants to the City Council. At the same time, I've taken over the protest group run by her late brother."

"What? Bath Against Developers?" Scotland was shocked.

"Yes and no. It's now called Traditional Bath."

"Christ almighty, Ian, I don't care what it is now called; whatever has possessed you to do that? No, you don't need to tell me, because I know already. You're thinking between your legs rather than in your head." He paused. Ian could almost hear him figuring out the angles. "You don't have to sell your shares, they could always be held in trust. No one needs to know, and having someone on the inside could be very useful for the Club."

"No, I'm sorry Tom, I can't do that. It would cause an impossible conflict of interest."

"Come on, Ian. When has that worried you in the past?"

"I'm sure it will come as a surprise, but I want everything to be transparent." Ian tried to sound sincere and friendly.

"Well, it's obviously up to you, but you realise that if you quit the club, you'll have to sell your shares in the Georgian Rooms."

"Oh, I'd forgotten that," Ian said, feigning innocence. "So be it."

"When do you want to get this done by?"

"Today, really, if that's possible, because I start with BRP on Monday."

"That's a bit quick, Ian." Scotland paused again, but Ian knew his colleague. "That gives no time to get a proper valuation of the company, management accounts, or any of that stuff the accountants and lawyers love to do at great expense."

"I'm not that worried about worth. Do you think someone would be interested in taking them off my hands at what they cost me to buy?" Scotland was hooked: it was just a matter of reeling him in.

"If you're certain, Ian, I'll take them myself."

"Oh, that's very good of you, Tom, and it's a weight off my mind. Thank you so much on behalf of Fiona and myself: she made it clear that everything must be totally above board."

"My pleasure," the older man responded. "I'll have the share transfer ready for you to sign in an hour's time, in that way she will know that you're a man of your word." Ian sensed he was smirking again.

A very costly exercise, Ian thought as he put the phone down, let's hope that Romer was right.

Three days later, his faith in the policeman proved well-founded when he saw the front page of the *Bath Chronicle*.

POLICE SWOOP ON BATH ILLEGAL GAMBLING DEN, MANY LEADING CITIZENS ARRESTED & CHARGED

* * *

At just after midnight in the early hours of Sunday morning, ...

Clearly, the police force came before Freemasonry, Ian thought as he read the lurid article – made sense, the latter being only a stepping stone to the former.

CHAPTER THIRTY-SIX

Trish loved the little flat over the shops at the bottom of Bathwick Hill and had grown ever fonder of her flatmate, Norman Piggot. By chance, she'd found herself sitting next to the charge nurse at the Memorial Service in the Abbey three months earlier. At the time, Trish was puzzled by his grief but assumed that either the rear admiral or the earl had at some time been under his care at the RUH. Now she knew better.

Years ago, her mother had been the Fisher's daily, and Mrs Traynor had planned to show her own respect for the rear admiral. Whilst aloof, he had always treated her as one of his crew. On the day, her sciatica had been bad, and she had persuaded her daughter to take her place.

Trish's later remark about wanting her own place had prompted Norman's offer of the small, spare bedroom in his flat. She had jumped at the opportunity and the chance of regaining her independence.

Gradually, and cautiously at first, their friendship blossomed as they started to confide in one another. Over time, her feelings for Ian became obvious, and Norman wasn't surprised – it explained the long days and nights she had spent at his bedside in the RUH.

Initially, the charge nurse was reticent about his own personal life, until one evening, he told her of his love for Alistair, the 4th Earl. Despite never meeting in public and always behind the closed doors of the flat, they had come perilously close to being prosecuted by Bath's ever-zealous policing of homosexual activity. One particular grey Ford Anglia seemed often parked nearby overnight.

Norman was a superb cook, and he spoke fondly about the meals he would make for Alistair, after which he stayed the night and they would make love.

"It was the happiest time, and for once in my life, I felt safe," he told Trish while they drank wine in the tiny kitchen and he prepared their evening meal.

"It seemed the most natural thing in the world that we should be together. To others, Alistair could come across as pompous or aggressive, but with me, he was so gentle and kind: like him, I had had some terrifyingly violent experiences with one-night stands."

The meal of grilled sea bass with young spinach and mushrooms had been wonderful. Now, in the little sitting room nursing a glass of Chablis, Trish asked gently,

"Didn't his wife miss him when he spent his nights here?"

"I expect so, but for him, it was a marriage of convenience – he wanted protection from the police, so he didn't care: I don't think he even liked her very much. Mind you, I felt sorry for Anne and assumed that, coming from a naval background, she would understand – after all, sailors have been falling in love with other sailors rather than with women since time began."

"You must miss him so much."

"Dreadfully, I will never find anyone like him."

"Don't give up. You will love again, Norman, and at least you won't have to hide away when the new Sexual Offences Bill becomes law."

"Perhaps, as Alistair was fond of quoting, our love was one that could never be spoken, and even if it becomes legal, there will always be much shame attached to same-sex relationships. We will still have to keep out of sight of 'respectable people' – behind closed doors and, of course, it only applies to consenting 'homos' over twenty-one."

Trish continued to nurse her wine and didn't respond – he was probably right: puzzlingly, homosexual men were deemed reprehensible and reprobate, yet lesbians were totally ignored, and, thanks to Queen Victoria's naivety, didn't even exist according to English law.

"But enough about me," Norman said. "I think we need to sort out your problem with Ian."

"I'm not sure there is anything to sort out," Trish sighed. "The only romance I've ever had with Ian has been in my imagination, so there's nothing I can do about it."

"That is where you are wrong, my beautiful and clever friend." He stopped fondling his beard and stretched across and took her spare hand in his.

"I think you know that you've got to give the idea of him up, Trish, because it's a lost cause: he is Fiona's. You need to find someone else, someone real who will love you as you deserve to be loved."

"I only wish …" She knew he was right. It felt like she, too, was in mourning, but in her case for something that had never existed except in her dreams.

CHAPTER THIRTY-SEVEN

At first, he had managed with a junior secretary, but as the work mounted, Fiona relented and eventually agreed that he needed an experienced and efficient senior office manager.

Ian rang the Mafeking Street number he had for Trish, but it was her mother who answered the telephone. After leaving the bunch of flowers for Elsie Traynor when he moved out of the house, he'd repeated the gesture a few times if passing nearby: it was obvious that she still had a soft spot for him. He was fond of her too and felt, as with his own mother, that she had had a raw deal from life, badly treated during years of menial work, her only aspiration to do the best for her daughter.

"What a lovely surprise to hear from you, Ian," she said before explaining that her daughter had also moved out. "She still pops in, because of course she's always been a good girl our Trish, but she left soon after Christmas. It was very sudden, just after that awful bomb at the golf club. Now she's sharing a flat with a male nurse, you know the one – that chap who looked after you so well in the RUH."

"Norman Piggott?" Ian remembered seeing them together at the memorial service.

"That's him. Well, he's got this place at the bottom of Bathwick Hill. It's above a shop and quite nice, really, over two floors and with its own front door. They have me over for Sunday lunch sometimes – he's a smashing cook but as queer as a coot, so nothing in it for her."

"Have you got a telephone number?" Ian could tell that the woman wanted to chat on and was lonely without her daughter. He felt guilty that he didn't have the time to talk longer as he wrote down the number she gave him. Much as he liked the charge nurse, he wondered why his ex-secretary was living with him and tried to call Trish. There was no reply. After several further attempts, he finally caught up with her that evening.

"Trish?" It had been months since they had last spoken at the Nurses' Ball before Christmas.

"Ian, what a surprise. And how nice to hear from you after all this time," she said brightly. "I assume you must want something."

"How well you know me." He wasn't sure that she was as glad to hear from him as she claimed.

"That's exactly why I've called – are you still temping through an agency?"

"Yes. Why do you ask?" she replied cautiously.

"Well, now I found you …" he was trying to be positive. "I've moved back into our offices at fifteen Queen Square," – he used the word "our" deliberately – "and wondered if you'd like your old job back."

"Same old Ian." She sounded irritated. "As always, there's no 'How are you, Trish?' or 'What have you been up to since you did all in my power to make me well again?' Instead, you're selfish as always, straight to the point of needing something for yourself." There was a pause. "So, do I assume that you're back in the property business?"

Maybe Fiona was right, he thought, and it wasn't such a great idea to have Trish back. But he also knew that he'd never find such a secretary elsewhere. As far as he was concerned, he had been right to wait until things were back on an even keel before speaking to her and inviting her to return.

"Never been out of it, I just needed time. So now, in addition to the business of Forsythe, Morris & Company, I'm also a part of the Bath Regeneration Practice."

"The name rings a bell. I don't know why." She sounded disinterested.

"It's a consultancy run by Fiona Symons. I introduced you to her at Ian Scotland's World Cup party at Widcombe Manor last year, remember?"

"Oh, yes – the sister of the Lundy man, the young Earl who got blown to pieces at the golf club." She paused and then said,

"I thought you hated the family because of the way they treated your mother? Or does that no longer count if you can make money out of them?"

"It was only the son and his mother who were so awful to us." He felt uncomfortable but persevered and went on to explain how he got to know Fiona when he first came to Bath from London some years ago. He waited for Trish to make a comment, but she said nothing.

"Are you still there?" he asked.

"Yes, I'm thinking." There was another silence until she asked,

"Where are you living these days?"

Now it was Ian's turn to pause, but he there was no point in lying.

"With Fiona at twelve Great Pulteney Street."

He heard the intake of breath.

"In your old house?"

"Yes – but it's hers now. She's got a lease on it. It's a bit complicated."

"I bet it is," Trish said before adding, "I'll think about the job offer and let you know."

The six boxes from Malcolm Austwicks's office had remained untouched, stacked in the corner of Ian's offices on the ground floor of fifteen Queen Square for some weeks. Fiona and he had spent hours, even days, dealing with the backlog of work at Traditional Bath. Then, one evening when things had slackened and Fiona had gone to see her mother, Ian had brought the first box, entitled *Company Matters*, home so that he could go through it at his leisure.

As he lay the box on the drawing-room floor, he noticed the carrier bag with the HMV logo and remembered the purchase he'd made a day or so earlier but still hadn't found the time to enjoy.

Gently, he took out the newly-released album and studied its colourful sleeve. He'd never seen anything like it before. Each of the four Beatles wore a heavy moustache and stood centre stage, dressed in different, dazzling, satin military costumes. Behind and beside them was a collage made up of dozens of cut-out photographs and waxwork models of famous people. He recognised Bob Dylan, Marlon Brando, Tony Curtis, Marilyn Monroe, Marlene Dietrich, Sonny Liston, Laurel and Hardy, HG

Wells, Oscar Wilde, Lewis Carroll, and Dylan Thomas – the list went on and on.

He'd been an avid fan of the group since he'd seen them before they were famous in 1959, first time away from Liverpool, at a tiny gig of no more than a few hundred at Windsor by the river, then again on their only visit to Bath. Musical Express was saying that this, their eighth album, was unlike anything that had gone before.

Reverently, he took the black vinyl disc from its extraordinary sleeve and placed it on the record player's deck, turning the volume to high. Determined not to miss a note, he was surprised by the sound of a whole pit orchestra warming up for a full ten seconds and the restlessness of a large audience awaiting a live concert. Then it came in all its Edwardian pastiche magnificence.

"It was twenty years ago today ..."

The box of papers brought home from the office was completely forgotten.

"Sergeant Pepper's Lonely Hearts Club Band ..."

Ian sat entranced for the the next forty minutes. He was sure that he was listening to one of the greatest LPs ever released. Track after track of sheer brilliance, ending as it started with a supposed brass band playing "Sergeant Pepper's Lonely Hearts Club Band".

His uncle's company matters forgotten, he listened to the record all over again before pouring a whisky and reaching across for the box. Unpacked, it produced three piles of documents, each about a foot high placed on the floor around him. He picked up a note and recognised Issac's handwriting, not seen since the letters to him at school all those years ago.

Attached to the note was a brochure, the front cover of which bore the same blue Bath Estates logo shown on the top of each box. It took Ian half an hour to read the original prospectus dated 23 September 1944, with its twenty or so densely-printed pages inviting would-be shareholders to join the venture. Odd words and sentences had been underlined in ink by his uncle and then ticked as each had been dealt with. The pamphlet's final page had been detached, only its perforated edge remained.

Ian had been involved in the preparation of many such documents when he was qualifying at Woods & Parker at Berkeley Square in London, and was impressed. The chairman was the 2nd Earl of Lundy, Alistair's late grandfather, and he recognised some of the other names including Malcolm Austwick, Christopher Johnson, and Peter Groves, now all elderly men but no doubt in their prime when Bath Estates was conceived.

While the detailed aims of the company were somewhat vague – no doubt deliberately so – reading between the lines, its objective was pretty obvious: simply and without fuss, it planned to quietly buy up every available property that had been destroyed or damaged in the Blitz at the knock-down value of a bomb site, and then redevelop it.

He put the prospectus down and picked up the handwritten letter.

Austwick & Company
Queen Square, Bath

I. Abrahams
Lundy House   *PRIVATE & CONFIDENTIAL*
North Road
Bath   *24 September 1944*

My dear Isaac,

10% Shareholdings in Bath Estates Ltd

Thank you for your letter returning the completed back page of the Prospectus, together with Naomi's cheque for £10,000. I note that the shares are to be acquired for Yann Morris and held in trust until his twenty-fifth birthday.

Yours sincerely,

Malcolm Austwick

Ian recalled that it had been Malcolm Austwick who had arranged his scholarship to Pitt College when he was eleven and still known as Yann.

On the rare occasions that he heard his first name, he still turned round to answer but didn't regret having changed it to Ian despite his mother's disappointment: it made him sound less foreign, more English – and in any case, a person's first name wasn't that important.

Given the ten original shareholders, the seed capital of one hundred thousand pounds, and the rest of the financing arrangements – enormous sums of money in 1944 – Ian wondered why the company had failed.

He stood up, went to the decanter to pour another large malt, and had listened to his new LP twice more by the time he finished reading all the contents of the *Company Matters* file and knew the answer.

It was a sorry tale that was all over in four years. The 2nd Earl of Lundy had died and been replaced by his inadequate son, Marmaduke, the 3rd Earl.

Not for the first time, Ian was reminded of the old aphorism 'clogs to clogs in three generations': the first generation founds the business, the next builds it and the third spends it.

Alistair's father and the company had bought far too much property too quickly using borrowed money. In addition, post wartime building restrictions made development impossible under Atlee's socialist government.

Unable to even let the properties because of such severe rationing and austerity, it proved impossible for the company to meet the ever increasing interest payments due on the outstanding loan of two million pounds. Receivers had been called in and instructed to sell everything.

Nothing ever changed, Ian thought. The advice given to him by Marcus Rose all those years ago had been, "Never do a deal where time is your enemy."

There was one last letter at the bottom of the pile from Christopher Johnson.

Bank of Bath, Milsom Street, Bath

I. Abrahams
Lundy House
North Road
Bath

21 February, 1949

Dear Isaac,

BATH ESTATES LTD IN RECEIVERSHIP

Now that it's all over and the Receivers have sold everything possible – probably about a quarter of all the assets – the Bank is prepared to dispose of the rump to anyone interested. As the only remaining other shareholder, you have what is called pre-emption rights, which means you have the right of first refusal.

Accordingly, if you are interested in buying the remaining 90% of the company you do not own, get Malcolm to call me; I am sure we can agree an acceptable price.

Yours sincerely,

Christopher Johnson
Manager

PS: As I said to you in confidence over lunch yesterday, the Bank takes the view that Bath Estates Limited is a worthless liability and just want shot of the problem. Given that the board have accepted ten pence in the pound for the assets, I would be prepared to recommend a price of £1000. I will leave you to decide if it's worth the punt. CJ

Clearly, Isaac had thought it a worthwhile punt and negotiated hard, because attached to the back of the letter was a receipt for eight hundred pounds.

Ian repacked the box, thinking about his uncle and aunt to whom he and his mother owed so much. He remembered reading his mother's letter when he was boarding at Beaconsfield School and her later telling him how death was like a pebble causing ripples in the pond of life: the ripples ended, calm water returned, and time healed. He'd struggled at nine years of age to understand how being blown up by a landmine was like throwing a pebble into water. That was sixteen years ago, he thought, and still there was no peace in the Middle East.

He was reminded of this again just a few minutes later when he switched on the television to catch the BBC news. The screen was filled with a newspaper's front page.

NASSER WANTS A DECISIVE BATTLE TO CRUSH ISRAEL

Pictures of Nasser strutting amongst tanks and ranks of Egyptian soldiers followed. The newsreader's voice started.

"This was the headline six days ago when President Nasser – joined by Jordan, Iraq, and Syria with their combined forces of half a million troops, three thousand tanks and eight hundred planes – boasted he would 'wipe Israel off the map'. But today, outnumbered by five to one, tiny Israel, under Moshe Dayan's command, has achieved total victory."

Dozens of pictures of Israeli jet planes, tanks, and jubilant soldiers in combat followed in quick succession, ending with Dayan's famous face with its black eyepatch.

"Within three hours of dawn last Monday, Israel had totally annihilated the Egyptian Air Force. Then, over the following three days, its forces passed through the Sinai Dessert and drove the Egyptian Army back across the Suez Canal: many Egyptian officers have deserted, which has resulted in eighty percent of the army's Soviet-built equipment to fall into Israeli hands.

"Elsewhere, in a spectacular helicopter raid, the Golan Heights have been abandoned by the Syrians. Jordan has surrendered the whole of the West Bank, along with that part of Jerusalem it previously occupied. Tonight, Israeli troops and their generals celebrate at the Wailing Wall. The United Nations is now brokering a ceasefire following this extraordinary achievement in just six days."

Ian wondered why the BBC was ready to tell viewers that the Russians supported Egypt but not that Israel had relied on America and much of the free world's assistance: it seemed that only Churchill understood the importance of special relationships.

As for Israel, without American aid, the Jewish state couldn't survive economically, let alone strategically. Perhaps Uncle Isaac and Aunt Naomi could now rest in peace in the knowledge that Israel was safe at last, although he didn't know where their final resting place was. It occurred to him that although born in Britain, they had no memorial in England or their adopted city of Bath.

Over the following days, Ian discovered that the five remaining Bath Estates boxes contained the detailed plans and title deeds of everything the company had bought. It owned more than three thousand properties on seven hundred acres of mostly-derelict land and buildings, which was a staggering ten percent of the eleven square miles of the entire city of Bath.

He particularly noticed there were also some large fields outside Combe Down, a village about two miles south of Bath, and he put them on his property list for an early inspection. They could be close to the new university and the extensive Admiralty office complex, which had been set up before the Second World War.

Then it dawned on him what must be done. The very company lovingly bequeathed to him over twenty years ago would become the memorial to the couple who had done so much for Bath, especially during the bombing of April 1942 and after he was born. He would resurrect Bath Estates Ltd with its widespread and untouched property. He and Fiona could create a hugely-successful business of which a part would be the Abrahams Foundation, a charitable trust dedicated to improving the lives of the poor and underprivileged of Bath.

CHAPTER THIRTY-EIGHT

Lady Anne Fisher left the flat at the top of fifteen Queen Square to slowly, very slowly and carefully, descend the grand staircase to the ground floor. It had become increasingly difficult for her to get up and down the stairs, and she felt clumsy holding onto the banister rail hand over hand as she took each step by turn. Standing, she felt an uncomfortable weight bearing down into her groin, and enormous and ungainly when she walked. She knew it was more of a waddle than a walk, and even her gynaecologist was surprised at how large she'd become. As a result, with the exception of the weekly hospital visits, she rarely left the flat. Instead, she relied on Fiona and a couple of other friends to visit and bring her what she needed.

She knew what had to be done. Ever since Fiona had told her that Ian had moved back into Alistair's office on the ground floor and confided in her that they had become lovers, she had to talk to Ian before the baby was born.

Eventually, she reached the beautifully-crafted, wooden ground floor and knocked on the oak-panelled door.

"Come in." Ian looked up from behind a mound of papers on the conference table as she entered the cavernous room. He immediately stood up, walked across, and guided her with care to one of the straight-backed, wooden chairs instead of the sofas. He was surprised by her arrival and uncomfortable, but her own physical discomfort had to be worse. She was pleased once seated that her pelvis was relieved from carrying the weight of her unborn child.

"Anne, good to see you." He was obviously trying his best. "Can I get anything to make you more comfortable? A pillow perhaps? A glass of water?"

"You're very kind, Ian, but I'm fine." She wondered where he would have found a pillow and was pretty sure that he could have more happily delivered a glass of whisky rather than one of water.

"It must all be happening very soon now, how are you feeling?" He asked earnestly.

"Enormous, gigantic, huge!" She couldn't help but laugh at his question.

"And all of this," she looked down at her bloated belly, "is due to a single mad but great night some thirty-seven weeks ago!" He looked aghast, and she laughed again. "Please don't look so worried, Ian. I'm not here to complain or cause any problems. In fact, quite the reverse." She took a deep breath and went on to explain that since Alistair's death, she'd come to realise what an enormous favour Ian had done for both her and the Lundy family – she even described it as "a most enjoyable' favour".

She had listened to her mother-in-law's sour comments about Ian's relationship with her daughter but knew that he made Fiona happy.

"She obviously loves you, Ian, and clearly, you are very much in love with her. I envy you both but have come to ask you personally for something very important for me and my baby."

"Which is?" He looked to be in pain as he asked the question.

"Your silence. Your eternal silence. Everyone must believe it's Alistair's child." Ian's palpable relief made her smile, although she started to become aware of her bladder sending messages that it was time to get back to the flat. "Especially if it's a boy. The very survival of the Lundy dynasty depends on it. Have you told anyone what happened that night?"

Ian shook his head.

"Not even Fiona?"

"Especially not her. Have you?"

"Just one person." In an instant, she could feel tears pricking her eyes. "My poor, sweet, dear daddy – and I swore him to secrecy, although he couldn't tell anyone now." She began to struggle up onto her feet. "Ironic, isn't it?" she mused. "None of this would have happened if Alistair hadn't panicked."

"I don't understand. Panicked about what?" Ian asked.

"The Sexual Offences Bill. It gets royal assent next month – it decriminalises homosexuality. If only he'd waited, he needn't have married me. There's even talk of legalising abortion, but it is all too late."

She sighed, and Ian was immediately at her side again as she laboriously stood up.

"One more thing about the baby …" She got no further before feeling a warm trickle run down her inner thigh. There was no pain, and she was reasonably certain that her bladder hadn't let her down.

"I think my waters have broken." She spoke calmly. No one had told her that the fluid would be so warm, and as she looked down, she saw that it was not clear liquid seeping onto the dark-blue carpet but what looked like blood.

Margaret Jones was waiting outside the casualty department of the Royal United Hospital and was the first of the team to enter the ambulance after it had backed up to open its doors. Only recently qualified, the young midwife ignored Ian, who had accompanied Anne.

"The contractions only started on our way a few minutes ago," the ambulance man reported. "But the bleeding has got much worse."

Minutes later, the obstetrics team had an emergency on its hands. Placenta praevia was uncommon – of course they knew how to cope with the complication where the placenta sheered off the uterus wall, but it was potentially very dangerous. An immediate caesarean section was the obvious solution.

No one was prepared for twins: the mother had never said anything, and when her notes were later located, there had been no suggestion of multiple births during her antenatal care. The placenta of the firstborn, a girl, was lying across the internal os, and both she and the little boy that speedily followed were very poorly: they were taken away immediately and put on oxygen.

Even though they had completed the deliveries at break-neck speed, the mother lost an inordinate amount of blood from the raw surface wound of the womb. They rapidly performed a hysterectomy, but it was to no avail, and nothing could be done to save her life.

Lady Anne of Lundy died forty-two minutes after entering the operating theatre while Ian waited in the hospital corridor.

CHAPTER THIRTY-NINE

"Fiona?"

Instinctively, she knew something was dreadfully wrong.

"Where are you?" she asked.

There was a murmur but no distinct answer.

"What's happened?"

Ian finally spoke so quietly that it was difficult for her to hear what he was whispering. "At the RUH … It's Anne … She's dead … during the birth."

Then she realised he was crying, something she had never heard before – even when he had relived his mother's death. Wanting to be supportive but feeling numb, she started to shake and struggled to control her own voice. "Oh, no … and the baby?"

There was another long pause, broken by quiet little sobs. She dreaded the answer but asked again, "Ian, did the baby survive?"

"Yes, but they're both very poorly."

"Both?"

"She had twins, a girl and boy."

Fiona didn't remember ending the call and driving to the hospital. Clutching a stony-faced Ian, she looked through the glass screen at the two tiny beings in incubators, and afterwards, the still expression on the ashen face framed by long, blond hair was seared into her memory. Never to be seen again after today, she felt sad and hopeless. She couldn't understand it: what could Anne have done to deserve such an awful end to her young life?

As if on auto-pilot, she made a perfunctory call to her mother and then tried to work out how best to let Rosemary know what had happened to her sister. Finally, she left a message on Malcolm Austwick's home answerphone.

Later, hours and hours later, the hospital team suggested Fiona and Ian leave the hospital and go home as the babies, whilst very sick, were stabilising and nothing was likely to change. Margaret Jones, who was tending them, promised to ring if it did. They drove along deserted streets and arrived at Great Pulteney Street just as dawn was breaking. Exhausted but past sleep and unable to face another cup of tea, Fiona poured them both some brandy and put her beloved Beethoven's Violin Concerto to play softly on the stereo.

They sat together on the sofa as the music filled the room. It ended, and in silence, Ian put his arms around her and gently, they kissed. When she opened her eyes, he was looking at her intensely and spoke slowly and quietly.

"What a sad, sad day. Lovely, kind, friendly Anne gone; never to be seen again, leaving two helpless babies. Oh, Fiona, my darling Fiona, what next?" His voice trailed off.

"Ian, Ian …" She tried to help this man she so loved, but it proved too much: she gave in and started to weep.

"Please don't, Fiona." It was good to have him so close, trying to comfort her. He kissed her wet cheeks as if trying to dry the tears.

"My darling, what would I do without you?" He pulled her closer, "Never, never, never leave me. Promise?"

"Why would I leave you?" she sobbed. "I love you. I want to spend the rest of my life with you."

"You mean marriage? You want to marry me?" He sounded incredulous.

"No, I can't ask that." She wasn't sure this was the moment to drag up the past but knew it had to be done sooner or later.

"Why?"

"Well, firstly, my age. I'm so much older and …" She paused, and he interrupted.

"That's not a problem. And?"

"The second reason is far more difficult. It goes back to that first Christmas we spent together, you remember?" He nodded.

"How could I forget? I told you then that I loved you, but you just told me I was too young and disappeared off to go skiing."

She became fearful that what she had to tell him would bring everything crashing down. "I didn't go to skiing, I went to ... the baby we made ... I went for a termination." She pulled away to look at his face, but it didn't change as he reached for his glass before replying.

"I know. I guessed that from the postcard you sent from a clinic suggesting that I owed you nine hundred Swiss francs."

Of course. She'd forgotten having sent that nasty, spiteful message and the rancour because of the suffering and pain he had caused her.

Ian continued. "I was gutted at the time – my own flesh and blood, the only living thing related to me, being flushed down a foreign sluice. But it's not a problem now. After all, we can always make more babies."

Her heart sunk, and she got up fetched the cognac bottle and refilled their glasses. "I'm afraid the abortion wasn't straightforward, and the specialist at the clinic told me that I would never become pregnant again. Ian, I can't give you children, and I know how much that will mean to you. You have no living relatives – your mother died, all the rest were murdered in Auschwitz ..." Her voice trailed off, and in that moment, she guessed it was all over.

Instead, he took another sip from his glass and said, "That makes no difference. I love you and I want to marry you. But now there's something that I need to tell you too."

With the liquor warm in her stomach and overly tired, she could only start to feel the relief of his words and wasn't prepared at all for what came next.

"Fiona, I am the father of those two little mites in the hospital."

Before Ian could say more or Fiona could fully appreciate the weight of what he'd just said, the telephone rang. She assumed it was the hospital and, dreading the worst, picked up the receiver.

"My dear, I hope I haven't woken you, but I've just heard your message." It was Malcolm Austwick.

"No, we've been up all night and only got back from the hospital an hour or two ago." She was back on auto-pilot.

"How awful. Is there any news on the babies?"

"No – the midwife said she'd ring if there was any change, so no news hopefully is good news."

"Well, let's pray that's so, and in any case, I need to see you urgently. Can you get to my office in half an hour – at eight o'clock? I've asked your mother to be here too. It's very important – and does the "we" mean that Ian Morris is with you?"

"Yes."

"Good, I should be obliged if you would bring him."

With the phone receiver back in its cradle, Fiona knew she would have to make a decision about Ian's revelation. She felt wide awake again and completely sober.

Margaret Jones should have gone off duty at the end of the night shift but could not tear herself away from two cots in the tiny post-natal emergency room. She made regular checks on the oxygen supply and the vital life signs of the two babies: she had promised to call Miss Symons if there was any change. At one point, she felt her head dropping to sleep, but then the door opened and the Ward Sister came in.

"Any change?" she asked. "I've had the family solicitor on the telephone."

The midwife shook her head and instinctively felt for the scrap of paper with Miss Symons's telephone number in her starched skirt pocket.

Malcolm's secretary had arrived early to work as requested and tended to their various needs: Earl Grey tea for the Dowager Duchess, white coffee for Miss Symons, black for Mr Morris, and just water for her boss.

Stony-faced, Emily, the widow of the Third and mother of the late 4th Earl, looked straight at Ian with open hostility, and there was loathing in her voice.

"What are you doing here? You are not part of this family."

"Hush, Emily, all will become clear," Austwick said soothingly and went on.

"I apologise for calling this meeting so early, but as Anne's executor, I had no choice. The reason is not the tragic and unexpected death of Anne late last night but the totally unexpected birth and survival of the twins. Much else can wait, but they cannot. I spoke to the hospital just before you arrived, and they have survived the night with their tenuous grasp of life continuing. So, we must pray and assume one or both of them survive."

The elderly solicitor picked up and unfolded the previously-unnoticed will and resumed.

"For now, I will simply tell you of Anne's wishes in the event of her pre-deceasing her child – it seems not even she knew she was bearing twins. In such an event, and I will quote, 'It is my earnest desire that any child is brought up in the Christian faith and that my sister-in-law, the Honourable Fiona Symons, and Mr Ian Morris, who has been a good friend, become testamentary guardians."

The Dowager Duchess reddened and initially pressed her lips firmly together but eventually spoke nevertheless.

"And what part am I to play in bringing up my grandchildren and, in particular, the Fifth Earl?"

"That depends," Austwick answered.

"On what?" she asked testily.

"Whether they live, and if so, if your daughter and Mr Morris agree to become their legal guardians."

Ian looked at Fiona and slowly nodded his head, and in barely more than a whisper, Fiona answered.

"We agree …" She paused. Then, stretching out her hand, she covered Ian's and, with a stronger voice, went on. "Well, Mother, now is as good a time as ever for me to tell you something else you will not approve of. Following last night's tragedy, Ian asked me to marry him, and I have accepted."

CHAPTER FORTY

Ian and Fiona left the solicitor's office, crossed Queen Square, and let themselves into number fifteen; none of the staff had yet arrived. For a few moments, they stood in the magnificent ground-floor office, clinging to each other, overwhelmed by the events of the previous twenty-four hours. Slowly, they pulled apart.

"I'll get us some coffee," Ian said, making for the kitchen, "then we can sit down and try making sense of everything."

Fiona started collecting up the discarded detritus left by the ambulance crew and shuddered at the dark patch of Anne's dried, congealed blood. She would ring the carpet cleaners later and, in the meantime, covered the stain with some of the unpacked empty boxes lying by the conference table.

Ian set the tray down and next to the two cups of steaming black coffee. Silently, they sat and drank. He was the first to speak.

"Let's pray that the two new babies will survive – and we both need to be strong, if only for their sake."

Fiona nodded slowly, reminding herself that the twins were conceived several months before her love for Ian had blossomed: she would never have known if Anne had survived. Nevertheless, it was so difficult to know that another woman had fulfilled his greatest desire for a child when she couldn't. On another level, she was pleased that the children were continuing to cling to life and that both she and Ian were to be responsible for them.

The mantelpiece clock struck nine and, sighing, she stood up to get the large leather diary she had given Ian as a last Christmas present.

We have to be strong and realistic, which means continuing with our daily lives, she told herself before saying aloud, "What have you got on today?" She handed it to him, knowing that she should check her own agenda too and wondered whether she really did have the strength to just carry on as normal.

Ian opened the diary for June 22 1967 and read out the three entries he had penned in.

11.00 am: Al Giles, first year's results of The Bath Way? Donna?
1.00 pm: Sandwich lunch – Trish Traynor coming back?
2.30 pm: The Bath Preservation Trust strategy meeting
3.00 pm: Stephen Vernon

"That last one is the difficult one – much more than just listening and going through the motions: we've got to decide on our best approach in dealing with the all-important Bath Preservation Trust."

Fiona, having completely forgotten about the strategy meeting, marvelled at how Ian had returned to the work mode: she took a deep breath and went to fetch the notes she'd made from her office.

On her return, she saw Ian sitting at the conference table reading some documents with his coffee cup beside him. She picked up her own and sat down opposite.

"So, tell me about the Bath Preservation Trust." He looked across at her and smiled. It was a wan and tired smile but full of love.

"OK. First for the history and background: it's a totally independent charitable organisation. It grew out of the Old Bath Preservation Society set up in 1909 and successfully stopped the demolition of the north side of Bath Street, exposing the Council's attitude that Bath architecture was ugly and expendable and best be cleared away. The Society was dedicated to preserving Bath, devoted to ensuring new developments did not mar the city, was not funded by national or local government but powerless to legally stop or change developments in Bath. It set up a charitable trust in 1934 to fundraise and buy property in order to resist the Bath Bill being passed by Parliament."

"The Bath Bill?" Ian interrupted. "What was that?"

Fiona checked before continuing.

"It was becoming apparent that the city's original layout with its narrow streets and terraces was unsuitable for cars and shoppers. The Corporation therefore proposed to extend Milsom Street to the Assembly Rooms, demolish Old Bond Street, and widen Broad Street along with much wholesale destruction elsewhere to make way for a new east/west road."

"That sounds radical," he said.

"Very." She continued. "Especially when it was discovered that most of the members of the Corporation had approved the bill, without even reading it. They'd only been given a brief oral summary of the list of streets affected. Uproar ensued, and with the aid of the *Times*, the *Bath Chronicle,* and much of the rest of the national press, the bill was thrown out. The Alderman responsible was forced to resign – it was a huge victory for the /Trust."

Ian interrupted again.

"And I suppose after that, as they say, the rest is history?"

Fiona continued. "The Trust became highly effective, putting forward its own agenda for enhancing the city and fiercely protecting the Green Belt surrounding it."

"So, where does it get its power from?" Ian asked.

"I'd say its authority stems from the nature and the sheer number of its members," she replied, looking at him. "It's taken very seriously as a representative body of the city's good and great. And on that point, I have an idea."

"Go on."

"My uncle, one of Father's brothers, is a retired judge and very much an active member this crowd, who are definitely old school. I think the trustees may be persuaded to listen to them. Shall I see if I can get him and a few others for the meeting this afternoon?"

"That's a brilliant idea, especially as we've got Stephen Vernon coming anyway." Vernon was an expert on historic building renovation.

"I don't expect the meeting with Trish should take long, so I should easily be finished and free by one thirty."

"Good," she said. "But first of all, I think we should go home. You need a shave, and we both would benefit from a shower and change of clothes."

CHAPTER FORTY-ONE

They sat, just the two of them, at one end of the large conference table in Ian's office in fifteen Queen Square. Al Giles was jubilant and knew he had every reason to be. If asked, he would have said that for some reason, Ian was subdued, tired, not his usual sparky self. Surely, it couldn't be anything to do with the business at hand: in the space of just six months, *The Bath Way* had proved to be an outstanding success, exceeding all the original projections.

Circulation was up by sixty percent, at eight thousand copies a month. It now boasted more than a hundred pages in each edition, with half of it pure advertising and most of the rest advertorials – all in full colour.

"It's the Twelve Tribes idea that originated from the Nurses' Christmas Ball that has proved such a winner." He opened the latest edition at the contents page where they were always listed in all their glory.

THE ARTS	*Arty Farties*
BUSINESS & MANUFACTURING	*Wheelers & Dealers*
CHARITIES	*Do Gooders*
EDUCATION	*Those who can't*
LAW & ORDER	*Cops & Robbers*
MEDIA	*Hackers*
MEDICINE	*Healers & Feelers*
MILITARY	*Pips & Stripes*
POLITICS	*Three-line Whips*
PROFESSIONS	*Guineas Club*
RELIGION	*God Squad*
SPORT	*Heavy Breathers*
TOURISM	*Globetrotters*

Ian noticed that there were now thirteen; clearly, Donna Lodge was not to be left out.

Al continued. "No matter what profession, the good citizens of Bath are only too willing to part with their half-crowns to read about their own triumphs and, more importantly, see what the competition is up to."

He could see that Ian was impressed as he flicked through the relevant pages. For each tribe, Al had persuaded an important, if not the most prominent player in Bath to act as an unpaid editor and to contribute editorially. Naturally, where appropriate, each of their organisations bought the facing page for a suitable advertisement.

"This is great, Al, but I think you should consider another possibility – two stand-alone supplements all paid for by advertising."

"Covering what?"

"House sales and tourism."

Al thought about it for a moment and then saw what Ian was getting at.

"I like it. I think it could really work.'

"Good. I'm glad you do, because I want you to meet the person who's going to make the tourism part happen."

Al felt a bit non-plussed by the idea of someone else being involved, but Ian stood up and went through a rear door, returning a moment later. A small, dark-haired young woman who barely looked over twenty accompanied him. She was smartly dressed in a blue business suit, but what Al noticed most as he stood up to shake her hand was her intense, deep-blue eyes.

"Al, meet Donna Lodge. Donna, this is Al Giles."

They shook hands and sat down, facing one another, with Ian between them at the head of the table.

"Donna used to work for a local travel agent, but as from yesterday, she's the managing director of Visit Bath, a new company I've set up to grow tourism in Bath." Ian looked towards Donna, who reached into her briefcase for a notebook and pen and addressed Al directly.

"Tell me," she clicked the biro down and flicked through to a specific page in the notebook, "what's the minimum size of a supplement that you could produce?"

Al was non-plussed – he was unused to dealing with women as his equals, let alone being cross-examined about his magazine.

"Eight pages, so sixteen sides."

"Good. I can immediately commit for twenty six issues," she referred to the open page in front of her, "say a mix, half colour, half black-and-white with minimum quarter page adverts, one third editorial with fifteen percent photographs. I'd like the first edition in a month and then fortnightly." She looked up at him. "Do you have any problem with that?"

He hesitated, completely taken aback; unused to taking orders from anyone, let alone this slip of a young girl. Ian broke the silence.

"Well, Al, can you do it?"

"Yes, but the cost …" Had she any idea what this would entail?

"Oh, don't worry about that," Donna said. "When can you let me have a fixed cost for the next twelve months?"

When Al didn't immediately respond, she looked sharply at Ian. "You promised me a completely free hand as to content, that all matters tourist will be covered exclusively in the supplement."

Shocked by the suggested reduction in his authority without any prior consultation, Al looked at Ian.

"Are you happy with this?" Only he could do the in-depth research and marketing that would be required for the supplement launch.

"I certainly am. I trust Donna completely and rest assured that, once you get to know her, so will you."

Donna smiled at the compliment, and Al noticed how her eyes now lit up her whole face. Well, he thought, at least she's pleasant to look at, and a nice figure, too.

"Fair enough," he said. "I'll do some figures and come back to you. Where are you based?"

"Here, for the time being – at what you would call the centre of things, you might say. Just through there." She pointed to the rear office before turning her smile to him – and still, she pushed. "Tomorrow for the figures?"

Al nodded and wondered how his thunder had been so deftly stolen.

"I'll leave it to you two to work out the detail. And it looks like you've got a thirteenth tribe, Al."

"What do you mean?" he asked.

"Your new Tourist Editor, Miss Donna Lodge. What will you call the tribe?"

Before Al had a chance to think, Donna came straight back.

"Globetrotters?" she ventured.

Al remained silent.

"Excellent," Ian agreed. "Anything else?"

"We need another tribe just for women."

"For discussion another time. Thank you Donna, Al," Ian said, rightly believing that the editor had been pushed far enough for one day. He stood, effectively drawing the meeting to a close.

After they'd left, Ian carefully tore the list of the Twelve Tribes out of the magazine, wrote *Tourism 13 Globetrotters – Donna Lodge* and paused, then added at the bottom *14 Blue Stockings?* He put the list in the middle drawer of his desk. He knew that tourism was still in its infancy, but this was a promising beginning – he very much liked Donna's style; she could and would certainly rattle cages.

Donna had no difficulty in filling the first issue with hotels, bars, and restaurants vying with each other for advertising, with several so-called Bath experts flattered to be asked and committing to editorial.

Gradually, Al got over his loss of total fiefdom, especially as the success of the supplement proved so popular with the tourists: it drove up the general circulation of the whole magazine. Over time, Al's antagonism had turned to attraction for his fiery co-editor, and in turn, she bullied him less and less. Much to Ian's amusement, it wasn't long before the local grapevine told of frequent late-night editorial conferences at Al's flat.

CHAPTER FORTY-TWO

Next on that strange day in late June 1967, Trish arrived for lunch as planned.

"Your favourite." She placed the paper bag on the conference table. "Cream cheese and gherkin on rye." She wanted him to feel comfortable before making her case and wondered why he looked so dreadful. She was about to ask if he was feeling all right but didn't get the chance, because with a brusque nod of the head at the sandwich, he came straight to the point.

"So, are you going to come back and work for me?"

Her sympathy vanished with his curt manner, and she responded accordingly.

"Not *for* you. Maybe with you, but that depends." She didn't wait to be offered a seat before choosing a chair directly opposite him.

"Oh?"

"I have no intention to ever again being in the helpless position you left me in after the assault. Not only did I lose my income, but I could not stop anything – eviction, writs, bailiffs: I was powerless."

Ian held his hands up to protest, but she ignored him and continued.

"I lost my flat before I could find another job but still came to visit you day and night at the hospital. I did everything I could to help you recover and even had you lodge at my mum's place when you were discharged. But once back on your feet, you simply left without warning, not even bothering to say a proper goodbye. Did you ever stop to think how you would've managed in those months without me? No, because the only person who matters to Ian Morris is Ian Morris. Now, out of the blue and months later, you get in touch offering me my old job back, as if it was yesterday and you're doing me a favour. Really? Firstly, how about telling me what's going on with the Honourable Fiona Symons?"

Ian was aghast by the outburst and even chastened. He looked even more drawn than when she'd arrived a few minutes earlier and still hadn't touched the sandwich.

"I don't see what business it is of yours," he said quietly, "but we are living together."

"I'm not interested in your love life." This was untrue, but she did want to get to the conversation which had brought her back to him. "I mean business-wise."

"I've switched sides and gone over to the preservationists. I'm joining Fiona's company."

"So, you want me to work for her?" This was the last thing Trish had expected or wanted.

"No, not at all. I'm involved in numerous projects as well as Fiona's consultancy, the Bath Regeneration Practice, which advises the City Council on all redevelopment. I've also taken over her late brother's protest movement, Bath Against Developers, but this is no longer a bunch of modernist haters. It's been renamed Traditional Bath." He paused, then continued. "Its aim is to regenerate historical interest and tourism in our city with sensitive renovation and development."

"So, where do I fit in?" Trish ignored his obviously well-rehearsed public relations patter. Unconvinced by the transformed Ian Morris, her scepticism was confirmed in his next reply.

"My estate agency, Forsyte Morris & Company will deal with all the resultant property business, and I see you back in your old role. What do you say?"

This was the old Ian, the one she knew, and so she moved onto her demands.

"I think I've made it clear that I wouldn't come back in my old role. For a start, I want more money. That's not all, I also want a share of the profits and, equally important, status. I want to go onto the notepaper with you. That's all."

"Oh, 'that's all'?" He was looking at her, and she knew he was thinking how much she'd toughened up – not just when she'd first come to work for him as an innocent, nineteen-year-old girl straight from secretarial college five years ago but since he'd walked out of her in Mafeking Street the previous summer.

"How much more money do you want and what sort of profit share?"

"Fifty percent more salary and a ten-percent profit share until I qualify. Then we will renegotiate." She had caught him off guard and relished how astonished he was at the idea.

"You ... are going to ... qualify?" he asked. "What as and how?" Expecting her to answer with some form of company secretarial role, he was completely taken aback by her reply.

"Like you as a Chartered Surveyor, within two years, under the new Direct Entry University Scheme." She was on the home run and knew it. "I can enrol as an external student, and I will need at least a day off a week plus two weeks every so often to attend, revise, and sit the examination."

"When you talk about 'going onto the notepaper', what do you have in mind exactly?"

"An associate until I qualify and then a full partner. Forsyte Morris & Company will become Morris, Traynor & Company."

The look on Ian's face made her wonder had she'd pushed too far.

"You have got to be joking," he said, but then he sat back in his chair.

She knew he was thinking the idea through, weighing up how much he needed her against what he was being asked to give away: he probably doubted that she could or would ever qualify.

"No, Ian, I've never been more serious. You can take it or leave it." She let the silence hang so that he knew not only that she meant it but that the the meek, adoring assistant of the past was gone.

"Agreed," he said slowly. "When can you start?"

"As soon as Patrick McCloy has drawn up the contract." She was determined never to be left vulnerable again and have everything in writing. It had been very tough, but she knew that Norman's advice about keeping personal feelings out of business negotiations was right – oh, so right.

Two weeks later, she returned to her old office at fifteen Queen Square. As her first job, she had the notepaper reprinted. Later that first day, when Ian asked her to arrange the marriage invitations, she reminded him that she was no longer a secretary: organising his personal life was not part of the terms and conditions set out in the contract prepared by Patrick McCloy.

CHAPTER FORTY-THREE

Half an hour after Trish left, Fiona came into Ian's office and shut the door behind her.

"The delegation is in the waiting room."

"How many did you manage to get at such short notice?" Ian asked.

"Six, and Stephen Vernon will be waiting in my office so that you can call him in at the right time."

Fiona had chosen carefully, limiting the invitation only to senior trust members who were friends of her family and occupied high places in the city's hierarchy. An elderly, discreet bunch, they all knew or knew of Ian Morris and generally viewed him as a young barbarian poised at the city walls, only interested in making money from the destruction of Bath.

Fiona brought them in and settled them, deliberately placing herself and Ian next to each other in the middle of the conference table rather than at its head. She waited until a junior secretary had provided their assorted beverages and stood up.

"Welcome, gentlemen," – Fiona was the only woman present – "and thank you very much for finding the time to join us today at such short notice. Looking around at you, I think I've known you all for my entire life, and if I may, I wish to start this afternoon's meeting with a personal request. As you have no doubt heard, last night, Anne, my sister-in-law and the widow of my brother, the late 4th Earl of Lundy, tragically died in childbirth. Twins, a boy and girl, survive and are still in a critical condition at the Royal United Hospital. I would respectfully ask that we stand for a minute's silence to remember her and pray for the survival of the two new fragile members of the Lundy family."

All stood, some closed their eyes, and one crossed himself. Once they had resumed their seats, Fiona continued.

"Thank you, and now for happier news. We will be making a formal announcement shortly, but I thought you should be among the first to know." She stretched out a hand and took Ian's.

"Ian and I are to be married."

There was an intake of breath, but the men involved recovered quickly, and there were mutterings of congratulations around the table.

"Now, the raison d'être for today's invitation: I will pass you over to Ian." A few of the men cleared their throats as she took her seat and Ian rose. He thanked everyone for their attendance and explained that it was their value of the city as well as their importance to the Bath Preservation Trust which had precipitated the meeting.

"I believe that the Trust accepts that it cannot save every building in Bath and so must concentrate on the best. We at Traditional Bath support this aim wholeheartedly. But you know as well as I do the forecasts: Bath's present population of eighty-five thousand is set to double in the coming decades. There aren't anywhere near enough houses for the city's present population, let alone the projected need of at least another seven hundred new homes every year for years to come. In addition, much of the existing accommodation is hopelessly sub-standard and must be made fit for people to live in."

The elderly judge interjected.

"Are you are suggesting the Trust turns a blind eye to the ninety five percent of the buildings it cannot protect, leaving you to knock everything else down?"

Then one of the others added.

"Leaving your lot to make a fortune in the process? We would be betraying our aims if we agreed to the wholesale demolition being promoted by the City Council."

"I'm not suggesting wholesale demolition, far from it. I–" Ian was interrupted again.

"What then?" The judge looked at Fiona. "And what do you think?"

She took up the baton instantly – after all, the curmudgeonly, old man was her uncle, and Ian had the facts to back his scheme.

"Remember the old saying 'Every new house is a dream for someone and a nightmare for the neighbour'?" She smiled warmly at her uncle. "Uncle, please listen to Ian for a little longer: hear him out."

She sat down, Ian continued.

"Rest assured that I do not want to belittle what Sir Lee Mayall and Sir Christopher Chancellor accomplished, nor do I overlook the fact that Michael Briggs is doing a fantastic job – as are all trustees of the Trust. But this is preaching to the choir, there is so much more to be achieved. Whole streets of small Georgian houses have been bulldozed without a murmur from the Corporation. As you rightly have surmised, the developers are quivering with excitement at the amount of money to be made.

"What Fiona and I have in mind is, firstly, a controlled modernisation of the existing housing stock, and secondly, infilling – building tastefully on all those extensive gardens so beloved by our Georgian ancestors but which have become too large for their ageing owners to manage. None will involve the holy of holies, the sacred Green Belt around Bath."

A leading city architect chipped in, his tone patronising. "Bath stone is so expensive, and ask two Bathonians to define 'tastefully' and you will get at least three opinions!"

Some of the others laughed, but Ian went on. "Our definition is simple. All new construction would be Georgian, albeit I accept using pastiche cast rather than natural Bath stone, but as close as we can practically get to John Wood senior and junior's original designs."

Silence prevailed, but Fiona thought the men's body language and faces said it all – scepticism and suspicion. They didn't believe Ian, and so, as agreed before the meeting, she casually said, "Oh, and we mustn't forget another thing – soot."

"What do you mean, soot?" It was the partner of a major conveyancing practice.

"We all know that the buildings are filthy," she said. "They're black from the soot of hundreds of years of coal fires. They must be cleaned if they are going to be preserved for future generations."

"But that would cost a fortune, far beyond the purse of individual owners, and take years," the solicitor retorted. "Now *that* is an impossible pipe dream!"

"I don't agree. Lundy Enterprises Ltd will be able to do this work. But perhaps before we get to that …" Ian walked over and opened the door to the adjoining office.

A tall lean man in his mid-fifties entered. "Gentlemen, may I introduce Professor Stephen Vernon from Oxford University, one of the country's leading experts on stone renovation. I have taken the liberty of inviting him to say a few words."

"Good afternoon." The professor's manner was relaxed and assured as one used to lecturing his lessers. Fiona couldn't help but notice how his grey hair and thick, horn-rimmed glasses emphasised the impression of distinction and learning. He spoke without notes and was obviously an academic whose views needed to be treated with respect.

"Some time ago, Miss Symons and Mr Morris commissioned my department to produce a report on the state of the stonework of the buildings in Bath and in particular, the desirability and feasibility of cleaning off the muck of centuries. The report will be ready shortly, but in the meantime, they have asked me to summarise its findings.

"The soft and mellow limestone of Bath has been used since Roman times, but it was only in 1726 that Ralph Allen began buying up all the small quarries on Combe Down, south of Bath. Bath stone has always been much favoured because it is a 'free' stone, meaning that it can be cut or sawn in any direction. In addition, it weathers to a beautiful, creamy, golden colour and develops a patina on which harmless lichens can grow.

"The problem of dirty buildings in large cities has been caused by the use of coal fires for over two hundred years. In more recent times, the situation has been made far worse by the exhausts of motor cars. In the particular case of Bath, the continual gushing of sulphur dioxide and nitrogen dioxide from engines has been aggravated by the city lying in a basin surrounded by hills. I will not bore you with the detailed chemistry but suffice to say the effect is worse where there is continual heavy traffic, as on the trunk routes crossing this city such as London Road or in the canyon of Broadgate Street.

"Nevertheless, careful cleaning can reverse the whole terrible process quickly and dramatically. There are numerous methods, including jet or soft washing, hot or cold water, steam, and high or low pressure hoses. The method of cleaning is critical, as over-cleaning and over-saturation of this highly porous beautiful stone must be avoided at all cost. My department is presently testing all of these, and the specialists' recommendations for Bath will be in our final report."

Professor Vernon paused.

"So, that is the general position, and I come to the specific questions we have been asked to address, which are feasibility, time-scale, and cost. Is it feasible? Certainly, the answer is yes. Once we've decided on which method to use, the technology already exists to restore Bath to pristine elegance.

"How long will it take? The cleaning process isn't rapid, and Bath's daily life has to continue uninterrupted throughout the project. As a result, and given the thousands of buildings involved, I estimate it will take the best part of twenty years.

"How much will it cost? At around two thousand pounds at today's prices for a medium-sized Georgian property, I calculate the cost will be a minimum of six million pounds." There was an audible gasp.

"Finally, with regards to where this huge sum of money will come from given my preliminary enquiries at local and national government level, I am confident it will be forthcoming. After all, we are talking about irreplaceable architecture and a priceless slice of British history that is renowned globally." Vernon sat down and Ian spoke.

"We're going to break for a cup of tea, during which time the Professor will be happy to answer your questions."

Thirty minutes later and after fielding a barrage of questions, Stephen Vernon departed. Fiona took her time in finishing her tea to wait for the right moment before addressing the elderly cohort around her.

"Many of you will know of Lundy Enterprises Ltd, the company set up in 1906 by my great grandfather, the 1st Earl."

A number of the men nodded.

"Its ownership passed to me when my brother died, and although it has been dormant in recent years, my husband-to-be has joined me on its board.

"Many of you will know Clive Wilcox, who has worked with Tom Scotland for years. Following Tom's recent retirement, after the unfortunate incident at the Georgian Rooms, Clive has joined us as the new managing director of Lundy Enterprises." The men didn't seem much interested by this news. She pressed on.

"Equally important is the fact that substantial funds are being put in place for it so that, once again, this company can undertake major construction projects in Bath. Additionally, it will specialise in the best method of stone cleaning in Bath as advised by Professor Vernon, who has agreed to be a consultant to the company."

Now they were interested, she thought and sat down to more positive mumblings.

Ian took over.

"I don't have to remind you of how close we came to the disaster of Abercrombie's plan being implemented after the war when the loss of so much of the Georgian city was saved by a single vote – thank goodness for the chairman casting one. All those empty bomb sites which have remained untouched from twenty-two years ago – the time has come to do something about them."

This was the cue for Fiona to sum things up. Ian took his seat.

"From our perspective, the Bath Preservation Trust seems to continually battle against accusations that it's trying to preserve everything. We are suggesting that it find a balance between a modern approach and a need to defend the deserving architecture. At the same time, it must break the grip of the developer. We know that with high land costs, developers are under pressure to get the most money back by building as much as they can on every inch of ground, which often means skimping on design, materials, and size. With this in mind, perhaps it would be better to introduce the word 'conservation' rather than maintain 'preservation'. A Bath conservation trust could then concentrate on making sure that anything new is worthy of our beautiful city."

"Gentlemen," she took a breath and smiled warmly at them all again. "Ian and I didn't invite you here to ask for your or the Trust's consent. Frankly, we don't need it – and unless managed, market forces may well overwhelm Bath. We thought it only fair that we should advise you about what we have in mind for Lundy Enterprises Ltd so you can take this into account when thinking about the Bath Preservation Trust's future path."

"So, what do you think?" Ian asked after they had left.

"They listened," Fiona replied, "Stephen Vernon was very impressive, and I think we've said enough to convince them. But only time will tell how much they can and will influence the Trust. Let's go home, I'm shattered, and we both need a proper night's sleep."

With the day's work over, her thoughts returned to the death of Anne and survival of the tiny babies.

"Malcolm still hasn't been able to get in touch with her sister, and if I don't hear something soon, I'll need to sort out a funeral." She could feel her eyes pricking with tears. "At least I'll know what to do this time. It only seems like yesterday when I had to arrange Alistair's and the Rear Admiral's memorial service."

True to form, Ian didn't wait for the Preservation Trust's blessing and immediately began to investigate the properties owned and bought by Bath Estates after the Second World War.

In 1962, Trish had organised the production of the wooden map-cabinet, some eight feet square from Martin Tracey at the Framing Workshop in Walcot Street. It had been fixed to her office wall and went unnoticed by the bailiffs when the lease of fifteen Queen Square was forfeited. Trish had kept her key. How Ian delighted in using his matching one to reveal the detailed map which showed every building and piece of land within the city boundaries – all in the glory of a scale of fifty inches to the mile.

It took Ian and Trish took much time and effort to identify the three thousand or so freeholds owned by Bath Estates Ltd. After several weeks, the job done, they had coloured each in red and numbered it: matching index cards had been produced showing all the relevant details extracted from the boxes of files and Marcus Rose's ten leather books. Each card was subsequently categorised by Ian for immediate, medium, and long-term action; be it sale, renovation or development, or for housing and commercial use.

Fiona was proved right by an extract from the Trust's subsequent annual report.

> "There is scarcely a street where its future is not threatened by that ill-omened word 'development', and yet mercifully, little has happened.
>
> An amenity society such as our own has a narrow path to tread. Uncompromising preservation can only lead to total impotence to influence inevitable development, while too great an acceptance of the profit motive would sacrifice the very reasons for its existence.
>
> Happily a firm middle road is practicable ..."

Tentatively at first, Bath Estates started submitting planning applications for a few houses and blocks of flats on the land which it owned: unopposed, over the coming years, the trickle turned to an unstoppable flood involving thousands upon thousands of flats and houses on the seven hundred acres of land in the eleven square miles of the city.

CHAPTER FORTY-FOUR

Margaret Jones had been a marvel and spent every spare minute she had on duty with the twins, ensuring that the two tiny beings thrived. Each day, Ian and Fiona went, always together, to the Royal United Hospital, and more often than not, Margaret was there, bringing them up to date with the babies' progress.

Then, one wonderful day in late summer, Margaret had personally brought them home to twelve Great Pulteney Street. Another date that Ian would remember for another reason: 27 August 1967 was the day the BBC announced the death of the Beatles' manager, Brian Epstein.

In her quest for a nanny and prompted by Margaret, Fiona had followed the well-trodden path of the English upper and middle classes leading to *The Lady* magazine. Published in 1885 by Thomas Bowles, grandfather of the Mitford sisters, it was reputed to be the nation's longest-running women's weekly, famed for finding domestic servants, particularly nannies.

Now the successful, twenty-one-year-old candidate, Miss Anna Jacka-Thomas, in her formal Norland College winter uniform of brown dress and matching brown leather shoes, welcomed the party into her territory, the nursery. She and Fiona had overseen the upper room's redecoration and provided everything the children could possibly need and more over the coming months.

With Anna tidying the nursery, Ian and Fiona were alone with the babies. With Ian's arm around her waist, Fiona stood gazing in wonder at the two cots with blue and pink ribbons – not that anyone needed a reminder of which one was which. The boy had jet-black, spiky hair, and the girl's blonde down was gradually beginning to curl. Fiona watched Ian as he, too, marvelled at them.

"Such pride, anyone would think you were the father," she teased. She was surprised at how quickly she'd grown accustomed to the knowledge that he had fathered the twins without any jealousy. Perhaps it was partly because of her guilt in the joy of having children at the expense of her sister-in-law's death and partly because she knew how important it was to Ian to have one, let alone two, living relatives. Nevertheless, she couldn't ignore the constant yearning to give birth to a child of her own; it was a concealed open wound that would never heal.

Not wishing to tempt fate, up to now, they hadn't chosen Christian names for the babies. Given that they were part of the Lundy dynasty and so would inherit their surname, it seemed only right that some forenames should come from Ian's family.

"Let's wet their heads," Ian interrupted her musings, and they went down to the drawing room. They clinked champagne glasses and drank in silence until Fiona spoke.

"Here's to your black hair and Anne's fair locks. I've been thinking about their future … and ours. Before the registration of births, the christening, and signing the formal adoption papers, we need to work out something else."

"Which is?" He looked at her expectantly.

"It's about our wedding. I've had second thoughts."

His face fell, and for a moment she wondered what the problem was. Then the penny dropped.

"Don't look so worried, sweetheart, not about marrying you! I've decided that I don't want a register office – I want to do it all properly and soon. Even if you are pregnant when you go up the aisle, normally one gets married and then has children. Looking at those two upstairs, who are officially orphans, the least we can do is start them off with a halfway happy, normal family unit." She wondered, but only for a moment, whether or not to mention her other reason and chose to be honest. "I want a proper church wedding. It would be better for my mother."

Ian grimaced, and she knew that he could not, nor would he ever forget, let alone forgive how her mother had made his mother suffer all those years ago.

"She's getting worse almost by the day," Fiona explained.

"What do you mean? She seemed her usual awful self when we were at the meeting in Malcolm's office the morning after Anne died."

"I've mentioned it before, but she's becoming senile. It's called Alzheimer's disease, and there's no cure."

Whatever her mother's faults – and she had many – Fiona still loved her. The elderly Dowager hated the idea of Fiona and Ian getting married at all, but at least if it was a big church wedding, the Dowager Duchess would be hard pressed to suggest that it wasn't a proper marriage.

Fiona thought again about not being able to produce a son for Ian and a grandchild for her mother: a lump began to swell in her throat, and she was on the verge of tears. Then she realised how lucky she was, brightened, and continued more light-heartedly.

"And I'm still terrified that you will tire of me and run off with a younger model, so I want something worth remembering."

Ian kissed her gently on the lips. "Not a chance, you're stuck with me."

"For better or worse, richer or poorer until death do us part," she prompted.

"Fiona, there's nothing I wouldn't do to make you happy, but there is a real problem about a church wedding." He grimaced again. "I'm Jewish."

"I know, but you're not a practising Jew."

"You're right, only by birth and race. I lost my faith in any deity, or what little there was left of it, after witnessing my mother's slow, agonising death."

"That's no problem, then," she replied. "My family are the same and only ever go to church at Christmas – unless there's a wedding or something. MP knows that we live in a heathen and secular age."

"MP?" Ian asked.

"The Reverent Michael Porter, the vicar of Appledore and the island of Lundy, the nearest thing my family have to a father confessor. Don't worry, he'll work out how we can kill at least three birds with one stone."

"Three birds?" he asked again.

"Your conversion to Christianity, our wedding in the sight of God, and the christening of the twins," she said, smiling sweetly at him.

The banns of marriage were duly read three times at Bath Abbey, and there being no objection, the wedding was fixed for December, which allowed more than enough time for Ian's conversion.

Ian was amazed at how quick and easy it was to become a Christian. Apparently, all that was required was a brief talk with MP and to sort out the time and place for the christening. Given that he was an adult, godparents were not required.

Hence, early one Friday evening in November, Fiona and he booked into the Royal Hotel, a delightful seventeenth-century inn on Barnstable Street in Bideford. They were soon ensconced in its snug when the Reverent Michael Porter bounced across to meet them.

"So, what do you believe in, Ian?" The pastor picked up his pint of Badgers Best, thinking Ian would need a few moments to think.

But Ian's response was immediate. "Land."

"I beg your pardon?" The glass hadn't even reached the vicar's lips.

"Freehold property has been the only reliable thing in England for the last two thousand years."

Seemingly unfazed, MP grasped his ale again and took a couple of hearty gulps. Then, after once again placing the pint glass back onto the table, he reached into a cardigan pocket for a much-used, battered copy of the christening service, which he handed to Ian. "Best you know what you are getting into!"

The three of them then enjoyed a rather drunken dinner together.

At the local church the next morning, MP did the honours with the holy water, and afterwards, they celebrated an even more liquid lunch at the hotel, with Ian and Fiona returning to Bath later that evening.

It was all a very far cry from the years of study of the Torah and teaching required by would-be converts to Judaism, Ian thought, as he stored his baptism candle in his bedside table.

He tried not to think of his poor mother and her aspirations about him becoming a rabbi: instead, he remembered what Nietzsche had said: "What men did for God, they now do for money," – or in my case, for a woman, he thought.

CHAPTER FORTY-FIVE

To celebrate the first anniversary of its publication in December 1967, ten thousand copies of *The Bath Way* were printed, containing one hundred and twenty pages in full colour. Its entire first page, usually devoted to a soft-focus portrait of the most socially-eligible local bride-to-be, was replaced with a wedding photograph set against a backdrop of Bath Abbey. Below this was printed,

THE WEDDING OF THE YEAR
THE SOCIAL EVENT OF 1967

The next six pages contained dozens of photographs of the happy couple, groups of their guests, the Pump Room with its tables piled high with wedding gifts, and the wedding breakfast.

The magazine had surpassed itself by the lines of glowing comment, which were interspersed among the images.

Witnessed by the hundreds inside Bath Abbey, the marriage was solemnised by family pastor the Reverent Michael Porter, vicar of Bideford and the island of Lundy, of the Honourable Fiona Florence Abigail Symons, only daughter of Marmaduke the late 3rd Earl of Lundy and the Dower Duchess Emily, and Mr Ian Morris of Pulteney Street, Bath. Helen Beer presided at the organ, robustly providing the majestic, matrimonial music which filled the length of the great building. The bride, attired in a beautiful gown of white crêpe de chine was attended by six bridesmaids and her maid of honour, Mrs Linda Fraker. She was given away by Mr Malcolm Austwick, and Mr Ford Fraker acted in the capacity of best man. Large crowds of well-wishers gathered outside the Abbey.

The bride wore a travelling costume of mole grey and a white trimmed hat.

The honeymoon is to be spent in the West Indies, at the Coral Reef Club in Barbados.

Few, if any, would have seen any connection with the full-page advertisement placed by the *First Bath and District Perfect Thrift Building Society (established 1840)* of fifteen Queen Square, offering favourable mortgages for house buyers and all other types of property. It had been the London banker Toby Stafford's brain-child, because Bath Corporation had run low on funds and had cut lending to home-buyers by three quarters.

Instead of just getting planning permissions and selling onto a builder, Bath Estates would now construct and sell the houses and flats. Unable to find a suitable lender, Toby hit on the idea of buying and owning their own building society so that every would be buyer was assured of a mortgage.

The First Bath, as it was known, was a fully-terminating society and would cease to exist when all its members had a house – which was about to be the case. As Stafford explained, all Ian had to do was become a member and pay off its existing manager. They would then own a vehicle that was totally controlled by Bath Estates, every penny received from loan repayments going to the Society. The bankers would love the security and creative accounting would take care of the rest: the thousands of individual mortgages to be granted would provide a five-percent dividend every year for twenty-five years.

Ian thought back a few months as he walked down from the hotel reception to their bungalow on the tropical beach.

"I suppose you'll want a honeymoon after such a fancy wedding," Ian said after a particularly-fraught meeting about guests, the wedding outfits, and caterers: he, for one, would welcome a break after all the fuss.

"Most certainly," Fiona replied.

"A few days in the country – why don't we go back to the Royal at Bideford? Quiet, off the beaten track; what do you think?"

Fiona hadn't thought much of the idea at all and wished above all else to exchange the bleak, dark, English winter for warmth and sunshine.

"I want to go where my parents used to take us every year when we were growing up," she said. "Come Boxing Day, the Rolls Royce would be outside the front door, with the servants lined up and waving us off. Those were the days: we were rich and without a care in the world; I just took it all so for granted."

Ian made no comment knowing that "servants" would no doubt have included his mother. It brought back his own memories of how Fiona's mother had insisted on female staff curtseying and the horror of, as a child of eight, coming back from boarding school for the first time to the tied cottage provided by Fiona's parents: particularly, he remembered the galvanised Elson chemical bucket behind the backdoor. Fiona reminisced about luxurious, tropical holidays, and his thoughts went back to privies outside a hovel in the woods of the Rowas Estate.

Fiona had taken his silence as agreement. "Barbados it is, then."

Ian said nothing and wondered if their differences were really bridgeable or whether he was making a dreadful mistake. But then, he couldn't imagine life without her and so knew that he needed to make it all work.

Fiona Symons, now Morris, fingered the novelty of the wedding ring on her finger and smiled. She had forgotten how wonderful the Coral Reef Club was; the family had first stayed when Budge O'Hara and his wife had opened the luxury hotel in the fifties. With its old-school, understated, and very English approach to comfort, it was the quintessential country house in the tropics and probably the best on the island.

Along the coast from Holetown, it continued to attract some British aristocracy, but now more and more of its well-healed visitors were business people from both sides of the Atlantic. On the veranda of their luxurious cottage surrounded by the glorious gardens with the purple bougainvillea and palm trees in the warm afternoon sunshine, she was at peace with the world. It was a million miles away from the Bath winter they had fled from thirty-six hours earlier.

Ian quietly came up behind her and placed his hands over her eyes.

She gently removed them but still held one in both of hers. "I was just thinking how perfect everything is. You, us, the twins back home. I so love not being poor anymore and this exquisite place. And it's all due to clever you." She kissed his hand and let it go.

"And you," he replied, sitting next to her. "After all, Pera Road, which began it all, would not have happened without your help."

Fiona said nothing and Ian continued.

"But that's only the start. All being well, there are millions of pounds to be made out of Bath Estates."

He thought about his good fortune because of Abraham and Naomi. Then, there was all the surplus railway property owned by Beaconsfield Properties and Green Park Station, which he hadn't even told Fiona about.

She interrupted his thoughts. "Your ambition terrifies me sometimes. Please promise that you won't let it destroy our relationship or Bath."

"I promise," he sat on an accompanying sun lounger, "and that, my darling, reminds me why I went up to the hotel reception desk."

He withdrew an envelope from his shirt pocket. "My wedding present for you," he said and handed her the opened airmail letter before adding, "and also, so it's less confusing, for Ruth and James." He had loved the fact that Fiona thought it only fair to name the twins after his parents.

Fiona withdrew the compliment slip from Malcolm Austwick's letter, which read *Welcome to the family!* Attached to it was a buff-coloured, official declaration with a large, red seal.

STATUTORY DECLARATION OF NAME
CHANGE

I, IAN LUNDY of 12 GREAT PULTENEY STREET,

BATH formerly known as IAN AND YANN MORRIS ,

do solemnly and sincerely declare that:

1. I absolutely and entirely renounce relinquish and abandon the use
of my said former names of IAN AND YANN MORRIS and
assume
adopt and determine to take and use from the date hereof the name of
 IAN LUNDY in substitution of my former names of IAN
AND YANN MORRIS .

2. I shall at all times hereafter in all records, deeds, documents, and
other writings and in all actions and proceedings as well as in all
dealings and transactions and on all occasions whatsoever use and
subscribe the said name of IAN LUNDY as my name in
substitution
for my former names of IAN AND YANN MORRIS so
relinquishing as aforesaid to the intent that I may hereafter be
called known or distinguished not by the former name of IAN
AND YANN MORRIS but by the name of IAN LUNDY
only.

3. I authorise and require all persons at all times to designate, describe,
and address me by the adopted name of IAN LUNDY .

It was signed by Ian and witnessed by Malcolm Austwick.

"And what would your mother think?" Fiona asked later over
dinner.

"I think she'd understand," he said. "She always said that one's
character was more important than one's name. After all, she did the same
thing to help make things work …"

Fiona looked puzzled.

"Oh, I don't suppose I've ever told you but, Morris isn't my real
family name. It was originally Morrishowl: the immigration official in Hull

where my father got off the ship from Poland after the First World War, couldn't spell it and so just wrote Morris."

"Morrishowl, Morrishowl," Fiona said slowly, savouring it. She lifted her wine glass.

"Here's to Morrishowl." Pausing, she added, "Morrishowl to the Lundy name in only two generations. Wow. That's impressive, Ian Lundy."

"Thank you, Mrs Lundy."

CHAPTER FORTY-SIX

1968, a new year: it was good to be back at work after a month of idleness in the sun and to see Trish again.

"How was the honeymoon?" she asked.

"Great but expensive," Ian replied as he settled behind his desk. "Now, I've got to pay for it. Bring me up to date."

It had been a pleasure working with Trish over the previous months, and knowing him so well, she had anticipated the question and handed him a single sheet of figures. Its twelve headed columns and fifteen horizontal lines below showed the money in for the last month and projected for the next twelve: eleven of the dozen columns showed a profit at the foot of the page. He quickly looked them over.

"Well done, Trish, these look great, but why the loss this month?"

"You'll see I've added a new outgoing heading – advertising, an executive decision I made in your absence regarding *The Bath Way*. Al rang me just after you left about the property supplement. He wanted to launch it this month but was very nervous about the possible lack of interest from potential advertisers. So, I told him we would take the whole supplement, all sixteen pages for six issues, and he was over the moon."

"I bet he was. What's that going to cost?" He knew that she'd have a good reason for the extra outlay.

"Nothing, I've sold it all. Once I put the word out that our agency was taking the front page, all the other estate agents couldn't wait to jump in. I wouldn't mind guessing that the supplement covers virtually every house sale in Bath, not to mention the new flat developments."

Yet again, as he had done in Barbados, Ian realised how good she was and what a disaster it would have been to lose her. The original spark between them had never gone away. The excitement of success bound them together, but now it was deeper than that, and not for the first time, he asked himself, why it had been Fiona that he had fallen in love with. He and Trish spoke the same language, had the same ambitions born out of lack of privilege. But unlike Trish, Ian knew that he had required something more – loath to explore the idea further, he pushed the thought away.

"I had plenty of time to think while lying on a beach with nothing to do."

"You? Nothing to do?" Trish laughed.

"It's time for your partnership and everything else you asked for six months ago."

"Really?" Her eyes lit up. "Are you sure, Ian? You know I haven't qualified yet."

"I've never been more certain. You were absolutely right, I hadn't given you enough authority in the past, and I'm not going to let that happen again."

"Thank you Ian, that's very generous," she said softly.

"Good, I'll get McCloy to prepare all the paperwork. And by the way, it's no longer Ian Morris. I've changed my name to Ian Lundy by deed poll – so, the firm is Lundy, Traynor & Company."

"Yet again a new name," she said, laughing.

They agreed to go for a celebratory drink with Fiona after work, but as soon as she returned to her desk – and for the third time – Trish, feeling extraordinarily happy, ordered yet another new brass plate for the front door.

The three of them were in their local, the Barley Mow. Just around the corner from Pulteney Street, it was an ungentrified English pub – cosy, casual, and unmessed with at the corner of Bathwick Street and Daniel Mews. The walls were covered in ancient metal signs for beers and tinctures, with the tables and chairs a mishmash of Victoriana around a roaring fire. The live music was in full swing, and the attentive landlord, Nick Etheridge, served their drinks.

"Here's to your partnership," Fiona said, toasting Trish. "I want you to know that I was all in favour when Ian asked me about it in Barbados."

"I didn't know he had discussed it with you. Thank you, Fiona, so good to have your support," Trish replied curtly.

Ian felt the tension between the two women and so hastily changed the subject. "Trish, how's your friend Norman these days?"

"All right." Trish relaxed. "He has a new boyfriend and is less fearful now that the new law legalising homosexuality has come in. I'm sure he's right that it'll be a long time, if ever, before it's properly accepted. Time came for me to move out."

Ian had lost touch with the charge nurse who had looked after him so well and been so kind and attentive at the Royal United Hospital.

"I'm so glad he's found someone else to replace that ..." – he was going to say "bastard" but remembered Fiona was with him – "his last friend, he deserves a little happiness in his life. So, where are you living now?"

"St John's, they've been marvellous. I have a lovely little flat in Chapel Court until I find something else. I think I'd like to buy somewhere – maybe one of the blocks that we're involved in."

"Makes perfect sense with the money from the new partnership," Fiona added.

Ian's thoughts stayed with St John's Hospital as the two women jousted. Whenever he wandered into Chapel Court in the centre of the city, he was transported back to how Bath might would have looked eight hundred years ago.

Named after St John the Baptist, it had been founded by Bishop Fitzjocelyn of Bath in 1174, gifted to him by a grateful monarch – the Bishop's fluent Italian had persuaded the Pope that Henry II was innocent of Thomas Beckett's murder. Later elected Archbishop of Canterbury, Fitzjocelyn became paralysed on his journey to take up the position and sadly died.

The hospital for the poor had been going for nearly eight hundred years, and it was almost certainly the city's oldest, largest, and richest charity. Its massive medieval land holding inside the old city's walls at

Westgate had been long built on and the acres of farmland outside turned into hundreds of houses for Bath's middle class over the last hundred years.

Being so close to the healing hot spa waters of the Hot Bath and the Cross Bath, St John's survived the calamitous Black Death of the fourteenth century and, thanks to nearby St Bellotts Hospital in Beau Street, it eventually tamed leprosy. Luckily, its secular nature kept it out of Henry VIII's grasp and untouched by the Reformation two centuries later.

Just after eleven o'clock on Saturday, April 25 1942, the first of six German bombs of over a thousand pounds each blew off the whole west elevation of the charity's Elizabethan Abbey Church House in a matter of seconds. One of the hospital's greatest treasures and the oldest building in Bath, it took ten years to restore and, unusually, some old-timers felt the new facade was an improvement on the one destroyed.

When the hospital's ownership of so much prime property on and around Milsom Street became apparent from his map, out of curiosity, Ian had obtained a copy of their latest accounts. Reading between the lines, he reckoned that the value of these holdings in 1965 was an eye-watering five million pounds, used to provide alms houses and accommodation for the needy.

"Ian," Fiona brought him back to the present, "I was just saying that Trish must come to us soon – it's about time we held a proper dinner party."

Later, as they walked arm in arm back to Great Pulteney Street, Fiona cautioned him.

"You may say I'm stupid, but Trish is still smitten, and the sooner we find someone for her, the safer I will feel."

CHAPTER FORTY-SEVEN

The dinner party was "very much for the business", as Fiona put it, and the first they'd ever arranged together. It seemed to be going well – she always fancied that eight people were ideal around the circular table.

On her left, Toby Stafford, Ian's urbane banker friend, was getting on well with Trish, who, thankfully, seemed taken with him.

On her right, she had placed her friend Richard Wyatt, one of the Mayor of Bath Corps of Honorary Guides. He was deep in conversation with – she relished the thought – Ian. Hopefully, Richard was furthering her crusade in persuading her husband that Bath was worth more standing and restored rather than flattened by bulldozers.

To her satisfaction, seating Donna Lodge between the two men had worked – Fiona could see her tourist brain whirring away as she lapped up Richard's every word.

Fiona knew Debbie Smith, Ian's suggestion to make up the numbers, from childhood, but not well, because Debbie was a Roman Catholic, and they had attended different schools and mixed in different circles. Her late parents had always worked abroad, and Fiona assumed there was family money given her house in Brock Street and that Debbie was a lady of leisure.

Seating Al Giles next to Debbie also seemed to be working well, although he seemed irritated by the attention Donna was paying Richard. Fiona was intrigued, for according to Ian, the two were locked in a constant battle over their respective editorial territories at *The Bath Way* – something of a love-hate relationship, she guessed.

"You were at Eton, weren't you?" Fiona asked Toby for Trish's benefit.

He nodded but didn't elaborate.

"Did you see much of my brother Alistair?" She immediately regretted having brought up her brother's time at the school.

"Yes, we were in the same house, but he was only there for a short while," Toby replied. "I think he left after the first year or so."

Fiona quickly changed the subject and said to Trish, "You should get Toby to take you to his alma mater sometime – it's a very impressive place. How many prime ministers has the place produced? Twenty?"

"Not quite," he replied and turned to Trish. "Would you like to see my old school?"

"Very much," Trish smiled in reply, grateful to learn what an alma mater was.

Mission accomplished, Fiona looked to her right to hear Donna ask a favour of Richard.

"As you probably know, *The Bath Way* now has a tourist supplement. Could I persuade you to do a short article for the next edition?"

Richard thought for a moment and agreed as long as he could have complete editorial control.

"I wouldn't want the Corps harmed in any way," he explained. "Have either of you ever taken the tour?" he asked Donna and Ian.

Fiona smiled as it sounded like a doctor prescribing a cure. Donna had, but Ian shook his head.

"Well, we must remedy that situation, Ian. Let's make a date, and I'll do one of my specials for you. How about tomorrow? Or when would suit you?"

Ian slowly nodded his agreement, and Fiona was delighted as her husband replied, "Not tomorrow, but soon, I promise."

Clearly, Richard had worked on the article overnight, for it was delivered to Donna by hand before lunch the next day, and it made a great front page for her supplement.

'GLOBETROTTERS' - THE MAYOR OF BATH'S CORPS OF HONORARY GUIDES

Most volunteers are retired men and women, who take groups of people on a two hour walking visit that includes many of the city's highlights. No charge is made for the tour, nor tips accepted.

Each day of the year except Christmas morning, dozens of the guides set out from the Pump Room in all weathers. In addition, during the longer days of the summer months when Bath is at its most splendid, there are early-evening walks.

These are ordinary men and women who are proud to share their enthusiasm and love of their city. There is no uniform, and an honorary guide is simply recognised by the blue shield badge he or she wears. This bears the coat of arms for the city representing its wall, its river, its thermal spring, and the sword of Saint Paul, one of the patron saints of Bath Abbey.

The Guides were first mentioned thirty-five years ago after the Mayor of Bath and local historian, Alderman Thomas Sturge-Cotterell, had been regularly showing visitors around Bath on Boxing Day and Easter mornings. Credited as the man who invented modern-city tourism, he loved Bath's history and heritage and even took a trip to Rome to help promote Italy's ancient links with the city.

Sturge-Cotterell went on to produce and publish an historic map of Bath showing the locations of famous buildings and those houses where celebrated occupants had previously resided. The properties were clearly identified by bronze metal plaques fixed to their exteriors. This again was Sturge-Cotterell's idea, and he approached a local architect, Samuel Reay, to design them. Each bronze plaque cost less than five pounds, and the project was funded by the city's Corporation towards the end of the last century. The first of the forty-five plaques commemorated Sir William Herschel, the astronomer who discovered Uranus. That was at nineteen New King Street and was unveiled in 1898. It is believed *that London's own blue-plaque scheme to denote buildings with prior renowned residents was probably modelled on that of Bath.*

By the time of his death in 1950 at twenty-two Great Pulteney Street, Sturge-Cotterell had assured that the walks by honorary volunteers was firmly established in Bath.

More recently, and within the last decade, formal training sessions lasting three months were introduced for new volunteer guides, and local experts were engaged to give lectures on a wide range of subjects.

As far as anyone can remember, no walk has ever been cancelled …

The manager, Yamca, fussed over them as they settled for lunch at Joya in New Market Row. She ran one of the best Italian restaurants in Bath – it was Toby Stafford's favourite

His period of secondment to Bath University had finished three months earlier, and he had returned to the Cassofiori Bank in London and a promotion. Shortly afterwards, Ian had travelled up to Leadenhall Street and enquired as to the possibility of moving his business to this private bank. Toby was pleased – apart from his liking for this man of his own age, Ian's desire for the expertise and kudos of a City Bank, coupled with the privacy and discretion such an establishment offered, made good sense. Aware of his rapidly-expanding empire, Ian felt sure that the incestuous relationships between Bath's various professionals and institutions made conflicts of interests unavoidable and indiscretions inevitable. Toby also saw an opportunity to become involved in Ian's blossoming enterprises.

The minimum assets of one hundred thousand pounds of liquid funds required to open an account with the Cassofiori proved a temporary difficulty but was solved by Toby arranging an appropriate indemnity from a Lloyds underwriter. The banker's first suggestion had been a complete review of all Ian's business ventures. He was using this review's completion as an excuse for lunch. It would also give him the opportunity of meeting Trish Traynor again after their trip to Eton.

"So, what's the verdict?" Ian asked once the waitress had served their drinks.

"Well, I'll give you the good news first." Toby knew how Ian hated criticism.

"My people think you've done extremely well and have a great opportunity to turn a good business into a great one. The various income streams are capable of making you very wealthy."

Ian sipped his Campari soda. "And the bad news?"

Toby sighed, knowing Ian would resent what he was about to say, but he had no choice. "The business lacks an overall strategy and is therefore vulnerable. There are too many worrying management gaps, which means it could easily spin out of control."

Ian's self-satisfaction disappeared, and Toby watched his defences go up. He had expected this and waited for some sort of sarcastic response – it wasn't long coming.

"Is that all – the business, my business is out of control? Are you sure there isn't anything else I've got completely wrong?" Ian barked.

"Most of the issues are easily fixed, but the most important thing missing is a long-term goal. You need to reconcile your present frenetic efforts with what you hope to eventually achieve. What is it that you want from life? For instance, how and where do you expect to be in say five or even ten years' time?"

Ian didn't immediately respond. Their starter from the fixed lunch menu, a Carbonara, arrived. Both men ate in silence. The pasta was superb, and Toby understood why the restaurant was such a success.

Once his plate was empty, Ian started to talk. "Three years ago, the answer was simple," he said. "All I wanted was to be rich, so rich that I would want for nothing – enough of what they call fuck-you money. I needed to justify my mother's years of struggle and the humiliation of poverty. I sought revenge, to punish Alistair Lundy and his mother – literally wipe them out and everything their type stand for."

Toby said nothing, just listened.

"Now, everything has changed. Alistair's dead, his mother has dementia, and I've married into the family. I've adopted the heir to the title and his sister, even changed my name to Lundy and became a Christian, would you believe? Apart from that last thing, my mother would approve." He laughed mirthlessly. "So, what do I want?"

Again, Toby remained silent.

"Up to now, it's all been so obvious, so simple – and with every new idea, the money just pours in. I have the Midas touch where all turns to gold, and the city of Bath is there for the taking. So, what is the ultimate point?"

"Rare and medium rare," Yamca arrived with two plates of rump steaks.

"I'm the rare one," said Ian.

"Only steak-wise," Toby smiled when they were left alone. "You're not so rare, Ian. Many of the Bank's clients are self-made men and have become hugely successful. Richer beyond their wildest dreams, but they still crave more. I've had similar conversations with them, and it usually comes down to power, influence, and respectability. We at Cassofiori describe the last as the Manor House Syndrome."

Ian was familiar with the saying. He laughed, immediately lightening the mood.

"Toby, I promise you that the last thing I want is to give it all up in exchange for some dilapidated, roof-leaking manor house in deepest Wiltshire, running the local hunt, and lording it over the natives. Ralph Allen said much the same thing two hundred years ago."

"So, are you suggesting we should regard you as a modern-day Ralph Allen?"

Ian chuckled. "You said it, not me."

Toby raised his glass of Valpolicella. "First Beau Nash, now Ralph Allen – where will it all end, I wonder. Cheers." He became serious.

"How much do you think you will spend on advertising this year?"

"I don't know. It will be what it will be," Ian answered.

Toby's silence re-enforced the point. Eventually, Ian felt compelled to add,

"About ten thousand, I suppose."

"What do you know about the advertising business? Or, to be specific, agency commissions?"

"Nothing."

"Well, that's the first thing that should be addressed. You need to set up an advertising agency, so that whenever you or your organisations place an advert anywhere, and I mean literally every single advert, you will get a commission of fifteen percent. At your estimation, that will be fifteen hundred pounds this year. Next, what do you expect your profit to look like next year?"

"Probably twelve thousand – I'd certainly hope not less. Trish would know. She started doing management accounts once I made her a partner in the agency business."

"Good move – she's a very smart young woman," Toby said. Attractive too, he thought. "So, what does that tell you about the way forward?"

Ian appeared puzzled and didn't answer. Toby thought for a moment, seeking how to provide a clue. He looked around the now packed and noisy restaurant.

"OK, Ian. Tell me, what are your thoughts about this restaurant?"

"Great. Superb Italian food, excellent service – a little goldmine."

"How can you possibly know that?" Toby was tucking into the steak – superb beef cooked to perfection.

"It's always full."

"But have you considered that it might be better if it was less full, even completely empty?"

Ian didn't answer but took another mouthful of steak, so Toby continued.

"Come on, Ian. I'm sure you've heard the expression 'Turnover is vanity, profit is sanity, but cash flow is reality.' If every meal served here costs just one penny more than it's sold for, it would be better to sell no meals. Even worse would be a scenario where projected costs are unknown: then, the restaurant owners wouldn't even know whether they should open or not."

"But surely that's why we pay accountants to produce annual accounts."

Toby smiled and shook his head. "You know Ian, for someone so market-canny, you are incredibly management-illiterate. Accounts are a just snapshot of a single moment in the past, one minute to midnight on the last day of the year. Worse still, they are often adjusted, which really means rigged, to minimise the tax payable by the shareholders."

"So, what are you suggesting I do?" Ian asked.

"Well, for a start, you could look for a good finance director."

Ian groaned before asking, "And where do I find one I can live with?"

Toby's smile got broader still. "I thought you'd never ask! You're looking at him. I can even demonstrate how I will cost you nothing."

"Go on."

"Do you know how large insurance brokers' commissions are?"

Ian said nothing.

"At least twenty percent of an annual premium but often higher."

Toby then explained how every house and flat that Bath Estates built could be sold on a ground-lease for, say, ninety-nine years. "No need to give away the freehold of the land. God bless William the Conqueror and our feudal property laws. The ground lease will contain various restrictions, many obsolete such as not hunting in the Royal Forests but also some much more important – including one that would require every house owner to insure the property through your company. That way, you, as in Bath

Estates, get to choose the insurer and keep commissions. Do you see what I mean?"

Ian saw it immediately. Strange that he had not thought of it himself, it was so obvious.

"Yes, it does make good sense and you're right that with everything growing so quickly, we need someone to spot the angles and keep track of the costs"

"So, do I come onto the payroll?" Toby had loved his time in Bath and was keen to return permanently. "And are we ordering coffee?"

"Definitely, Toby. But I'm afraid it's no to the coffee. I've promised to join Fiona for a Mayor's Guide tour and need to get going."

Toby was happy to settle the bill, and, knowing that neither Ian nor Fiona would be at fifteen Queen Square, he would wander over and tell Trish the news.

CHAPTER FORTY-EIGHT

Richard Wyatt was as good as his word. Urged by Fiona to be thorough, his special tour took much longer than usual. He was accustomed to a great deal of walking; he enjoyed it. Sensibly dressed in stout boots under his flared jeans, a reefer jacket, and brightly-knitted gloves, he was well protected against the January weather, comfortably striding along Parade Gardens. His thinning hair was covered against the chill wind by a woollen hat presented to him by a grateful regular.

Ian, in his business suit, overcoat, and leather gloves, felt overdressed and cold. The tour spanned nearly three thousand years, starting with the legend of Bladud and leprosy in 860 BC, and finishing with Bath University receiving its royal charter in 1966.

As usual, Richard spoke completely without notes. He began by describing three local great events – the battle of Dryham in 577 AD, Alfred the Great three centuries later, and lastly, England's first coronation of a King – Edgar, crowned in Bath in 973 AD.

Ian was intrigued and then much interested to learn of, as Richard put it, Bath's twenty-five big moments.

After three hours, the exhausted, cold, and tired listeners mutinied and demanded a high tea in Milsom Street. Still, Richard wasn't finished, and the three listened politely as he continued to hold forth over Welsh rarebit on toast and Earl Grey.

"So, let me tell you about where we are sitting here, in Somersetshire Buildings." Richard's knowledge seemed endless. "Daniel Milsom was a school master and wine cooper who owned an extensive house outside the northern wall at the top of the road." He gestured north towards George Street and in the direction of the Assembly Rooms.

"Behind it – here to the south – was his large, very large garden; it stretched all the way down to the bottom of this street. Now, two hundred and seven years ago to the day, on 20 February 1761, he did a spectacular deal with the City Corporation. He agreed to build Milsom Street: it was to be some fifty-three feet wide, and for this, he would be granted building leases for five grand houses – to be erected on this very spot by Thomas Baldwin, the city architect ..."

"Enough!" Fiona protested, "I'm all guided out, Richard. Finish your tea before it gets cold."

Ian happily turned to her, put an arm around her shoulder, and kissed her cheek. "You see, darling? Nothing changes, the developers have always been part of Bath," and as if to nail the coffin lid down, he asked Richard innocently,

"Do you happen to know the terms of the ground rent leases?"

"I certainly do," Richard answered triumphantly, "ninety-nine years at four shillings for every foot of frontage onto Milsom Street."

CHAPTER FORTY-NINE

Fiona had gone to gone to visit her mother at Combe Grove, and Ian sat alone in the drawing room as night fell.

He had planned to watch television. '*Til Death Us Do Part* made him laugh and Johnny Speight's dialogue was brilliantly funny, but Alf Garnett's continual reference to yids and coon's blood made him wince: he wasn't in the mood for a comedy programme involving racism and immigration. This was especially poignant given the recent arrival of an additional twelve thousand Asian refugees driven from Kenya. These desperate people, who arrived in only what they stood up in, were greeted by fear and resentment stirred up by Enoch Powell's "Rivers of Blood" speech; horrendous – he would never forget the politician's classic quote,

"Those the gods wish to destroy they first make mad."

Ian's mother had been a penniless migrant; because of her, he had made good, and yet it still wasn't enough.

He thought back to a recent meeting with Cecil Weir, the Council's housing-officer-cum-social-worker. Weir had told him about one young, homeless lad – despite being born and bred in the UK, it had proved virtually impossible to house him because of apathy and racism.

Malik Ceiros, the result of a brief encounter between a Somalian sailor and a Cardiff prostitute, had never met the father he was apparently named after. His mother had died from drug abuse before he was out of short trousers.

Now approaching twenty, he had been living for a nightmare year on the streets of Bath, and he survived by begging: passers-by gave him small change simply to get him out of their sight. It seemed that many of the "good citizens of Bath" preferred to believe that people such as him didn't exist and that there were no poor in their beautiful city.

Constantly moved on and off the street by police, Malik apparently spent most of his nights sleeping with another lost soul in the small courtyard behind the Forum Cinema. He was young and, behind the curtain of floppy, curly hair, quite a good-looking boy, so he needed to avoid the weirdos and the drunks who wanted to kick the shit out of him for a bit of fun after the pubs emptied.

Ian wandered around the house. He felt restless and tried to work out why. He acknowledged that, give or take a few days, it had taken him seven years to discover that wealth and financial security were not enough. Ever since his lunch with Toby, he'd been thinking about one question: what did he want from life?

Then there'd been the tour with Richard when he'd experienced the guide's passion for history and architecture. It had highlighted the gap between Fiona's enthusiasm and his lukewarm attitude about the city's past, which, out of consideration for her, he concealed most of the time. He had to accept that there was no quick fix for his lack of understanding and empathy, even though he knew Fiona was right about Traditional Bath: quite simply, he preferred modern buildings.

Finally, he thought about whether her yearning for a child could ever be overcome: despite her evident love and affection for the twins, she desperately wanted to have her own and his child. Fiona rarely mentioned it, but he sensed that every time she cuddled either Ruth or James, she remembered. As always whenever Ian identified a problem, he sought an instant resolution, but the position was insoluble.

But what if the Swiss doctors who told Fiona she would never conceive again were right? Damn it, he decided he would hire the best doctors in Harley Street for a second opinion, whatever the cost. Then he cursed himself for yet again thinking that money could always solve everything.

As the business had expanded, become more specialised, and new staff were hired, he was conscious that Fiona's involvement had diminished. This was not only due to her ever-increasing enjoyment of the twins – her daily routine was rarely challenging, and Ian wondered if this made her dwell on being unable to bear her own children. In the meantime, her mother had become more burdensome as the dementia worsened.

Knowing that little could be done immediately about Fiona's desire for a baby, he sought another solution, and an idea came to mind. The lease of Great Pulteney Street had only a couple of years to run, and they had, from time to time, discussed buying something. Fiona hankered after her early life in the country, saying that the rural life would be much better for the children – adding that, anyway, the goldfish bowl of the city was not for her. Ian was not fussed either way as long as he could get to work easily.

All their seeking came to nothing. Neither wanted the hassle, disruption, and unquantifiable restoration cost involved with converting ancient, old houses often sub-divided with odd-sized and numerous poky rooms. It then occurred to them that they could build a new house, and the idea of a modern home greatly appealed to Ian. To his surprise, Fiona remarked how she would love to design and build them a house in the country. Perhaps a distraction was exactly what was needed, Ian thought – but sadly, their search for a suitable piece of land proved equally futile: everything proved impractical or untouchable, being in the Green Belt and listed.

The idea came alive again some months later when Ian noticed something in Trish's weekly agenda under *New Sale Instructions*. It was just a single line.

"Derelict quarry watchman's house and land at Murhill."

"Not much to tell," she had said. "A letter came in two days ago describing it as a ruin with just the stone walls and roofless – it dates back to 1805 when the stone quarry first opened. The house was abandoned when worked stopped in the 1930s, leaving just a lot of land and streams running down to the river and canal. From what I can tell, the only thing going for it is a fantastic view solely enjoyed by the sheep grazing there."

Ian had heard of the old Murhill quarry with its tramway down to the Kennett and Avon Canal, along which the stone had been taken three miles south-west to Bath and then onto Bristol. He remembered reading that some of the stone had even been used for the facade of the Temple Meads Railway Station in Bristol.

"Who's the seller?" he asked.

"Probate. It must be some trust that Austwicks are winding up."

"How much do they want for it?"

"They're waiting for us to tell them what we think. If you like, I could get out there to inspect tomorrow."

Ian thought for a moment.

"Don't worry, I've got an easy day," he said. "I'll go and have a look myself."

A few hours later, he finally found a telephone box near the Winsley Post Office and fished into his pocket for some change. He found the strange new shilling with *five pence* written on it and what had been two shillings or a florin, now called a ten pence, and rang Fiona.

"Are you busy?" he asked.

"Not particularly. The twins are having their nap, but Anna's here. Is there something you need me for?"

"I'll pick you up in about twenty minutes." He was starting to feel excited. "I want to show you something."

Fiona gasped as she looked down over the Limpley Stoke Valley.

"It's perfect, but I don't think the town planners will ever let you build."

"Let them try and stop us." He emphasised the "us" and went on. "Don't worry, I'll take care of them. The recent designation of the conservation area won't help, and I accept that the city will be difficult, but with the right architect, there's absolutely no reason why the quarryman's house can't be replaced. It's not as if no one has ever lived here, and let's hope the Preservation Trust won't be too narrow-minded. It will all come down to first-class design and materials – but is this something that you'd be happy to take on? I won't be able to devote much time to it."

She hesitated but then said enthusiastically,

"Yes, all right – why not? It could be amazing if we got there. But as you say, we need the all-important architect …"

"I'll put the word out." Ian, back in his comfort zone of solutions, was delighted to see that she seemed keen. "How do you feel about Frank Lloyd Wright?"

"I thought he was dead."

"He is, but I bet there's some modern young man out there itching to design and build a new Fallingwater."

It was Professor Stephen Vernon who found him after Ian's chance remark on the telephone when they were discussing the following stone re-cleaning project.

"You're looking for the best architect in England for modern houses? I would say that Mark Watson is your man." Vernon went on to describe how, after surviving D-Day and the war, Watson came home and won a travelling scholarship which took him back all over Europe to study buildings old and new. He had become one of Britain's most important post-war architects with commissions in the Middle East as well as England.
His breakthrough came when he built his own home, a single-storey modernist house – it won a RIBA medal.

"Yes, he's definitely your man," Vernon concluded. "Brilliant, expensive, and difficult but worth every penny if you can cope with and afford him. Mind you, before you start, make sure that you like what he's done, because he's single-minded and won't care a damn whether you accept his obsession with so-called Brutalist architecture. He's very much a take-it-or-leave-it sort of person." He paused and laughed. "It will be, as they say, a Marmite relationship: you'll either hate or love each other."

CHAPTER FIFTY

Toby trod very carefully in the weeks after Fiona's dinner party but was fascinated by Trish – she was quite unlike any other young woman he had ever met. His friends, mostly Old Etonians, had girlfriends from similar backgrounds to their own, and most, thanks to wealthy parents, didn't need to work for a living. Things were slowly changing, but these trendily-dressed "Sloane Rangers" adorned art galleries and up-market boutiques rather than engage with the gritty world of business frequented by Trish.

A further complication arose, because like himself, most of his women were from Roman-Catholic families, some dating back hundreds of years. This meant that relationships were chaste but had the advantage that they shared similar family values.

At first, he used his recent appointment as finance director as an excuse for meeting Trish, who was becoming ever more important in his big idea on how to develop the business. He managed to extend these meetings into the odd working lunch, and then one night, after a particularly-gruelling day together, he suggested a drink after work.

They walked around to the Abbey Hotel and sat outside to enjoy the beautiful May evening as Bath's mini rush-hour came to an end. Despite being in the heart of the city, Toby noticed that they could still hear birds singing in the trees of Parade Gardens opposite and even see, away to the east, fields of cows.

"What an amazing place," he said, "so unlike London and everywhere else. Here we sit in the middle of this Georgian wonderland with its hot springs, surrounded by wildlife – not to forget its surrounding seven green hills, just as in ancient Rome."

"You're right," Trish replied, "and I'm embarrassed to admit that I barely notice it anymore. I was born in Bath, grew up here, and have been in the city all my life: I take it all so for granted; I know nothing else."

They each had a couple glasses of wine, and Toby was pleased that Trish agreed to a meal even though she insisted on going Dutch. They went into the hotel for dinner, and as the meal progressed, Toby felt an increasing fondness for the petite brunette opposite him. With bright, hazel eyes and a few freckles across her pert, snub nose, he surmised she could easily have some Celtic blood, even possibly the odd Catholic in her ancestry – at least he hoped so.

Tipsy for the first time together, their conversation drifted away from work and to the personal. Trish told him about her background, her lack of a father, and her mother's struggle, who just about got by on a series of part-time, menial jobs: the single most important thing for Trish was her career and the success it brought. It gave her the financial independence that had been denied to her mother and which she craved above all else.

Inevitably, the conversation turned back to a discussion about Ian, and it was clear even to Toby's slightly befuddled brain that Trish's admiration of Ian went well beyond the business. She was very fond of him, but Toby couldn't work out whether there had been anything between them in the past: he discerned a sense of wistfulness which suggested not.

He told her about his time at Eton and Oxford before going into banking. He explained that he had simply done what was expected of him, and although his sisters were the first generation to have gone onto higher education, he had merely followed in his father's footsteps, as had his father before him.

Her background was so foreign, and whilst Toby realised that his world was a million miles away from hers, there was the bond of shared ambition – Ian. More importantly, Toby really enjoyed being with her, and they laughed a lot together.

He tried to persuade her otherwise, but she was adamant, and they split the bill. Trish declined his offer to walk her back to her flat. Feeling a bit sorry for himself, he returned to Miles Buildings, his beautiful but empty house and the appropriately-dour music of Leonard Cohen.

CHAPTER FIFTY-ONE

Dr Caroline Thomas was considered to be one of the foremost experts in gynaecology, with referrals from across the country. One such was a Mrs Lundy, who was here with her husband in her Harley Street waiting room. She re-read the notes from the Bath consultant.

Mrs Fiona Lundy, aged thirty-six, underwent an illegal termination of her first and only pregnancy in Switzerland seven years ago. Due to a post-operative infection, Mrs Lundy did not recover as hoped and was subsequently informed that it was highly unlikely that she would be able to conceive in the future. She presented to our clinic earlier for a series of tests after having kept a menstrual and temperature diary for the previous twelve weeks. My conclusion is that, despite her advancing years, she ovulates regularly, but her fallopian tubes have been irreparably damaged. This would be consistent with the earlier infection, and I did explain to Mrs Lundy that her chances of a geriatric pregnancy are extremely slim. However, she and her husband requested further investigations ...

Doctor Thomas did not look forward to the conversation with Mr and Mrs Lundy.

To take her mind off the depressing meeting at Harley Street, which realistically was impossible, Ian took Fiona to lunch at the Carlton Club. He had managed to arrange to meet the elusive Mark Watson there later in the afternoon, so he was pleased they had something else to talk about over the sombre lunch.

Ian recognised Watson as soon as he was brought into the drawing room by the club porter: they'd met before, but he couldn't recall where or when. The architect was dark-haired, of medium build, and probably in his mid-forties. He looked more like a country squire than a business professional. Wearing corduroy trousers, a twill shirt, a hand-knitted tie, and a tweed jacket, he was out of place in the elegance of the London club but exuded such self-assurance and poise that gave Ian confidence that he knew what he was doing. What was more, Watson remembered.

"You weren't called Lundy in those days," he said as he took a seat. "And you didn't have a beautiful wife either – or at least not with you." He smiled appreciatively at Fiona. "It was in Kingston, Jamaica, about five years ago at the Courteney Bay Hotel. I'd just finished the thing for Ian Flemming and was taking a break. I seem to recall you were doing something with a sugar plantation."

"Of course." Ian was struggling to think who could have introduced them back then, when Watson asked, "So, what can I do for you? Have you got your eye on something else in Jamaica?"

Fiona answered. "Much nearer to home, Mr Watson. We own a piece of land – around fifteen acres – about two miles south of Bath. It slopes down over a magical valley of fields, rivers, and woodland. I want to build an English Fallingwater there and have been told you are the only person clever enough to do it."

Fiona's on form, thought Ian: the flattery, not that Watson would see it as such, made the architect ever more attentive.

"That sounds very interesting, Mrs Lundy – or may I call you Fiona? I think the sooner I come and have a look, the better."

CHAPTER FIFTY-TWO

Mark Watson was never one to waste time when an interesting project beckoned. Two days later, as dawn was breaking over southwest England, he pulled his white Morgan sports car off Winsley Hill and parked near the ruined quarryman's cottage. He got out to stretch his legs, and his gaze swept down over the Limpley Stoke Valley to Freshford, instantly realising that he'd found the ideal setting for his next masterpiece.

There were only two obstacles – the client and the Bath planning office. The first would be all about cost but less difficult for him to placate than the latter's love affair with everything built before 1850 and constructed of Bath stone.

He'd driven through the darkness of the early hours in order to see the sun rise over the land. This was essential a useful tool, especially if, like today, it promised to be a fine morning. It helped him visualise the all-important bond to be created between his building and the surrounding countryside – absolutely perfect, the house could face due south. Light would flood the enormous glass windows in all the rooms from daybreak to nightfall.

By the time Fiona arrived, the architect had a very good idea of what he could achieve.

"Good morning, Mark." She walked across the top of a field to meet him. "So, what do you think of the site?"

"And a very good morning to you too, Fiona," he replied. "It is, as you described, magical – absolutely perfect."

He reached into his inside jacket pocket to take out a small sketchbook and pencil.

"Now, I need to find out exactly what you expect of the house – how many and what people are to live in it, bedrooms, any quirky habits; that sort of thing."

"Five bedrooms, each with its own bathroom," she replied. "That will allow one for our nanny, one each for the twins as they get older, and a guest suite."

"And the other rooms?"

Fiona went on. "I want a grand drawing room, as big as possible as we plan to do a lot of entertaining; a good-sized dining room, say to seat at least twelve; and, most important of all, the greatest modern kitchen you can design: marble tops, and in it, I want the latest oven, refrigerator, and every other labour-saving gadget you can dream up."

She had clearly put much thought into what she was after, and Watson then asked if there was anything special that she would like incorporated into the fabric of the building.

"A log-burning stove, something Swedish?" she ventured. "And my husband has a large quantity of books – some rare – so, a small library would be good, and we both love music: I've always fancied one of those futuristic sound systems with an outrageous number of loud, show-off speakers."

"And then outside, the point of it all," she opened her arms over the panorama which stretched down the valley and filled the entire horizon, "a waterfall." She looked at the architect and fell silent.

"Is all this possible?"

"Anything and everything is possible, Fiona. It always comes down to the cost and planning permission." He did some calculations in the sketchbook. "The building alone, excluding anything unforeseen the engineers find in drilling for the waterfall, will be one hundred and fifty thousand pounds. Then, you will need to add on my own and all the other professional fees."

Fiona eye's widened. "That's a monumental amount of money, over double what Ian and I expected. Based on the usual building rates in Bath, the cost of …"

Mark Watson smiled as he thought how predictable her reaction was. "That's exactly what it will be Fiona, a monument. Nothing about the home I build for you will be usual. It will be at least seven-and-a-half thousand square feet, built around a stunning, central drawing room measuring perhaps forty-five foot square. The building cost cannot be less than twenty pounds a square foot, and although I can't be precise, I would suggest you will have little or no change from two hundred thousand pounds."

"I see," she said. "I'll obviously have to discuss this with Ian. If we agree to go forward, what's next? Should we speak to the planning office?"

"Under no circumstances. That's my job, and it's far too early." He was pleased that she hadn't immediately changed her mind because of the projected costs – this frequently happened with clients. Always he lost business as a result of his honesty but was unwilling to compromise his reputation. "However if you decide to go ahead, I'll prepare the usual contract for signature and then draw up some sketches to show you what I have in mind."

As Fiona walked towards her car, Watson questioned the chances of the Lundys being able to raise enough capital for the project. He doubted it – they were comfortably off, yes, but not that wealthy. He took a final look at the vista and wondered if it was worth taking a few photographs in case they did get back in touch. Why not – the site was truly amazing.

"Toby, I need two hundred thousand pounds," Ian said as he walked into the finance director's office.

"Whatever for?" It was common for Ian to arrive in such an abrupt manner, but Toby was taken aback by the sheer size of this latest request. He immediately stopped tapping figures into his desktop calculating-machine and sat back to listen.

"Fiona wants to build a house." Ian didn't take a seat but remained standing with his hands in his pockets.

"What's it made of, gold?" Toby joked but could see that Ian was not smiling. "What house can cost that much to build in 1968? How big is it?"

"Seven and half thousand square feet, ultra-modern, like Lloyd Wright's Fallingwater, in Winsley overlooking the Limpley Stoke Valley. Toby – I am deadly serious about this."

"I can see that. OK, let me think – and do sit down, you're making me nervous." There was no doubt that Ian and Fiona were worth at least a hundred thousand pounds, if not two, and if or when the house was completed, it should double their wealth. He had been meaning to speak to Ian about his big idea, but the right moment hadn't arisen: this might be the ideal opportunity. He laughed.

"What's funny?" Ian asked after he finally sat down.

"You're making me think of Ralph Allen again and his mansion at Prior Park." He paused for a moment and then said, "I think I can find a way to raise two hundred thousand pounds for *your* Prior Park."

Mark Watson was pleasantly surprised by the letter from Fiona Lundy enclosing a cheque for five hundred pounds, expressing the hope this would be sufficient for him to produce the preliminary sketches.

CHAPTER FIFTY-THREE

Ian's need for money made the timing of Toby's big idea perfect, and when the time came to explain it, he had Ian and Fiona's undivided attention.

"The first step is to immediately tidy everything up – the whole sprawling mass of land, buildings, construction, insurance, publishing, and all the rest of your various businesses – made into a single holding company. Get Peter Groves to set it up and transfer everything into it. I mean absolutely everything – every share you and anybody else owns in all your numerous ventures." He was about to continue when Ian interrupted.

"Called what?" Ian asked.

It was a detail at this stage but important nevertheless. "The magic word needed is holdings," he said. "Nothing complicated – the fewer words the better; explaining where, how, and what it does."

Knowing well how Ian's mind worked and his love of detail, Toby said nothing but waited and watched as Ian jotted in his notebook before looking up.

"I've got it – Bath Fiscal Holdings Limited," he said. "It's got the where, the what, and I take it that "holdings" is the how."

"That's perfect," Toby confirmed. "Holdings will have a hundred ordinary shares of one pound each of which Fiona a you will own ninety-six, with the remaining four going one each to the rest of us – Al, Donna, Trish and me. Next, we have to get everything valued."

"What do you think that will come to?" Fiona asked.

"It's difficult to say, but I'm sure it will be adequate," he replied.

"Oh, come on, Toby, you must have an idea. You would have found it irresistible not to have worked it out; otherwise, you wouldn't be even suggesting this move. A ball park figure?" she teased. She knew him so well.

"A million, maybe more."

She gasped, but Ian showed no surprise and Toby continued.

"Holdings will then issue a debenture to some friendly local interests. I suggest ten at ten thousand pounds each which will raise one hundred thousand pounds for your grand-mansion plan."

Fiona interrupted. "Sorry, Toby, but can you explain what a debenture is?"

"In essence, it's a loan that's secured on the company's assets and pays a guaranteed rate of interest. In this case, I would suggest five percent a year. Its beauty is that, unlike ordinary shareholders, the debenture holders have no say in how the company is run. You keep full control."

This time, Ian spoke. "But we need double that amount for the house."

"That's not a problem once you've got the first one hundred thousand pounds," Toby said. "I will then get you a fifty percent mortgage on the new house, which will provide the rest."

"How difficult do you think it will be to find the ten investors?" Ian asked.

Toby smiled. "Already done."

Ian pursed his lips, evidently irritated at not having been consulted, but it was only momentary.

"Who?"

Toby knew that he had been right to foresee and provide all the answers before talking to them. He counted them out on his fingers.

"Old friends – Malcolm Austwick, Peter Groves, Christopher Johnson, Patrick McCloy, Roger Palmer, Tom Scotland, Al Giles, Debbie Smith, Ford Fraker, and, last but not least, myself."

Ian turned to Fiona. "What do you think, darling?"

"I think it's brilliant," she replied.

"So do I." Ian looked back to Toby. "Well done. Congratulations, let's do it. By the way, you were right."

"What about?" Toby was delighted to get the go-ahead.

"I did need a good finance director, and now I have a superb one. Thank you."

CHAPTER FIFTY-FOUR

Fiona was really pleased to see the invitation that had come with a hand written note from Linda Fraker:

"Hoping you can join us, it will be just a select few and should be great fun. xx"

Dr. Dallas Pratt

Requests the honor of your presence

for

A Nantucket Island Thanksgiving Dinner

on Thursday, 28 November, 1968

at

The American Museum,

Claverton Mannor, Bath

Dress: Lounge Suits   7.30 pm for 8 pm

R.S.V.P.

Linda was Fiona's closest friend in Bath ever since their joyous reunion when the couple had eventually arrived from Boston to take up residence in their St James' Square home. The two women spent much of their free time together, and Linda was forever promoting the "special relationship" between the British and their cousins across the pond.

This involved a voyage of discovery for her English friends and family, such as a Fourth-of-July party amidst a sea of Stars-and-Stripes bunting, while Ford attempted, without much success, to teach their guests the mysteries of baseball.

Inevitably, their husbands became close. Ian continued his love affair with the United States and all things American: this had been the case ever since his first visit to the country when he was twenty-one. On his way back from Jamaica after having bought a sugar plantation on behalf of Marcus Rose, he had spent a few days in New York: he felt the New World was exactly that and had so much more to offer – it lived up to everything Hollywood portrayed on the silver screen.

His subsequent trips to Washington DC and the top-flight lawyers on K Street who handled the Jamaican venture only reinforced his enthusiasm. He was introduced to many millionaire businessmen, politicians, and lawyers who convinced him that the United States were a land of unlimited opportunity – so unlike England, hidebound in tradition, where above all else who you were related to and which school you attended mattered. In the United States, class played no part in success unless your family were very rich, very famous, or very old – probably in that order of importance.

From time to time, Ian would discuss emigrating to the US, but Ford strongly advised against it.

"Look at the country. Take off your rose-tinted glasses, my friend – you know nothing of the poverty, race, and how the almighty dollar is everything. Easier to become a big fish in the small pond of London and then exploit that mystique in the vast New World.

"Most Americans, starting with beautiful, young women, fall for the so-called sophistication of the British, which usually just comes down to the accent and collar-length Beatles haircuts. Remember, Americans are obsessed with anything new, but novelty quickly fades and they rush on to the next craze – never a look back."

Fiona was always amazed by Ian's conviction that the American way of doing things and all things American were modern and best, with everything British coming a poor second. She checked her diary. They had tickets to see the musical *Hair* on the day following the dinner but were free on the twenty-eighth. Without even speaking to Ian, she immediately accepted the invitation – she was that confident of her husband's obsession.

Although Linda and Ford had mentioned Dr Dallas Pratt in conversation, she remembered her mother's training for dinner parties prevailed. So, in preparation for the party, she rang Al Giles, whose files on the great, the good, and not-so-good in Bath were second to none.

"What do you know about Dr Dallas Pratt?" she asked

"Of American Museum fame?"

"That's him," she said

"Hold on." There was a short pause before he came back to her and started reading the most salient points from his index card.

"I interviewed him about a year ago at the museum. He's from an enormously-wealthy New York family and named after an ancestor who founded the city of Dallas in Texas. He's fifty-four now and very much into animal welfare. He qualified as a doctor and psychiatrist in the thirties and served in the latter role in the war," Al went on.

"He's been an avid collector since childhood, and he showed me the magnificent death mask of John Keats given to him by his grandfather, which started his craze. He had a long-term companion and partner called John Judkyn, a British Quaker. They collected stuff together before buying Claverton Manor and then opening the American Museum in 1961. Sadly, shortly afterwards, Judkyn was killed in a car crash in France. Pratt didn't mention Judkyn to me, but I've heard it said that he's never got over his loss."

Fiona took advantage of the pause.

"That's fine, Al, more than enough."

"Why do you ask?"

"Ian and I are invited to a private Thanksgiving dinner with him. It's through the Frakers," Fiona told him.

"If you get the chance, do make a mention of *The Bath Way;* I'd love the chance of a follow up interview."

"Will do. Many thanks, bye."

CHAPTER FIFTY-FIVE

Mark Watson's sketch plans were beautiful; they were like pieces of art. Headed *FALLINGWATER MURHILL – THE PROPERTY OF MR & MRS I LUNDY OF BATH*, the rooms had been painted with different, light water-coloured washes according to use.

Fiona looked at the main elevation that would face south, overlooking the entire valley. It had twin flat roofs covering enormous glass pavilions on two floors, supported at each end by vertical pillars of dark, reddish-brown bricks. To one side, there was a third pavilion of only a single storey.

The glass used in every wall and the very thin flat roofs cleverly gave an impression that the whole building was floating over the ground rather than cleaving to the side of the valley. This disguised its enormous size and bulk and thus belied the usual brutalist description of the modernist style. She thought it was one of the most beautiful buildings she'd ever seen.

Turning her attention to the room layout, and in particular the stunning drawing room which occupied the entire first floor of the main pavilion, she was mesmerised by its two vast glass walls. Each was held by an uninterrupted, single glass frame. She wondered how such gigantic sheets of glass could even be made and transported in one single piece. Next to it, in the second pavilion, was the glass-walled dining room and kitchen with an exterior stone-terrace, again looking down at Freshford and idyllic for al fresco eating. The glass walls continued over the entire upper floor in the principle bedroom, bathroom, and dressing room.

She picked up the telephone and dialled Ian's direct line. The drawings had arrived in the post after he'd left for work that morning.

"How's Toby's big idea getting along?" she asked, finding it difficult to conceal her excitement.

"He's been working with Trish on it day and night. I haven't been involved much but think we're just about there. I gather the investors' money is coming in today. Why do you ask?"

"I'm hoping you're not too busy to have lunch with me." She didn't tell him about the drawings, because she delighted in seeing his reaction when he saw them.

"There's nothing they need from me, and I get the impression I am only in the way," he replied. "So, I would love to, especially when the invitation is from you."

They met at the Hop Pole in Limpley Stoke and chose one of the larger tables in the garden outside the venerable old pub. Ian spread out the sketch plans while they ate. He was stunned and raised his glass.

"To Fallingwater – your baby."

"To Fallingwater – our child," Fiona corrected him.

CHAPTER FIFTY-SIX

As Toby predicted, the hundred thousand pounds needed for Fallingwater was raised without a hitch. Everything was signed up by the end of the Friday afternoon in late August – no small thanks to the assistance received from Trish Traynor. The whole burden of delivery had fallen on the two of them and entailed working relentlessly over the previous weeks.

All day, the investors had been coming into the office, signing the debentures and handing over their cheques for ten thousand pounds. Trish found the whole operation fascinating and was thrilled to have been so involved. Ian had disappeared before lunch and not returned, but she had happily spent the afternoon with Toby at the conference table, surrounded by the mountains of paperwork inevitably produced by such a deal. Now, with just the money to be deposited in the bank's night safe, they could relax.

Toby completed, signed, and passed the last piece of paper to Trish.

"And this is for you." Toby handed her a cheque for the sizeable bonus. "Not bad for two months' work. With your looks and this in the bank, every penniless gigolo will find you irresistible"

Taken by surprise, Trish laughed.

"Thank you." Emboldened by the closeness that had grown between them from working so closely together for weeks and elated by success, she quipped back,

"You are far from penniless, Toby, so I wonder what the future, woman-wise, holds for you."

"We shall have to wait and see." He smiled and looked at her. "Have you got anything planned for the long weekend?"

"Oh, in all the excitement, I forgot," she admitted. "But of course, Monday's a bank holiday. Like the last few weekends, I kept it free, just in case we hadn't finished and I was needed."

"That's good – because you are needed." He was still smiling, "I need you to do one last thing with me in Bradford upon Avon."

Thinking it must be something to do at Patrick McCloy's office in the town, she nodded. "OK – what is it?"

"Christen my new boat – I take delivery in a couple of hours."

Trish watched him – no longer the finance director or ex-banker, he was just a rather grown-up-looking little boy playing with his new toy.

It was obviously one he knew something about, because in no time, they'd left the marina and were puttering slowly away from the town. The fifty-two-foot narrowboat was exquisite, nothing like the old canal boats with their garish colours which she was used to seeing along the Bath towpaths. It was sleek and stylish, with everything up to the waterline painted white and all above dark blue, capped with a deep-brown mahogany roof.

She was astounded by the sheer luxury. The entire front third of the boat was a sitting room with two deep, leather armchairs either side of a cast-iron wood-burning stove. Then came the dining room and galley in the centre, with the back third of the vessel containing a double bedroom with en-suite shower and flushing lavatory.

"It can sleep five people," Toby proudly told her and showed her how the dining room ingeniously converted into another double bed and then how a single bunk could be made to magically appear in the sitting room. What struck her was how modern everything was; it could have been designed by Conran. It was every bit as smart as, if not smarter than, the newest luxury flat in Bath. Nor did its perfection stop at the furniture: everything had been chosen with such care – expensive linen, china crockery, and Danish cutlery. She laughed when she saw there was even a hairdryer hanging in its own space on the bedroom wall.

Before leaving the city, they had stopped at Paxton & Whitfield in John Street to pick up one of their special hampers and then again at Great

Western Wines for some champagne. Toby cruised just far enough into the countryside to find privacy and moored up. She unpacked the picnic hamper onto a little table outside on the stern, and they ate and sipped their wine in peaceful seclusion with only birdsong for company. Trish could not remember when she had felt so happy.

"This is wonderful, Toby," she said, raising her glass to him. "Thank you so much for bringing me here."

"No, Trish – thank you," he replied. "For all the long hours and late nights you've put in over the last months. I couldn't have done it without you."

"I don't believe you, but it's very flattering, and I thank you in return for all that you have taught me."

Daylight went and with it the heat of the day. They moved into the sitting room and opened a second bottle of champagne. Hours passed with reminisces and much laughter: Trish realised that she didn't want to leave. Nothing was said, but Toby simply dismantled the dining room table, and the second double bed appeared.

"This is where I sleep," he said. "You can take the master suite, as the boat builders grandly call the bedroom."

She tried to protest, but he simply led her to the back of the boat and kissed her lightly on the lips before returning to the dining room.

Trish put her fingers to her mouth, remembering the brief touch of his lips and wished she'd taken the initiative and kissed him in return. Then she took her clothes off and slipped naked into the luxury brand of new, unused, linen sheets. She thought again about the kiss and hoped there would be a next time as she started to drift off to sleep. Never having slept on a boat before, she was mesmerised by the sound of the water lapping at the iron hull next to her pillow and didn't hear the gentle knock on the door.

It seemed so natural for him to slide into the bed next to her and kiss her again. This time, she kissed him back and felt his hands travel lightly down to her breasts. His lips went to her ear and he whispered,

"Trish, I love you."

"Toby," she whispered in return, "I love you too, but I've never done this before."

"Well, are you sure you want to now?" he asked.

She answered by kissing him again and pressing her body against his.

CHAPTER FIFTY-SEVEN

"Have you seen this?" Ian asked over the breakfast table. He poured both of them a cup of coffee and handed her the November edition of the *The Bath Way*, open at its lead-feature page.

ANOTHER MILESTONE FOR THE AMERICAN MUSEUM

Over three hundred and fifty years old, Claverton Manor, with the church, much land, and its vineyard, remained in Sir William Bassett's family for a hundred and fifty years before Ralph Allen bought it in 1758. Previously owned by his wife's family, it had been sold when father and son fell out.

Bequeathed to his great nephew, Allen Tucker, it passed to John Vivian, a solicitor, in 1816, who demolished the sixteenth-century property and constructed the present, magnificent building in a different position and with superb views across the Limpley Stoke Valley.

It stayed within the Vivian family until ten years ago, apart from a break of about five years, when it was briefly let to James Wilson. Mr Wilson, who had founded The Economist magazine in 1843 was the Liberal MP for Westbury until it "went Tory".

In 1874, the manor passed to Vivian's great-grandson, Henry Duncan Skrine, who, in 1897, organised a fete for the Primrose League, and twenty-three-year-old Winston Churchill made his first political speech in the gardens.

During the Second World War, Claverton became home to a celebrity: Squadron Leader Kenneth Horne of the Royal Air Force became quizmaster to a BBC radio show, and by 1944 had started the comedy series Much Binding in the Marsh. *Then, three years ago and to the joy of many, he created* Round the Horne.

For the eternal benefit of Bath, the manor house was bought in 1958 by Dr Dallas Pratt and Mr John Judkyn, who subsequently co-founded the American Museum.

The piece went on to explain the museum's aims and describe a current display describing the country's annual Thanksgiving celebration rituals.

Fiona read the article as she drank the coffee and tucked into a bowl of muesli. Both were finished before she gave her opinion. "Mmm, it's interesting, I suppose, but not exactly exciting nor a coincidence given that we're going there this evening. I wonder if Dallas Pratt sent Al a press release."

"Possibly." Ian sounded doubtful. "According to Ford, he shuns personal publicity, and I'm sure there's more to this dinner than meets the eye." He had buttered some toast and reached for the marmalade.

"What do you mean?" Fiona asked.

"Ford was a bit mysterious about it when we spoke last week, but apparently, it's a very select party – just five couples and Pratt in his private suite on the top floor of the museum. He mentioned Nantucket Island again for some reason. I knew about Nantucket from Linda – it's been his family holiday home for over a century. She loves the place. It's very exclusive, a tiny island off Cape Cod, and they always spent most of the summer there. She suggested we might like to go over and stay with them next summer. I told them you'd love the idea."

Ian laughed, stood up, went around the breakfast table, and kissed her.

"How well you know me. I can't wait to see America again."

The only three English guests were Fiona, Ian, and Linda Fraker. Dallas Pratt presided over the evening but said little, and he was noticeably older than any of his guests. The other men were all tall, lean, and athletic, with Boston accents, and, Ian guessed, about Ford's age. He assumed they'd all been to Harvard or another Ivy League institution, and their young wives probably Vassar, beautifully groomed and straight out of the Daughters of the American Revolution drawer.

Ian studied the men as they introduced themselves over drinks. Harry said he was from the US State Department and a professional diplomat. Liam was a naval attache from the US Embassy in Grosvenor Square. Finally, there was Hank, who simply said he worked for the military as a strategist. He was prematurely bald, wore horn-rimmed glasses, and was tall, perhaps six foot five or six: Ian felt incredibly short standing next to him.

"So, how well do you know Ford?" Hank asked.

"We get on well, but originally, it was our wives who were friends," he replied. "And you?"

"Our families go back a long way. We were at Princeton together. Football, baseball, ice hockey – we played them all, and I'd say Ford was good enough to go professional in any and all of them. Instead, he played the long game and became the hot-shot Boston banker. We catch up most summers in Nantucket. Do you know the island?"

"No, although my wife informed me only this morning over breakfast that she has accepted an invitation for next summer." The announcement of dinner could not come too soon, if only because he could sit down and continue his conversation with Hank on more level terms.

The tall American continued. "It's an interesting place – boasts the highest real-estate prices in the United States and not a brick to be seen – just wooden clapboard houses and only four thousand islanders.

"From what I hear from Ford, you're a natural deal maker and should thrive there. It's a private bastion of free enterprise and possibly one of the last for the very rich, old American families. It's a world away from the Irish Kennedy dynasty on Cape Cod," he laughed before adding, "they say you're not allowed to set foot on Nantucket if you or any member of your family of the last three generations has ever voted Democrat …"

Then thankfully: "Dinner is served."

It became clear to Ian, seated next to Harry's wife Olivia, that her husband was a professional diplomat, whilst Emma, Liam's wife, was very vague about her partner's exact occupation – Secret Service, Ian guessed.

He looked across at Fiona. She, like himself, was studying the menu card and the unusual fare that awaited them.

MENU

Squash soup
with
cast-iron skillet corn bread

———

Savoury broiled oysters

———

Broad-breasted white turkey
with
sage & mushroom stuffing

Apple & cranberry cobbler
Chestnut fritters
Sweet potato & green bean casserole

———

Pumpkin pie

———

Beaujolais nouveau
Apple cider

Dallas Pratt tapped his glass; the room fell silent.

"Ladies and gentlemen," the white haired man raised his glass, "our Founding Fathers."

Then, after the toast had been drunk, he added, "For the benefit of our three English guests, I would add, if it hadn't been for a case or two of tea, we, your American cousins would still be part of the British Empire. More's the pity, you will say." He raised his glass. "Our loss."

"So, what was all that about?" Fiona asked later as they were driving home. "Why do you think we were invited?"

Ian thought for a moment before answering. "American Trade and Vietnam. It all came out over the Port, when Dallas was giving you ladies a private tour of the museum." Ian went on to explain that it was Harry from the State Department who had explained: the numbers were phenomenal.

"This year alone, American investment in Britain is likely to be nearly seven billion dollars, can you imagine. That's nearly twice what they're putting into Germany. Think of some of the great English companies that they are involved with – Rootes Motors, Smith Crisps, Gallagher, and Rowntree's was a very close shave. They don't want the gravy train to stop but the City of London is up in arms.

"Then, there's Vietnam and those violent anti-American demonstrations outside the US Embassy in Grosvenor Square in March and again last month. They really spooked the Yanks. Not having been called up for National Service or involved in a war, I suppose I can't get my head around what this war means to them."

"When you say 'them', who do you mean?" she asked.

"A very impressive team of elite Boston bankers, a dozen Wall Street big hitters, all Dow Jones, plus some top Republicans. Apparently, the whole idea was dreamt up a few months ago in the sunshine of Cisco Beach on Nantucket, hence its name, Nantucket Project.

"They say that they're worried and seeking friends in England to quietly look after their interests." He looked across at his wife. "They asked if I could help in the south west of England, centred in Bath."

Fiona was incredulous.

"Bath is a sleepy provincial town, a backwater. They're nuts if they think anything's happening here. If you ask me, they have realised that Vietnam is a war that can't be won and are trying to find excuses. What on earth do they think is going on in our little old city?"

"Not according to Hank. He says that with the Admiralty in Bath and with left-wing Bristol so close by, it could be a perfect target."

"Really?" Fiona sounded unconvinced. "So, what did you say?"

"I said I'd think about it."

Three days later, Ian rang Ford Fraker and agreed to join the Nantucket Project.

"Great news, I'll let the Firm know."

"The Firm?"

"Langley; Fairfax County, Virginia, about eight miles south of Washington DC – CIA," he replied. "They checked you out thoroughly before you were invited to the dinner."

Ian was quite shocked but said nothing to Fiona.

Ford's answer had been short and simple: "… any and everything, good and bad, which might affect 'the special relationship' between our two great nations."

Although an ardent capitalist and admirer of the American way of life, Ian had always stayed away from politics: there was no profit in it, quite the reverse. Most of his acquaintances were the same, businessmen, and although none would have voted the Wilson shambles into government, they concentrated on making money and donating some of it to the Tory Party.

However, he was completely unaware of what the average man in a Bath street thought, if anything, about America's involvement in Vietnam, but he had a friend who would have a good idea. Mike Watts was a stall holder in the Guildhall Market, and Ian met him a week later.

The Guildhall was the oldest shopping venue in the city and had traded on its High Street site for over eight hundred years. The nail, a table on which deals had been sealed for centuries, and "paying on the nail", still survived near the market's entrance.

Ian and Mike had both been born in Bath but led very different lives. Their friendship had been formed years earlier and deepened when Ian had supported Mike's battle and eventual victory over the competitors who wanted to close the historic market down. Mike spent all his time immersed at the coal face of the local community: he was the litmus paper for the mood of the man and woman in the street, be it posh Milsom Street or the lowly London Road.

The trader smiled broadly as they shook hands and wandered into the market's café. He looked like a weather-beaten farmer dressed in his open-neck shirt, grey moleskin waistcoat, and straw hat.

"So, to what do I owe this pleasure? You don't often slum it down here with us ordinary folk," Mike said, overemphasising his West Country drawl. They both chewed on the best bacon sandwiches to be found anywhere in Bath. Despite being a non-practising Jew, until he met Mike, Ian had shied away from pork, but all this changed after his first Guildhall bacon butty – shellfish was soon to follow.

"This is going to sound a strange request," he said between mouthfuls. "Is there much anti-American feeling around Bath?"

"Well, I'm not quite sure what you're getting at, Ian," Mike replied, "but I think most people couldn't care less. There are a few hippy types – you know, like the CND and Peace Movement – who hate the way the Yanks dominate the rest of the world. What are you asking, exactly?"

"Some friends of mine are asking." Ian finished his sandwich and licked some bacon grease from his thumb.

"Well, I've always known you were unusual, but it now looks like you've acquired some really strange mates." Mike looked at Ian quizzically.

"See that?" He pointed to a nearby notice on the market's wall. It was a bye-law dating from 1864 that read, *No person shall throw or fling vegetables garbage or any missile in the market.* It took Ian a moment to work out what he was getting at. Mike continued.

"OK, so what do you want to know?"

"Those that you reckon who could make trouble for the Americans if they got the chance, and how many of them there are here in Bath.'

"All right, I'll have a think and ask around."

CHAPTER FIFTY-EIGHT

Fiona and Ian returned to Barbados for their first wedding anniversary, and of an evening would sit on their veranda overlooking the sandy shoreline, listening to the gently-lapping waves of the sea.

They'd left the never-ending rain, high winds, and sub-freezing temperatures of England for the balmy, tropical breeze of the Caribbean. The twins were sleeping in their cots under the vaulted rattan roof of their beachside bungalow, with nanny Anna nearby, and Fiona was at peace with the world.

A Scrabble set lay on the table between them, and they were ready to commence one of their epic contests. These could last for hours, simply because, ever striving for the best score, neither would accept a time limit for their turn. Ian sipped his fruit punch as Fiona took out seven tiles in the bag of letters: they weren't the best, and she was to lay first.

"Who would have thought we'd be here now, playing happy families when eighteen months ago, we wondered if the twins would even survive their first night of life – it's hard to believe." She immediately saw the word "mess" and then "remiss" – that would leave her with only one tile, an E. "That reminds me: we must put James on the list as soon as we get back." She started to lay the word onto the board when she thought of "messier" and triumphantly added the final tile.

"All seven out first go," Ian groaned.

"And what's the list when it's at home?" Ian asked absentmindedly, concentrating on the letters on his tray.

"You know," she reached for seven more letter tiles, "it's the system under which any old boy can pre-register his son."

Letters forgotten for the moment, Ian sat back on his chair and looked at her blankly.

She too took her gaze from the game and realised that Ian didn't know what she was talking about.

"For Eton, the finest school in the world, and where most of the boys only get in because their father went there."

"Why would we send James to Eton of all places? It will turn him into a snob!" Ian seemed irked by even the suggestion. "Anyway, what makes you think it's the finest school in the world? What's wrong with King Edwards in Bath?"

"The answer to your first question is very simple – because the last three Earls and their brothers have all gone there."

"That proves my point," Ian interrupted, "a bunch of privileged individuals who didn't have a clue how the real world worked and were totally incapable of earning a living."

"You are so wrong." This was one argument she was determined to win. "Find me another school that has produced so many greats – twenty plus prime ministers, not to mention the innumerable writers, scholars, doctors, economists, composers, actors, journalists, sportsmen, and so many more. It's produced Nobel Prize winners and some of the most successful businessmen. Look them up if you don't believe me, but better still, ask Toby. He's an OE, and presumably, as our finance director, you accept that he's capable of earning a living."

"OK, OK. I just want the best for him." Unusually, Ian sounded defensive, but she knew this was so very important. He took a sip of his punch and added, "Let's not forget Ruth."

"She is going to my old school, Cheltenham Ladies College. No debate – it is the best."

"And where do you propose they should go before Eton and Cheltenham Ladies College?"

"I'll have to check, prep schools change – it often depends on the headmaster." She was relieved that Ian appeared to have been persuaded. "But first, we'll have to choose a pre-prep until they are seven – which should be in Bath, whether or not they board."

"No – and now I do know what I'm talking about." This was the old Ian, back onto the offensive. "We're not sending them away at seven. It's too young, and I couldn't bear it."

Aware that he'd been sent away to school at the age of five, Fiona was not surprised by his reaction. "Ian, it's not about you or me," she said gently. "We must do what's best for them, but let's leave it for now. I don't want anything to spoil our holiday."

Ian didn't answer. But unable to put it out of his mind, he sent a telegram to Toby.

THINKING OF ETON FOR JAMES STOP YOUR THOUGHTS WELCOME STOP IAN

The reply came back within a few hours.

NO BETTER STOP FINEST OB NETWORK IN WORLD STOP
HOLIDAY READING BEING SENT STOP TOBY

True to his word, Toby airmailed the book to Barbados: it covered the history of the celebrated school from its foundation over five centuries earlier by Henry VI until the present day. Having little else to do, he started to read it. Finding it heavy going, one afternoon, he turned to an appendix listing some of the school's most notable old boys of the twentieth century. Howard Edgington's name – the headmaster of Ian's old school, Pitt College, and to whom he owed so much – was amongst the names.

Another appendix attributed the famous sayings about the school over the ages.

The Duke of Wellington was credited with "the playing fields of Eton". He looked out at the sunlit, azure sea – unlike the Polish potato fields and a peasant girl of twelve, he mused, thinking of his mother.

CHAPTER FIFTY-NINE

Toby had proposed marriage, and Trish had instantly accepted. She wanted to spend the rest of her life with him.

Fiona and Ian had departed with the children nine days earlier for Barbados, and she couldn't wait to tell Ian on his return: he would be so happy for her.

It was a culmination of an amazing four months with this wonderful man – her man and someone who understood her. He accepted that she had a desperate desire to succeed above all else and was so proud of her because she did. They discussed everything and nothing, laughing and arguing at the same time. It seemed too good to be true, but they dared to believe.

There had been no discussion during that first weekend on the canal boat, but they both knew: on their return to Bath, he waited while she gathered up a few essentials from her St John's flat and moved into his little house in Miles's Buildings. No mention was made of Trish having given up the flat, and to avoid comment, they deliberately organised to arrive at and depart separately from the office.

Trish had no religious beliefs but accepted that Toby's faith was very important to him. He assured her that his family posed no problem with him marrying a non-Catholic and that the priest's permission would be forthcoming: all that was initially required was her undertaking that any children would be brought up in the true faith.

"But not for a long time yet," she said as they decorated the office Christmas tree. Toby wanted an early spring wedding so that they would no longer be "living in sin". Trish, on the other hand, was very happy with the present situation and could see no urgent reason to get married.

"Who knows," he quipped, half joking and placing the stepladder near to the tree, "I might even be able to persuade you to convert."

Framed by the magnificent wooden staircase, the fir reached upwards from the ground to the first floor of the Queen Square townhouse.

The staff had gone home for the night, and so it was just the two of them stretching the chain of fairy lights over its branches.

"I wouldn't hold your breath on that one," she replied as she started up the ladder. "But who knows? Five years from now, when I'm ready for a baby, maybe I'll have changed my mind." She stretched down to take a bauble from him. "Can you find the star for the top?" she asked.

Opening her eyes, she saw a very anxious Toby, and behind him, the half-decorated tree with the Christmas lights hanging. She was lying on her back and realised that she'd fallen off the ladder that had toppled over beside her.

Toby was stroking her head. "Don't move," he said. "I've called an ambulance. I should never have let you up the ladder. I'm so sorry."

She tried to rise, but he held her down firmly.

"Please, darling, wait. Just in case. Let the ambulance crew check you out."

The flashing blue light soon filled the hall windows, and the next thing she felt was the ambulance man feeling her neck, shoulders, and down her back. He looked at Toby.

"Are you sure she lost consciousness?" he asked.

"Yes, I'd say she was out for no more than a couple of minutes." Toby replied.

"Well," the ambulance man looked back to Trish, "I can't find where you hit your head, but it's the hospital for you, young lady. They'll want to check you for concussion."

Coincidentally, Norman Piggott had agreed to relieve the overload by taking an extra shift in Accident and Emergency that evening. He was evidently surprised to see his old flatmate arrive on a stretcher with her good-looking but worried boyfriend in tow.

"Trish! What a pleasant, or should I say unpleasant, surprise – what have you been up to?" He drew the curtains around the cubicle, and she smiled when he instinctively raised his hands towards his neat beard as he looked down at her. For a moment, she struggled to find her voice but then began.

"Decorating the tree, fell off the ladder …" Again, she blacked out, but when she came round, to her horror and embarrassment, she realised that she'd wet herself.

"Don't fret, it's quite normal." Norman had obviously seen what had happened. "It's just shock."

He turned to Toby and ushered him through the curtains. "Maybe, for the patient's dignity, it would be better if you waited outside while we get her ready for the doctor. I'm sure we can find you a cup of tea."

While he was gone, another nurse arrived with fresh sheets, deftly removed Trish's soiled clothes, and left her clean and tidy in a hospital gown. Norman returned with the young doctor – unshaven; preseason Christmas-party drinks and fights had taken their toll.

"Trish, this is the on-duty doctor who wants to take a look at you before we get you up to x-ray," Norman explained.

The doctor sat down next to the bed and took hold of her wrist to check her pulse. "How do you feel?" he asked.

"Fine." She couldn't explain what had happened. She really did feel normal.

"I think you fainted and fell off the ladder. Do you have a history of fainting?"

"No." She shook her head.

"Are you frightened of heights or suffer from dizziness?

Again, she shook her head.

"I'll just have a listen." He placed the stethoscope on her back and listened. "That all sounds good." He paused and had a thought. "Has there been anything unusual with your periods recently?"

"I'm a bit late, but that's not unusual. I'm often irregular, and sometimes, they can be painful."

The doctor stood up without saying any more and spoke quietly to Norman.

"We'll probably have to take bloods but to start with, a urine sample – I think she may be pregnant."

CHAPTER SIXTY

Trish lingered for three days, but the paracetamol in her liver proved fatal.

POLICE STATEMENT

Concerning	:	Death of Miss Trish
Traynor of		
		50 Miles's Buildings,
Bath		
At	:	Royal United Hospital,
Bath		
On	:	19 December 1968
Time of statement	:	7.18 pm
At	:	Bath Police Station
On	:	19 December 1968
By	:	Tobias Newman Stafford of
		50 Miles's Buildings,
Bath		
Relationship		
(if any) to deceased:		Fiancé

Statement:

I, Tobias Newman Stafford, discovered my fiancée lying on the bed at our home at about 11 pm on Monday, 16 December. She was unconscious and unable to move or speak. I could not rouse her. On the bedside table was an overturned, brown pill bottle, labelled 60 paracetamol tablets that was empty. Next to it was a half-empty bottle of red wine with a wine glass beside it. Both were overturned, and wine red wine was spilt on the bedside table which had dripped down onto the carpet. I immediately called for an ambulance and travelled with my fiancée to the Royal United Hospital.

Under protest, I attach a letter in an envelope addressed to me personally found on my bedside table. I confirm that the handwriting is that of my fiancée. The circumstances leading up to my fiancée's death are as follows: on the previous Tuesday, 10 December, my fiancée was admitted to the Accident and Emergency department of the Royal United Hospital after she had fainted and fallen while decorating our office Christmas tree. The cause was diagnosed as pregnancy. Whilst I was overjoyed at the prospect of a baby, my fiancée was not. She thought it would mean the end of her successful career as a company director of a thriving Bath property business. She wished to terminate the pregnancy, but I am a practising Roman Catholic and could not agree with such a course of action. We argued constantly until, on the night before she took the overdose, I became very angry and hit her across the face. I had never struck her before, and she fled to another bedroom and locked the door. She didn't go to work the next morning. I telephoned the house three times during the morning to apologise. I wanted to suggest she have the baby but give it away for adoption. Each time, there was no reply. She called in the early afternoon and told me she had that morning had an abortion. I was very angry and told her that I could not forgive her for murdering our child and never wanted to see her again. I wanted her out of my house. After I left work, I went to the pub, only returning home at about 11 pm when I found Trish.

Signed: *Tobias Stafford*

Witness: *DI J Romer,*
               Bath Police Station

Attachments: Suicide letter (copy)

               RUH report (pregnancy)
               Clinical report (termination)

CHAPTER SIXTY-ONE

The line was terrible; oscillating and fading in and out, but for all of that, the person-to-person telephone call from Toby left Ian and Fiona in shock and brought them home from Barbados on the first available flight.

During the hours of sleepless travel, Ian endlessly played and rewound the mental tape-reel of his mind chatter. The interview when he had first met Trish. Was it really as long ago as 1961? So much time had passed since she had come for the job interview. She had explained everything – how, despite passing the eleven plus and thus gaining entry to Hayes Grammar School, her mother's poverty had meant leaving before she could sit A levels and go on to university.

She had joined him just two weeks after qualifying at the Pitman Secretarial College and never looked back – they had forged a fabulous partnership. Over the six years, they had grown close and shared so many moments of triumph: no one else, not even Fiona, could understand the bond between them – driving ambition, to the exclusion of all else. Trish was as determined to succeed as he was and totally understood his constant striving for achievement.

When it all came tumbling down, she was there at his bedside. Did he ever fully acknowledge her devotion, let her know how vital she was? Could he ever work again without her support?

As the plane flew into the dawn, Fiona gently gathered Ian's head to her breast and tried, to no avail, to ease the grief.

All day at the inquest, Ian, seated between Trish's mother and Fiona, listened to Toby giving evidence. His friend was ashen-faced, often barely audible, his voice reduced to a whisper, and at times, he was utterly incapable of continuing. The lurid newspaper headlines deepened the guilt.

The journey to the church behind the hearse seemed unreal. Ian did his best with his eulogy, which he had taken hours to write and rehearse. It all came to an abrupt halt as his eyes found the stark wooden coffin in which her cold lifeless body lay. Silently, Fiona rose and led the sobbing man back to the pew.

A bleak, uncelebrated Christmas and New Year passed. Ian just sat at home, listless and brooding, any questions sought from him either ignored or reluctantly answered with a monosyllabic reply. Even the twins' laughter and happiness didn't move him. She became convinced he was on the verge of a nervous breakdown.

Fallingwater saved him.

CHAPTER SIXTY-TWO

Ian point-blank refused to return to Queen Square, so when the office re-opened in January 1969, Fiona went in his place. Toby had resigned, and with both men absent, Fiona struggled to manage, delegations to the demoralised staff being all but impossible. She felt she was coping – that was until the planning refusal for Fallingwater was leaked to the *Chronicle*.

Mark Watson had warned her to expect it, but the pure vitriol of the newspaper headline still upset her.

BATH REJECTS

BRUTALIST ARCHITECTURE

Lundy

Following its planning department's recommendation to reject Mark Watson's radical design for the mansion at Murhill, not a single council member voted in favour. In the words of one councillor,

"Our fine Georgian city should not tolerate such a monstrosity – not a single piece of our beautiful, honey-coloured Bath stone used, just brick and glass despoiling forever the wonderful Limpley Stoke Valley. It's the thin edge of the wedge: grant permission, and next thing you know, these barbarians ..."

Fiona made an appointment to meet the architect at Murhill and brooked no argument from Ian: she insisted that he join her.

It was a grey morning, damp and chilly, so Ian said he'd stay in the car, but she was determined otherwise.

"I need you, Ian," she said. "This is our project for our family and our life. It's for all of us, and I cannot handle it without you. You persuaded me to do this, and I simple will not allow you to opt out – I warn you, if you do, we abandon the whole thing right now." He reluctantly did her bidding, shook hands with Watson, but stayed obstinately silent.

"I did warn you. This was totally expected." The architect shrugged off the refusal and his clients' gloom. "Don't look so depressed; this is just the beginning! We'll go to appeal, and with luck, we'll get an inspector from London who will agree with us: nostalgia for the past, narrow-mindedness, and parochial opinions of taste are not valid reasons for stopping us building Fallingwater."

"How long do you think it will take?" Fiona asked.

"Quite some time in putting together the instructions for the counsel and briefs for expert witnesses. I'd say six months in preparation and three more for a decision."

Fiona's heart sank. "And how much will it cost?"

"I'd estimate between two and three thousand pounds," Watson answered.

At the mention of money, she saw Ian react, and although he didn't say anything, the way his eyes focussed and the slight shake of his head – just for a moment, Ian was back. Finally, a spark.

Immediately, her face brightened. "Onward and upward, then."

In the car on the way back, and to Fiona's surprise, Ian began talking. It was as though he had woken from a deep sleep and was struggling to shake off a nightmare. He gazed out at the beautiful houses fronting Bathwick Hill.

"What is wrong with this city?" It took Fiona a moment to realise that he was venting his frustration about the rejection.

"We offered them a perfect opportunity to drag Bath out of the eighteenth century and into the twentieth, and they just don't want to know. Not only are they absolutely not interested, worse still, we're branded as barbarians, heretics – presumably fated to burn on a bonfire in front of the Abbey."

"Why are you so shocked?' Fiona didn't mind the rant – she was delighted that, at long last, he was engaging. "Watson had told us to be ready for the refusal, so what did you expect?"

"A fair hearing would have been reasonable," he fumed. "How about some of them having minds open to change? Just a few people ready to accept that maybe, just maybe, a beautiful modern building designed by one of Britain's greatest young architects is good enough for Bath."

"Ian, get real. If you think that our Mr Mark Watson is about to unseat John Wood and his son, forget it," she said.

"Factions. Self-seeking, self-interested factions," Ian seethed. "That's all we've got. It all goes back to Al Giles's very clever tribes but adjusted for the biggest tribe of all – bigoted, bloody narrow-minded residents."

Fiona interrupted him. "You know it's not that simple. Firstly, you have to divide the people who live in Bath between those born here, including incomers who have lived here for years, and the newly-arrived. Surprisingly, the first seem to be the least vociferous, probably because they have seen it all before. The incomers, the Johnnys-come-lately are our problem. But enough cynicism," she continued as she drove them back to Great Pulteney Street, "thankfully, there's Traditional Bath and its members. Yes, they want to preserve the beauty of Bath, but, as we've discovered, most of them are realists. They know it can't all be Georgian pastiche and will agree to new, different, and modern – as long as its design and quality is worthy of Bath. Fallingwater is both."

"I agree, but what do we have to do to convince them?" he said despairingly.

Encouraged, a few days later, Fiona cautiously raised the question of the business and how she desperately needed him back at Queen Square.

"I'm not sure I can go on without Trish or Toby," Ian replied. "I probably need more time."

"I think you've had enough time feeling sorry for yourself, and I know that Trish would agree with me. I'm sure Toby can be persuaded to return."

"How?" he asked.

"For exactly the same reason – Trish. Tell him that you don't accept his resignation. Explain that without her, he's needed more than ever and that she'd want him to carry on with his vision. He probably knows that already. He's an honourable man, and you both need to move on."

Fiona was right, and the two men returned to the Queen Square office to work together a few days later. Nevertheless, it was tough, and later in the week, Ian was pleased with the timely invitation from his favourite bookshop, Mr B's. Nick had found another book about Churchill, and Ian used it as an excuse to leave the office early. Since Ian's first purchase some three years earlier, Nick had been true to his word, enabling his Churchill collection to grow to over a hundred books and pamphlets, including, ironically, a foreword to the Chartered Surveyors' handbook from years past.

CHAPTER SIXTY-THREE

A chance remark about his Churchill collection and his admiration of the wartime leader at the American Thanksgiving dinner had prompted an invitation for Fiona and him to attend the International Churchill Society dinner at Blenheim Palace in March 1969. Out of curiosity, they accepted and to their surprise, found themselves placed on the table with Mary Soames, the youngest of Churchill's five children.

It was a sumptuous affair with Pol Roget, Churchill's favourite champagne, provided with the compliments of Odette Pol Roger from her domain near Épernay. The guest list was august – an international Who's Who. Ian counted ten Commonwealth prime ministers, at least five top members of the newly-formed Nixon administration, various members of the British Cabinet, European heads of state, and a substantial representation from the media.

The aim of this newly-formed society was to be the eternal guardian of Churchill's reputation and promoter of his vision for future generations. Flattered to have been be asked and swept along by rubbing shoulders with the famous in a sea of good food and unlimited champagne, Ian willingly accepted an offer of membership to its British chapter. Would he, a retired brigadier asked, be interested in becoming involved in tours of the Cabinet War Rooms?

"Yes," he responded to the ex-military, back-bench Tory MP, without hesitation. He neither knew what the War Rooms were nor what "involvement" meant but soon gathered that he would be expected to give tours of the place to visiting VIPs.

"Don't worry," the brigadier reassured him. "Colour Sergeant Jones, who runs the place, will soon lick you into shape. He's a mine of information. Any questions, Lundy?"

"When would you like me to start?" Ian asked tentatively.

"First of all, I'll get my secretary to fix up for you to come and see me at the House of Commons. I heard from our security people that our

American cousins cleared you a while ago, so that's good enough for me. You can sign the Official Secrets Act, and then off you go, my boy. You'll be one of the few of your generation to learn how Churchill really waged and won the war against the Nazis."

The visitor's buff card simply read,

FRANK DUFFER Jnr
Special Advisor

Ian thought the name sounded familiar but wasn't sure why when the Daimler picked up the elderly, bespectacled man from the Dorchester Hotel. The American was impeccably dressed but in a three-piece suit of Donegal tweed, as if his guest was under the impression he was joining a Highland shooting party. Interestingly, and somewhat incongruously, Ian also noticed the exclusive Phi Beta Kappa Society fob hanging from the gold watch-chain spanning the ample waistcoat.

They exchanged a few pleasantries, and before long, the car drew up outside the bunker entrance in Birdcage Walk, where Jones was standing to attention.

"Colour Sergeant Christopher Jones," Ian introduced them, "Mr Frank Duffer Junior from the United States of America." The ex-marine saluted, and Duffer nodded his acknowledgement.

The bunker, Jones explained as he began the tour, had been in continual use twenty-four hours a day from the moment it opened a week before Britain declared war on Germany on 27 August 1939 until it closed on Thursday 16ᵗʰ 1945."

The underground Cabinet Room where Churchill had been forced to command from was exactly as it had been in October 1940 after 10 Downing Street was bombed. It was a small, low room with an oblong table covered in blue serge and surrounded by twenty or so chairs.

Jones let the American sit in Churchill's low-backed, wooden armchair. Duffer was clearly deeply moved by the scratch marks on the end of its wooden arms where the strain of meetings had told. The colour sergeant then showed him where Atlee had sat on Churchill's left, with Ernest Bevan and Lord Beaverbrook opposite.

They moved on to the cupboard with its *vacant/occupied* lavatory sign on the door, which was used by Churchill to talk on the telephone directly to President Roosevelt. Then the Map Room with the funny little cartoon of Adolf Hitler doodled on its main map by a bored serviceman, Churchill's bedroom with its chamber pot, the Chiefs of Staff Conference Room, and the BBC broadcast room followed. Lastly, the Dock, the subterranean lower floors, where staff and marines slept in dormitories of bunks between bare brick walls and concrete floor, often no more than four foot high.

Afterwards, Ian took the American to lunch at the Carlton Club: he had obviously been fascinated by the whole visit.

"It's mind-blowing stuff," Duffer said. "If we had something like this in the States, it would have been sold to Walt Disney and turned into what we call 'an experience', but you Brits are so low-key."

As they parted, Duffer grasped Ian's hand. "It's been great, Ian; please let me reciprocate. The Smithsonian is worth a visit when you next come to America, and please bring your wife. Please give her my regards, I hope she has good memories of our time working together."

"OK." Ian was perplexed by the final comment. "But how do I get in touch with you?"

"Oh, I thought you knew," Duffer smiled. "Just address everything to the White House, Washington DC."

In the car back to Bath, Ian had time to think about what Duffer had said: he must not forget to pass on his regards to Fiona. Then, as usual, his mind reverted to business and how he could make Bath prosper again. The city had been in decline for over two hundred years, ever since the Prince

Regent had taken himself off to the south coast and the sea air, and what little industry remained was shrinking at an alarming rate. He thought about what the American had said about Disneyland. A theme park would never work but two thousand years of heritage and history should.

Donna Lodge, Al Giles, and Toby met in Ian's office. Donna had the floor because Ian had charged her to do the historic research.

"The tourist office was set up in the 1930s by a few men at the Council – generally, Conservatives and Freemasons. I could have missed something, but since then it seems to have been very much a hit and miss affair: there are few statistics with no one really in charge.

As far as I can establish the position, and it illustrates my last point, is that in 1964, about three hundred thousand visitors came to Bath. No one knows where this figure comes from, possibly it's the total ticket sales at the various Council venues. Nor does anyone have any hard statistics on how those visitors got here or how long they stayed. I couldn't get any reliable information from anyone; British Rail, the coach operators, the hotels, or even the boarding houses.

"I've identified around a hundred attractions; there are probably double this number within twenty-five miles, excluding the festivals. Again, it's very piecemeal, everyone doing their own thing, keeping their cards close to their chest. With regard to the festivals, there's a continual struggle for sponsorship – having said that, the Bath Blues Festival later this year has booked Fleetwood Mac and Led Zeppelin."

Donna sat back in her chair.

"So, to sum up: tourism is disorganised, fragmented, and chaotic–"

"But with potential for massive expansion," Ian interjected. He waited to see if anyone had further comments before continuing. He was firing on all cylinders; after all, he had had enough time to think about the idea.

"So, we need to set up an entirely-new entity to promote every aspect of tourism," he spread his arms wide, "and cause a big splash in the city, across the country, and around the world.

"As a first priority, we urgently require an information centre in a prime location – ideally by the Abbey and the Roman Baths so that it's somewhere every visitor passes. Then, we need to link it to other information centres in Britain, already famous as historic places of interest and popular with tourists – especially Americans. The Tower of London, Oxford, Cambridge, Stratford-upon-Avon, Chester, and Edinburgh immediately spring to mind, but there are plenty of others. Next, Bath has to be promoted in those places where foreign tourists come from – be it German spa towns, Europe, the Commonwealth, or North America. Donna, I think you're the person to head up this operation. OK?"

He didn't wait for an answer.

"Now, Al, I want you to be in charge of all publicity; advertising, and promotional literature – maps, guides, and programmes – not only everything needed by Donna but anything else you think that could be a runner. I see *The Bath Way* being pivotal. All right?" He still didn't wait for a response before continuing.

"Both of you need to work out the staffing requirements and a rough budget and let Toby have the figures by the end of the day. I do realise they'll be little more than guesstimates." He paused before ending the discussion.

"Let's meet again. Same time tomorrow."

Everyone stood to leave, but Ian asked Toby to stay.

"So, what do you think?" he asked when they were alone.

"Good but very expensive," the finance director replied with his usual slant.

"I think we all need something to concentrate on." Ian looked at his friend. "How are you doing?"

"Not good, but I'll survive."

There was an awkward silence – neither handled emotions well. Eventually, Ian spoke.

"Whatever figures Donna and Al give you, double them, and tomorrow, we'll work out where the money is to come from. And what should we call the new company?"

"It'll simply be a subsidiary of the holding company – Pure Bath?"

Ian smiled.

"I like it – but it rings a bell. I think it may already being used by someone."

"I'll check," Toby replied and also smiled before adding, "is that all BN2?"

"BN2?" Ian asked.

"Your Beau Nash Two, for like him, you wish to mastermind tourism." He stopped for a moment to add to RA2. "The 'second coming' is almost upon us – all we need is JW2."

Ian laughed.

"Speaking of the John Woods, have you seen this?" He tossed over a copy of the previous day's *Chronicle*.

MP Kent gets consent for largest residential development near city centre – a hundred and eighty private homes south of Wells Road. On eight acres, …

Toby read the front-page article.

"It would appear that we house builders are winning," he said.

By May, the information centre was up and running in a location overlooking Abbey Courtyard. In September, Donna was able to report that sixty thousand tourists had gone through its doors in July alone. At the same time, work started on an ambitious new museum at the Royal Crescent to depict eighteenth-century life in an affluent city-home.

Elsewhere at long last, an answer to the winter flooding which often covered the bottom of the city, came the start of the Pulteney Weir scheme, costing nearly half a million pounds.

The story had even made the sports pages of some nationals.

The river gives back its dead had been the headline after the long-lost moose's head had been discovered when the Avon was drained.

Stolen years earlier by a northern rugby club from Bath one particular wild night, the thread-bare mascot resurrected the excuse as a trophy for an annual rugby match between the two but was so frequently stolen by drunken fans that the fixture was abandoned and the head thrown back into the Weir.

The wrecker's ball claimed another victory with the demolition and sale of Trim Street but was held at bay when Whitehall refused to allow the south side of Kingsmead Square to be knocked down.

"The first murmurings of organised civil protest against the Council" was how Ian described it.

CHAPTER SIXTY-FOUR

Watson was right. It took nearly a year and cost five thousand pounds, but the planning inspector agreed and granted consent for Fallingwater. This was achieved because Fiona had managed to convince so many Traditional Bath members not to oppose the appeal – some even gave it their support.

Work began after they got back from Barbados in January 1970. The building site was a scene of manic activity, noise, and exhaust fumes as bulldozers, diggers, and dumper trucks dug out half the hillside ready for the foundations.

It all came to a sudden halt when no less than four springs suddenly bubbled up through the ground, disgorging hundreds of gallons of water an hour. Within a day, a lake about four feet deep filled the whole excavated site. Then, the ice-cold water, which the experts said had fallen as rain millions of years ago and came from thousands of feet below ground, overflowed and poured down the hill to the river.

"More like Niagara Falls rather than Fallingwater," Mark Watson dryly remarked, and Fiona wondered if it could be fixed or if the project would have to be abandoned.

"Everything can be fixed, as always it comes down to money," the architect reassured.

The experts came and delivered the bad news. The structural engineers had warned that the planned construction method could mean the whole hillside was in danger of drying out and collapsing, taking any new house down the valley with it. The answer was to pile foundations thirty feet deep, or even further, until they hit solid rock.

She related the whole sorry tale to Ian over dinner.

"What's the damage?" he asked. Well used to overruns in any building works, even he was shocked by the answer.

"Add three months to the programme and at least another twenty thousand pounds." Fiona looked at him. "Have we got the money?" she asked fearing she was about to lose her dream.

Ian thought. A total of two hundred and twenty five thousand pounds including the appeal costs, and from experience he knew that was not the end of it: there would be other unforeseen expenses. Mentally, he put a price of a quarter of a million pounds on the build.

"No," he answered truthfully, "but we'll find it. I'll have another word with Toby in the morning. He'll find a way; he always does. Tell Mark to carry on."

"I don't know, Ian, the bank won't lend anymore," Toby explained. "The cost of the tourism operation has proved much more than we estimated. Yes, after nine months, it's making money – just – but its cash flow is wafer thin, and all we can do is pray that we have a good summer and lots of visitors."

"What about me personally borrowing more from the Cassofiori Bank?" Ian asked.

"No chance. You've already hocked everything you and Fiona own."

"But you're always telling me we're rich."

"Asset rich but cash poor," the finance director explained. "I'm afraid this is beyond me, but I'll have a word with the head of Corporate Financing at the bank in London.

Fiona, Ian, and Toby travelled up to Leadenhall Court. It had taken three months for Toby to produce the seemingly endless information – updated accounts, detailed asset valuations, and cash-flow projections – required by the Cassofiori Bank.

Opposite them in the large conference room sat the Corporate Finance team of six men headed by Michael Whitcroft. He was a man of about forty who evidently enjoyed his food and was immaculately dressed. Relaxed, Whitcroft was every inch the city gent.

"Good morning and thank you for coming." Smoothly, he introduced his colleagues. "I suggest we make a start as there is much to cover. We've gone through everything to complete the due diligence, and I am pleased to tell you, Mr and Mrs Lundy, that I agree with Toby. A public offering of shares in Bath Fiscal Holdings Ltd on the London Exchange could work and the Bank would be pleased to handle the placing.

"Before we go ahead, I think it is most important that we address what this will mean to you both personally. So often, I have had meetings in this very room with highly-successful people like yourselves, who took the step too lightly. Yes, it will make you very wealthy, but you will no longer own nor control the company, this company which you have both created and birthed – your baby."

Ian heard Fiona's intake of breath and regretted the unfortunate metaphor.

"Furthermore," Whitcroft continued, "remember you will be employees, bound by contracts for at least a year, probably two, and subject to the wishes of a board of directors and institutional shareholders. Are you going to be comfortable with that?"

"Of course," Ian answered.

"Mrs Lundy?"

She nodded.

Toby had pre-warned them to expect the question, but he had explained that once the company was successfully floated, they would be able to finish Fallingwater and should never have to worry about money ever again.

Whitcroft continued. "Good. Now we have dealt with that point, we need to move onto the question of a local stockbroker. Toby, I think you have some thoughts?"

"Thank you, Michael," Toby spoke. "As we have discussed, there is already considerable appetite in Bath itself and the surrounding area for the shares, so the appointment should be a local firm. Bradley & Company, established in George Street, is by far the best choice, a husband and wife team that has been around for years and is well respected. Robert Bradley is the dealer, and Janet, the analyst, is particularly successful and backs winners time after time. If we succeed in getting her on side, the floatation should be home and dry. I'm planning a meeting shortly."

Janet Bradley retired to her office, hung out the *Do not disturb* sign on the door and locked it.

The Lundys and Toby Stafford were well known among Bath's business community, but she had only met them once, briefly, at that morning's meeting. She had found Ian Lundy rather arrogant and preferred the manner of his wife and the finance director when they discussed the proposed share issue. But Robert was mustard keen on accepting the instructions: too often, he prioritised the large commissions to be earned from placing and trading the shares over the interests of a client.

However, she, in turn, knew that their reputation depended on choosing the right businesses, and Ian Lundy was obviously the key player on this occasion. For her part, she had the only thing she needed – 28 April 1942, Ian Lundy's date of birth. She sat at her office desk and made a telephone call to ensure that she would have a copy of his birth certificate in two days to verify where he was born. Then she turned to a fresh page in her foolscap note pad and wrote,

An Astrological Profile of Ian Lundy (previously Yann Morris)

Next, using its only key, she unlocked the steel cabinet and took out her leather-bound charts and books and made a start.

Two weeks later, she had completed the task and regarded it with satisfaction.

Ascendant Sign: Cancer 29°, giving Leo most of the 1ˢᵗ Home prominence:

Virgo prominent 2ⁿᵈ House:
Liking for team work in business. The influence of Leo will include friends in their financial plans or perhaps make money through large corporations or group endeavours.

Taurus dominates the 10ᵗʰ House:
Where the Sun, Mercury, Saturn and Uranus dwell. (Sun & Mercury as original minus cross outs).
Saturn and Uranus conjunct. Powerful aspect, giving combination of ambition demanding recognition. Can be ruthless realising ambition. Far-sighted, disliking routine work. Can have fixed opinions, but adaptable. Taurus influence with Saturn gives interest in banking and investments. Uranus influence prepared to take considered risks.

11ᵗʰ House Jupiter:
Gives enjoyment to many friends and acquaintances.

Pluto in Leo in 1ˢᵗ House:
Sign of leadership, energy, and power. Sun Square Pluto a difficult aspect, produces ambition for power, inclined to impose will on others, softened by the influence of the Cancer Ascendant.

Moon in Libra:
Has a need to bring balance to all aspects of life, has Charm and Diplomacy. At best when working with others, loves and looks after family.

Everything went back into the locked steel cabinet, and, quitting her small back office, she strolled into her husband's much grander affair overlooking George Street. He looked up and asked,

"Ian Lundy?"

"Despite my initial misgivings, I've got no reservations – I believe that he will be fine. He comes out with flying colours in both attitude and aptitude, so we can go full steam ahead. I'd advise putting every client on our books in and around Bath into the shares."

CHAPTER SIXTY-FIVE

"How many?" Even Ian was astounded.

"We propose to issue one million new ordinary shares at one pound each," Toby repeated.

"And how many will Fiona and I get?"

"Your eighty existing shares will be replaced by eight hundred thousand new shares at one pound each, making your holding worth eight hundred thousand pounds. With the completion of Fallingwater for a quarter of a million pounds, congratulations – you'll be a millionaire by the age of twenty-eight. By the way, how is the grand mansion doing?"

"Fiona reckons we'll be in by October, as long as it doesn't rain too much over the summer and the glass suppliers don't mess her about."

"I'll keep my fingers crossed."

"So, what happens now?"

"The roadshow. You and I travel the land and meet the thirty or so institutions that we have to persuade that you and the company are a good bet, or in city jargon, have potential and are worth investing in. All the remaining shares must be placed with them if the float is to get underwriting."

"Underwriting?"

"An old city way of ensuring that there is no risk and much profit – that way, everyone wins," Toby said.

It took four gruelling months – London, Bristol, Birmingham, Manchester, Edinburgh, Glasgow, and the many other towns and cities where there was clients' money to be had.

Each trip took them to a different place, with countless hours spent in cars and trains, with a different hotel room each night. An identical roadshow presentation was repeated every time – so often that the initial enthusiasm waned and Ian became bored listening to himself.

Countrywide journeys were also interspersed with meetings in Leadenhall Court with the lawyers, accountants, and public-relations people. Michael Whitcroft and his team masterly steered them through the maze of interminable detail and Stock Exchange Rules.

Then there was the press, the financial journalists with their devious questions, hoping to trip him up with the numbers. Like the travelling, the pressure was non-stop, but one glorious evening, Ian was able to relax. He had got drunk in a city far away from London with one of the financial journalists – a kindred spirit: well into his cups, the newspaperman disclosed his skill for picking the shares he tipped with remarkable success for the newspaper's readers.

"Nothing to it, my friend," he told Ian. "I pin up a copy of the share page from the *Financial Times* and throw darts at it: I tip the ones on which the darts land."

In early September, Ian and Toby returned to Bath absolutely shattered. They had succeeded. The institutions had promised support; this would provide the new company with a war chest of two hundred thousand pounds for further investments in Bath.

Bath Fiscal Holdings Plc floated on the London Stock Exchange at one past eight on Thursday, 1 October 1970. The issue price of one pound quickly rose by three shillings, producing a further profit for Ian of a hundred and twenty thousand pounds in the first two hours of trading.

CHAPTER SIXTY-SIX

Enthralled by the six enormous speakers, each three feet high, and the sound system in the drawing room at Fallingwater, Ian turned the volume down on Cat Stevens' "Morning has broken" and opened the brown envelope which had been hand-delivered.

Hope you like this!

The yellow sticker was attached to the November edition of *The Bath Way*. Ian had promised an exclusive to Al Giles, and the stunning photograph encompassed the whole front cover.

"FALLINGWATER"
A MASTER PIECE – A SIGN OF THE FUTURE FOR BATH?

A first for a news story in the magazine's existence, it was a magnificent picture taken at night, looking up at the broad facade. Internal golden light poured through the vast windows which formed over three quarters of the elevation overlooking the Limpley Stoke Valley.

The front page headed *THE LUNDY'S AT HOME* showed a tranquil Fiona seated at the end of one of the enormous, grey sofas. By her side, perched on its arm, was Ian, and the twins dressed in matching outfits stood in front of them – a perfect family setting.

Fantastic photographs of the rooms, specially dressed for the wide-angled camera lens, filled the next five pages. Underneath and by the sides waxed a lyrical commentary.

Barely three miles from the centre of the city lies this radical new mansion created by the renowned young architect Mark Watson, (pictured above), very different in style and materials, unlike anything ever built before in Bath.

Mr Watson is thought by many to be one of the most important modernist architects of the twentieth century. A travel scholarship allowed him to study buildings old and especially new throughout Europe.

Like its namesake by Frank Lloyd Wright, built in 1935 in Pennsylvania, America, Fallingwater has created a relationship within the seclusion of this beautiful wooded valley and springs. Its flat roofs blend into rather than dominate the surrounding countryside, says Watson.

Walk with us through the split levels of the three pavilions, each connected by floor-to-ceiling glass, providing stunning views of Freshford village church.

Cleverly, the Lundys have enhanced their home with bespoke, fitted, contemporary furniture below ceilings of sycamore, yew, rosewood, and cedar.

The house is built for grand entertaining.

The enormous drawing room of over fifteen hundred square feet was first shown empty in all its glory, followed by a picture with it packed with people at the house warming party.

Under the title "The Tribes of Bath", everyone, on page after page, followed – headed with Al's beloved created nicknames for Bath society, invented in the first edition covering the Nurses' Ball.

Arty Farties, Wheelers & Dealers, Do Gooders, Cops and Robbers, Hackers, Healers & Feelers, Pips & Stripes, Three-Line Whips, Guineas Club, God Squad, Heavy Breathers, and *Globetrotters.*

Each page was subdivided, showing small groups, glasses in hand chatting and smiling, with the name of each person superimposed on the scene.

We say congratulations to Mrs Fiona Lundy, who managed the whole project and has achieved such success, often in the face of ill-informed local opposition.

As usual, the Lundy family depart in a few days for Christmas in Barbados and a well-earned rest. It certainly has been a busy year for them. Throughout 1970, the Lundys have combined all their numerous and highly-profitable ventures in Bath – building, banking, property investment, publishing, tourism, to name but some – into a single company, Bath Fiscal Holdings. Backed by some of the UK's largest institutions, this company was successfully floated on the London Stock Exchange two months ago, giving every Bathonian and others a wonderful opportunity to invest in this great city's future.

This magazine wishes the family the season's greetings and a happy and prosperous 1971.

Next morning, Ian scribbled a reply.

Al, I couldn't have asked for anything better – you've done a superb marketing job. Bradley and Co report a surge in share sales to small, local investors. No doubt as a result of this article, and the reason for the recent rise in the share price. Well done!

See you when we get back,

Ian

CHAPTER SIXTY-SEVEN

The afternoon temperature was just right for December, like a summer's day in England. Ian sipped his Planter's Punch and looked across the beach at Anna and the twins building sandcastles on the perfect sand. Not for the first time, he pondered the success over the previous five years, which enabled the family to spend weeks yet again in Barbados, away from the dreary English winter.

Ian put the book down. The warmth closed his eyes and allowed his mind to wander. Reading was his greatest love: books had taught him so much; he was never without one.

It had all started twenty or so years earlier. At the age of five, Ian, or Yann as he was called then, could read like an eight-year-old and had the use of the vast private library at Cassofiori House, the blind home at Box, the village outside Bath, where his mother had been housekeeper. Every free moment of his holidays was spent reading in the stillness of that wonderful collection of books.

The library at Beaconsfield, his prep school, proved a worthy replacement. Here, he found Fielding, Defoe, the Brontës, George Elliott, Trollope, and many others.

When he went on to Pitt College in 1953, he discovered Wells, Hardy, Cronin, Kipling, Laurence, Orwell, and Huxley. As always, once discovered, he utterly devoured all the works of each new author, never moving on until he had read everything he could lay his hands on.

Then came a defining moment. In 1958, he won a Rhodes Literary Prize, and his prize was a strange novel called *Van Loon's Lives*. Published in 1942, the author, Hendrick Willem Van Loon, was a Dutch-American who had been born in Holland in 1882 and emigrated to Connecticut, America.

The book contrasted the barbarism of Hitler and the Nazi war-time occupation of the Netherlands with the Dutch civilisation of more than a thousand years. It filled a huge gap in Ian's literary knowledge.

Loosely based on *Plutarch's Lives*, published in 1517, Van Loon demonstrated his imagination and immense scholarship in a uniquely entertaining way: by leaving a note under a stone, he could invite anyone from the past to dinner, irrespective of when and where they had lived, and seat them together.

In turn, Elizabeth I, Erasmus, Confucius, Plato, Thomas Jefferson, Einstein, Thomas Moore, Descartes, George Washington, and so many more all came to his old family summer house in the province of Zealand. Peter the Great took Marconi's wireless apart, and two archbishops, rivals at the Carnival of Nicea in the fourth century, became so abusive they had to be locked up in separate cells by a local policeman, only to have disappeared the next morning.

Ian scoured second-hand bookshops for every work mentioned by Van Loon, be it a Greek classic, *Utopia*, or *In Praise of Folly*. Once read, the book was kept – his alto-ego, an ever-increasing library, which stayed with him.

The endless drudgery of correspondence courses and night school study for qualification was relieved by outrageously-funny authors such as JP Donleavy and Tom Sharpe. Then, he discovered what was to become his greatest love – Evelyn Waugh.

The rustling caused him to open his eyes.

"Mind if I join you?" It was Budge O'Hara, the owner of the Coral Reef Club.

"Delighted." Ian waved him into Fiona's vacated chair.

"Digs comfortable, anything you need?"

Ian laughed at the description of Canefield, the hotel's most luxurious plantation suite on the beachfront.

"Want for nothing."

Budge looked at the book.

"*To Serve Them All My Days*," he read aloud. "I noticed it on the bestseller's list for 1972. Good read?"

"I like Delderfield, always have. Great social histories, usually from the politically-left's viewpoint. This one is no different – South Wales coal miner, injured and shell-shocked in First World War, becomes history teacher at minor public school in North Devon, etc. etc," Ian answered, "but too dated."

"What do you mean?"

"He is writing about an England that no longer exists. Everything has changed and is continuing to change profoundly and so quickly."

"Go on."

"My generation were called the Silents. National Service abolished, we could concentrate on our careers, more interested in financial security than activism. We conformed, made no fuss. There were fewer of us born than in the previous generation, and we entered the job market in the prosperous late fifties, early sixties – jobs galore and, most importantly, war-free.

"Yes, my generation is the lucky one, hence the Swinging Sixties. Another big change was the rise of feminism. Compulsory, free contraception became law last year, and big changes to make divorce much easier are planned. The permissive society, sexual experiments, pre-marital sex, one-parent families, the decline of marriage, tolerance of homosexuality – the whole Pandora's box is open and cannot be shut.

"With the birth of a counter-culture, reverence for the old disappeared, replaced by fascination with the new – the newer the better – driven by the young. Don't be fooled: people of my age – yes, they pay lip service to anyone over fifty who has power, but the only thing that really matters to them are fame, success, novelty, money, or whatever else turns them on.

"They have no time for or respect birth, privilege, inherited wealth, and all such outmoded connotations. They view our ancient institutions such as the law, the church, or military as completely out of touch, irrelevant, and often with ridicule. 'Angry young men' – it started with *Look Back in Anger*, John Osborne's play about ten years ago. Did you ever see it at the Royal Court when you were in London?"

Budge shook his head.

"Surely it's not that bad – I didn't notice anything different when I was last back in the UK on leave."

Ian thought for a moment, seeking an example to make his point.

"Did you spend much time in London?"

"No fear, hate the place. I have to spend a few days at my club in St James' to entertain the travel agents, then back to glorious Wiltshire and the parents' home. Why do you ask?"

"Ever heard of Portobello Road?"

"It's a sort of place for bric-a-brac in West London, isn't it? Never been there myself."

Ian laughed.

"A bit more than bric-a-brac – the in-place at Notting Hill, a thriving antique market where everyone under thirty goes to for trendy, second-hand clothes. Do you know what is the hottest seller?"

"No idea, tell me."

"Military uniforms – the grander the better, the more medals the better. Fiona and I went to a dinner party before we came out here – black tie, sit-down, posh affair. Had to go: we had sold a well-known pop star the house in the Royal Crescent.

"Never any suggestion it was fancy dress – our host was very rough and at least five years younger than me. He wore a First World War infantry-officer's dress uniform complete with ribbons, including an MC and bar, all bought from a Portobello stall.

Half way through dinner the pop star stuck his finger through a small hole above the heart, no doubt made by the enterprising stall trader. 'Where he died, stupid bugger,' our host announced, 'preferred it to the judge's wig and gown and the archbishop's stuff,' he added. No one said anything or batted an eyelid – didn't dare, we all had taken his money and hoped for more."

The hotel owner looked shocked.

"I must go and sort out the new guests – the London plane came in about an hour ago – perhaps we could pick this up later?"

"Sure, I'm not going anywhere!"

"When did it start?" Budge asked. Dinner was over, and he and Ian were sharing a decanter of Cockburn's, overlooking the moonlit ocean.

"After the Second World War, economically, England followed where America led. The realisation for me was a magazine picture – the centre double-page of *Time* – I remember the date, July 1967. Downtown Detroit, America was a scene of utter devastation and thousands of National Guard in full combat gear – five, maybe ten rows deep spanning the entire street. A sweltering-hot night of violent rioting and looting, it was described as the worse race riot in US history and the end of the myth."

"What myth? I don't understand."

"Overnight, when peace came in 1946, American industry converted its massive war production into producing everything its aspiring white middle classes could want for – the suburban house with a white picket fence, filled with every conceivable modern appliance. Ten years of the American Dream."

"So, what went wrong?"

"Black people were excluded. I first noticed a real change about five year ago after Fiona and I were married and adopted the twins; I suppose it was the responsibility of having an instant family. Like the rest of the country, the white, middle-class, middle-aged citizenry of Bath revelled in 'the shock and horror of America' at every turn and twist, sanctimoniously reported in detail by Auntie."

"Auntie?"

"The British Broadcasting Corporation."

Budge, who was like most expats, relied totally on the World
Service of the BBC, religiously tuning in every night.

"So, what's next?"

"The Swinging Sixties are over. Now, we have the baby boomers,
sired by the hundreds of thousands of lustful returning servicemen of the
Second World War and years of sexual abstention. They regard themselves
as entitled, a special generation. Very outspoken, most reject traditional
values. A privileged lot, indulged, subsidised to the hilt by post-war
governments in everything – education, health, employment, housing – they
want and expect the world to constantly improve. I am told it's the same all
over the western world." Both men were silent, then Budge spoke.

"That's exactly what has happened to the hotel business here in
Barbados. Fantastic growth and expectation: its traditional, pre-war English
aristocracy and wealthy still come – still British but much fewer titles and
less breeding, more Canadians and some Americans."

"A global clientele?" Ian suggested.

"Exactly."

"Interesting. A friend of mine, a banker, sent me his research paper
before I left on this very point. Would you like to see it? In confidence, of
course."

"Very much so."

CHAPTER SIXTY-EIGHT

Five years after Bath Technical College was inaugurated in 1966, it finally became Bath University: the city granted it a ground lease of Claverton-Down for 999 years at a peppercorn rent. The evening celebration began with the University Treasurer presenting the mayor with an inscribed, silver box containing six peppercorns, one plus five for the arrears of back rent.

To mark the occasion, Ian had established the Abrahams Foundation's Scholarship for Business Studies – an undergraduate grant worth a thousand pounds, to be awarded annually.

Now in the quiet of his office a year later, Ian read the paper that Toby Stafford had presented in his continuing capacity as a guest lecturer to the university: many of the great and good of the business world had been invited.

THE GLOBAL EFFECT

Over the last six years, the post-war financial environment has changed dramatically. The business world has become global, and London's influence has declined further, principally replaced by New York.

Investors need to take less interest in local UK issues and far more notice of worldwide events. In the past, these have been viewed as purely affecting America.

Ever-greater news coverage of events in the United States, and their ever-faster communication around the world, has made their impact greater.

Set down below are some examples.

As if to emphasise the point, vivid scenes flashed up in Ian's brain as his eyes ran down the list.

WORLD EVENTS

1968

4 APRIL   MARTIN LUTHER KING ASSASSINATED

Who would ever forget the balcony outside room three hundred and six of the Lorraine Motel…?

5 JUNE   *THE ASSASSINATION OF ROBERT KENNEDY*

The horrendous picture covering the whole of the front page of the London Evening Standard with the mortally-wounded presidential candidate laying, arms outstretched, on the kitchen floor of the Ambassador Hotel in Los Angeles.

1969

20 JANUARY   *NIXON'S INAUGURATION AS THE THIRTY-SEVENTH*
                    PRESIDENT OF THE UNITED STATES

In his office was the photograph of the Frakers standing between the newly-elected president and Frank Duffer Jnr.

21 JULY   *MISSION COMMANDER NEIL A ARMSTRONG*
                 BECOMES THE FIRST HUMAN TO STEP
                 ONTO THE SURFACE OF THE MOON

So many people had stayed up through the night to watch those grainy, black-and-white pictures as the astronaut stepped off the bottom rung of the module steps with the American national flag of Stars and Stripes, unruffled in the windless atmosphere.

1970

12 SEPTEMBER   *FOUR JET AIRLINERS BOUND FOR NEW*
                     YORK AND LONDON HIJACKED BY THE
                     POPULAR FRONT FOR THE LIBERATION OF
                     PALESTINE. THREE FORCED TO LAND AT
                     DAWSON FIELD, A REMOTE DESERT ISLAND
                     IN JORDAN, WHERE THEY WERE BLOWN UP

Miraculously, all three hundred and ten passengers and crew survived, but he remembered thinking, would it ever be safe to fly again after watching the three enormous jets being blown up on television in front of the world's press?

19 OCTOBER   *Oil found in the North Sea*

The only British item on Stafford's list …

9 NOVEMBER   *CHARLES DE GAULLE DIES THIRTEEN DAYS*
              BEFORE HIS EIGHTIETH BIRTHDAY

Thank goodness, no more "Non" to the UK's application to join the Common Market.

Three events in 1971 caught his eye. In January, Idi Amin seized power in Uganda. A month later, the UK denied citizenship for Commonwealth migrants, and three weeks before Christmas, a Belfast pub was blown to pieces.

CHAPTER SIXTY-NINE

The first annual general meeting of Bath Fiscal Holdings Plc started promptly at 11 am in the Assembly Rooms in Bath on 31 March 1972. An hour into the meeting, Ian rose to make the Chairman's Statement to the packed room. Gratifyingly, journalists from the *Financial Times,* the *Times,* the *Telegraph,* and the *Investor's Chronicle* filled the chairs reserved for the press.

"It has been an extraordinary period for your company. Without exception – and I will leave you to study the detailed figures in the annual report and accounts – profits in every single division of your company, be it property, banking, insurance, construction tourism, or publishing, all have increased significantly …"

Sitting on his right-hand side, Toby had no worries: Ian loved speaking to large audiences, and they had practiced this speech to perfection. He spoke slowly, left space for applause, and then let it build.

"There is not a single aspect of legitimate trade, business, or leisure in this great city with which your company is not involved. This enterprise, your enterprise, and Bath are joined at the hip. Both prosper, and I intend to see that this continues for years to come. Thank you."

He sat down to a standing ovation from the grateful shareholders and business owners who were the citizens he had been talking about.

Once the applause had subsided, he stood up again. "Now, if anyone has any questions …"

As usual in such public meetings, the first question had been planted by Toby in order to give the board a chance for self-congratulation. Robert Bradley rose.

"Firstly, on behalf of Bradley & Company and the numerous shareholders we represent, may I congratulate you and your board for such outstanding results in the company's first year. My question is very simple: what is your view of the year to come?"

"The company enters the second quarter of 1972 in rude health," Ian responded. "Its profits are up by five percent. Most fortunately, many of its buildings are let under leases, where the rents it receives are historic, fixed five years ago. Substantiated rent increases of at least fifty percent can be expected during the next twelve months.

"Based on the strength and certainty of these guaranteed increases in its income, your company has been able to advantageously rearrange and substantially increase its borrowings. This will facilitate the funding of our extensive construction programme in and around Bath. This will involve building two thousand plus of the houses and flats for which the company has gained planning permission.

"By this time next year, importantly from the shareholders point of view, this should allow your board to double the dividend."

A few more questions, none of any significance, followed.

Ian closed the meeting to more applause, and his audience was eager to proceed to the main reason for its attendance – the veritable feast of the shareholders' lunch laid out in the next room.

CHAPTER SEVENTY

Air Commodore Brian Stanbridge's top-secret, coded memorandum clattered through the printer in the cipher room of the Admiralty HQ at Empire Buildings at 1207 hrs on April 2 1972.

Alone in the basement was the cipher clerk, Chief Petty Officer Furlonger, who tore off the printout and set about decoding it. When finished, he made an additional copy, placed the original in the special envelope marked *Eyes only commanding officer*, and sealed it.

A SOVIET NUCLEAR ATTACK ON
THE UNITED KINGDOM

The United Kingdom is a primary target because it is the only state in Western Europe which is part of NATO. There can be no effective civil defence against a large-scale nuclear attack on Britain.
The government and some of the population realise this. Listed in Appendix One are the one hundred and six targets, comprising thirty-eight towns/cities, thirty-seven air bases, twenty-five control centres and six naval sites, which will be hit by over a hundred and fifty land and submarine missiles.
London will be devastated by probably three or more nuclear bombs of five megatons, each three hundred times more powerful than the fifteen kiloton US atomic bomb that killed a hundred and forty thousand people in Hiroshima. Glasgow, Birmingham and Manchester will suffer similar fates.

Before delivering the envelope, he re-read the copy, together with Appendix One, and noted that it included Bristol, which meant that Bath too would be wiped out. He folded it carefully to a quarter of its size and concealed it into the lining of his cap. He planned to deliver it this evening to Bristol after checking out the new recruit who worked at the Guildhall Market.

Ian thought the Americans were looking for reds under the bed where none existed, but prompted by a call from Ford Fraker, he decided to telephone Mike Watts. He had arrived early at his office and knew Watts would already have been at the Guildhall for some hours.

"You must be telepathic," the market trader said. "I was about to call you, because I got what you wanted last night at the Lion, and your friends will want to hear this."

The Lion, as Mike called it, was the Coeur De Lion in Northumberland Place, said to be the smallest pub in Bath and the Guildhall stall-holders' favourite watering place. Ian wondered how they could all fit given its size and the number of stall holders involved in running the market.

"Shall I see you there later?" Ian asked.

"I think it would be better somewhere more private, and the sooner the better. I think the weirdos may have twigged," Mike replied, and they agreed to meet at Great Pulteney Street.

As soon as he put the phone down, Ian unlocked the safe and took out and re-read the paper which Toby's global research team in London had provided for him. Once he had heard from Watts, he would pass it to Ford Fraker.

Hatred of America:
Anti-American Feeling in England

Conclusion

There would appear to be no commonly-held reason, more than the usual tendency of human beings to hate those in charge and the need to find a scapegoat for their own failures. Once it was the British Empire, now it's the successful and all-powerful Unites States of America.

 In the United Kingdom, anti-American feeling is rife, especially among the elite.This intellectual hatred has arisen out of resentment of the United States' achievements with relatively few sacrifices in two World Wars. The result: American dominance versus much-reduced British influence.

 An added and constant irritant is the European youth's attraction to US culture and its classless opportunities.

In the attached six appendices, we set out in detail the historic and other detailed reasons summarised in this conclusion, together with the sampling survey and parameters employed.

Ian didn't re-read the appendices; he was only too familiar with the often justifiable criticisms about the US administration: there was its lack of consultation, high-handed treatment of supposed allies, isolationism, trade protectionism, and doing what was solely in America's selfish interest, without regard for anyone else. Then, there were the interest payments which the US continued to charge on its vast wartime loans to the UK; these still had decades to run. Ian knew that these home truths would not please Washington.

They sat at the breakfast bar in the kitchen, Mike Watts with his carrier bag, nursing a beer, and Ian with a malt whisky and note pad.

"The Yanks are right to be worried."

"Tell me."

"One of my lot had to join the Bath CND movement to get what you wanted. Posing as a simple, peace-loving bloke, happy to wear the armband, march with the banners, and shout the slogans outside the Abbey every Saturday morning.

"Being a drinker, he soon found himself with the more serious blokes – the weirdest bunch of oddballs and misfits which neither he, nor I for that matter, would believe existed in Bath. Bristol, yes, but not in our sedate, little, white-middle class city.

"Marxists, anarchists, and even the odd Trott: the whole death-to-capitalism mob, all violently anti-American. Forget peace and democracy; the shared aim is the destruction of the Yankee satan. The ugly crowd, as he calls them, are led by a man called Furlonger – keeps his cards close to his chest. He's Royal Navy, works in the Admiralty at the Empire Hotel.

"The Bath marchers meet in a little two-up-and-two-down Victorian house in Villa Street behind Lower Bristol Road – no secret, draped with a bloody-great CND banner outside.

"The people in charge are clever; they keep well hidden behind the scenes, but my chap got lucky. Being the newest of the recruits, the lowest of the low, he drew the short straw and had to stay behind to clean and lock up Villa Street after the meetings. One Friday night, a messenger arrived with a parcel – banners and other paraphernalia for the march next morning – by luck, a retired stall-holder from our market, old timer and widower, keen to earn a few bob by delivering stuff around Bath.

"They went for a drink, and, living on his own, the old boy was more than glad to gossip. After the second pint, my mate innocently asked where the parcel had come from. Always the same place, pick up from Bristol, Stokes Croft by Gloucester Road – the ban-the-bomb-nutters' place."

Ian knew the area, infamous for civil unrest and riots by communists and the hard left.

"That's where all the Bristol marches start from, sometimes led by, you know, the toff who gave up his title and seat in the House of Lords to become an MP – anti the royal family, pacifist, wants to nationalise everything so the American's can't steal our British companies. Even tried to abolish the Queen's head on the postage stamps when he was Postmaster General."

Ian interrupted.

"Tony Wedgewood Benn?"

Mike nodded.

"Or as Harold Wilson called him, Mr Zig-Zag-Loon."

Benn's rants were notorious. "Impossible to construct the Labour Party without Marx and the Communist Manifesto ..."

"And this is just a few of the things my lad collected," Mike said as he emptied the contents of the carrier bag onto the breakfast bar.

The Little Red Book, with Mao's portrait circled in yellow and the four large Chinese symbols below, immediately caught Ian's eye. He picked it up, because he'd heard of it but never seen a copy before. With it lay pamphlets and books carrying the CPGB printer's stamp of the British Communist Party.

"Here I was thinking that the Americans were being paranoid," Ian said, "and you've just scratched the surface of Bath and found all this – a communist working at the Admiralty who's possibly in league with a cabinet minister who could one day be elected leader of the Labour Party and then become Prime Minister."

Immediately after Watts left, Ian gathered everything up, rang Ford Fraker, and went over to see him.

Ten days later, Ian happened to be in town shopping with Fiona when he saw the CND was doing its usual distribution of pamphlets in front of the Abbey, and he took one. It showed the familiar mushroom of an exploding nuclear bomb.

STOP UNITED STATES SLAUGHTER!

AMERICA PLANS TO STRIKE RUSSIA USING FIVE MEGATON BOMBS - EACH 300 TIMES MORE POWERFUL THAN THAT WHICH DESTROYED HIROSHIMA, KILLING 140,000 PEOPLE. RUSSIA WILL BE FORCED TO DEFEND ITSELF, AND 38 BRITISH TOWNS & CITIES WILL PERISH INCLUDING BATH & BRISTOL.

As always, Ford Fraker passed everything onto the CIA.

Chief Petty Officer Furlonger was snatched from his bed in the early hours, never to be heard or seen again in the city. At Langley, Ford Fraker and Ian were credited with a major coup of which the citizenry of Bath never did, nor would ever, know about.

A few weeks later, towards the end of April 1972, a major-incident alarm came through to Bath Fire Station just before eight o'clock one evening. The service's Blue Watch abandoned its supper to mobilise every appliance, including both the turntable and aerial platform with the water ladders.

It was a wise decision, because the Guildhall market was well ablaze with thick smoke pouring from its enormous, domed roof: the commander immediately deployed men and hoses up the ladders to the eaves.

The blaze was unusually fierce, and it took time to bring it under control and eventually extinguish the flames. Luckily, the market had been closed for the night when the fire started, and so, human life had been spared.

A cocktail party in the adjoining Guildhall continued undisturbed until later that night, despite the presence of four thousand gallons of diesel oil stored beneath it and the flames.

Mike Watts shuddered when he and his fellow stall-holders inspected their workplace in the daylight of the following morning. It reminded him of the pictures of the Blitz damage to the city almost thirty years earlier to the day. The entire interior was gutted, with charred shards of wood pathetically dangling from steel frames. The remains of wet and burnt goods of every sort were piled up amidst pools of water from the firemen's hoses. He noticed broken glass on the floor and looked up to see that even the ancient and ornate glass windows had gone.

Some suspected arson. The final bill was a staggering fifteen thousand pounds, and Watts couldn't help but wonder if this was payback for exposing the Admiralty mole.

CHAPTER SEVENTY-ONE

Reading Al Giles's article in *The Bath Way*, Ian was reminded of Fiona's Family Trust.

COMBE-DOWN & RALPH ALLEN

In 1710, Ralph Allen, only seventeen years old, moved from Cornwall and became an assistant to a Bath post mistress. He was evidently very ambitious and talented, because just two years later, he won the contract for the postal service covering all of South West England and went on to make a fortune.

By 1726, he had used it to buy much of Combe Down with its enormous stone quarries that were ripe for extraction.

Within five years, he constructed a tramway one-and-a-half miles long, rising four hundred feet from the river in Bath up to Combe Down, following the route of what is now Ralph Allen Drive. The wagons (pictured) were thirteen feet long and each carried four tons of stone on five-inch iron wheels, rolling along the narrow railway gauge.

Over time, Allen bought out the opposition to create a virtual monopoly for Bath stone and used the profit to build himself a very grand mansion – Prior Park.

A consummate salesman, this not only provided Allen with a magnificent home but was a superb advertisement for his excellent and beloved Bath stone.

In 1729, Allen commissioned the row of eleven cottages to house his workers. He died in 1764.

Austwick's description of "worthless" rankled, because in Ian's experience, land was very rarely worth nothing. In addition, there was news that the Admiralty headquarters would finally be moving out of the Empire Hotel and into new offices at Combe Down.

Ian drove past Fir Field, where the far sighted Allen had planted fifty five thousand young fir trees to provide in time all the floor boards needed for the new houses in Bath. He found a parking space outside the Old Rank where he had arranged to meet Simon Burrow, the Secretary of the Combe Down Historical Society.

Armed with the map produced by the Society and aided by such an expert guide, Ian had been able to identify Austwick's so-called "worthless fields" located in and around the village by lunchtime.

Now in the Forester pub, presumably built for those who tended the trees planted by Allen, they ate their ploughman's lunch in the old bowling alley. A bygone sign required the putter-up to be paid one penny.

"Given your background, Ian, I ought to mention something else that might interest you." Simon pointed to the high wall across the road from the pub. "Behind that is the disused Jewish burial ground that once served a synagogue in Corn Street." Although Ian knew the street, he could never recall his mother nor uncle and aunt ever mentioning a synagogue in Bath.

Combe Down and its connection with Ralph Allen – one of Ian's great heroes – was an impossible place to build houses. Yes, it was an ideal location only two miles south of Bath, but everyone knew that stone quarrying, started in Roman times and greatly increased by the eighteenth century, had left much of the land hollowed out, full of caves, highly unstable, and far too risky to build on.

Maybe Malcolm Austwick was right, but hadn't he read something in the *Chronicle* about the Old Quarry in Stonehouse Lane and planning permission for twenty new houses? No harm in getting a geologist to do a half dozen or so ground tests, he thought as he drove back to Queen Square and parked his MGB behind the office. He knew just the right person, a Frenchman, Jean-Pierre Auge. He would give him a ring before he went home.

Ian's telephone was ringing as he entered his office.

"I have the First Bath and District Perfect Thrift Building Society on the line," the receptionist said. Ian smiled. He would never get over the name, a relic from the nineteenth century. "It's the manager. He wanted to speak to Mr Stafford, but he's not in. I suggested I get Mr Stafford to call him back, but he sounds very upset – said it's most urgent and insisted he speak to you."

He wondered what could ever be urgent at the District Perfect Thrift Building Society. It was Toby's world, but he was happy to talk to the man. Even though the Society was located in a building on the other side of Queen Square, for the life of him, Ian couldn't even remember ever meeting the manager or his name.

"Ian Lundy speaking. How can I help?" he asked.

What came next threw him. The manager was breathless and barely able to speak; odd words came tumbling down the phone line. "Crisis … run out of money … unable to borrow … Sections 123 and 127 of Companies Act 1967, lower lending ceilings … reduced ratios …" He carried on, but became evermore incoherent, and Ian sensed danger.

"Stay where you are, and I'll come straight over," he said.

To his relief, everything seemed perfectly normal as he entered the Building Society, just a few customers queuing with their deposit books. The head cashier recognised him and lifted the barrier giving access behind the counters. He walked past the man and opened the door marked *Manager* and stepped into the large office.

The manager had slid out of his chair with his head slumped, glasses askew, and mouth set open. Ian knelt down. He was still breathing but seemed unable to move anything except for his panic-stricken eyes. He quickly returned to the outer office, closed the door behind him, and quietly said to the head cashier,

"Call an ambulance. Tell them it's urgent. I think it's a stroke."

"Should we close the office early?" the head cashier asked after the ambulance had left with its siren and lights blazing.

"It's only half an hour until your closing time, last thing we want to do is alarm anyone. Keep everything as normal," Ian replied, keeping his voice calm, "but I'd be grateful if you could get Mr Stafford's secretary on the telephone and put her through to me in the manager's office."

To his relief, Toby answered.

The Society closed at its usual time, and the staff departed for the weekend. Toby and Ian worked through the night, and by dawn on Saturday, it was obvious that the Society had indeed run out of cash. They sat in the debris of coffee cups and paper from their twelve hours in the manager's office.

"No wonder the poor sod panicked. I just cannot understand why he didn't call me sooner," Toby said.

"How much is it going to cost us?" Ian asked.

"Nothing – we haven't got anything like the amount of money needed," Toby yawned. "In any case, it would be illegal to carry on, and you and I could go to prison if we did. Also, now that we know the situation, I am obliged to make an immediate call to the Bank of England."

"But it's Saturday morning – there'll be no one there," Ian yawned in return.

"That's where you are wrong." Toby picked up the telephone. "There is always someone there, in case of bad news."

It had taken just twenty-four hours. The Monday edition of the *Chronicle* carried the story; it was considered of such minor importance that it was tucked away halfway down an inside page.

SUCCESSFUL TAKEOVER BID OF BATH BUILDING SOCIETY

The Building Society Association announced this morning that the Wessex Building Society had been granted consent by the Bank of England for its takeover bid for Bath's highly-successful First Bath and District Perfect Thrift Building Society.

A spokesman for the merged Society said that this would enable much larger sums to be lent to the rapidly-expanding house market in Bath.

Toby explained it all over lunch at Joya later that Monday. He had deliberately chosen a table upstairs so as not to be overheard.

"I'm sorry, Ian, I should have seen it coming. Even now, most people haven't a clue. Why did it happen? Well, in the old days, Building Societies only lent money which savers had deposited with them. This meant that they needed and always had ten savers for every lender. Nowadays, that's no longer possible; not enough people can afford to save. The demand for homes and therefore mortgages is insatiable; Societies have to borrow.

"Banking has always been a slight of hand. The banks effectively invent money by lending and relending the same savings. As long as all the savers don't all ask for their deposits back at the same time, it works, because people trust them."

"But that doesn't explain why the First Bath went bust. How did that happen?"

Toby explained. "The Societies borrow from the banks short term – say, only for three months at a time – and then lend the same money long term to house purchasers for twenty-five years. It works as long as you can continue to borrow. But suddenly, the banks have become incredibly nervous – lending has dried up, and the banks are calling their loans in."

"Were the Bank of England surprised?" Ian asked.

"No, apparently, it's happening all over the country. So far, the solution has been manageable, and the big Societies have been ordered to take over the failing small ones."

"How bad is it?"

"Very bad."

"For us?"

"Not disastrous. Thank goodness for our rents, especially because of the large increase due by December, at least fifty percent. But shortly, if it's not already, it will be impossible for the man in the street to get a mortgage. And no mortgages means that we will not be able to sell our newly-built houses. Not only must we stop building immediately, we need to mothball everything already underway and close down every building site. Under no circumstances should we commit to or start any new construction."

"What? Not even Horton House? I was due to exchange contracts on Monday."

"Definitely not," Toby said. "Do not sign that contract or take on anything else. If we're careful, we can make do with our existing cash flow as long as there are no other nasty surprises. Finding new lending in the present climate would be nigh on impossible, and even if I could increase our borrowing, interest rates are about to go through the roof."

CHAPTER SEVENTY-TWO

Cecil Weir cycled to work in the June sunshine. As usual, he was thinking about what he could do about the city's chronic shortage of rented accommodation. Even his employer, the City Council, didn't seem to know or want to know just how critical the problem had become – it would become even worse in the approaching winter. Once again, he reminded himself that councillors reflected the views of the people who elected them into office.

The predominantly middle-class, white voters who owned their own homes resented subsidised council tenants and were extremely vocal. As far as they were concerned, there was no poverty or homelessness in Bath, and in the unlikely event some was found, it was solely due to people who were "too bloody idle to work" – it was as simple as that.

Weir knew better. It was a complex problem, often including chronic ill-health, disability, illiteracy, gambling, alcohol, and other substance abuse.

Few figures were available about slum housing, but Weir reckoned that of the seven thousand sub-standard homes, at least two thousand were in such terrible condition as to be totally unfit to live in. One in every five tenants had no hot water while even more had to share a bath or lavatory, and one in twenty still had to rely on an outside toilet.

Unable to persuade his superiors of the need for adequate resources, he had continued to rely on a few private charities. The Salvation Army and St John's had dealt with the position as best as they could for decades, but now, the situation was out of control.

He decided to use his occasional column in the *Chronicle* to explain how the present system was unsustainable: sooner or later, a crisis would arise, possibly with catastrophic consequences, and the issue could no longer be ignored.

After padlocking the bike and removing the bicycle clips from the bottom of his trousers, he walked up the steps into the grand entrance foyer of the Guildhall and along to his small office in the back of the building.

Amidst the chaos of paperwork on his small, wooden typist-desk a message had been left for him about a call that had come in from a police beat officer overnight. It concerned a smashed-in door on the corner of Back Street and Little Corn Street, a Victorian slum near the river. Closing orders were outstanding on all of these buildings because of the perpetually threat of winter flooding from the Avon.

Demolition to make way for a new car park was literally weeks away, but Weir picked up his torch and a pair of gloves from a drawer and made his way to the bottom of town. Along Somerset Street, past the Forum Cinema, down the steps, he crossed Ambury into Back Street. The sickly smell of raw meat and offal from Bath's sole surviving Victorian abattoir was overwhelming.

Little Corn Street was a roughly-cobbled road of squalid houses that had been slums from the day they had been built in the last century. Constructed as cheaply as possible from the stone spoil left over from grander buildings, the terraced houses comprised a single room on each of three floors. All of the small windows and narrow doorways were boarded up, except for one.

Weir had seen poor housing elsewhere in the city but none as bad as this so close to the city centre. He had to check that no one was sleeping rough inside the vandalised property before getting the council workmen to board it up again. Extracting the torch from his pocket, he entered and was greeted by empty filth.

Collapsed and mildewed plasterwork had piled up around the edges of the floors, exposing the skeletal walls. There was the sweet-sickly smell of rampant dry rot. He turned and was about to leave when he heard a rustling noise from above. It was almost certainly a rat, but he had to make sure.

Gingerly, he climbed the wooden staircase, checking the solidity of each step before trusting his weight to it. As his head rose above the level of the first floor, he inhaled the stench of fresh faeces. The torch beam swept across the failed attempt at a fire in the grate. Dim daylight, filtering through the gaps in the boards covering the window, illuminated the toppled cider flagon and the origin of the stench. It was a misshapen heap in the corner of the room, less than four feet from his head.

"What the fuck do you want? Piss off you, little runt!" It was a roar more than a voice, and the heap started to rise.

Of slight build, Weir needed no second invitation and fled down the staircase, out of the hell of that place, and to the telephone box on Broad Quay. Shaking, he dialled 999.

Unmarried, Jack Romer had dedicated his life to just two causes – the police service and Freemasonry. Before going to the station on that bright June morning, he reverently placed his apron and other lodge paraphernalia into his tan leather briefcase. This included the Centenary Jewel of 1833 with its blue ribbon and hanging metal medal as well as the 1933 bicentenary one with its grey ribbon and grander bronze pendant.

He would wear both at the Masonic temple in Orchard Street that evening for what would be the proudest moment of his life. His dogged detective work and loyalty over the years were finally bearing fruit.

It had been John Lum Stothert, chairman of the globally-renowned engineering company Stothert & Pitt, and Royal Cumberland Lodge Master, who organised the purchase of the building in Orchard Street for one hundred and fifty pounds in December 1866. It had originally been constructed a century earlier as the Orchard Street Theatre and became Bath's original Theatre Royal. This was the theatre that Jane Austen and Thomas Gainsborough knew and where performers such as Sarah Siddons and John Henderson acted in the works of contemporary playwrights, including Richard Sheridan and Hannah More.

Fifteen years after it became the city's new Masonic temple, the magnificent white reredos from St Mary's Chapel was acquired when the road to the new Green Park Station was widened. Later still, the Lodge's spiritual aspirations were fulfilled when the chapter acquired the organ and altarpiece from the city's Octagon Chapel.

Into this splendour of pseudo religion, Jack Romer, the son of a farm labourer, would that night be installed as Master of the Temple. Surrounded by this grand church ornamentation, he would be guided into the high-backed, bejewelled chair on the carpeted stage surviving from the Theatre Royal all those years ago. Witnessing this spectacle would be fellow Lodge members, many of the great and good of Bath: prominent members of every one of the tribes invented by *The Bath Way* – except women – would behold his enthronement.

The latest in more than ten generations of dignitaries and local men of all backgrounds and professions, Romer, who was born in a tied cottage close to Bath, in the village of Freshford, would join those illustrious men listed on the honours boards in the temple's anteroom, alongside some still familiar surnames – Attwood, Phillott, Bateman, Spry, Stothert, Pitt, Fuller, Sparrow, Ireland, Milsom, Cater, Stoffell, Fortt, and dozens more.

Tonight's ensemble would also include his police superiors, many from outside Bath, one of whom only yesterday had quietly informed Romer that his installation as Lodge Master could only hasten his promotion to Chief Inspector.

On arriving at the station in Manvers Street, Romer carefully stored his precious briefcase into his cupboard, which he then locked. He hoped for a busy day to quieten his nervous anticipation of the evening's event and was pleased to take Cecil Weir's call when it came through.

The detective inspector welcomed the distraction and the chance to get out of the police station for some fresh air. He had had to deal with squatters on numerous previous occasions, where all that was needed was a firm hand or, in very exceptional cases, a solid wooden truncheon. The housing officer had assured him that workmen would be there within the hour to re-secure the broken doorway, so he strode off towards Back Street – a man with a definite purpose.

Romer met Weir and the two council workmen with their handcart of wood and tools outside the address in Little Corn Street.

"Are you on your own?" Weir had expected more than just him.

"I don't need anyone else," the DI answered confidently, and to prove the point, poked his head through the doorway and shouted, "Come on out now. You're trespassing on private property."

Nothing happened immediately, but then, there was movement, and a slim, black man with a mop of curly hair came slowly down the stairs, clutching a plastic carrier bag of belongings. He seemed very sleepy and said nothing as he stood on the pavement hugging his possessions.

"Just you, lad?" Romer asked, and the young man shook his head.

"It's Desperate Dan." Despite his brown skin, he had a Welsh accent. "He wants to sleep; you won't get him down."

"Desperate or not, he'll come down if I tell him to." The DI laughed and walked back through the front doorway. "Don't make me come up and get you," he shouted into the house.

"Or what?" a bellow echoed down. "Fuck off!"

Romer's face turned white and then red before he disappeared from view as he leapt up the stairs. The small group waiting on the pavement heard yelling and a scuffle, then more shouting and a final, heavier thud, followed by the sound of footsteps crashing down the stairs.

"Well, hopefully that wasn't too painful," Weir said to the workmen, expecting Romer to reappear at the doorway. Instead, the dishevelled bulk of Desperate Dan materialised, barged them out of the way, and fled off towards Green Park Road.

Upstairs, Weir discovered the body of Detective Inspector Jack Romer, a large knife sunken into his chest with just the hilt visible.

The housing officer's subsequent telephone brought the emergency services en masse. Following Cecil Weir's description, the city was effectively closed down and encircled, but Desperate Dan was not to be found: forty years in the army had taught Regimental Sergeant Major Daniel Morgan where and how to hide.

It was two days before anyone thought to look in Romer's locker and found the tan briefcase.

CHAPTER SEVENTY-THREE

Just as Toby had predicted, after the collapse of the Building Society, not one of the company's newly-built houses was sold: no one could get a mortgage, and cash buyers were few and far between. Reports from other regions suggested that the crisis stretched across the entire country.

On the first Monday in June of 1972, the usual monthly board meeting of Bath Fiscal Holdings took place around the conference table in Ian's office. The sales figures made for grim reading.

"How many houses or flats have we actually sold or agreed to sell?" Ian asked.

"None. The only interest is in about three or four in Petronia House, Weston." This was a block of four brand-new flats, imaginatively named after Succa Petronia, the three-year-old-daughter of, possibly, a Roman gladiator or actor. Her tombstone discovered in Bath dated back to the first century AD.

Toby was checking through some papers as he spoke.

"The few real buyers have got wind of our problems and want big discounts. No actual offers, just interest at twenty percent below the asking price, which would mean a loss of at least fifteen percent, even if we actually managed to get an offer and complete a sale."

"We can't possibly accept that," Ian said. 'We're supposed to be in business to make a profit.'

"I don't think we will have any choice," the finance director replied. "Otherwise it will be open house for squatters. We are haemorrhaging cash," he laughed mirthlessly. "It's got to such a stage that even those who never pay their bills have stopped ordering."

Toby knew that Ian had left instructions with the company receptionist not to be disturbed, but the telephone continued to ring. Ian sighed in annoyance, pushed his chair back, and walked across to his desk and picked up the receiver.

"I thought I told you," he began but was obviously interrupted and said, "Good morning, Chief Inspector, what can I do for you?" He listened. "Yes, I heard the news," he said, "but I don't understand why you need us."

Again, he listened, and the shock showed on his face. "Well, of course, straight away," he said and replaced the handset.

He looked at Toby and the other board members.

"Apologies. I have to bring the meeting to an end, because Fiona and I are needed at the police station." Unusually for Ian, he seemed nervous as he explained,

"It would appear that the block of slum property where Detective Inspector Romer was stabbed to death yesterday ... belongs to Fiona."

Cecil Weir had managed to arrange an emergency bed for Malik Ceilos through the Salvation Army, but this was only a short-term solution – a matter of a week at most. Weir knew that the young man would soon be sleeping rough again unless a permanent home could somehow be found. Following the previous day's tragedy and its aftermath, Weir couldn't shake off the image of Romer's chest and the knife: he had barely slept. He had never envisaged murder. This was the catastrophe he had feared, but it still didn't stop him thinking if he could have done more to prevent it.

They were sitting in a stark room at Manvers Street police station waiting to be formally interviewed, and he looked at Ceilos beside him quietly drinking water from a paper cup. Not for the first time, Weir wondered what chance this malnourished and poorly-educated youngster had ever had of a decent life.

Fiona had never been inside the police station before and felt even more queasy as she and Ian were shown into the waiting room. Apart from a couple of tattered posters about safeguarding homes, the grey walls were bare, and the window looked out onto a treeless carpark below a colourless sky.

There were a half a dozen metal-framed chairs with plastic seats, and a couple of cheerless looking men sat side by side under the window. She guessed that one was about the same age as herself, in his late thirties with slightly-receding, brown, wavy hair. He wore cheap glasses and was quite a small man, dressed in a light-coloured mac over dark-brown trousers. He was clearly nervous. Beside him was a scrawny, young, black man who reminded her a little of Jimi Hendrix. His clothes were tatty and worn, but he seemed oblivious of his dreary surroundings. Fiona wondered what had brought these unfortunate individuals to the police station, not realising it was for the same reason as Ian and herself.

"Hello, Cecil, what are you doing here?" Ian obviously knew the chap in glasses who stood up, and they shook hands. Ian introduced Fiona. The housing-officer-cum-social-worker explained that he and the man beside him had to give witness statements, and it soon became apparent that the four of them were indeed at the police station due to the same dreadful crime.

Although Fiona had never met Cecil Weir, Ian had mentioned him in the past, and she had read his articles in the *Chronicle*. She listened as Weir spoke about Romer's horrendous death. The social worker said he hoped this would be the wake-up call for the Council, the young man next to him being a typical victim. More resources were needed desperately, both suitable living accommodation and money.

Fiona was moved by the young man's silence. She looked at his forlorn face and tried to understand what could have happened to him, with absolutely no one to turn to for help and nowhere to live.

Ian was thinking and came to a decision.

"How would a brand-new flat in Weston suit?"

"That would be amazing," Weir smiled, "but even after what's happened, I'm sure the Housing Department would refuse to pay for a room in such a posh location."

"I don't see how they can if it is free," Ian went on, "Petronia House, owned by the Abrahams Foundation, a charitable trust set up by my wife and myself."

Fiona's heart swelled as her husband elaborated: how much he'd learned and changed over the last few years. She was so proud. Weir's whole demeanour had altered; he had brightened, seemed taller.

"It's so refreshing to at last meet someone who appreciates the position and has sympathy for the poor and the homeless. It's so rare."

Puzzled, Ian asked, "What do you mean?"

"Oh, you know," Weir replied, "the usual attitude – 'one more freeloader who feels entitled to sponge off us, the hard working tax payer'. That sort of thing."

"What's your name?" Ian addressed the youngster.

"Malik," the young man replied. "Malik Ceiros."

Ian held out his hand. "Hello, Malik Ceiros. I am Ian Lundy; this is my wife, Fiona."

Fiona smiled at the young man in the knowledge that Malik's whole life was about to change for the better.

All due to the man she loved and whose child she was now certain she was carrying.

Get in touch

To find out more about the author and both novels please visit www.douglaswestcott.com

Please contact

Valley Spring Press

PO Box 2765

Bath

BA2 7XS

Or goswiftandfar@outlook.com

- To re-order, become a stockist or for any other queries.
- If you run or are involved in a reading group, multiple copies of the novel are available at preferential prices.
- To contact the author or for freely available talks and readings.

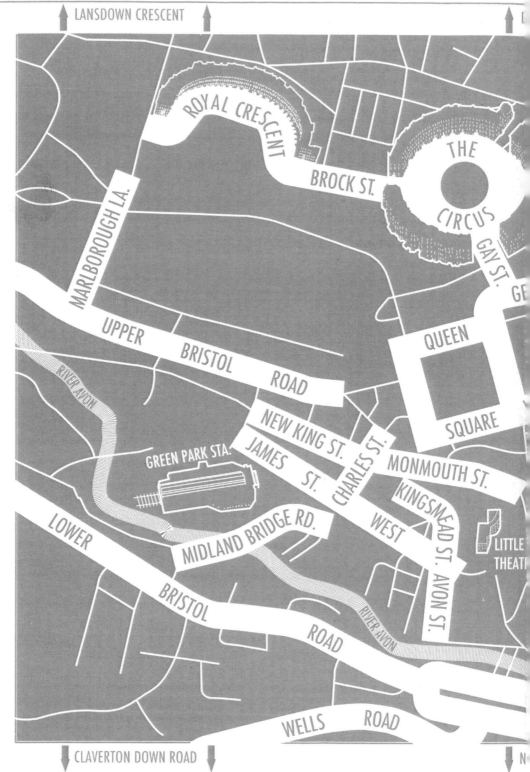

ROYAL CRESCENT

THE

CIRCUS

BROCK ST.

GAY ST.

MARLBOROUGH LA.

QUEEN

UPPER

BRISTOL

ROAD

SQUARE

RIVER AVON

NEW KING ST.

GREEN PARK STA.

JAMES   ST.

CHARLES ST.

MONMOUTH ST.

KINGSMEAD ST.

LOWER

MIDLAND BRIDGE RD.

WEST

AVON ST.

LITTLE
THEAT

BRISTOL

ROAD

RIVER AVON

WELLS   ROAD